BRIAN WORK

D1570743

INTO THE BLACK

Into the Black
Copyright © 2022 Brian Work. All rights reserved.

First Edition.

Published by Brian Work
http://www.brianwork.com

Cover designed by MiblArt.
Chapter title artwork by Marissa Trudel.

ISBN: 979-8-839996-58-8 (print)

Printed in the United States of America.

For Mom,
Who always encouraged me to dream
About the worlds beyond my walls.

Chapter 1

SYDNEY

I hitched Flik to a post outside the general store, keeping him as far as possible from the horses at the other end. He growled in annoyance as I hooked on his muzzle, but he knew the drill by now. Even after fifteen years, people in town still got jumpy as hell around Dad's raptors.

Yes, raptors. Vicious, giant, killer lizards. After my dad retired from the bandit life, he took some of nature's most dangerous creatures and turned them into horses that can rip your face off. Guess you could say he's a professional crazy person. Course, Mom's the one who brainstormed the first train robbery, so it's a wonder I ain't completely batshit.

The familiar smells of stale coffee and fresh leather greeted me inside the store. The owner, an old man with a beard down to his belly, looked up from his newspaper and grunted.

"Afternoon, Sydney."

I tipped my hat. "How's business?"

He looked around the empty store then back at me. "Booming."

"Get any new dime novels in?"

5

A wary look crossed his face. "Your mom told me to stop selling you those. Said they're putting bad ideas in your head."

I screwed up my face. "What are you talking about? She reads the same books."

"And look how she turned out." He pushed himself to his feet. "Hold your horses, boy. I'll get that pump handle wrapped up for ya."

I poked around the store while I waited, hoping to find something new and exciting for the first time in my life. The dusty jars of cactus juice sure didn't meet either criteria. One or two of the potted meats were new, but my mom taught me to never trust a tin of meat if you can't identify the critter on the label. I walked past the stack of newspapers, but a blurry sepia photograph on the front page made me do a double take. I snatched up a copy and stared at the photo of my uncle leading a man in handcuffs onto a train.

Trouble arose at the border yesterday as a thief from Esperan attempted to evade capture from members of Ascension, an Esperanian guild from San Domingo. Ascension tracked the man on horseback from San Domingo, where he allegedly stole an unknown artifact of sindari origin from the residence of Lord Ricardo Aguilar. Lord Aguilar was out of the country at the time and was never in any danger. Ascension's guild master, Darian Rankin, did not respond to a telegram for comment.

Leave it to Uncle Darian to get out of Laredo and spend his days catching bad guys. Sure beat the hell out of running errands for my parents.

I secured the pump handle in Flik's saddlebag. He let out a low chirp and twitched his head toward the

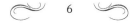

center of town. A crowd had gathered around a large, gaudy merchant's carriage with a banner on the side advertising "Jake's Magical Sindari Elixir." I groaned. Another joker rolling into town to peddle foul potions with supposedly magical properties. It should've been obvious to anyone with a lick of sense this guy was a fraud, but he'd gathered up quite an audience behind his carriage. I gave Flik a pat on the head and made my way into the crowd.

"If you've ever wanted to unleash the magic inside you, why then my sindari elixir is exactly what you're looking for," said the man with the bushy mustache who must've been Jake. "Are you sick of the sindari and elves hoarding their magic to themselves? Well, of course you are. We all are." He held up a vial of purple liquid. "And this here is the answer! At great risk to my own health and safety, I have traveled deep into sindari lands and stolen this magic potion straight from the vaults of the queen herself. One drink of this and the magical powers you've always dreamed of can be yours for twenty-four whole hours! The sindari have been guarding their secrets for centuries, trying to keep us pure blood humans from getting our hands on their precious magic. Well, no more! For only thirty silver, their powers can be yours!"

A murmur went through the crowd. The fact that they were buying this shit made me feel real bad about my hometown.

"Now, I know that's a lot to take on faith. Because I am an honest man, I'm willing to give one of you fine folks a free sample of my amazing magical sindari tonic to prove it really works. Can I get a volunteer from the audience, please?"

I would've volunteered, but that'd probably be cheating. I already had magic powers, after all. They weren't worth a damn, but that was beside the point. I didn't have enough elven blood in me for the good stuff. All I got was the leftovers.

Several hands went up throughout the crowd. Jake made a big show of choosing a volunteer before settling on a young woman near the front.

A beautiful young woman.

A beautiful young woman I'd never seen in my life.

I mean, come on. We live in a mighty small town. If that girl lived here, I'd have known.

Judging from the applause and disappointment from the rest of the crowd, they hadn't reached the same conclusion.

Yep. Real proud of my hometown right now.

Jake took her hand and led her to the front. "Now, young lady, before we start, are you in fact a pure-blood human?"

"Yes, sir, I truly am." Her demure attitude was far too heavy-handed and a couple generations out of date. I waded through the crowd to get a better look. She wore a hat pulled down over her ears, which was more than a little suspicious. Her eyes were blue, but that didn't necessarily mean anything. I didn't have pointed ears, but my purple eyes gave away that I wasn't entirely human. Elven blood was sort of a dice roll.

Jake handed her the vial. "Now, miss, you be sure to drink the whole thing down, else it won't work. And don't you spill a drop now. I don't fancy using my whole inventory on demonstrations."

The girl raised the vial in a toast and drank it down in one long gulp. "Mmm. Tastes like grapes!"

"The sindari may know magic, but ol' Jake knows a thing or two about good taste." A few laughs came from the onlookers. "So, how do you feel, young lady?"

"I feel... stronger. More powerful!"

A chorus of "oohs" came from the audience. I snorted. That line wasn't even good enough for one of my dime novels.

"More powerful in what way?"

"My hands..." The young woman turned them over and stared at them. "They're tingling. Warm... I think..." She extended her hand in front of her. A ball of fire formed and swirled around her palm. She pointed toward a cactus on the side of the street and loosed the fireball. The cactus burst into flames as the crowd burst into applause.

"Now that is some good magic if I do say so myself!" Jake held up another bottle. "Who else wants to unleash their inner magic? Only thirty silver for a twenty-four hour vial. Buy two and save 'em for a rainy day!"

I couldn't watch any longer. People were digging into their pockets for money, but I refused to let this guy walk away with any of it. I pushed my way to the front of the crowd.

"I'll buy three!" I shouted.

"Smart boy!" Jake pulled out three vials. "That'll be ninety silver."

"Just one question." I turned to the young woman. "How much for a date with you?"

She smiled. "Sorry, I'm not for sale."

"That's funny, cause you've done a helluva job selling his shit." I snatched the hat off her head. The assembled crowd gasped. There, plain as day, were the pointy ears of a half-elf.

I took a deep bow for the crowd, ready to bask in their applause. Instead, I looked up to see them backing away. I glanced back to the carriage, where an angry Jake had produced a dagger. As bad as that was, I was more worried about the half-elf brandishing a fist full of fire.

"Um..." I looked from one to the other and flashed my most charming smile. "Truce?"

The girl hurled her fireball. I dove out of the way and barely avoided getting turned into barbecue as the flame exploded into the dirt where I'd been standing. Then I did what any brave crime fighter would do.

I ran.

They saw through my brilliant plan and chased me down the street. I turned the corner at the general store and slammed into a solid, muscular form that knocked me right on my ass. As I went down, I caught the glint of metal on their chest.

Oh no. Oh no, not now. Not now...

I pulled my face out of the dirt. My mother stood over me, arms crossed in her brown leather duster. Her eyes were barely visible under the brim of her cowboy hat, but her frown was plain to see.

"Sydney? What are you—"

"Sheriff Winter!" someone called out.

Mom's head shot up as Jake and the half-elf turned the corner. As soon as she saw the dagger, Mom darted past me and drove a boot into Jake's kneecap. His scream almost drowned out the sound of cracking bone. Almost.

"Sydney! Home, now!"

Mom cursed as a fireball flew past her and landed in the dirt by my feet, showering me with bits of debris. I scrambled to my feet. Another *crack* was followed by a thud as Jake collapsed into the dirt. Mom spun away from the next fireball as I unhooked Flik's lead from the hitch and leapt onto his back.

I couldn't be much help to Mom in a fair fight, but my parents hadn't always been big on fighting fair.

I removed Flik's muzzle. He snapped his jaws as I spun him around to face the half-elf squaring off with my mom. She'd seen how quickly Mom disabled her friend and was being careful to keep her distance. That meant she wasn't focused on me.

"Flik, *revash!*"

The half-elf glanced my way. Her eyes went wide. "Bloody hell!"

Mom scooped a handful of dirt and threw it in the half-elf's eyes. The girl let the fireball loose in my direction, but it was too late. Flik and I were already airborne. Flik landed on top of her, pinning her to the ground. He brought his face down to meet hers and growled. I did a quick mental check that I'd fed him before we left home.

"I told you to go home," Mom said.

"I couldn't just—"

"Get it off, get it off!" the half-elf begged. "Oh god, don't let it eat me. Oh god, oh god..."

Mom glared at me. "Sydney..."

I sighed and tapped the side of Flik's neck. "*Lomani.*" He gave one last growl, but stepped off the girl. Mom grabbed her shirt and hauled her to her feet.

"You seem to be causing trouble in my town."

"I'm sorry, I'm sorry!" The half-elf's eyes were still fixed on Flik. "It won't happen again."

"Oh, I know it won't." Mom grabbed the girl's chin and turned her face so they were eye-to-eye. "You know who I am?"

"The... the sheriff?"

Mom smiled. "Congratulations, you know what a badge looks like. Read the name."

The half-elf looked down at Mom's badge. "Celeste Wint—" She froze. "Celeste Winter..."

"Now, I'm gonna ask you again. You know who I am?"

The girl nodded. Being eaten by a raptor was suddenly the least of her worries.

"Then I don't need to tell you how bad you just messed up." A pair of deputies arrived on the scene, and Mom shoved the girl into their arms. "I'll deal with y'all two later, but I just got one last question. You think you can answer that for me?"

The girl swallowed hard, but nodded.

Mom stepped up to her, staring her dead in the eye. "Did you just throw a fireball at my son?"

"Your..." She looked from Mom to me. Her panic shot up tenfold. "Oh god, I—"

After one hell of a right hook, Mom's deputies dragged the unconscious half-elf away.

No wonder I couldn't get a date in this town.

Mom sighed and turned to me. "The hell were you thinking, Sydney? You see a problem, you come get me. You shouldn't be getting yourself involved. You're only seventeen."

I hopped down from Flik's back. "Hey, I'm doing better than you and Dad were at seventeen."

"That's different and you know it. When I was seventeen—"

"You were robbing banks. Can't you at least be happy I'm trying to do, you know, the opposite of that?"

She rolled her eyes. "Yes, I'm thrilled your face ain't on wanted posters. That's a very low bar for a mother to set for her child." She grabbed my shoulders and looked me over. "You alright?"

"Yeah, I'm fine." I took a breath and dug into what was left of my dignity. "Thanks for the save."

"Don't mention it. You can pay me back by helping your dad with dinner tonight."

Someone cleared his throat behind us. "Got room at that table for one more?"

I dropped Flik's reins in surprise and spun around. "Uncle Darian!"

He laughed and wrapped me in a hug. "It's been a while, Sydney. Good to see you."

Mom was slower in her approach. "Darian..." They hugged, but mom looked tense as she broke it off. "What's wrong?"

Darian looked from her to me. "Where's Mathiu?"

"At the ranch. Why?"

"We need to talk." Darian set his eyes on me. "I have a job for Sydney."

Chapter 2

LANEI

I t had been easier to sneak through the streets of Rivalta as a young girl, before gaslights lit up every corner. Their amber glow violated the sanctity of the night, threatening to rob me of the anonymity I required. I pulled my hood tight and stuck to the shadows as best I could.

Even at night, the capital of Maldova was beautiful. Homes and stores adorned with copper and rose gold glinted in the gaslight. Carefully maintained parks popped up every few blocks, the last vestiges of nature in a city obsessed with the future. And on a hill above it all sat a palace so grand you could be forgiven for thinking poverty only existed in the lesser kingdoms. The whole facade was meant to make its citizens well with pride and its visitors green with envy.

And damned if it didn't work.

I'd never left the kingdom before. Most Maldovans never did. Why would we? All our lives, we've been told Maldova is the bastion of human civilization and progress in Nasan. From a technological standpoint, I knew that was true. But I still had doubts.

Leaving home was either the greatest decision or biggest mistake of my life. By the time I knew which, it'd be too late to turn back.

I circled the stables twice before I was satisfied the area was free of prying eyes. I checked the shutters on the rear window. Unlocked, as agreed. I slid inside.

The stables were dimly lit from a single flickering light overhead. Ridley's pen was easy to spot. The enormous Clydesdale stood three hands taller than the horses around him.

"Hey, boy." I produced a carrot from my cloak and offered it to him. He accepted with a grateful whinny. "You ready to become a fugitive?"

"Already planning for the worst?"

I spun around, my hand reaching for my sword. The handle of a pitchfork smacked my hand away. I winced in pain.

"Goddammit, Cassius." I rubbed at my sore hand. "You're going to send me to Petrichor with a broken knuckle."

The old disgraced knight stepped out of the shadows and planted the pitchfork in the ground. "You're out of practice."

"No, you're just an asshole." I eyed the bags in the pen behind him. "Is it all there?"

Cassius nodded. "Everything you requested."

"And my work?"

"Yes. Next time, don't make me run all over the city collecting your belongings."

I grinned. "Gotta get your cardio in somehow."

"I will have you know, my cardio is fine. But I don't relish the thought of being caught and questioned."

"That's why I didn't want it all in one place. Thought it was better to—"

Cassius pulled back my cloak, revealing my hair. He touched the freshly dyed blue streak. "What is this?"

"I... I wanted to make a change. It's not much, but..."

"It suits you." Cassius smiled. In the dim light of the stable, he looked his age. The gray in his beard seemed to extend to his eyes, giving them a faraway look. "Your mother would have been proud of you."

I cleared my throat and pulled the cloak back over my head. "We'll see. I won't have anyone to bail me out if things go south."

Being on my own was nothing new. I'd mastered the art of being alone in a crowded room, sometimes for better, sometimes for worse. But this would be a different kind of alone. Shit, if I didn't wind up dead or in prison, I could probably write this whole deal off as a success.

"You're resourceful. You'll figure something out." Cassius offered me a hand to climb onto Ridley's back. I didn't need it, but I took it anyway. He handed me a large bag, which I slung across my back. "Will you go straight to Esperan?"

I shook my head. "Too risky. I'm taking an indirect route through Laredo."

Cassius laughed. "Laredo... Well, you're in for a shock. It's a far cry from Maldova."

"Everything is." I squeezed Ridley's sides and he stepped out of his pen. "Thank you, Cassius."

"Stay alive. That's all I ask." Cassius opened the stable doors, letting in the night air. "Are you prepared for what lies ahead?"

I wasn't. But I had to be.

"Someone needs to burn it all to the ground. May as well be me."

Chapter 3

SYDNEY

Uncle Darian's visits usually involved him and Dad staying up until all hours drinking whiskey and telling stories. No matter how long it'd been, they always fell back into it like old friends. But tonight was different. Mom didn't say much the whole way home and Dad only cracked two jokes before offering Darian a cup of coffee.

Not whiskey. Coffee.

Something was up.

Nobody was ever going to look at us and mistake Darian for my blood relative. His dark brown skin contrasted with mine, which didn't have half the tan it should for someone who grew up in a desert. My father always said you had two families: The one you're born into and the one you choose. Darian was the latter. He and my dad had been getting each other out of trouble since they were kids, and they'd been close as brothers ever since.

My parents have always been straight with me about their past. Darian was part of their gang back when they cut a solid swath out of Laredo before they'd had enough of living like bandits and wanted to do good for a change. When I was born, my parents made Darian my godfather.

Bottom line, Darian was always there for my dad and always had his back. That's family, whether you share the same blood or not.

Darian took a sip of coffee and gagged. He cleared his throat and set the mug down. "Remind me to bring you the good stuff next time I visit."

Mom let out a laugh more bitter than the coffee. "Maybe next time you'll write ahead and let us know you're coming."

Dad put a hand on her arm. "Celeste..."

"No." She got to her feet and started pacing. "You said you'd give us plenty of warning."

"Things have changed," Darian said. "Aguilar wants to pull the trigger now."

"But we haven't started—" Mom looked at me. She shook her head. "He's only seventeen."

Dad smiled. "When we were seventeen—"

"I know what we did at seventeen!" Mom threw her hands up. "I was there. Will everyone please stop telling me things I already know?"

Darian lifted his mug to take another sip, but thought better of it. He set it back down. "It's Sydney's choice. I'm not here to force him into anything."

They all looked at me. I waited for an explanation, but, well...

"Yeah... I've got no idea what y'all are talking about. You're gonna have to give me a noun or something."

Darian sighed. "Petrichor."

I choked on the whiskey I wasn't drinking. The Petrichor Martial Academy in San Domingo was the premiere training ground for Esperan's guilds. The finest warriors, archers, magic users, tacticians, you

Into the Black

name it, that's where they went for six months of intensive training to be molded into the best of the best. I, however, was none of those things.

"I appreciate your faith, but I ain't got a mudsill's chance at getting into Petrichor."

"You're already in," Darian said. "You just need to say the word."

"I'm already..." I looked at my parents. "Did I miss something?"

Mom ground her jaw. "Your uncle's about to be missing his front teeth."

Darian glared at her. "Can we not do this right now?"

Mom held up her hands in mock surrender.

Darian turned back to me. "What do you know about the disturbances in the magical community over the last year?"

I blinked. "The what now?"

"That's what I figured. Not a lot of magic in Laredo." Darian cracked his knuckles. "I'll bottom line it for you. Right now's a dangerous time for non-humans. The sindari, elves, and throldkin have been targets of violent attacks throughout Esperan and Maldova, and to a lesser extent the rest of Nasan. Lord Aguilar's doing what he can to stop the violence in Esperan. As for Maldova, well... Lord Greyton hasn't done much to help anyone but himself."

How had I not heard about this? Chisholm wasn't so far removed from the rest of the continent, was it?

"I don't understand. They're hurting people 'cause they ain't human?"

"The world's changing, Sydney. The advances in technology over the last few decades have been extraordinary. Steam engines, the telegraph and phonograph, gas lighting... These were unheard of a hundred years ago." Darian stroked the edges of his mustache. "But it's not

19

enough for some folks. They see the other races' magic and hate that humans don't have it."

"Some of us do. I've got magic." I lifted my hand to demonstrate but thought better of it. "Sort of."

"You've got some elf in you. Pureblood humans don't have any innate magic. That's where the resentment comes in. Some of these people believe the magical races have gotten a free pass, not needing to innovate the way humans have. They twist that into believing the existence of magic is holding humans back."

"That don't make sense." I frowned. "How's magic holding us back if we've been making so many advancements?"

"There's that logic I taught ya," Dad said. "Bigots ain't big on that."

Darian sighed. "A lot of these people aren't necessarily evil, they've just been manipulated into believing they're victims."

"Manipulated by who?"

"Are you familiar with the Children of Omek?"

A shiver ran up my spine at the mention of Omek. Everyone knew that name. "Omek's been dead a hundred years."

Darian nodded. "It's much easier to kill a man than an ideology. The Children are an old cult that's regaining ground. They've taken credit for the recent attacks, and the fear they're spreading is starting to catch. We've been seeing an exodus from the northern kingdoms. Queen Valeria summoned the remaining sindari back to Rainess. The throldkin are returning to Wismore. And the elves... hell, at this point you could probably count the pureblood elves in Nasan on one hand. The rest have fled back across the sea. Even the half-bloods are feeling the impact. Anyone who looks visibly non-human has a target over their head."

Mom waved a hand at my face. "Look at his eyes! There's your target right there."

Darian held up a hand. "Eyes don't stick out as much as ears. These people ain't great at nuance."

"Oh, good." Mom flexed her fist and glared at her knuckles. "We're relying on nuance here. I'll show you what nuance—"

"Honey..." Dad placed a hand on her arm, but she shook it off and retrieved the whiskey from the shelf. She poured a glass for herself, sighed, and moved to pour a dram in Darian's mug.

"Oh, god no." He slapped a hand over the mug. "Don't tarnish good whiskey like that."

Mom rolled her eyes, but a smile flickered on her face while she got him a clean glass.

"Understand, this is an active, angry minority. Most Esperanians don't think that way, but that doesn't mean they aren't looking the other way, pretending it'll disappear on its own. It won't. Not if we don't do something about it. That's where you come in."

"Me? How do I figure in?"

"I need a student at Petrichor I can trust."

"I... okay..."

"Ascension recently learned that several of Petrichor's top graduates have been drafted into the Children of Omek. Lord Aguilar and I believe there's a traitor at the school recruiting students to their cause. I want you to help root them out."

I blinked. "I'm sorry, I thought you just said you wanted me to be a spy."

"I did."

"I'm not a spy. Hell, I'm barely subtle. And I can't fight worth a piss. Just ask Mom."

"You can learn those things. It is a martial academy, after all." Darian studied me for a few moments. "Look.

I'm not going to force you to do this. I chose you specifically because I trust you and your parents without question, and there aren't a lot of people I can say that about. I've watched you grow up. Maybe you aren't equipped for this task right now, but you've got the character and intellect to pull it off. The rest will come."

"It's your choice," Mom said. "You don't have to do it."

Dad nodded and took Mom's hand. "But if you do, we'll have your back."

Darian cleared his throat. "So, Sydney, tell me. Are you—"

"I'm in." I looked between the three of them. "You've got the wrong guy for the job, but I want to help."

"Goddammit." Mom wrapped her arms around me. "Why'd I have to raise you to do the right thing?"

"That's on you." Dad smirked. "I wanted to bring him up as a thief, but no, you said our boy ought to be better than us."

Darian smiled. "One of my men, Reno Isale, is the new hand-to-hand combat instructor. He'll be your advisor and go-between if you need to get a message to me. Outside of myself, Headmaster Kane, and Lord Aguilar, he is the *only* person you can trust. Do not tell anyone else of your mission. Understood?"

I nodded. "Understood."

"Good. You leave first thing tomorrow." Darian flipped open his pocket watch. "I got an hour before my train leaves. Come on, Mathiu. I'll help you get Flik ready." He turned to my mom. "Celeste."

"Darian." Mom gave him a long stare then sighed and hugged him. "I love you, but you know the drill."

"Anything happens to him, you kill me," Darian said. "Loud and clear."

"Good."

Darian placed a hand on my shoulder and gave me an approving nod. "Good luck, kid. I'm counting on you."

"I won't let you down."

I watched him walk out the door, praying I wasn't lying to him.

Chapter 4

SYDNEY

arian wasn't kidding when he said the train left first thing in the morning. It pulled into the station as the sun crept over the horizon. The stable car attendants threw a fit when they saw Flik, but Mom pulled a few golden strings and they agreed to stable him so long as his muzzle stayed on. They wanted to do something about his claws, but really, have you ever tried putting boots on a raptor? It doesn't happen. They like their claws nice and available. Dad got him settled in his pen while Mom and I checked my luggage.

"Be sure to write if you need anything." Mom reached to adjust my cowboy hat.

I ducked. "I'll be fine."

"I know you will. But I'm allowed to worry."

Dad hopped out of the stable car. "We're all set. Now, I want you to promise me you won't do anything stupid."

"Dad..."

"I'm serious." He gave me a stern look. "Before you do anything, ask yourself if it's something your mom or I would do. If it is, do something else."

I laughed. "I'll keep that in mind."

"We love you." Mom smiled at me, her eyes brimming.

"And we're proud of you," Dad added.

"I love you, too." I hugged them as the stationmaster blew his whistle.

"That's you." Mom held onto me for a moment longer. "Your father and I haven't always made the right choices. But we eventually got it right."

Mom let go and gave me a gentle push onto the train. I waved goodbye as the door closed between us.

The first three cars were all full, or at least full enough that I couldn't get a bench to myself. That made it all the stranger when the fourth car only had five people in it: four Maldovan knights playing cards and a muscular girl my age who looked like she could take any one of them in a fight. I'd never seen Maldovan knights before, but I recognized their heavy plate armor. No way that was comfortable in this heat.

One of the knights looked up from the card game and gave me a look that told me I wasn't getting dealt in. Too bad, 'cause I could've used the extra spending money.

I walked halfway down the car and slid into a bench. Metal rattled as one of the knights thumped his fist against the wall.

"Move along, hillbilly. This car's not for you."

I turned in my seat. He had a thick mustache that curled up on the ends. The tip on one end touched a scar across his right cheek. "Are you serious?"

"Do I look like I'm joking?"

"Depends. You making that face on purpose, or did it come like that?"

The knight scowled and stood. "You want to step outside?"

"We're on a moving train."

"And?"

Oh. Right. That was probably the idea.

"Don't let them bully you," the girl at the end of the car said, her face still buried in her book. "They may think they own everything, but they're not in Maldova anymore. They can't actually do anything about it." She looked up from her book and smiled at them. "Isn't that right?"

The knight narrowed his eyes, but grumbled and sat back down.

I moved a few rows ahead and sat on the bench opposite her. "Thanks."

"Don't mention it. You know how Maldova is. Always butting their heads in other people's business."

"Can't rightly say. I ain't met many Maldovans."

"That's been my experience. And as someone from there, I should know." She extended her hand. "Lanei Walker."

I shook it. "Sydney Winter."

"Nice to meet you." Lanei set her book aside. She was pretty, with light brown skin and long wavy black hair which had a blue streak falling down the side of her face. She also had numerous piercings, and I caught myself staring at them. Laredan girls rarely had more than a single piercing in their earlobes. Lanei also had two in the cartilage of each ear, along with a small hoop through her right eyebrow. Hadn't even left home and I was already getting culture shock. "Got to say, I'm glad to have someone else in this compartment. After those knights sat down, everyone else kept walking."

"I thought knights were supposed to be, you know... noble."

Lanei smirked. "You're thinking of Araspian knights. Araspia's an awful long way from here."

"Yeah, I suppose so."

She laid her arm across the back of the bench. "So, where are you headed?"

"San Domingo. I'm, uh..." I couldn't believe the words that were about to come out of my mouth. "I'm going to the Petrichor Martial Academy."

"No shit?" Lanei cocked her head to the side. "Me too."

I grinned. "That's awesome!"

It made sense. This girl looked like a badass. Her muscles were more defined than mine and she had a small crook in her nose, a look I recognized from both my parents. It'd probably been broken before.

"I've been counting down the days since I got the letter," Lanei said. "What about you?"

"My letter? Oh, yeah, it didn't come until, um... yesterday."

Lanei raised her pierced eyebrow. "You should've gotten that weeks ago. Did they say anything at your evaluation?"

"No, they said..." Think fast, think fast... "...normal things."

Oh yeah. I was going to be a great spy.

The door to the compartment jangled open and a half-elf stepped in. He was average height for a human, but there was no mistaking his race with ears like that.

The knights stopped their card game and glared at the elf.

"Keep walking, half-breed," one of the knights said. "No room for your kind here."

He shoved the half-elf forward, right over another knight's foot. The half-elf crashed to the ground. He scrambled to his feet and hurried away from them.

I started to stand.

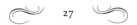

"Don't," Lanei said.

"But they—"

"Don't."

Lanei kept her eyes fixed out the window as the half-elf walked past. I expected him to chastise us for not doing anything, but he stared at Lanei, saying nothing. As he walked out the door at the opposite end, he turned around for one more look. Lanei continued watching the desert roll past.

"Hey," I said. "You okay?"

"It's been a long ride," she said. "Going to sleep a little before the next stop."

Lanei laid her head against the back of the bench and closed her eyes. I couldn't tell if she was faking it, but either way I gave her space and slid over to the other side of the aisle. I rested my head against the window. A nap wasn't the worst idea in the world.

I woke up to the train braking to a halt. The sudden stop jolted me halfway out of my seat. I had to grab the bench to keep from sliding off. Not the most graceful stop, but we didn't crash into anything, so it worked for me.

One look out the window told me we'd crossed into Esperan. My first time leaving Laredo and I'd slept right through it.

The architecture was unlike anything I'd ever seen. Other than the bank, the buildings in Chisholm were made of wood and not a whole lot else. But here, all the walls were covered in a light tan plaster, which made the buildings look classier than the ones back home. Archways extended off the outer walls and created a sort of covered pathway between the streets and buildings.

Even the roofs were different. Instead of flat wooden shingles, these were curved and made of fired clay.

Yep. I wasn't in Laredo anymore.

I took advantage of the stop to get out and stretch my legs. A few people milled around the platform, a combination of new passengers preparing to board and people who'd stepped out to get fresh air. I walked past them to check out the general store. I'd missed out on my first view of Esperan, so I might as well take a sec to see what this kingdom was about.

As it turned out, this kingdom was about food. Lots and lots of canned, jarred, and bagged food.

Sure, we had canned food in Chisholm. I mean, it's the middle of a desert. Most houses at least had a stash of preserved foods saved away for a not-so-rainy day. Kind of need that to not die. But our general store only stocked the necessities: Meat, vegetables, fruits, alcohol... Esperan had more room for luxury foods.

The shelves were lined with jars of candies, chocolates, syrups, jellies, pickles, sauces, and a whole bunch of stuff I'd never heard of. Bags on the shelves advertised everything from fried potato slices to roasted nuts. Uncle Darian sometimes brought snacks with him when he'd visit, but I had no idea they were this easy to buy. I figured he was bringing the fancy stuff.

I grabbed a bag of potato slices and a couple jars of candies that weren't too expensive. No point loading myself down. If there were this many snacks at a train station, they had to be growing on trees in San Domingo.

The first whistle sounded. Perfect timing. Now I could enjoy the rest of the trip with tasty treats to—

"You don't want to do this." The voice was faint, but I recognized it. Lanei.

"Don't tell me what I want," said a male voice.

"You're making a mistake."

I followed the voices into an alley behind the store. Lanei was there, backed against the wall. The half-elf from the train stood in front of her, his knife pointed at her throat.

"I know exactly wh—"

"Hey!" I called out.

The half-elf's head snapped in my direction. Lanei's hand flashed up and shoved the knife aside. She grabbed him by the back of the head and slammed him face first into the wall behind her. He crumpled to the ground.

I sprinted down the alley. "Are you okay?"

Lanei stared at the half-elf's unconscious body. "Better than him."

"I'll say." I looked around. "We should report it to someone."

"Leave him. The train's about to head out. It was only a mugging."

"How about them knights?" I gestured back toward the train. "They'll know what to do."

"No!" Lanei looked past me down the alley. "The last thing we need is Maldovan knights trying to take control of a crime in Esperan. You want to talk about an international incident?" She shook her head. "No. I'm fine. Just let it slide."

"But—"

The whistle blew twice more.

"Come on." Lanei nudged the half-elf with her boot until his body flopped over. She studied his face and heaved a sigh. "Time to go."

I wanted to protest, but she left the alley before I could say anything. Why would she join Petrichor if she didn't want to bring the guy who attacked her to justice? Unless justice in Maldova boiled down to kicking someone's ass.

I shook my head. Apparently, I had a lot to learn.

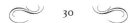

Chapter 5

LANEI

Goddamn half-elf poking his nose in my business. Goddamn knights with their goddamn eyes tracking my every goddamn move.

And goddamn, Sydney sure could talk up a storm.

It took some time for him to drop the incident at the station. He kept going back to it until I spotted the deck of cards in his pocket and asked him to teach me to play poker. That kept him occupied for a good while. I think he even believed he was teaching me.

I studied Sydney while he rattled on about poker hands. He was not what I expected from a Petrichor recruit. Nothing about him screamed elite fighter. He was in shape, but not muscular. He certainly didn't carry himself like someone with years of training under his belt. What was he then? Stealth and subterfuge? No, he came off too naive to have been recruited for that. He didn't look like magic was in his blood. Ranged, maybe? That was possible. I could see him firing a bow and arrow from horseback. The cowboy look lent itself to that.

Sydney set the cards down and pulled out the bag of junk food he bought at the store. "I don't know about you, but I could eat the north end of a south bound bear."

I blinked. "What are you..." My eyes widened as he dug a jar of little red candies out of the bag. "Are those Cherry Drops?"

Sydney checked the label. "Looks like."

"Oh my god." I snatched the jar out of his hand. "I haven't had these in forever. They were my mother's favorite. She used to have them shipped from Kialen when I was little." The world around me blurred. I bit my lip to bring myself back to the present. "Sorry. I think I turned into a five-year-old for a second there." I held the jar out to him.

Sydney shook his head. "Keep 'em. I can get more in San Domingo."

"No, I can't do that."

"Sure you can. Just pull your hand back and boom, done."

I hesitated. "Are you sure?"

He flashed a goofy grin. "They're calling your name."

"Thank you." I smiled. This cowboy wasn't so bad. "These are more addictive than snowdust." I unscrewed the lid and offered the jar to Sydney. "Seriously, though, you have to try one."

We each took a Cherry Drop from the jar. When I bit through the gummy exterior, the fruit explosion hit my tongue and I was once again a little girl sitting in my mother's lap in a world that still made sense.

"Hot damn." Sydney pointed to his mouth. "You weren't kidding!" At least his world hadn't burst yet.

The train slowed. I looked out the window. San Domingo stretched as far as the eye could see.

Sydney pressed his nose against the window, taking in the view outside. "Are you seeing this?"

San Domingo was undoubtedly beautiful. It lacked the marvel of Maldova's largest cities, but it didn't feel like it was competing with them. Esperan's capital combined the size and scope of Maldova with the genuineness of Laredo. But as I'd learned, there was always something hidden beneath the veneer. I was counting on it.

The station sat at the edge of the city, so the train ground to a halt before long. We stepped off and headed down the line to the stable car. I glanced over my shoulder. The knights exited behind us and walked to the center of the platform. Lovely...

Ridley was in the first pen of the stable car. He neighed at my approach and nuzzled the side of my head.

"Oh wow..." Sydney looked my horse up and down, amazement in his eyes. He whistled. "I ain't never seen a Clydesdale in person."

"This is Ridley." I reached up and scratched behind his ears. I glanced down the line of stalls, not wanting Sydney to dwell on how I'd managed to get such a nice horse. "Which one's yours?"

"Um... about that." Sydney led me to an enclosed stall at the far end of the car. The door shook as the creature inside rammed its body into it. It did it again as we neared. The nearby horses whinnied and shied away.

I slowed to a halt. "Is he okay? That can't be good for him."

"He's probably sick of being cooped up. Ain't never been on a train before."

The door rattled again.

"Damn. You should let him out before he hurts himself."

Sydney laughed. "Yeah, I ain't too worried about that." He unlatched the door and swung it open, revealing—

"Holy fucking shit!" I stumbled back, tripped, and landed on my ass. "Oh fuck. Holy fuck. That's a raptor!"

"Oh, yeah. This is Flik."

"A raptor ate your horse!"

"No, Flik is—"

"A fucking raptor!"

"Well, yes. But he's still—"

"A. Rap. Tor!"

"Um... Yes." Sydney scratched under the beast's chin. The raptor closed his eyes and cooed.

I blinked several times to make sure I wasn't seeing things. The goddamn raptor cocked his head to the side and looked at me like I was a crazy person. "How is he not ripping your throat out right now?"

"I mean, I do feed him."

"People?" What the hell kind of redneck shit are they getting into in Laredo?

"No, not... How's that the first place you go?" Sydney removed Flik's muzzle. He stretched his jaws as Sydney reached into his saddle bag and pulled out a piece of dried meat. "Here. Give him one of these."

I've done some dumb things in my life, but even I'd never put my hand anywhere near a raptor's mouth. "Will he eat me if I don't?"

"He'd say yes, but that's just 'cause he likes treats."

This boy was insane. That was the only explanation.

With great caution, I took the piece of meat and got to my feet. I crept up to Flik's pen and held the meat at arm's length, advancing one tiny step at a time.

"He's not gonna bite. I promise."

I narrowed my eyes. "If I lose my hand on the first day, I swear I'm gonna kill you."

I took a deep breath and stepped forward, dangling the meat directly in front of Flik's mouth with my fingernails. The raptor stretched his neck out and, ever so gently, plucked the piece of meat from my hand. He chewed it slowly, never taking his eyes off me, and then swallowed in not one but two gulps. I was pretty sure the damned thing was being condescending.

I stared in amazement. "Doesn't he try to eat you?"

"Not so much anymore." Sydney pointed out a few of the scars on his arm. Flik cooed and rubbed his head against it. "My dad met a human with a raptor back when he was a..." Sydney's eyes shifted back to me. "When he was younger. After I was born, he started training them. I asked for a puppy when I turned thirteen, but Dad gave me an egg instead. Said he was afraid one of his raptors would eat a dog, so he got me my very own predator. I've been taking care of Flik since he hatched." He shrugged. "I guess it's a little unusual."

"A little?" I scoffed. "A little unusual is finding an abandoned chest of gold on the side of the road. This is like someone leaving the palace doors open with a 'Free Treasure' sign out front."

"Is that a thing where you're from?"

"I'm just saying. Damn."

Sydney opened the gate to Flik's pen. He stretched and stepped out. I shifted to take a step back, but held my ground. If this overgrown lizard was going to be at Petrichor, I'd have to get used to him. Sydney strapped Flik's saddle onto his back and led him through the car. The horses shied away to the backs of their pens. All except for Ridley. The big horse whinnied, but didn't back away. Flik cocked his head and chirped a couple times. Ridley snorted in response and turned his head aside.

Sydney laughed. "I don't think your horse is a fan."

"Ridley can be stuck up. I think he was bred that way." I gathered up Ridley's things and glanced outside the car. The knights were still standing on the platform. I cursed. Bastards had been too close for comfort since I boarded the train. The last thing I needed was a confrontation now.

Thank god for cowboys and killer lizards.

I finished saddling Ridley. "Hey, I'm going to be a few minutes here. You go on ahead and I'll catch you at Petrichor."

"Yeah, okay. I'll see you there." Sydney tipped his hat.

I gave Flik a cautious pat on his neck. "Keep him out of trouble. He's going to attract attention, and probably not all the good kind."

Sure enough, gasps and astonished cries greeted Sydney and Flik within moments of stepping onto the platform. The crowd parted as they passed. They stopped at the baggage car, where a nervous looking attendant took Sydney's ticket, ran inside for his bag, and hurled it out the door without coming back out.

The knights looked ready to shit themselves when they saw Flik. Their hands went to their swords, but they didn't draw. Their eyes followed Sydney as he exited the platform. While they were distracted, I hauled my bag over my shoulder, led Ridley off the train, and took off in the other direction.

Not this time, boys. I've got places to be.

Chapter 6

SYDNEY

I dropped Flik off at the stables and promised to come back once I'd gotten settled in. However, I gave my sense of direction way too much credit. Petrichor was a large, sprawling series of buildings, and the dorms weren't all in one place. I finally found mine on the second floor of the fourth building I wandered into.

I'd never seen anything like it. The room had stone walls, arching windows, heavy oak furniture, gas lamps, and a large open area in its center. Each side had a bed twice the size of my bed at home, a tall dresser, a desk, and an empty weapons rack.

Were we supposed to bring weapons? Hopefully they were giving us some, because I had a great big nothing in the weapons department.

I grinned at the sight of an actual light switch. I flipped it. The gas lamp flickered to life. I hit the switch again and it dimmed out. Once more, and the light came back on. So cool...

The door opened. The guy who entered was roughly the same height and build as me, but with a darker complexion and long black hair hanging loose over gold studs in both ears. He took one look at me and came to a halt.

"Hi..." He stretched the word out into a full sentence.

"Hey. I'm Sydney." I stuck out my hand. He shook it, but his eyes kept searching the room.

"Kaden..." He walked back to the door, pulled out a piece of paper, and double checked something. He stepped back in, brow furrowed. "This is 14B, right?"

"Yeah, 14B."

"Huh..."

"Something wrong?"

"I think they put me in the wrong room." Kaden set his bag down on the bed. I raised an eyebrow, and he quickly shook his head. "No, sorry, it's nothing personal. I was supposed to be in a room with someone else. I'll leave my things here until I get it straightened out at orientation." Kaden ducked back outside and wheeled in two large cases, which he leaned against the bed.

"Were we supposed to have gotten roommate assignments already?"

"Well, no, but I was supposed to be with... a friend of mine got in too, and we requested to room together."

"Oh." I shrugged. "Sorry about that."

Kaden shook his head. "No worries. I'll figure it out." His face brightened, the whole roommate confusion behind him. "So, Sydney, right?"

I nodded.

"Nice to meet you. I'm Kaden. Kaden Ashworth."

He paused. I think I was supposed to say something. "Sydney Winter."

"Winter..." He thought it over. "I'm not familiar with the Winters. Where are you from?"

"Chisholm." That got me a blank look. "Sorry. Laredo."

"Ah, that's why. We only read about a few Laredans in school."

"My family wouldn't be in there." At least, I *hoped* my family wouldn't be in there. That'd be an awkward conversation at this kind of school. "Where are you from?"

Kaden cocked an eyebrow. "Araspia. You know... Ashworth."

I shrugged. Didn't ring any bells.

"Wait, wait, wait..." Kaden stared at me. "You don't know who my family is?"

"Uh, no. Sorry."

Kaden clapped his hands together. "Sorry? Dude, do *not* be sorry about that! It's such a relief to meet someone who's never heard of us. That just doesn't happen back home."

"Oh. Well, you're welcome then."

"Expectations are a beast, huh?"

"Yeah, I get that... Everyone expects you to follow in your parents' footsteps."

"Right!" Kaden laughed. "So what are yours, some sort of Laredan nobles?"

I shook my head. "Pretty sure we don't have nobles in Laredo."

"Oh. So what do they do?"

"They..." I thought about the easiest way to phrase it. "Well, my mom's a sheriff and my dad's a rancher."

"A sheriff?" Kaden rubbed at his jaw. "That's sort of like a knight, right?"

"Yeah, close enough. Same concept at least."

"And a rancher... Damn. So you must be, like, a major badass, huh?"

Color rose in my cheeks. "Don't know if I'd say that."

"Ha, modest! Don't worry, once classes start you can let your actions do the talking."

That's what I was afraid of. "Something like that."

Kaden laughed. "I like you. Hopefully we wind up on the same squad after this roommate thing gets worked out." He checked his pocket watch. "Fancy checking out the grounds before orientation?"

He flicked it closed and was out the door before I could respond.

"This is Araspia's first year sending knight candidates to Petrichor." Kaden led me through the corridors like he already knew the place by heart. "It's sort of a test run to see if they can meet the standards we're accustomed to. And I was chosen as one of the inaugural candidates."

I gathered that, seeing as he was here talking to me, but pointing that out wasn't going to win me any friends. Act impressed. "Oh. That's cool."

"I know! They selected four of us, including, get this... Yasir Levenheit!"

I blinked at him.

"Yasir Levenheit," Kaden repeated.

I shrugged. "Sorry."

"Son of Sayid Levenheit."

"Yeah, still not ringin' any bells."

"Seriously? First Knight of Araspia. Kind of a big deal."

"Don't really come up where I'm from."

"Huh." Kaden was quiet a moment. "Well, that's just weird."

"I mean, it's a whole different kingdom. I wouldn't expect you to know who's who in Laredo."

"Yes, but that's Laredo. I'm talking about Araspia."

I stopped and stared at him. "You know you sound like a dick, right?"

Kaden considered this. "I do, don't I? Sorry about that."

"No worries."

The Academy really was something. We passed several halls of dormitories and poked our heads into a couple classrooms. The most intimidating of them looked more like an armory than a classroom. Weapon racks lined the room, covering everything from the usual swords and axes to daggers, whips, and staves. The center of the room was a large open courtyard, presumably where students would duke it out. I hoped the weapons had blunted edges. If not, I didn't like my odds of walking out of here with all my limbs.

"Pretty nice, huh?"

I spun around so fast I tripped over myself. I hadn't even heard Lanei sneak up on us. Kaden didn't seem the least bit startled by her sudden appearance.

"Don't do that," I said.

"Don't do what?"

"Sneak up on people like that."

She snorted. "That wasn't sneaking. That was walking. You'd know if I was sneaking."

"How would I know? If you're doing it right, I'd never hear you."

"No, but you'd be flat on your back."

"Yeah, well..." I struggled for a comeback, but had nothing.

Kaden cleared his throat.

"Oh, right. Lanei, this is my roommate, Kaden. Kaden, Lanei."

Kaden took Lanei's hand and bowed with a grand flourish. "Kaden Ashworth. A pleasure."

Lanei raised an eyebrow. "Araspia, right?"

Kaden smiled. "Ah, so you've heard of me." He winked at me. "I've been trying to explain to our friend here—"

"Nope, never heard of you," Lanei said. "But when someone goes out of their way for archaic formalities, my mind goes straight to Araspia." She gave Kaden a wink of her own.

I stifled a laugh, but Kaden let his out, doubling over from laughter. "Oh, you're wicked. I like you." He nudged me again. "I like this girl."

"Oh good," Lanei deadpanned. "I'd be lost without your approval."

"Come now, you'd get over it," Kaden said. "Eventually."

"So," I said, "have you met your roommate yet?"

"What? Oh, no. They put me in a single. Must be an odd number of girls on my squad or something. Or, you know, however that works."

"That's a shame," Kaden said. "If you were rooming with my sister, you'd be with me and Sydney on the Araspia squad. And you'll never guess who else is on—"

"Yasir Levenheit." Lanei shrugged. "Meh."

"Meh?" Kaden's jaw hung open. "Meh? No. No, you cannot just 'meh' Yasir Levenheit."

"Meh," Lanei repeated.

"But..." Kaden stammered. "But... He's Yasir *Levenheit*. How can you 'meh' the son of Araspia's First Knight?"

"Talk to me once he's accomplished something on his own. Until then, I couldn't care less who his parents are."

"But... But..."

I fake whispered in Lanei's ear. "I think you broke him."

She smiled. "He should be so lucky."

"You two are unbelievable. Not impressed by lineage... Whoever heard of such a thing?"

"I know," I said. "We're the worst."

A hoarse voice spoke from behind us. "Not all of you."

A middle aged woman stood in a doorway across the hall, her narrowed eyes magnified behind the lenses of her glasses. She wore her gray hair pulled back tight, which complemented the permanent scowl that made her look like someone had spat tobacco in her soup.

Kaden bowed. "Instructor Russo."

Russo ignored him. Her eyes trained on me. "Apparently we're letting anyone in these days."

I stiffened. "I'm sorry, have we—"

"No." She strolled over to me, her eyes never leaving mine. "But I know your parents."

Oh.

Oh shit.

"I'm, uh... guessing you ain't old friends?"

Russo scoffed. "I've never cared for Lord Aguilar's association with Darian Rankin, but I didn't think he would be so blinded by that friendship to allow the spawn of Celeste and Mathiu Winter to disgrace the halls of this school." She spat on the ground. "The Celestial Riders, indeed."

I gritted my teeth. "That was a long time ago."

"Bad seeds don't change. They just sprout more poison." The heat from Russo's glare bored a hole into my skull. My temperature rose ten degrees. "Do you really expect me to believe you're anything more than concentrated poison?"

"You can believe—"

"That was a rhetorical question, Mr. Winter. Is your mind as dull as your parents' morals?" She inhaled through her nostrils, making a loud snorting sound. "That one was not rhetorical. Please tell me you aren't completely dim witted."

Lanei scoffed. "Well, you're a pleasant ray of sunshine, aren't you?"

Russo turned her gaze to Lanei. "Miss... Walker, is it?"

Lanei nodded. She held her ground.

"Well, Miss Walker, maybe you aren't accustomed to treating authority figures with respect where you're from, but I suggest you change that attitude immediately."

Lanei laughed. "After that little display, you're seriously going to talk to me about respect?"

Russo's icy demeanor cracked as she ground her teeth. "Yes, I am. And I believe you know why you of all people need a lesson in how to treat others." A smile formed on Russo's lips, but her eyes remained cold. "You will show me respect if you want your time here to be... tolerable. Do you understand my meaning, Miss Walker?"

Lanei bit her lip. She held Russo's gaze and let out a slow breath. "Perfectly."

"Good." Russo eyed Kaden. She brushed the side of her nose with her thumb then pointed at him. "Mr. Ashworth. You should be careful of the company you keep. One's choice of friends says so much about a person." Without waiting for a response, she stepped back into her classroom and shut the door.

We stood there, stunned. I was too embarrassed to say anything. Lanei clenched her fists so tight I could practically hear the strain on her knuckles. Kaden stared at the door in disbelief, looking back and forth between it, me, and Lanei.

He broke the silence. "Wow. I... don't think I can be friends with you two."

Fantastic. My time at Petrichor was off to one hell of a start.

Lanei spun on him. "Are you shitting me?"

"Yes," he said. "I am. Teach me your waaaaays." He smiled. "Seriously, everybody loves me. I can't even fathom what you two did to earn such ire from that woman."

"Some people were just born miserable," Lanei said.

"Terrible way to live. I like my way better." Kaden grinned. "Come on, let's go somewhere less dreary."

Kaden started off down the hallway. Lanei took a deep breath and, with great effort, unclenched her fists.

I knew why Russo hated me, but what had Lanei done to make Russo dislike her so much?

Chapter 7

SYDNEY

We still had time before orientation, so I suggested we visit the stables. I felt guilty for dropping Flik off in such a rush and wanted to check in on him. It was his first time away from home and I wasn't sure how he was handling it. He was probably homesick already. Questioning if he'd made a huge mistake and was in over his head. Thinking that at any moment he was going to be exposed as a fraud.

Flik. Not me. Flik.

From the outside, the stables looked like a fancy ranch house. On the inside, they were nicer than my house in Laredo. I don't mean they were nicer than the stables back home. I mean they were nicer than the house itself. These horses would be living in *style* for the next six months. Each stall was spacious and had artwork hanging inside. Actual artwork. Like, pastorals. Some of last year's horses must've complained the decor wasn't up to snuff.

I passed beneath a crystal chandelier in the center of the stables. "This all seems a little... unnecessary."

"Some of these horses must be prissy bitches." Lanei pulled a couple apples out of a barrel and tossed one to Kaden. "I know mine is."

Each stall had a bronze placard on its gate with the names of the horse and its owner. Lanei approached Ridley's stall and he stuck his head over the gate. He whinnied in appreciation and took the apple from Lanei's hand.

Kaden whistled. "Now *that* is a horse. Your family must be loaded."

Lanei winced. "He's not a vanity item."

"Maybe not, but... damn. Seriously, how much does a horse like that cost?"

"Does it matter?" Lanei reached up and scratched Ridley under the chin. "I don't keep him around because of his price tag."

"Come on," Kaden pressed. "I'm just—"

"Drop it." Lanei gave Ridley a couple pats on the head, and he retreated back into his stall.

"Yeesh, fine." Kaden walked down a few stalls to one with "Cosette" on the placard. Cosette was a sleek black horse with a white, diamond patch on her forehead. She nuzzled Kaden's hand, and he tossed the apple to her. She snatched it out of the air. "This is Cosette. Fastest horse you'll ever meet. Well, if you don't count my sister's." He nodded to the white horse in the stall beside Cosette's. "Which we don't."

Heavy footsteps sounded behind us as three more students entered. In the center was a hulking brute of a guy with long, greasy black hair and a flat nose. He was built like a bookcase, wide and sturdy, and wore brown leather pants with a brown shirt and black suspenders that were earning their keep. He was flanked by two slender figures who looked almost identical. Both had pale skin, long blond hair, and bright green eyes. Their clothing was different from anything I'd ever seen. The girl on the left wore a short leather skirt the color of wine, tall black boots, and a revealing brown corset covered with straps and brass buckles. The one on the right was probably a guy, but his features were as delicate as his sister's, so it was hard to tell. He wore breeches of the same burgundy as his sister's skirt, tucked into black boots of the same fashion, and a white shirt and dark purple tie under a brown leather vest with its own assortment of straps and buckles. They had goggles resting atop their heads and honest to god capes. These two wanted you to know they came as a pair.

Kaden nudged me in the ribs. "Warren Malenko and the Levesque twins. From Maldova."

Lanei cut them a quick glance and turned back to the stalls.

"How do you know them?" I asked.

"Oh please," Kaden said. "With the bad blood between Esperan and Maldova, I'm amazed Lord Aguilar allowed Lord Greyton's best knights to send their children to Petrichor. Almost as shocking as Lord Greyton permitting it in the first place. Don't you read the papers?" He paused. "Wait. You *can* read in Laredo, right?"

"Yes, we can—" I shook my head. "Lanei, do you know them?"

"Nope," she said, not bothering to give them another look.

Kaden frowned. "Wait. You're Maldovan?"

"Guilty."

"Lanei Walker..." Kaden thought about it. "I don't know the surname. Are either of your parents knights?"

"No."

"Then what—"

"Hello there!" I called out to the newcomers. Lanei snapped me a nasty look and Kaden mumbled something about the importance of formal introductions.

The three looked at me, but didn't say anything. The twins grinned, their lips curling up in unison. It was kind of creepy.

"I'm Sydney. This here's Lanei and Kaden."

Lanei raised a hand in acknowledgment, but didn't bother facing them. Kaden stepped forward and bowed deeply.

"Kaden Ashworth, future knight of Araspia. A pleasure to make your acquaintance." He held out his hand, but nobody made a move to shake it. Kaden let out an awkward laugh and pulled his hand back. "This is normally where you would introduce yourself."

The big guy crossed his arms. "Thanks for pointing that out. Here I thought you were waiting for a tip."

The girl stifled a laugh.

Kaden smiled. "Happy to clear it up."

The big guy wasn't amused. "I'm Warren Malenko." He jerked a thumb at the fancy pair beside him. "These two are Milia and Milich Levesque."

Milia burst out laughing. "I'm sorry, I'm sorry." Looking at me, she gestured around her head. "What is this?"

"Huh?" I asked.

"That... thing on your head. What is that?"

I raised an eyebrow. "It's... a cowboy hat."

"A cowboy hat," she repeated. "How cute." She turned to her brother and batted her eyes. "Isn't that cute, Milich?"

"Adorable," he said. "So common."

"So common," Milia confirmed. "Are you the stable boy for the term?"

"The stable boy?" I asked. "No, I—"

"Of course he's the stable boy," Milich said. "Why else would he be dressed like one?"

"I'm a student," I said. "This is how we dress in Laredo."

"Laredo?" Milia opened her eyes wide and raised her chin to Milich. He copied the gesture.

"What?" I asked.

"Oh, nothing," Milich said. "We were just discussing a rumor we'd heard that Petrichor accepts a charity case each year."

"Someone so pitiful he makes everyone else look wonderful by comparison."

"We just weren't expecting to find him so quickly."

Anger boiled up in me for the second time today. "I am not—"

"Oh, of course you're not," Milia said. "Surely it's some other poor boy here."

"Say, sister, have you seen anyone else dressed like a farmhand?"

"No, brother, I must say I have not."

"Well, then I can only conclude—"

"Will you two shut the hell up?" Lanei slammed her fist against the nearest stall. The horse inside neighed and slammed into the wall. "For the love of god, just stop talking. It's people like you who give Maldovans a bad name."

Warren pushed past me and Kaden to stand in front of Lanei. "What did you just say?"

Lanei stepped up to meet him. Not quite eye-to-eye, but more nose-to-chin. "I told your friends to shut the hell up."

Kaden cleared his throat. "Well, this is lovely meeting you all, but really, I think—"

"Do you know who I am?" Warren asked. "Do you know who my father is?"

"Do I look like I give a damn?" Lanei narrowed her eyes. "You seem a little slow on the uptake, so I'll give you a hint: No. I don't."

My eyes flicked between them. I would've thought something was about to go down, except the twins stood there as casually as if this was a polite conversation. Milia took a moment to adjust her bust in the corset, while Milich gazed at his nails.

Finally, Warren smirked and walked away from Lanei. "I'll look for you once training starts."

"At least he wasn't an asshole about it," I muttered.

Warren knocked his shoulder into me as he passed. I braced for it, but even the glancing blow from him spun me around like I'd been hit by a bull.

"Even if the schooling is atrocious, at least we'll be entertained," Milia said.

"Poor stable boy," Milich said. "I suppose you can't even afford a horse, can you?"

The bandit in my blood crept to the surface. I smiled. "You're right." I walked down the rows of stalls to the enclosure at the end that was locked and barricaded behind a steel door. "Well, mostly right."

Milia snorted. "Charity case."

I reached my hand into a barrel and plucked out an apple. I tossed it over my shoulder. "Hey, Lanei, you don't happen to have any fresh meat, do ya?"

"Fresh meat..." Lanei leaned back against a stall. "No, can't say that I do."

Kaden frowned. "Why would you feed your horse meat?"

Milia smirked. "Tsk. A stable boy who doesn't even know how to care for his charge."

I took the key to Flik's pen out of my pocket. "I only ask because my friend here hasn't eaten in a while. Ain't that right?" I banged my fist against the steel door. In response, Flik slammed into it. The bars shook.

Milich's eyes widened. "What is that?"

"Well, it isn't a horse," Lanei said.

"No, it surely ain't." I turned the key in the lock and removed the steel bars. They dropped to the ground with a heavy clank. I held the door shut, but Flik hit it again. I had to push all my weight against it to keep it closed.

"Sydney..." Kaden backed up behind Lanei. "What do you have in there?"

"Oh, nothing. Just a very hungry raptor."

Warren snorted. "Oh, please. If you're going to bluff, at least—"

I swung the gate open and Flik burst out. I caught him around his neck and swung onto his back. Warren jumped back into the twins, knocking them to the ground.

"What the fuck is that?"

"This is Flik." Flik screeched at the sound of his name. "And Flik is very hungry right now." I tapped his sides with my heels and he paced toward the three Maldovans. Warren's face went pale. The twins scrambled on the ground to find their footing. "I just wish I'd remembered to bring him some fresh meat... Hey, Flik, see anything you wanna eat?"

Flik craned his neck down as he approached them. Warren hauled Milia to her feet and they stepped away, but Milich backed himself into one of the apple barrels. Flik's tongue snaked out of his mouth, brushing against Milich's cheek. Milich screamed and knocked the barrel over as he tore out of the stables, Warren and Milia on his heels.

I turned Flik toward Lanei and Kaden. Lanei watched calmly, but Kaden had swung himself into Cosette's stall.

"What. The. Hell?"

"Don't worry. I just taught him that phrase to freak people out." I hopped off Flik's back and pulled a piece of dried meat from my hip pouch. I tossed it to him and his head snapped forward to snatch it out of the air.

"Well you succeeded!" Kaden climbed out of the stall, but caught his foot on the gate and tumbled to the floor. He lay on his back, shaking his head. "You are sick. Sick, sick, sick."

"That a problem?" I asked.

Kaden laughed. "Hell no! At least, not as long as we're on the same side."

Lanei smiled and held out a hand to Kaden. He accepted it and she hauled him to his feet. "Hopefully everyone else isn't like those three."

Kaden flipped out his pocket watch. "We'll find out soon. Come on, we need to get ready for orientation."

"Go on ahead," I told them. "I'm gonna stay here for a bit."

Kaden shrugged. "Suit yourself."

I walked Flik back to his stall and gave him a couple extra pieces of meat. I made a mental note to request an icebox in here so I wouldn't have to haul his food back and forth from the kitchens every day. Flik cooed, and I rubbed the side of his head, reassured that even if I wasn't up for this challenge, he was.

Chapter 8

SYDNEY

It took me all of three seconds to realize I'd missed a memo about orientation.

I wound up coming straight from the stables, which was a mistake. Turns out, this was a formal affair. Everyone else was dressed in the fancy clothes of their native kingdoms. And here I was wearing dirty jeans with a ragged green v-neck and my cowboy hat. Not like I brought anything nicer to change into.

I was off to a great start. But at least I was an authentic Laredan.

"Sydney!"

Lanei and Kaden waved me over. Nice as it was to see familiar faces, they were making me look like a homeless guy who'd just walked in off the streets. Lanei wore a red halter dress that showed off her toned muscles. Other than her piercings, the only jewelry she wore was a turquoise pendant on a black choker. Kaden, meanwhile, was decked out in gold. The gold studs in his ears had been replaced with gold studs with diamonds. He wore a gold chain with a ruby pendant and large gold rings on multiple fingers of each hand.

Even the tabard over his clothes looked like it had real gold woven into its stag sigil.

Kaden flinched back when he saw me. "What are you..." His eyes widened and he grinned. "Aha! Defying authority by refusing to conform to society's standards. I love it!"

"Oh, yeah." I slapped at the dirt on my thigh. "That's... exactly what I was going for."

"Brilliant!" Kaden laughed.

"Yep. Just trying to stand out by... not... standing out."

Lanei smirked. "You had no idea this was a formal thing, huh?"

"Not a clue."

Kaden shook his head. "Your great wit has taken a hit today, my friend."

"That's okay. If I need to hit back, I'll borrow your big ol' rings. One look at those will have 'em laughing too hard to put up a fight."

"Touché."

"So, what have I missed?"

Lanei shrugged. "Kaden watching the door like a hawk and announcing everyone who comes in."

"Hey, this is important stuff," Kaden said. "You'll thank me when squads are announced and you know who everyone is."

Lanei rolled her eyes. "Yes, I will cherish both minutes that saves me. Honestly, I—"

"There he is!" Kaden squealed, jumping to attention and latching onto my arm. "That's him!"

"Who?" I asked.

"Who? *Who?*" Kaden sighed. "That's Yasir Levenheit! How can you not recognize him? He looks just like his father!"

"Again, not Araspian."

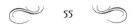

Kaden harumphed and straightened himself out.

Yasir's entrance captured the whole room's attention. He was unfairly good looking. His long black hair was slicked back, minus a few stray hairs that fell loose and framed his chiseled-from-granite face. Even beneath his formal wear, you could tell the rest of him was just as chiseled. Despite all the status Kaden had attributed to him, Yasir wore simple black leather pants with an unornamented green velvet doublet. He strode into the room, chin held high, and flashed a smile that I swear sparkled.

"Okay, so I guess he looks good. What's the big deal?" I looked over at Lanei. She was still staring. I nudged her.

"Huh?" She blinked. "Who said what now?"

"I can't believe he's really here!" Kaden whispered through a plastered smile. "And I'm going to be on his squad! Just think how much I can learn from him!"

"I thought we were here to learn from the instructors," I said.

"Well, yes, we are," Kaden said. "But do you honestly think there's anything they can teach him that he doesn't already know?"

"Uh, yeah. That's why he's here."

Kaden waved a hand dismissively, his eyes still tracking Yasir until he vanished behind a crowd of people. Kaden turned back, eyes positively beaming. "This is going to be the coolest thing ever!"

A girl with Kaden's same bronze skin and amber eyes slapped him on the back. She wore a green velvet dress under leather armor that covered her shoulders and arms. Like Kaden, she had a stag embroidered on her dress, albeit without the gold flair. "Did you finally get a look at your hero?"

"Yes!" Kaden said. "I am so excited!"

"Good. Now get it out of your system so I don't have to listen to it for the next six months."

Kaden grinned. "Guys, this is my sister, Devi. Devi, this is Sydney and Lanei."

"Nice to meet you both." Devi extended her hand. I shook it, which made Kaden snicker.

"You'll have to excuse him. He's from Laredo. Manners aren't really his thing."

"Hey, my manners are just fine," I said.

Lanei rolled her eyes. "If it makes you feel better..." She took Devi's hand and made a dramatic show of bowing as she kissed the back of the other girl's hand.

Devi laughed. "Careful. Kaden will be scandalized if anyone suspects his formalities are slipping." She leaned in to whisper in my ear. "I was too busy learning to fight to worry about that." She elbowed her brother in the ribs.

"Sydney was put in my room by mistake," Kaden said. "Have you seen Vigo? I need to talk to him so we can get the administration to sort this out."

"Oh, uh, yeah..." Devi rubbed her hand against the side her neck. "Vigo is in a room with Yasir."

"What?" Kaden shook his head. "No, that can't be right. We're supposed to be roommates."

"I don't know. Wait until they announce squads and see what's going on."

"There's nothing to wait for. We're all supposed to be together. Four Araspian knights and some random magic user. That was the whole idea." Kaden looked to me. "Unless you're the magic user. Are you the magic user?"

"God I hope not," I said.

"See? There's got to be a mistake somewhere." Kaden looked like he was about to have a panic attack. "Come on. Let's see if we—"

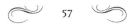

A loud gong rang out three times. The amplification system crackled and popped as a tinny symphonic recording began playing. The music swelled, and the faculty walked onto the stage. The sight of Instructor Russo made me cringe.

The last man out walked to a microphone at the center of the stage.

"That's Ricardo Aguilar," Kaden whispered. "Lord of Esperan."

Lanei craned her neck to get a better look. Ricardo didn't look like any lord I'd ever imagined. He wore no robes or gems, just plain brown pants with an old orange doublet. He looked more like a street merchant than a lord.

"At least I'm not the only one who didn't know this was a formal event," I whispered back.

The music cut out.

"Good evening." The amplification system echoed and squealed, causing several people to cover their ears. Ricardo laughed. "New technology. Still working out the kinks. Hello!" He spread his arms wide. "And welcome to the Petrichor Martial Academy! I am pleased to see so many talented young faces with us today. The next six months will likely prove to be the most challenging of your lives, yet I trust this will be a transformative experience for you all."

He gestured to a pair of portraits on the wall behind him. One was of himself, looking much the same as today, right down to the casual clothing. The other was of a man in purple robes with dark brown skin and gray hair. "When Lord Daron Kane and I started this school, our goal was to create a place to train the finest warriors in all of Nasan and mold them into the greatest purveyors of law and justice in the land. I am proud to announce that this year we have students representing all eight kingdoms of Nasan, including, for the first time ever, knight trainees from Araspia and Maldova!"

A burst of applause from the audience, although nobody cheered as loud as Kaden. On my other side, Lanei clapped politely.

"Now," he continued, "rather than bore you with a tedious detailing of what awaits you, I'll pass things over to the headmaster so she can bore you instead." A light chuckle of laughter came from the crowd. "Ladies and gentlemen, Sadie Kane."

"Daron Kane's sister," Kaden whispered under the audience's applause. "When Lord Kane died, she abdicated her place in Kialen's line of succession so she could continue her brother's work here."

Headmaster Kane stepped up to the microphone. She wore rich purple robes similar to those in her brother's portrait. Streaks of gray colored her black hair.

"Thank you, Ricardo," she said. "I will try to keep the tedium to a minimum. First, I would like to welcome our newest instructor, Reno Isale."

She gestured to the big man at the end of the dais, who was to be my contact. Reno was easily the tallest and brawniest person on stage, as well as the youngest. His head was shaved, giving him a no nonsense look, and tattoos covered the tan skin of his left arm. But his right arm... What I first thought was a bronze gauntlet was instead a false metal arm from the elbow down. Gears and pistons whirred and turned as the metal fingers twitched. It was an incredible sight to behold. When I looked up, I saw him staring back at me. He nodded in acknowledgment. I returned the gesture.

"Seeing as Lord Aguilar makes jokes at my expense each year for being longwinded, I have decided to make this brief," Headmaster Kane said. "Not for your sakes, but to force my friend to come up with new material."

Lord Aguilar choked on his wine. He wiped his mouth on his sleeve and wagged a finger at her.

"You have each been assigned to a squad," the headmaster continued. "Each squad will have a squad leader and a lieutenant, as well as an advisor who will oversee your training. Those advisors will be Instructors Isale, Russo, Lightfellow, and Verdicci." She looked out over the crowd. "Your squadmates will be your friends and allies during your time here. Know them. Trust them. No one here can do this alone."

Lanei smirked.

"The instructors will now announce their squads," Headmaster Kane said. "Thank you, and I hope you all make the most of the experience that is about to be afforded to you."

Headmaster Kane stepped away from the podium and took a seat beside Lord Aguilar.

Russo stepped up to the podium. "Squad Leader Warren Malenko from Maldova. Also from Maldova, Milia Levesque and Milich Levesque. From Ravenstone, Katya Wight and Selena Toombs." She sniffed and walked off the stage without another word.

Kaden laughed. "Well, that seems fitting."

Lanei heaved a sigh of relief. I didn't blame her. Her countrymen were dicks.

A man with the attire and demeanor of an Araspian knight stepped to the microphone. Like Yasir and Kaden, he was also ridiculously handsome. Maybe that was a prerequisite for knighthood over there. He flashed a smile.

"My name is Miklotov Lightfellow, and I am honored to be your melee weaponry instructor. I will be advising the following students this term—"

"This is it!" Kaden practically vibrated. "Wish me luck!"

"From Esperan, Robia Castillo. From Rainess, Anji Latherian. And from my native Araspia, squad leader Yasir Levenheit, Vigo Luchese, and Devi Ashworth. I look forward to working with all of you this year."

"But... No..." Kaden shook his head. "There has to be some mistake. I'm supposed to be on that team!"

Devi rested a hand on his shoulder. "I'm sure all the teams are good."

He shrugged her off. "It's not about being 'good.' I'm supposed to be with you guys. And Yasir! That was supposed to be me in there."

"I'm sure they have their reasons."

"There are no reasons! This is a disaster..."

"Chill out," Lanei said. "It's not the end of the world."

"Not the—" Kaden pursed his lips. "How am I—"

"Shhh! I want to hear this."

Kaden shut up, but he didn't look happy about it.

The next instructor was young, beautiful, and wore a black leather dress that hugged everything just right. But when she started speaking with a low, silky smooth voice my hormones went crazy.

"I am Lucia Verdicci from Maldova. And while I am happy to instruct each of you in the arts of stealth and deception, I am quite disappointed to have no actual Maldovans on my squad." She cast a sour glance at Headmaster Kane. The headmaster glared back in response. "But I suppose concessions must be made. I shall be advising Nakato Walden, Zeke Mathey, and Jeyla Isthiru from Kialen, and Chavo Gutierrez and Vanessa Santos from Esperan. Miss Walden will serve as squad leader. Thank you."

Lanei snorted. "I think I'm glad I'm not on her squad."

"Can I be?" I murmured. Lanei smacked me upside my head.

Reno was the last of the instructors to speak. "I won't bother introducing myself again. My squad leader will be Lanei Walker from Maldova. We've also got Sydney Winter from Laredo, Kaden Ashworth from Araspia, Tenkou from Wismore, and Ayana Isale from Esperan."

"See?" Devi nudged Kaden. "Familiar faces, at least."

"This isn't right..." He pouted, shoulders hunched in utter dejection.

I shrugged. "Sorry, man."

"No, it's not you guys. It's just... This wasn't the plan."

"I need to go meet up with my squad." Devi looked pained for her brother. "I'll catch you later."

"Say hi to Vigo for me..."

Devi squeezed Kaden's shoulder and walked away.

"Did he say Ayana Isale?" Lanei asked. "What do you think, a sister?"

"I guess," I said. "What about the guy from Wismore? Just Tenkou? No last name?"

Kaden's eyes went wide. "Holy shit... Turn around."

I did, and my jaw about hit the floor. Weirdly enough, it wasn't the giant lizard man who startled me. I'd met a throldkin once when I was a child, but she'd been a hunched old woman. Tenkou was even taller than Reno, with rough, dark green skin over a frame of solid muscle. He had yellow eyes and a pair of stubby horns, and wore brown leather pants and a fur lined vest.

So yeah, okay, that was weird, and a lizard person should've been the most startling sight of the evening. Except a young sindari girl stood next to him. She had pale purple skin, red eyes, and hair such a dark blue it almost looked black.

But that couldn't be right. There *were* no young sindari. They were a dying race. All the male sindari had been dead for a hundred years, and humans couldn't father their children. Plus she was short, not even coming up to my chin, and sindari were supposed to be tall. But then she brushed her hair out of her face and I saw her long, pointy ears.

She was half elf...

I stared at her. She stared right back at me, eyes wide. I didn't know whose jaw was lower.

"A real cowboy..." she whispered.

Before I could process anything else, she squealed and hugged me.

"It's so good to meet you! I'm Ayana. You must be Kaden. Or Sydney. Which one are you?"

"I..." Cute sindari girl. Hugging me. "I'm..."

"The talking wonder is Sydney," Kaden said, coming to my rescue. Sort of. "I'm Kaden."

Ayana unlatched from me and hugged Kaden. "It's a pleasure to meet you, Kaden!" She turned to Lanei. "And you must be Lanei!"

"Don't—"

Ayana wrapped her arms around Lanei, whose eyes bugged out like she'd drunk poison.

"I thought sindari were supposed to be all regal and shit," Kaden whispered to me.

"I..." I had nothing. I was out of words.

"We're going to have the best time ever! I can't wait!" Ayana clapped her hands and bounced up and down on her toes.

"She has been like this since I met her," the throldkin said, his voice a rumbling bass that could've shaken the ground. "I am Tenkou."

Kaden stuck out his hand. "Kaden Ashworth." Tenkou looked at the hand with a puzzled expression. Kaden pulled it back. "Uh, we'll work on that."

Lanei pulled away from Ayana and brushed off her dress. "Hey, uh, not to address the big glaring question, but you and Reno are... related?"

Ayana beamed. "Yes."

"Can I ask how?"

"Oh!" Ayana's cheeks turned a darker shade of purple. "No, no. It's nothing like that."

"Nothing like..."

"He's my brother." Ayana laughed. "I mean, ew. Ew."

Lanei turned to me for help.

"I think what Lanei means is that he's human and you're..."

"Oh, that!" Ayana slapped her forehead. "Right, yes, that. I was adopted. Sorry, I always forget that throws people off."

I had a million questions, but I didn't think I could ask any of them without sounding like a damn fool, so I just smiled and nodded.

Fortunately, Reno showed up in time to keep my foot out of my mouth. "Good, you've all met. Classes will start—" He was cut off by Ayana giving him a big hug. Reno sighed. "Ayana, could you, you know... not undermine my authority right now?"

"Oh, right." She stepped back and saluted him. "Stern big brother time."

Reno rolled his eyes. "Your classes start tomorrow. You've got me first thing, so be there on time and well-rested. I will not go easy on you because you're my squad." He looked at Ayana. "Or family."

Ayana saluted again, this time not hiding her grin.

Reno handed each of us an envelope. "Here are your schedules. As I said, Lanei will be squad leader. Sydney, you'll be her lieutenant."

Oh, wonderful. One more chance for people to realize I'm out of my league.

Lanei smiled and rubbed my shoulder. "Don't worry. I'll be a just ruler."

Reno gave her an uneasy look. "You'll do as I say. All of you will. I won't let someone get hurt 'cause you aren't taking this seriously. Now, that said, Sydney, go get a round of drinks so we can make a toast."

I nodded and headed to the refreshment table at the back of the room. Maybe lieutenant was just shorthand for "errand boy." I could handle that.

As I poured, someone handed me a tray. "You may need this."

"Oh. Thank you." I took the tray and was about to resume pouring when I did a double take. "Lord Aguilar!"

"Shhh." He pulled his hat down further. "I'm trying to be incognito. Honestly, if this is how you handle subtlety, I'm going to need to talk with Darian about how he chooses his spies."

"Right, of course. Sorry, Lord Aguilar."

He laughed. "I'm joking. And call me Ricardo. Lord Aguilar was my father."

"Er, yes. Okay."

"Keep pouring," he said. I did. "I met your parents once."

"Oh?"

"It was a long time ago. Back when they were still wanted criminals."

"Oh..."

"Your mother saved my life. Did she ever tell you that?"

She hadn't. That seemed like something worth telling. I shook my head.

"Really?" He shrugged. "Huh. It was quite a tale. You'll have to get it out of her someday. Point being, when Darian told me he was considering you for this task, I was certain you were the right choice."

"I'll try not to let you down."

"Good. If you were *trying* to let me down, I'd be most disappointed." He arranged the glasses on the tray. "Trust Reno. Trust Headmaster Kane. Suspect everyone else." He looked back toward my squad. "Everyone. Do you understand?"

I nodded.

"Then I'll leave you to it. Reno will be reporting to me, so keep him posted on your progress. I'm counting on you." He handed me the tray. "Good luck."

I nodded and walked back to where my squad was waiting for me. After the lord of freaking Esperan just told me he was counting on me.

So, you know... No pressure.

Chapter 9

/LANEI

ifty paces from the stables to the main hall... Nothing a good sprint couldn't cover quickly. The courtyard was open, minus a fountain in the center that provided minimal coverage. The hedges lining the buildings allowed for space to hide in the alleys between them. Decent for sneaking, bad if you're trying not to get shot.

I placed my hand on the outer wall and flexed my fingers against it. The grout was recessed enough that I was able to get a half-decent grip. That could come in handy...

"It's not fine. How is everything always 'fine' with you?" Kaden's voice carried across the courtyard. I slipped into the shadow of the building as they approached.

Kaden was walking alongside a larger young man with broad shoulders and solid muscles who looked like he had been tailor made for a suit of armor. His friend Vigo, I presumed. Vigo's messy brown hair and the tuft of facial hair under his bottom lip were at odds with Kaden's perfectly tousled appearance.

"You're getting the same training as the rest of us."

"That's not what I mean. We had a plan! This was our time!"

"It's six months." Vigo placed a hand on Kaden's shoulder. "It'll fly by."

Kaden huffed. "Right. Because that's the—"

I stepped out into the courtyard before they had a chance to notice me in the alley. "Oh, hey, Kaden."

"Lanei!" Kaden almost tripped over himself as he came to a halt, but he gracefully turned it into a bow. "Ah, Lanei. Perfect. I would like to introduce you to Vigo Luchese, my fellow Araspian and future knight of the realm. Vigo, I present Lanei Walker of Maldova, the leader of our illustrious squad."

Vigo gave Kaden an odd look, but proceeded to bow. It wasn't half as graceful as Kaden's, but it sufficed. "A pleasure to meet you."

I returned the bow. "You as well."

Vigo moved behind Kaden and grasped his shoulders, pushing him a step toward me. "Please know that I take zero responsibility for Kaden. His eccentricities are his own and no fault of mine. I place him in your care. My apologies and condolences to you."

"He's joking." Kaden attempted to squirm out of his grasp, but Vigo held firm. "Tell her you're joking."

"I am deadly serious." Vigo gave me a conspiratorial nod. "Zero responsibility."

Kaden stomped on Vigo's foot and slipped out of his grasp. The bigger man laughed.

"I swear, you're worse than my sister." Kaden straightened his tunic. "What sort of Araspian has manners as rough as yours?"

"The sort that isn't from Araspia." I tapped a finger against my cheek. "Luchese... That's a Maldovan name, isn't it?"

Vigo nodded. "My parents were loyal knights of Maldova until that fascist Viktor Greyton took over." He spat on the ground. "My father was one of the only knights brave enough to speak out against him. After he was executed, my mother and I were exiled. We took refuge in Araspia. That is the only home I claim." Vigo took a step toward me. It wasn't a specific threat, but he was well aware that he had a hundred pounds on me. "I don't know where you stand on Maldovan politics, but if I hear you defend that piece of shit, you and I are going to have a problem."

My blood boiled more with every word Vigo spoke, but I did my best to keep my face free from emotion. "I am sorry for your loss. It sounds like he was a brave man." I took a step toward Vigo. Even if I had a role to play, I wasn't going to let anyone make me play the coward. "But if you think stepping up to me is the right move here, you're even braver than he was."

Vigo studied me for a few moments before cracking a smile. "I'm being aggressive, aren't I?"

"A bit," I said.

"A bit," Kaden echoed, peering over Vigo's shoulder.

"My apologies." Vigo took a step back, raising his hands in concession. "As Kaden said, my manners are a work-in-progress."

"We have that in common." I extended a hand. "I don't suppose they have an etiquette class here."

Vigo grasped my hand and shook it. "God, I hope not. I couldn't bear to be one of Kaden's students."

"Can you not..." Kaden took in a dramatic breath and exhaled. "You are absolutely ruining my first impression."

"We already met," I said.

Kaden sighed. "Second impression."

"Twice."

Kaden clenched his fists and brought them to his mouth. "Two of you... what on earth did I do to deserve two of you?" He shook his head and made his way to the mess hall, Vigo following behind him.

Another link to Maldova... That could complicate matters.

Chapter 10

SYDNEY

Kaden was already awake, dressed, and fussing with his hair in the mirror by the time I rolled out of bed. I looked at my clock to see if I had slept in, but no, it turns out he was just a freak of nature who didn't need sleep.

"Morning," I mumbled.

"Morning," he said. "I was starting to wonder how late you were going to sleep."

"When'd you get up?"

Kaden looked at the clock. "About an hour ago. Enough time to go for a run around campus."

I shook my head. "You're crazy."

"I'm prepared. Who knows what they're going to throw at us?"

That was a good point. I mean, I was in good shape, but so was everyone here. On the other hand, I liked sleep. So...

"What classes are you enrolled in?" Kaden asked.

I yawned. "What do you mean?"

"Your class schedule. The one Reno gave you yesterday."

"I thought we had the same classes?"

Kaden sighed. "No, man. I mean, we're in classes with our squadmates, but we're not all taking every class. Here." Kaden handed me his schedule. "See? I'm only in four classes. Strategy is just you and Lanei, and there's no point sticking me in a magic class. Kinda like I'd place odds Tenkou isn't taking Stealth & Deception. That's my specialty, so I'll be working separately with Instructor Verdicci on that."

I hadn't even looked at my schedule. I pulled it out and scanned over it, but... "Huh."

"What?" Kaden asked. I handed it to him. "Wait... This can't be right. You're enrolled in all six classes. And they didn't give you a specialty. That's... unheard of." He grinned. "Dude, you must be a badass."

Or I'm spying on the entire faculty and student body and they want me around as many people as possible. But I couldn't say that, so I shrugged it off like the badass I was supposed to be. Guess I knew why I'd been made squad lieutenant now. The idea made me queasy. I couldn't help thinking Kaden "Up At 5 a.m." Ashworth would've been a much better choice.

Lanei and Ayana beat us to the training room. Lanei took shots at a punching bag while Ayana perched on a barrel, kicking her legs back and forth.

"Good morning!" Ayana called out. Lanei caught the punching bag and faced us. She wiped the sweat off her forehead with the back of her hand.

"Morning!" Kaden said.

Seriously, how was everyone so chipper and awake this early in the morning?

"No Tenkou yet?" I asked.

Lanei jerked her thumb across the room to a row of weight benches. The first three held empty bars. Tenkou lay on the fourth, pushing up a bar that appeared to have *all* of the weights on it.

"Holy shit..." Kaden muttered.

"Yeah, you don't want to know how many reps he's up to," Lanei said. "It'll make you feel all sorts of inferior."

I moseyed over to Ayana. "Glad I wasn't the only one who didn't get a workout in before class."

"Oh..." Ayana bit her lip. "Oh, yes! Yep, you and me. Not working out. Because we are totally good without that. Yes indeedy."

I raised an eyebrow. Lanei laughed.

"She was here before me."

Ayana blushed. She made that look good. "Sorry. I didn't want you to feel like you were slacking off." She clapped a hand over her mouth. "Which I totally don't think you were doing! Slacking off, that is. You have no slack. You are Mr. Slack-free." She smiled awkwardly. "Somebody stop me, please."

Lanei grinned. "Why? You're on such a roll."

The door swung open and in walked Warren's squad. Warren led the way, with Milia and Milich slightly behind on either side and the two Ravenstone girls bringing up the rear. The pecking order was clear.

"What are they doing here?" I whispered to Kaden.

"We must have this class with them."

"I thought it was just us?"

"No," Kaden said. "Squad training is just us, but the classes are all shared with another squad."

Warren smirked. "Oh, this is going to be fun."

Ayana waved. "Good morning!"

The twins came to a dead stop. Milia feigned gagging. "What. Is. That?"

"I haven't a clue," Milich said. "Is it sick?"

"Don't get too close. You wouldn't want to catch it."

Ayana's smile faltered for the first time since I met her. The twins snickered to each other.

"What did I say?" Ayana whispered to me.

"Nothing," I said. Much louder, I added, "they're just assholes."

Milia grinned. "Oh, look. They've given the stable boy a new pet."

There was a loud *clang* as Tenkou dropped the weight onto the rack and stood to his full height. The twins stopped snickering. Tenkou stalked across the room to join us. He looked at Ayana, then back at the twins. He didn't need to say a word.

The twins took a step back, but Warren held his ground. One of the Ravenstone girls, who was nearly as big as Warren, stepped up beside him.

The door opened again and Reno entered. He frowned at the standoff. "If this is how you introduce yourselves, you're in for a long six months. Now sit your asses down, all of you."

Ayana plopped down immediately. The rest of us followed suit, although Tenkou, Warren, and the Ravenstone girl kept their eyes on each other.

"Good," Reno said. "A couple things before we get started, so you know who I am and why I'm here. My name is Reno Isale. I spent five years with Ascension. If you're here, that name should mean something to you. If it doesn't ring a bell, you need to do your homework. Guilds don't get any better than Ascension." Reno flexed his metal fingers. "I don't say that to talk myself up. I say that so you know I'm not just some guy off the street. I was Ascension's muscle and Darian Rankin's right hand man. If there's anyone who can teach you how to handle yourself in a fight, it's me."

Milich leaned in to Milia and said, too loud, "A cripple is supposed to teach us to fight? Father will have something to say about this."

Ayana let out a tiny growl. I thought I saw a ripple of energy pass over her clenched fist. She let out a breath and slowly counted to ten, delicate purple lips moving without sound.

Reno folded his arms over the barrel that was his chest. "You got something to say, Levesque?"

Milia batted her eyelashes. "Me, sir? I didn't say anything."

"Your brother, you fucking moron," Reno said. Milia looked genuinely taken aback. I bet she didn't hear that much at home. "Milich, you got something to say?"

Milich's forehead twisted up like he was debating whether or not to answer. He made the wrong choice. "I just want to make sure you're qualified. Sir." He grinned. "In Maldova, our trainers are a bit more... complete."

Reno locked eyes with him until Milich broke contact. "Stand up, Milich."

Milich looked at his sister, a silent message passing between them. He slowly got to his feet.

"First thing's first. I want to see where you're all starting from, so I can make you more... complete... fighters. Milich here's been kind enough to volunteer to go first. Step into my ring, Mr. Levesque."

Milich hesitated a moment before stepping into the center of the room. He faced Reno and squared off.

Reno laughed. "Oh, you're not fighting me. That wouldn't be fair." He looked over at my squad. "Now, who should I put you up against?"

Tenkou stood and took a step forward. He towered over Milich. Tenkou exhaled through his nostrils, making Milich's hair flutter.

Milich gulped. "But—sir... Shouldn't I fight someone my size?"

"The bad guys don't give a damn about fighting fair," Reno said. "Lucky for you, I'm not going to make you fight someone bigger than you. Tenkou, have a seat." Tenkou nodded and sat down. Reno looked at his sister. "Ayana. You're up."

The tension in Milich's body evaporated. A jackal's grin spread over his face as Ayana stepped into the ring. He bounced back and forth from foot to foot, jabbing at the air while Ayana took a moment to stretch.

"Ayana, how tall are you?" Reno asked.

"Five foot."

"Milich?"

"Five nine."

"Tenkou?"

"Bigger."

"I'd guess six six." Reno looked at Milich. "I point this out because there's as much a size difference between you and Ayana as there is between you and Tenkou. Ayana, do you think it's unfair for you to fight Milich?"

Ayana stretched her arms over her head. "Yes."

"Are you going to fight him anyway?"

"Yes." She grinned. "I don't care if it's unfair for him."

Milich laughed. "Right."

Reno stepped between them and raised his metal arm in the air. "I've only got two rules in here. One: No permanent damage. That includes broken bones. Two: If someone taps, fight's over. Got it?" They both nodded. Reno dropped his hand. "Fight!"

Ayana stayed still as Milich circled her. She pivoted to keep facing him, but didn't move beyond that. Milich chuckled.

"Something funny?" Ayana asked.

"I was just wondering what color you're going to turn when I choke you out."

"Oh, I see. Because my skin's already purple. You're right, that is—"

Milich punched her in the face. I jumped to my feet, but Reno put a powerful hand on my shoulder and pushed me back down. "Her fight, not yours."

Milich danced around Ayana. He threw two more jabs, which she narrowly avoided. She pressed a thumb to one of her fangs, checking it.

"Tell me..." The grin was still on his face. "Do you bleed red?"

Milich took another swing, but Ayana sidestepped and landed a kick to his midsection. He staggered back, and that was all the opening she needed. Ayana wasn't powerful, but damn was she fast. She caught him with a right, a left, kicked him in the thigh, spun around and backhanded him in the mouth. A spray of blood flew from Milich's split lip. Ayana stepped back and allowed Milich a moment to touch his mouth and see his blood.

Ayana smiled. "Kinda like that?"

That was when Milich lost both his temper and the fight. I'd seen it countless times when people tried fighting my mom. That lesson had been repeated to me over and over through my childhood. I still hadn't quite learned it. Clearly, Milich hadn't either.

He cursed and charged. Before he could tackle her, Ayana leapt into the air. She came down on top of Milich, planting her foot on the back of his head and driving his face straight into the ground. Ayana didn't give him a chance to recover. She spiked a knee into his back, wrapped her arm under his chin, and yanked up. Milich weakly tapped her arm three times.

"That's it!" Reno called. Ayana held on a moment longer before unceremoniously dumping Milich back to the floor. Milia ran to her brother's side and helped him to his feet.

"What?" He stared at his blood on the ground. "How..."

Ayana brushed herself off. "Oh, I'm sorry. I should've warned you. I've been taking private lessons from my big brother for years." She beamed at Reno. "And if you insult him again, I'll show you all the super secret ways he taught me to kill someone." She paused to consider that. "Well, I'd only show you one of the ways. You'd be too dead to see the others."

Milia gave Ayana a poisonous glare as she sat her brother down with the rest of their team.

Ayana sat down beside me. "I've never threatened anyone before. How'd I do?" I gave her a thumbs up.

Reno stepped back into the center. "Lesson one: Do not underestimate your opponent. Ever. I don't care if you're as big as Tenkou or Katya," he said, indicating the giant from Ravenstone. "The moment your ego drowns out what's in front of you, you've lost. In here, that means getting your ass kicked. Out there, it could be your death. Got it?"

Nods from our side of the room. Reluctant ones from Warren and the Ravenstone girls. The twins were too busy seething to respond.

"Alright," Reno said. "Here's how it's gonna go. Warren versus Tenkou. Lanei versus Katya. Sydney versus Milia. Kaden versus Selena. Who's up first?"

Milia let go of her brother's hand and got to her feet. She bared her teeth. "We're up, farm boy."

I made my way to the ring. This was it. Do or die. Time to show everyone what I was made of.

Milia's cocky smile was gone. Seeing her brother go down had done something to her. Her eyes were cold and calculating. I recognized that look. It was the same one Flik had when I took him hunting.

The only thing I remembered after Reno yelled "Fight" was a cracking sound somewhere in the vicinity of my skull.

Chapter 11

SYDNEY

When I came to, I was still lying on the training room floor. A dull ringing filled my ears. It took me a few moments to shake the cobwebs.

Reno sat at his desk, adjusting screws in his arm. Everyone else was gone. I sat up. It only took two tries.

"What happened?"

Reno set down the screwdriver. "You got your ass kicked is what happened."

"I did?"

"You got a better explanation for how you wound up unconscious?"

I shook my head.

"Well, there you go."

"How long was I out?"

"About ten minutes." Reno took a seat on a barrel beside me. "Could've continued class, but I didn't want everyone thinking it was okay to knock each other out." He gave me a hard look. "Plus, I wanted to talk to you. This gave me an excuse to get rid of everyone."

"That's what I was going for." I touched my skull to make sure it was in one piece. "Just trying to help you out here."

"Yeah, well don't. You look like an idiot."

Valid point.

"Okay," Reno said. "I need you to be straight with me. Was this a fluke or is that going to be a regular thing?"

I'm not sure if it was my insecurity or the possible brain damage that made me slow to respond.

Either way, Reno shook his head. "Shit. Are you kidding me? You're the best Darian could find?"

"Hey!" I tried getting to my feet in protest, but couldn't quite muster it. "That's... Look, it's my first day, okay?"

"Yeah, and it was hers too. That's not an excuse." He sighed. "Alright, so you're a work in progress. I can live with that, but you better be willing to work your ass off."

"I am."

"Good. I'll keep you updated if I get intel from Darian. Anything you notice, you report to me."

I nodded. "Can do."

"One more thing." Reno stood, a mountain over the heap that was me. "If you drag Ayana into this, we're going to have a problem. Got it?"

I rubbed at my forehead. "Looks like she can handle herself just fine."

Reno smacked my hand into my own face. "That's because I've taught her to handle herself. This world isn't friendly to someone who looks like her. So if you put her in a situation where she has to handle herself, you're gonna be the one paying for it. Understand me?"

I nodded.

"No. Tell me you understand."

I pulled myself to my feet. "I understand."

"Good." Reno slapped me on the back. The force nearly knocked me back down. "Then get out there and start your training. We've got work to do."

I spent the next couple hours in the stables with Flik. I wasn't hiding from the others to avoid being mocked for getting knocked out. I just liked the smell of hay and day old horse. It reminded me of home. Really.

I timed my arrival to ranged weaponry class so I got there just as the clock ticked over. Plus side, I couldn't possibly be so bad with a bow that I'd hurt myself. Down side, my brilliant plan didn't account for the instructor being late.

Lanei, Kaden, and Ayana rushed me when I walked in. Well, Ayana rushed. Lanei and Kaden more sauntered.

"Are you okay?" Ayana asked, her eyes wide with worry. She grabbed my chin and moved my head from side to side, examining it.

"Ah! Yeah, I'm okay." I pulled my face away. "Just a little head trauma."

"That was quite a shot," Lanei said. "The way your head snapped back, I thought she might've broken your neck."

"Nope, neck's just fine. Head hurts and vision's a tad blurry, but the neck's fine."

"Good. Don't go pointing any arrows my way today."

"This is all my fault." Ayana looked like she might cry. "If I hadn't hurt Milich like that, Milia wouldn't have been in such a bad mood when she fought you."

I shook my head. "That's crazy. There's no way this is your fault. She beat me fair and square, that's all."

"Yeah, okay." She reached out to touch my face, but pulled her hand back at the last second. "But I'm still going to feel bad about it."

"Don't." As much as my pride didn't want to be fussed over, I didn't hate the attention. I forced a smile. Her red eyes brightened as she smiled back.

Kaden snickered. He stood there, arms crossed, a big smile on his face.

I sighed. "Go ahead. Say it."

"Dude, you got knocked *out!*" Kaden burst out laughing. "You should've seen your face! It was all 'Oh man, I got this' and then it was all—" He closed his eyes, stuck out his tongue, and fell sideways to the ground, where he resumed laughing. I tried kicking him, but he rolled out of the way.

"Yeah... Can we not go advertising that to everyone?"

Lanei shrugged. "It's gotta happen to everyone eventually. Besides, I'm sure Milia's already told half the school. You're better off owning it."

"That's right!" Ayana beamed at me. "You should be proud you got back up."

"I didn't die. My big achievement for the day is not dying. Fantastic." I looked around. "Where's Tenkou?"

"I'm guessing they don't make bows his size," Kaden said.

"Oh." I was relieved to see we weren't stuck with Warren's squad again. Yasir, Devi, an Esperan girl, and a half-elf boy hung out on the other side of the room. "Yasir and company?"

Kaden's shoulders dropped. "Yeah..."

Devi strolled over. "How's the face, Sydney?"

I glared at Kaden.

Devi shook her head. "Milia was bragging about it in the hall."

"Told ya," Lanei said.

Ayana looked across the room at the half-elf who stood a few inches taller than her. His spiky blond hair showed off his long, pointy ears. He made no attempt to conceal what he was. Growing up in Rainess, he'd probably never needed to. "Who's that?"

Devi followed her gaze. "That's Anji. He's good people." She winked at Ayana. "Want me to introduce you?"

"What? No!" Ayana blushed. "I just... Don't meet a lot of other half-elves."

Devi raised an eyebrow. "I thought you were half-sindari?"

"Well, yes, but I'm half something else, too."

"Oh. Right." Devi tried messing up Kaden's hair. He ducked out of the way. "You ready for me to show you up?"

"You ready to... not... show up?" Kaden pursed his lips then sighed. "Yeah, that was dumb."

"It was."

"Shut up." Kaden looked past her. "Where's Vigo?"

"They didn't put him in ranged. I think they wanted him to focus on close quarters stuff."

"Oh." Kaden sighed. "Do you..."

His voice trailed off as the instructor walked in. Caesar Hortez looked out of place at a school that taught combat and deadly weaponry. His short, black hair was streaked with silver, and he had a beard to match. He looked like an average shopkeeper, but carried himself with a confidence that didn't match his unassuming form.

"Students. Pick up a bow and a single arrow and stand over there." He gestured to a line opposite the targets. "I presume you all know how to use a bow. Shoot the target."

We did. Mine went high and struck the hay above the target. Lanei and Ayana both hit the outer ring.

Kaden's arrow landed snugly in the third ring. Further down the row, Anji hadn't fared much better than me, but Yasir and Devi each placed theirs in the second ring. The Esperan girl with a pierced bottom lip shot a perfect bullseye.

Caesar studied her. "And you are?"

"Robia Castillo, sir." She stood straight as a statue under his inspection.

Caesar nodded. "Ranged weapons are your specialty, are they not?"

"Yes, sir."

"Very good." He handed her a second arrow. "Do it again."

Robia notched the arrow and drew back the string. She let out a breath and released. It struck the target a hair outside the bullseye.

Caesar gave her an approving look. "I can work with that." He turned to the rest of us. "None of you managed to shoot each other, which tells me you aren't hopeless. I can work with that as well. I need a volunteer." Several hands shot up. Mine did not. "To act as a target." All but two went down. Mine remained firmly at my side.

Caesar looked between Robia and Lanei.

"Robia." He handed her an apple. "Stand by the target and hold this at arm's length." As Robia took her place, Caesar notched an arrow. He didn't bother taking aim, just casually lifted the bow in her direction and loosed the arrow. It jerked the apple out of her hand.

"Very good." Caesar looked at Lanei. "Miss... I'm sorry, what was your name?"

"Lanei Walker," she said, gravel in her voice.

"Yes, that's it." Caesar held out a lime. "Not as large a target, but I think I can still hit it."

Lanei snatched it from him and walked to the targets. She held the lime out as Robia had.

"Oh, no, they've already seen that trick. Balance it on your head."

Lanei gave him a dirty look. "Try not to shoot me. I don't need any more piercings right now." She rested the lime on her head.

"Then I suggest you don't move," Caesar said. "The slightest movement and this could go very badly for you. You may want to close your eyes."

Lanei didn't. My heart pounded in my chest. Somehow, Lanei looked unphased.

Once again, in a single swift movement, Caesar brought up the bow and loosed the arrow. It speared the lime from Lanei's head without incident. Lanei closed her eyes and let out a slow breath.

Caesar turned to the rest of us. "By the time I'm done with you, you will either have the ability to perform the same feat or the bravery to face down an arrow. Where you stand is completely up to you. Let's begin."

Chapter 12

SYDNEY

After the pile of fail that was my first day, I just wanted day two to be tolerable. Unfortunately, the time for my first class, Stealth and Deception with Instructor Verdicci, was listed as "dawn." So, you know, that was vague. Kaden wanted to play it safe and get there before sunrise, which meant waking up at the ungodly hour of "too damn early." I made the mistake of joining him for his morning run. By the time we were done, Kaden was awake and refreshed, but my lungs were about to burst out my chest.

Not the kind of start I was hoping for.

We ran into Lanei on our way to class. Her eyes were still heavy with sleep and she dragged her feet with each step. She wore a long leather trench coat to guard against the chill morning air.

The schedule didn't list a classroom, only to meet on the outskirts of the forest outside the school. Through the fog, I was able to make out Instructor Verdicci's squad waiting for us.

The Kialen girl with dark brown skin was their squad leader, Nakato Walden. The two students from

Esperan were Vanessa Santos and Chavo Gutierrez, an athletic looking pair who seemed friendly and, judging from their touchy feelies, probably more than friendly with each other. The other Kialen girl, a dark-skinned half-elf named Jeyla Isthiru, threw nervous glances our way and rearranged her hair to cover her ears.

Lucia Verdicci appeared with the sun, materializing from the fog. She didn't approach from the school, but from the forest behind us. No telling what she was doing out there at this hour.

"Good morning," she purred. No, like, her voice actually purred. It was this low, beautiful sound that couldn't possibly have come from a human being. "I am Instructor Verdicci, but you may call me Lucia." She walked between us, shaking hands and greeting everyone by name. "Please forgive the hour. I promise this will not be our usual meeting time. In fact, there is no set time for this class. You will be notified when and where to meet. Often in the middle of the night."

When she looked in my eyes and shook my hand, I went somewhere else... it was like stepping outside the morning after a fresh rain.

She leaned in, her breath warm on my neck as she whispered, "Usually in the middle of the night."

I shivered.

She greeted Kaden last. As she shook his hand, his eyes widened and he jerked back.

"Hey!"

Lucia smiled at him. "Very good, Mr. Ashworth. You are one of mine, are you not?"

Kaden gave her an agitated look, but nodded all the same. "Yes. Stealth specialty."

I elbowed him and raised an eyebrow; in answer, he rolled his eyes and raised his ring-adorned hand.

"Good, good." Lucia turned to the rest of us. "Six out of seven. I hate to think I'm losing my touch. I suggest the rest of you check your belongings."

A series of curses rippled through the class as realization dawned. A strand of brown hair fell over my face, which was weird because my hair was in a ponytail. *Was.* I reached back. How the hell had she managed to remove the leather band without me noticing? Everyone was embarrassed and humbled at being tricked.

Everyone except Lanei.

Lanei's face was steady as she patted herself down. A moment of clarity came and her hand shot to her throat. When it came away empty, blood rushed to her face.

Lanei turned on Lucia with a fury that caught me off guard. "Give it back. Now!"

Lucia smiled and pulled Lanei's turquoise choker from her pocket. "Is this what you're—"

Lanei snatched it from her hand. "Don't you ever touch that again. *Ever.* Do you understand me?"

"Miss Walker—"

Lanei slapped our instructor. The sound echoed through the clearing.

"Ever!" Lanei shoved past her and stormed away, clutching her necklace in her fist.

I almost followed her, but stopped short when I caught sight of Jeyla. The half-elf girl cowered behind Nakato, fingers locked in a vice grip on her friend's arm. The trembling girl's face was a mask of terror that made my blood run cold.

Chapter 13

LANEI

Kane sat at her desk, tapping her finger on a folder with my name on it. No doubt that folder contained everything she knew about me. How much of it was true, I didn't know. Probably depended on how good her sources were. Either way, I wasn't going to play her game. This was complete bullshit and she knew it. So I hooked my leg over the arm of the chair and waited.

Kane heaved a sigh. "Oh, good. You're being petulant."

I glared at her. "I am not—"

"You are. Spare me the theatrics." Kane picked up the folder and waved it at me. "We have overlooked a great many things for you to be here. And yet, you have responded by assaulting one of your instructors."

"Oh, please. I slapped her. If I'd assaulted her, she'd be in the infirmary right now."

"No, she wouldn't. You either overestimate yourself or have no idea what Instructor Verdicci is capable of. Probably an unhealthy dose of both." Kane set the folder back on her desk. "I'm going to set your past aside. We're going to settle this without giving it any further consideration. Fair?"

I didn't know if Kane could be objective enough for that, but what choice did I have? I nodded.

"Good. Then let's get on with this."

Kane's hand vanished under her desk. A few moments later, the door to her office opened and Lucia Verdicci strode in.

"Hello again, Miss Walker." Lucia smiled, no trace of a mark on her perfectly contoured cheek. I should have slapped her harder.

I scowled. "Do you expect me to apologize?"

"No," Kane said. "But you're welcome to." I held her gaze while she waited for an unreasonable amount of time. Guess she hadn't read my file too closely. Kane sighed. "Very well. Lucia?"

Lucia slithered around behind Kane's desk, the predatory smile never leaving her lips. "Miss Walker, I am afraid we started off on the wrong foot. That should not have happened. We are both Maldovans, after all." She traced a finger over my folder, keeping her eyes locked on mine. I gripped the arms of the chair to keep myself from lunging for it. She was the last person I wanted knowing my past. Lucia pushed the folder aside. "But actions must have consequences. Don't you agree?"

"Yes. But I already slapped you for what you did, so I figure that makes us even."

"An overreaction on your part, no doubt."

I held her gaze. "Try it again and see what happens."

"Enough." Kane narrowed her eyes. "You would do well not to antagonize the woman who will determine your punishment."

I blinked. "What?"

"Your offense was against Instructor Verdicci. As such, she will determine and administer your punishment."

"But you're the headmaster."

Kane leaned over her desk. "Then slap me and see what happens." She waited. I knew enough about her family not to take her up on the offer. "Thank you."

I turned my gaze to Lucia. "So, what, are you going to make me run laps or something? Slap me around in front of the class to make an example of me?"

"Oh, Miss Walker..." Lucia walked back around Kane's desk and sat on the edge. She placed one foot on the edge of my chair. "You really don't know who I am, do you?"

Chapter 14

SYDNEY

Lanei was in the melee weaponry training room polishing her sword when I arrived with Kaden and Tenkou.

"Hey," I said. "You okay?"

"Fine." Lanei didn't look up from her task. "Don't want to talk about it."

"You were pissed," Kaden said. "I didn't think Lucia was going to—"

Lanei pointed her sword at him. "Don't want to talk about it."

"Fair enough." Kaden held up his hands and backed away. Lanei resumed polishing.

Tenkou studied us. "I missed something."

"Stealth class," I said.

"Ah." And that was it. No curiosity, no questions, just respect for Lanei's wishes. Must be a throldkin thing.

"This class is going to be good," Kaden said. "Sir Miklotov Lightfellow is practically a legend in Araspia."

"Ain't he a bit young to be a legend?" I asked.

"That's why I said 'practically.' He's one of Araspia's most renowned knights of the past fifteen years. I'm frankly amazed Petrichor was able to get him."

"Is there anyone here you don't know everything about?"

"Yeah. And they put me on a squad with all of them. Seriously, I'm at least passingly familiar with everyone else at this school, but you lot are a big question mark to me."

"Shame." Lanei rubbed at a smudge. "You might have to get to know us before you pass judgment."

"Don't worry, I'm starting to piece together a picture."

She glared at him. "You can keep that picture to yourself."

Yasir and his squad walked in before an argument could break out. It looked like their whole team was in this class. Robia entered alongside Yasir, whispering in his ear. Anji followed behind them with his head buried in a book, while Devi brought up the rear with a muscular guy who had a small patch of facial hair under his bottom lip. Must be Vigo. Kaden left our group to talk with them.

Lanei and Tenkou had brought their own weapons to class. Lanei's sword was a long rapier, while Tenkou carried a carved club that was almost as big as me. Yasir's squad also came fully equipped.

"Uh, was I supposed to bring my own weapon?"

Lanei looked up. "It wasn't required, just suggested. I think he wants to see what everyone prefers. I doubt we're using real weapons on day one."

"Oh. Good."

I didn't want to go up against a real sword yet. Plus, I didn't have a weapon of my own. I'd practiced with swords and daggers, but never had enough knack for either to convince my parents to buy me one. Or let me use theirs.

"That is fortunate," Tenkou said. "I would hate to shatter so many pretty swords so soon."

Lanei smiled. "Brother, you couldn't even get near me with that club of yours."

"We shall see."

Yasir and Devi stopped stretching and stood in a stiff, formal salute as Instructor Lightfellow entered. Kaden and Vigo were so wrapped up in their conversation it took an elbow from Devi for them to realize he was there. They scrabbled to join the salute.

"That's not necessary, but I do appreciate it." Instructor Lightfellow gestured for them to be at ease. "Yasir, how is your father?"

"Quite well, thank you," Yasir said. "He sends his regards."

"Good man. When next you write him, tell him I am honored he has decided to entrust the Petrichor Academy with your training."

"It was at your urging that he finally relented."

"I am glad to hear it. Devi and Kaden, I have been fortunate to know your mother as well. A fine knight. If you are half as skilled with a sword as she is, we can all count ourselves lucky." He turned to Vigo. "I never met your father, Vigo, but by all accounts he was a fine man."

"Thank you." Vigo gave an appreciative nod.

"My apologies," Instructor Lightfellow said to the rest of us. "Respect for family and lineage is an important part of our culture. I assure you, I will treat everyone in this class equally, regardless of who your parents are. That is my promise to you."

I could swear he looked at me as he said it. I shifted uncomfortably and bumped into Lanei. She nudged me back.

"Now, I would like to see what everyone can do with a sword. Have you all had at least basic instruction?"

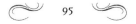

Nods and words of agreement circled around the room. "Very good. In that case…"

Tenkou raised his hand with a timidness that didn't match his size.

"Tenkou. Yes?"

He cleared his throat. "I… have never used a sword."

Robia stifled a laugh. Instructor Lightfellow cut her a look.

"Miss Castillo. Would you like to comment?"

Color rose in her cheeks. "No, sir. That's just… surprising."

Instructor Lightfellow nodded. "We will be studying a number of weapons in this class, and I should be surprised if any of you were masters of them all. The sword is the weapon of choice in many cultures, but not all. History is full of noteworthy throldkin warriors, and I would be hard pressed to name more than one or two who preferred the sword to a club or ax. Tenkou, I do not expect the sword will ever be your weapon of choice, but I will ensure you are comfortable wielding one."

The big man nodded. "Thank you."

Instructor Lightfellow set us off to sparring with practice swords while he assisted Tenkou. Even the largest sword looked like a toy in his hands. He looked ridiculous wielding it, but he picked up the form quickly.

While helping Tenkou, Instructor Lightfellow still managed to keep an eye on the rest of the class. He'd be mid-sentence, call out an encouragement or correction to someone halfway across the room, and go right back to what he was saying. About every note he gave me while I sparred with Kaden was one Kaden had already given me himself.

"Um, try not to take this the wrong way," Kaden said, "but aren't you supposed to be some sort of badass?"

I took a hard swing, but he parried like it was nothing. "Hey... shut up."

"No, I just..." He landed a blow on my side. "I figured with your background you'd..." Another on my arm. "Be kicking my ass by now." One more to my leg.

"I'm just..." I lunged, he sidestepped. "Feeling you out..." Parry. "For weaknesses." He jumped over my blade.

Kaden laughed. "Keep looking."

Instructor Lightfellow called for us to switch it up. I fared decently well against Anji. He had skill, but wasn't as experienced as the Araspians. We traded blows back-and-forth until a chorus of battle cries echoed across the room. Kaden and Vigo had teamed up to fight Yasir two-on-one.

Kaden was good. Vigo was good. But Yasir was on a whole 'nother level. He moved with blazing speed and stayed two steps ahead of them. By the time we switched, Kaden and Vigo were panting and bruised, while Yasir wasn't even breathing hard. He bowed and shook their hands before moving on to dominate someone else.

I didn't have much luck after Anji. Devi and Vigo took enough pity not to humiliate me, even though they could've turned me into a human pincushion. Robia's skill wasn't limited to the bow. It was clear why she was Yasir's lieutenant. The others were polished and refined, but she was fast and unpredictable. The way she moved kept me off balance the entire fight. To make matters worse, she talked trash the whole time. And it was good trash talk, too. Even if I hadn't fared well against the others, I had at least been able to stay on my feet with sword in hand. Robia was a whirlwind.

After she disarmed me for like the dozenth time, I realized the fighting around us had stopped, but the sound of steel-on-steel was loud as ever. Robia turned her back on me, and I followed her gaze to where Yasir was tearing it up with Lanei. Their sparring match had turned into a full blown battle with a level of intensity unlike anything I'd seen. They drove hard at each other, leapt over obstacles, and tossed barrels into the other's path. As far as I could tell, neither had scored a hit on the other.

The fight lasted several minutes. Even Instructor Lightfellow paused Tenkou's instruction to observe. The rest of us turned into personal cheering sections for our squad leaders. Lanei was strong, but Yasir was stronger. Yasir was fast, but Lanei was faster. And neither made mistakes for the other to capitalize on.

Yasir pushed an advance on Lanei, attempting to corner her. As he drove her back, she vaulted off a barrel and flipped over his head. He brought his sword down as she landed, but she rolled with the momentum and swung her blade up to meet his. The swords met with a piercing shriek as both blades shattered. Lanei and Yasir stared dumbly at each other. They dashed to the weapon racks.

Before they could grab new swords, Instructor Lightfellow let out a sharp whistle and applauded them. "Well done, both of you. Well done. That was quite spectacular."

Lanei and Yasir looked ready to go again, but reluctantly eased away from the racks and shook hands. For the first time today, both were out of breath.

"That was fantastic," Yasir said, running a hand through his hair. "Where on earth did you learn to fight like that?"

Lanei shrugged. "Just... sorta picked it up."

"Well, bravo." Yasir grinned. "Bravo."

Lanei flushed. "Thanks."

"I'd say that is as good a note as any to end class on," Instructor Lightfellow said. "Keep practicing, every day. I expect to see improvements from all of you."

"Yes, sir," Yasir said, his eyes still on Lanei. He opened his mouth to speak, but Robia stepped between them.

"Come on." She took him by the arm. "I think we've earned ourselves a good meal."

"Oh, yes." Yasir bowed to Lanei. "It was a pleasure, m'lady."

"You too." Lanei brushed back the strand of blue hair that had fallen over her eyes. "But call me that again and I'll show you a real ass kicking."

Yasir flashed his million dollar smile. Robia scowled and dragged him away, followed by the rest of their squad.

Kaden beamed. "That was amazing! You went toe-to-toe with Yasir Levenheit! Do you have any idea how cool that is?"

Lanei rolled her eyes. "Chill out. I didn't win."

"Yeah, but you didn't lose either," I said. "He wiped the floor with everyone else."

"Oh, don't you start with the hero worship, too." Lanei shoved me into Tenkou, who caught me with a large, scaly hand. "One Kaden is enough."

Kaden nodded. "That's true. Two me's would be too much of a good thing."

"Two you's would be too much of a lot of things," I said.

Kaden laughed.

As we left, I leaned over to Lanei. "Seriously, though. Where'd you learn to fight like that?"

"Like I said, I just picked it up."

I shook my head. "That ain't picking it up. That takes practice."

Lanei shrugged and gave me a sly smile. "Guess I've had practice then."

Chapter 15

SYDNEY

I had to drag myself into magic class the next morning. I'd stayed up late sparring with Kaden and Tenkou, and now my whole body ached. Somehow Kaden still managed to wake up for his early morning run. I told him to kiss my ass when he tried waking me to join him.

There was only one magic class for all four squads. Ayana, Tenkou, and I were there to represent ours. Nakato's squad had Nakato and Jeyla, while Anji was the only one from Yasir's. Warren's squad didn't have any.

"They all knew each other from before," Nakato said when I asked her about it. "Their parents requested they be placed together, so there wasn't an opening for a magic user. Their loss."

Magic was pretty foreign to me. I mean, I had latent ability, but it was like trying to read a language I didn't know. This would be my first time seeing much of it firsthand. Growing up in Chisholm, most everyone I met was pureblood human, so magic was hard to come by.

The majority of Nasan's magic users, myself included, got it from elven ancestry. Anji and Jeyla had strong elven features: long pointy ears, purple eyes, and shorter stature than the average human. My bet was they were straight up half-elves. Like me, Nakato could pass for a pure human without much trouble. She was taller and leaner than average, and although her brown eyes were flecked with purple, her dark skin made her elf blood hard to detect unless you looked closely.

Elven magic was highly focused. You more or less only got one thing you could do, but you could do it really well. That one thing could be channeling lightning or flying or running super fast. But, generally speaking, the less elven blood, the weaker the magic. All told, it was a safe bet mine was a good ways down the line. Ah well. At least I could count on living longer than a pure human. Even a few generations back, my elven heritage would give me another ten years or so. Either way, I'd still look good when I hit middle age.

Pureblood elves followed the same rules, but it wasn't unheard of for them to master multiple types of magic after years of study. They lived for a few hundred years, so "years of study" had a whole different meaning for them. Magic was stronger across the board for pure elves than human-elf hybrids. Sadly, most of today's elves didn't seem interested in using their magic for anything useful. Maybe it was different across the sea, but it sounded like the elves in Nasan were more interested in enjoying life than mastering their magic. You were more likely to find an elf using his magic for art or entertainment than helping people.

The sindari were supposed to have the strongest innate magic, and in the legends they wielded it with great power and flexibility. There had been legendary sindari warriors whose feats had become the stuff of myth, but those weren't the names associated with sindari magic these days. That honor belonged to the false god and former king, Omek. Guess I shouldn't have been surprised magic made people twitchy.

I didn't know much about throldkin magic because people hadn't written much about it. Or, at least, not much I had access to. Their magic was more shamanistic than the elves' and sindari's, but that was about all I knew.

Tenkou, Ayana, and I couldn't have looked any more different if we'd tried. I wished there was a joke about a cowboy, a sindari, and a throldkin entering a bar, because we were primed for a punchline. None of us were remotely the same height. Tenkou wore tan rawhide pants with a fur-lined rawhide vest, compared to my denim pants, tight brown shirt, and cowboy hat. Ayana made up for our drab colors with a bright green sleeveless dress that had some intricate design woven into it with shiny yellow thread. Her dark blue hair was pulled back and braided so it fell to one side. She also carried a plain looking staff, and by "plain looking" I mean a tree branch with a gemstone crudely bound to the tip with wire.

Kasia Windamier glided into the room with unnatural grace. She was a slender elf with pale skin and brightly glowing lavender eyes. Her long silver hair fell halfway down her back, blending in with her silver dress. She greeted us with a warm smile full of its own brand of magic.

"Welcome." Her voice was a calm, spring breeze. "I am pleased to see such a diverse group of students with us this term. We are here to support and encourage one another, so in this classroom you are not to be concerned with squads. There is already too much turmoil in the magical community for us to divide ourselves further.

Instead, let us focus on what we have in common: A unique connection to the mystical forces of our world." She smiled again. "I have read the reports on everyone's abilities, but I would like to see them for myself. Who would like to go first?"

Nakato stepped forward. "It's not much. I only had a great-grandmother who was an elf."

"Magic is not always about raw power," Kasia said. "It is often about finding new and creative ways to use what is available to you."

Nakato nodded, closed her eyes, and swirled her arms above her head. The air around me dropped in temperature. A thin fog formed around her, shrouding her in darkness. Even in the light of the room, her features were concealed.

"I'm sure Instructor Verdicci will find that most useful," Kasia said. "We will work on finding other ways to harness your power."

Jeyla went next. The nervous half-elf summoned up a few fireballs, and created a small funnel of fire that was like a flaming tornado of death.

Anji showed off his telekinetic powers. He really was showing off. He waved his hands about, picking up objects and hurling them across the room at incredible speeds. He even lifted Tenkou off the ground before a growl from the big man made him realize that was a dumb move. He'd clearly been well trained from a young age. But then, he was from Rainess, the only kingdom in Nasan that still valued magic.

Tenkou was up next. He walked over to a punching bag that hung from the ceiling.

"This is my strength without magic."

He reeled back and threw a hard punch. The bag flew up so high it was parallel to the floor before swinging back into place. He caught the bag and steadied it.

"And this is when I imbue myself."

Tenkou closed his eyes and muttered quietly to himself. His fists emanated a faint yellow light. A humming sound rang in my ears. It didn't seem like it was coming from Tenkou, though. It was just... there. All around me.

Tenkou opened his eyes. They, too, glowed with yellow light. He hauled back and threw another punch. It wasn't any faster than the last one, but this time the chain holding the punching bag snapped, sending the exploding bag flying across the room, showering us all in coarse sand. The magical light faded.

Kasia raised her eyebrows. "Fascinating..."

"There is... something else." Tenkou said. "Something that was not in my file."

Kasia nodded for him to continue. He removed a small horn from his belt, uncapped it, and poured the contents into his hand. He used it to paint symbols on the floor. When he finished, he sat in the middle of them all.

"This may take some time," he said. "Please remain quiet. I must concentrate."

Tenkou rested his hands on his knees and closed his eyes. We waited for something to happen. We waited longer. And longer. After several minutes of uncomfortable silence, Anji took a breath to speak up, but Kasia held out a hand.

Fifteen minutes later, I let out a yawn and closed my eyes. Ayana leaned her head against my shoulder. My body flushed, and I opened my eyes. I jerked back, but it had nothing to do with her.

Tenkou still sat in the same place. But he was... also... standing above himself. The second Tenkou was faint, transparent. It walked across the room, through a table stacked with books, and stopped in front of Kasia. The image of Tenkou bowed then returned to the physical, seated Tenkou. It laid a hand on his shoulder and vanished. Tenkou's eyes opened. He let out a long breath, as if he'd been holding it the whole time.

"Astral projection," Kasia labeled for us. "That is quite a gift."

"I cannot do it for long." Tenkou bowed his head humbly. "Nor can I go far from my body."

"We shall work on that. All in good time." Kasia turned to me and Ayana. "Two left."

I was in no hurry to prove I didn't belong, so it was fortunate that Ayana hopped up. She swung her makeshift staff around as she stepped into the center of the room.

"Ayana, what are you holding?" Kasia asked gently.

Ayana looked at the piece of wood in her hand. "It's my staff. Do you like it? I made it myself."

"Under whose guidance did you make it?"

"Nobody's. I just figured I needed some kinda focus. You know, like in the stories." Ayana twirled the staff around. "I haven't figured out how it works yet." She held it up for Kasia to see. "But it looks cool, right?"

There was muffled laughter from the other side of the room, but Kasia smiled. "It is a fine start. I will help you fashion it into a proper staff."

Ayana's eyes lit up. "Really? Thank you!"

"Now, Ayana, your file did not specifically list your magical abilities."

"Oh, yeah, that. My brother didn't want it in there for some reason. He was afraid you'd think I was weird or something." Ayana lowered her voice. "But between you and me, I just don't think he understands them."

Kasia raised an eyebrow. "Them?"

"Right. Yes. One sec." Ayana closed her eyes and raised her staff. The staff was probably just for show, as it didn't seem to be channeling anything. A few moments later a swirling ball of purple and black haze appeared in front of her. It expanded until it was half her size. Ayana opened her eyes, looked into the haze, and called, "Vadazach!"

A small red demon crawled out of the portal and dropped to the ground. Everyone in the room jumped back. Anji and Jeyla assumed combat stances, and even Kasia looked ready to leap into action. The demon yawned and stretched his little arms. He wasn't big; in fact, he barely came up past Ayana's knee. He had cloven feet, a long tail, and curved horns protruding from his forehead. The little demon even wore a pair of brown leather pants.

"Ayana!" Kasia's eyes were wide. "What are you doing?"

"Oh, sorry," Ayana said. "Introductions. Everyone, this is Vadazach. Vadazach, these are my new friends."

Vadazach glanced around the room, unimpressed. He took note of the aggressive stances. "Gee, they're a friendly bunch o' bastards, ain't they?"

"Vadazach!" Ayana wagged a finger at him. "Manners."

The little demon rolled his eyes. "Yeah, yeah."

Kasia gave Ayana an incredulous look. "You're a summoner."

"That's why Reno figured you'd think I was weird."

"How is that possible?" Kasia narrowed her eyes at the girl. "The demon realms were sealed off centuries ago when the summoners lost the ability to bind the demons to their will. How did you manage to bind him?"

"Bind him?" Ayana scrunched up her face. "What do you mean?"

Vadazach laughed. He jerked a thumb toward Kasia and looked back at Ayana. "This is gonna get real good in about ten seconds."

"No summoner has been able to bind a demon for hundreds of years. How did you learn to control him without any training?"

"Oh!" Ayana smacked her forehead. "I see the confusion. I'm not controlling him. I just let him out."

"You what?" Kasia's fist glowed red. She placed herself between the demon and the other students.

Vadazach snickered. "Told ya."

Ayana looked confused. "Why would I want to control him? He's my friend. You don't bind your friends. That's just rude."

"You mean to say you turned an imp loose in our realm?" Anger flared in Kasia's eyes. "Do you have any idea how dangerous that is?"

"Oh, relax. He's not going to hurt anyone."

"I mean, I could if it'd make you feel better." Vadazach stretched his arms over his head and stumbled forward in an exaggerated walk. "Grr! Argh!"

"Stop it, Vadazach. You're not fooling anyone."

Vadazach shrugged and used the claws on his left hand to sharpen the claws on his right.

Kasia narrowed her eyes. "Ayana, what do you mean when you say this demon is your friend?"

"I mean he's my friend. He's been my friend since I was little."

"Since you were..." Kasia blinked. "How long have you been summoning demons?"

Ayana shrugged. "Since I was five. They were my friends when the other kids wouldn't play with me." She smiled at the imp. "Vadazach was the first demon I met. He was the first person who didn't judge me for looking different from the other kids."

"I also set the other kids on fire," Vadazach said. "Don't forget to mention that."

"What?" Kasia's fist glowed red again.

Ayana waved her hands to stop her. "He's kidding! He's kidding! Vadazach, tell her you're kidding."

Vadazach sighed. "Alright, fine, I didn't set them on fire. I just burned a couple girls' pigtails off."

Kasia gave Ayana a stern look.

Ayana blushed. "Okay, that part's true. But he only did it because they were being mean to me! And I may have asked him to do it."

"She totally asked me to do it," Vadazach said.

Kasia studied the demon. The little guy flexed for her. "He is a demon. How can you be sure you can trust him?"

Vadazach stopped flexing and glared at Kasia. "Trust *me*? Lady, we were perfectly happy in our little realm before your kind showed up and enslaved us to do your dirty work. Don't act all high and mighty with me." He turned up his nose at her. "Sure, we may like chaos and destruction, but at least we're honest about it."

Ayana nodded. "He has a point, you know. I mean, did the old summoners ever try asking nicely?"

"Asking... what?"

"Asking nicely," Ayana repeated. "They're actually pretty friendly once you get to know them."

"No, we're assholes. Just a big buncha assholes." Vadazach leaned in to Ayana. "Hey, what're ya doin'? I got a reputation to uphold."

"Oh, sorry," Ayana whispered back. To us, she said, "I'm sorry. They're assholes. But friendly assholes."

Kasia considered this for several moments. "This is unprecedented. I will need time to digest this. Can you... send him away so we can move on?"

Ayana nodded. "Sure."

"Aw, and here I thought we were going to build a campfire and sing songs." Vadazach looked me up and down. "Check out cowboy here. I bet he knows some good songs. You know some good songs, cowboy?"

"I'm... not much of a singer."

"Yeah, no kidding." Vadazach held out his hand. "C'mon, gimme five."

I looked at him for a sec, shrugged, and gave him a high five.

"Yeah, there we go. See? At least one of you's got some class."

Ayana waved the demon back over to her. "Come on, Vaddie, time to go."

"Yeah, yeah, alright." Vadazach rocked back and forth on his hooves. "Hey, uh, before I go... You got anything for me?"

"Of course." Ayana reached into her pocket and pulled out a candy bar. She handed it to the little demon. "Here you go."

Vadazach took a bite of the candy bar, foil and all. His eyes rolled back like he was in heaven. Or, you know, whatever the demon equivalent was. "Chocolate and almonds. Man, you just can't get that shit where I'm from." He looked back at Kasia. "You know, if you'd just given us a cartload o' this stuff back in the day, we woulda leveled whole cities for you assholes for free. Just saying. Your loss." The imp gave a little bow and jumped into the portal. It sealed up behind him.

Kasia stared after the imp, mouth agape. "I have lived for hundreds of years and that may be the strangest thing I've ever seen." She shook her head. "Ayana, we shall discuss your... friends... later. Sydney, it is your turn."

My mouth was dry as I prepared to be laughed out of the room. "It's, uh... kinda worthless."

"No power is worthless, no matter how small."

"Don't be so sure of that." I held out my hand and tried to focus. Bringing up my magic took longer than usual, because nerves, but eventually a small ball of light formed over my hand. I jiggled it from side to side. "Yeah, so... that's about it. I get it if you don't want me to come back for—"

"Sydney..." Kasia's eyes remained focused on the light. "Why on earth would you call your power worthless?"

"Um, because I make little fireflies?" I shrugged. "I mean, I can read in the dark, but that ain't really something to write home about."

She let out a breath. "Have you never had your powers examined by someone who actually knows magic?"

"Don't have many of those where I'm from. What's the big deal? It's just a little light."

"That's not light." Kasia looked into my eyes, a sense of wonder coming over her. "That's *The* Light. But I've never heard of anyone wielding it who wasn't a sindari or pureblood elf."

"I don't understand."

"It's the Light of Life, Sydney." Kasia Windamier held out her palm and a ball of light similar to mine appeared. It swirled up into the air in a tall column, radiating a pleasant warmth. "You're a healer."

Oh.

Well, that's...

Damn.

Chapter 16

SYDNEY

I was still in a daze when I walked into strategy class and fell into my seat next to Lanei. She gave me a strange look.

"Hey, cowboy. You alright?"

"Ever have one of those days where you question everything you've ever known about yourself?"

Lanei shook her head. "Nah. I'm pretty much perfect as is."

"Oh. Well. Seems my 'as is' ain't as 'is' as I thought it was."

Lanei blinked. "I have no idea what you just said."

I ran down my experience in magic class, how my magic had suddenly gone from worthless to potentially useful if I could figure it out.

Lanei gave me a funny look. "I didn't realize you were a magic user."

"Well, until an hour ago it wasn't worth mentioning."

"No, I mean... You look human."

"I am human. Just with a little extra flavor mixed in." I pointed to my eyes. "This here's about the only sign."

"Oh. I didn't realize..." Lanei shrugged. "Either way, good news for you. Nice to have an edge over the rest of us."

I laughed. "I've seen you in action. An edge ain't gonna get me anywhere near your level."

"Then it's a good thing I'm on your side, huh?"

She wasn't wrong. Had to figure everyone here had something going for them.

Nakato and Chavo sat in the back of class. Chavo had a sketchpad in front of him, which he kept adding drawings to and showing Nakato. It made her laugh, but he was cracking himself up.

Yasir and Robia took the seats at the front. Yasir looked annoyingly studious, sitting up straight in his chair with pen and paper neatly laid out before him. Robia took the opposite approach. She leaned back in her chair, boots propped up on the table as she absently twirled a throwing knife in her hand.

Adelaide Russo entered with Warren and Milia in tow. She pointed to the seats closest to the door, and they obeyed. Russo stepped to the podium and looked over the eight of us. Her eyes settled on me.

"Mr. Winter. How you were placed in this class is beyond me. Do you honestly believe you belong here?"

Milia laughed. The words 'go fuck yourself' crossed my mind, but I bit them back.

Instead, I looked around the room and held up my schedule. "This is Self-Righteous Lectures 101, right?" I turned the sheet upside down and squinted at it. "Yeah, looks like I'm in the right place."

If looks could kill, the one Russo shot me was pure murder. She stalked over and backhanded me across the face. The force knocked me clear out of my chair and sent me sprawling.

Lanei jumped to her feet. "Hey! You can't—"

"I will not tolerate disrespect in my classroom." Russo's voice was cold. "If you have a problem with my methods, I suggest you leave to make room for someone with thicker skin. It is impossible to lead effectively if you are overly concerned with others' opinions of you. That is your first lesson." She turned her gaze to me. "And as Mr. Winter can now attest, you *will* learn my lessons, one way or another. Is that understood?"

I stretched my jaw and got to my feet. "Yeah, I gotcha."

She backhanded me again. This time I spun into Nakato and Chavo's table. Nakato steadied me, keeping me from toppling over them. I planted my fists on the table and strongly considered getting myself expelled. Nakato caught my eye and gave a sharp shake of the head.

Russo returned to the front of class. "The correct answer is 'yes, ma'am.' Why don't you try it out and see how it feels?"

I gritted my teeth and bit back my pride. "Yes, ma'am."

Russo turned up her nose and snorted. "Good. Then if you're done acting out, I'd like to begin my class."

I faceplanted onto my bed when I got back to my dorm that evening. I didn't want to be reminded of anything except the sweet nothingness of sleep. Before I could even close my eyes, the door swung open and Kaden burst in.

"No," he said. "No, no, no. You are not sleeping. Not now, not ever."

I mumbled into my pillow. He yanked it out from under my face and tossed it aside.

"Nope. Get up. We've got things to do."

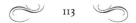

I lifted my head enough to not have a mouthful of sheets. "I am too damn tired to train anymore. Just let me die until tomorrow."

"We aren't training." Kaden lifted my shoulder and rolled me onto my side. "We're celebrating."

"What on earth could we possibly have to celebrate?"

"We survived the first round of classes! That is celebration worthy."

"We're not supposed to leave campus midweek."

"I mean, sure, if you're one of those people who believes in things like rules. But I think we both know you're not."

Got me there. "Who else is going?"

"The whole squad!" Kaden said. "Well, just me and Lanei so far. But she's working on Ayana, and I think with your help we can convince Tenkou. But unofficially, yeah, everyone's going."

"You don't take definitions literally, do you?"

"Nope," Kaden said. "Too constraining. So, what do you say?"

An hour later, I found myself at Dragonfly in San Domingo, sitting at a table with Kaden and Ayana.

Kaden gestured around the place. "See? Aren't you glad you came?"

The verdict was still out. I'd never been to a club before. Chisholm had a saloon, but it wasn't much more than a bar with tables for pool and poker. My father took me there for a shot of whiskey on my seventeenth birthday. That was the only alcohol I'd ever drunk. The people here looked like professional drinkers.

Dragonfly was much more than a saloon. It had not one, but *three* bars spread throughout the place. There

was a whole room for pool tables, and another for poker and blackjack. Tables lined the walls, and the remainder of the club was dominated by dance floors that were crowded even in the middle of the week. Loud, tinny music pumped in through the expensive looking speakers situated in every corner. The tech in this place alone was worth more than my hometown.

I definitely wasn't in Laredo anymore.

Ayana bounced in her seat. "This is so exciting! Reno never let me go to clubs. He called them dens of sin and corruption, but all I see is a bunch of people drinking and dancing and making out, so I don't get what the big deal is."

I adjusted my hat to get a better look at her. "What did you think he meant by dens of sin?"

Ayana shrugged. "I dunno. Ritual sacrifice?"

"The night's still young!" Kaden said. "We might get lucky."

Tenkou and Lanei returned from the bar holding a bottle of liquor made of black glass with a boar's skull painted on it. Tenkou slammed the bottle down, and Lanei set five shot glasses beside it.

"Niadhogr," Tenkou said.

"Bless you."

Tenkou rolled his eyes. It had a much more dramatic effect than when humans did it. His eyes rolled all the way back into his skull so only white showed. "Niadhogr is a throldkin liquor, brewed in the jungles of southern Wismore. It will remove the hair from your chest."

Kaden's eyes went wide. "Like, literally? Because that'd make—"

"It is an expression."

"They just had the one bottle," Lanei said. "Supply and demand only works when there's an actual demand. And it was expensive, so you better drink it and like it."

Tenkou pulled the cork free. Smoke rose out of the bottle. The smell was like a punch to the face.

"Ahhh," he said. "Still fresh."

I covered my nose. "What the hell is in that?" Whatever that liquid was, it didn't smell like something that should occur in the natural world.

"Ancient recipe. It is a mystery."

Kaden coughed. "Thank god."

Ayana, meanwhile, breathed in the smell like it was morning coffee. "Well, I think it smells lovely."

Tenkou filled everyone's glasses to the brim and raised his. "Drink deep and live long!"

Ayana raised her glass with a smile, and Lanei followed suit. She didn't look keen on the smell, but I doubt she wanted to see her gold go to waste. Kaden and I exchanged a glance, but lifted our glasses anyway.

"Cheers!" Lanei said. We clinked glasses and tossed back the shots.

Now, I'd only ever had whiskey, so I didn't know how other alcohols tasted, but I knew it wasn't supposed to be this. Niadhogr tasted like spicy fruit mixed with... trees? Or grass? Something that was definitely not a normal part of a liquid diet.

And holy shit was it potent. I felt the burn as soon as it hit my mouth. Kaden coughed and dropped his glass. Lanei looked like she'd been punched in the face. Ayana swirled hers around in her mouth, a contemplative look on her face. Tenkou slammed his glass down on the table in triumph.

"Ha!" He picked up the bottle and poured another shot of the smoking liquor. "Who will join me in another round?"

Lanei looked at the bottle like it had betrayed her. "Maybe it's an acquired taste..." She held out her glass for more, although it looked like it caused her physical pain.

Ayana swallowed and let out a contented sigh. "That's delightful!"

"Nope," Kaden said. "Nope, nope, nope. I don't know what that is, but I don't want it in my body ever again. Ever. Never ever." He pushed himself away from the table. "I'm getting a real drink." He wagged his finger at the bottle. "Bad Niadhogr. *Bad*."

Before I could join him, Tenkou pushed another shot in front of me. "Let us drink to victory!"

I was already stumbling when I left the table to join Kaden at the bar. It hadn't taken him long to attract a beautiful girl to his side. Her low-cut top left little to the imagination, and even less when she leaned over like that. She laid one hand on his arm and traced it up his bicep. Kaden retracted his arm and casually brushed back his hair. When he spotted me, he yanked me over.

"Sydney! Have you met Sydney?"

I didn't get the same doe eyes she'd given Kaden. "Hi, Sydney," she said, although she was already turning back to him.

"Uh, hey."

Kaden placed his hands on the girl's shoulders and turned her back to me. "Sydney here is from Laredo. How wild is that!"

"Mmm, very wild." She reached up to take Kaden's hands, rubbing back against him as she did. "Want to dance?"

Kaden may have mouthed something at me, but I was too distracted by the gyrating girl to tell what it was. He cleared his throat. "Hey, I'll be honest. I'm just here with my friends tonight. I'm not really looking for anything else."

The girl stuck out her lower lip. "Aww. Well, if you change your mind..." She leaned in and whispered something in his ear that brought more red to his cheeks than the alcohol did. She trailed a finger down his chest and strutted away.

I whistled as I watched her go. "You know, I wouldn't hold it against you if you decided to take off."

Kaden shook his head. "Nope. I orchestrated this little outing, so it's my duty to see it through to the end. Team building and all that, you know?" He handed me a shot of whiskey.

I waved him off. "No more for me. That throldkin stuff was strong, and I ain't a drinker."

"Nonsense." Kaden raised his glass. "You only live once. What's the worst that could happen?"

Something was different when we got back to the table, but I couldn't put my finger on it. Tenkou and Lanei were chanting something unintelligible as they slammed their fists on the table and tossed back more shots. Ayana sipped on her smoking glass of Niadhogr like it was lemonade. The big green slime demon next to her drank straight from the bottle and let out a loud belch.

Nope. Still couldn't put my finger on it.

With effort, I climbed back into my seat. Coordination was broken. Don't know how I broke it, but it sure wasn't working. I could fix it tomorrow. I looked at the others. "What fixes coordination?"

Lanei laughed. "Aww, look at Sydney. He's already drunk. That's adorable."

Kaden grinned. "Three drinks in and he's three sheets to the wind."

"My sheets are fine, thank you." I pouted.

Ayana slapped her palm to her forehead. "Where are my manners. Sydney, have you met Malbohr?"

"No. Who's Malbohr?" I looked around the bar, but nobody jumped out at me.

The big green slime demon stuck out a slimy green hand. "Malbohr glad meet you."

I shook his hand. "Ohhhh, that Malbohr. Yeah, yeah, I know Malbohr!" I pulled my hand back and stared at it. Why was my hand slimy? I looked at Malbohr again. Then at Ayana. Then at Malbohr. I leaned over to Kaden and, in the sneakiest way possible, whispered, "Whose squad is Malbohr on?"

Ayana smiled. "Malbohr is a friend of mine."

"Ohhhhh." It all made sense. "Friend from home. Gotcha."

Malbohr nodded. "Malbohr used eat little man people. Now Malbohr make friend them. Malbohr good demon."

Ayana patted Malbohr on the head as he took another swig of Niadhogr. "Yes, you are."

Kaden shifted his seat further from Malbohr.

The next hour was mostly a haze.

I remember Malbohr eating a full bottle of whiskey. Not drinking. Eating. He had to go home after that.

I remember Kaden getting us all out on the dance floor. I wouldn't call what I did dancing.

I remember Lanei knocking out some guy who wouldn't take no for an answer when she refused to go to a private room with him.

And I remember the guy who turned to his friends as they walked past our table and loudly said, "Can't believe they're letting throldkin and sindari in here now."

Tenkou scoffed and brushed the comment off, but it sucked the life out of Ayana. The smile that'd been plastered on her face all night vanished. She sunk down in her chair and tried to hide her face.

The guy noticed her reaction and puffed himself up, pleased as can be. "At least she's got the decency to be ashamed."

I pushed myself up from the table. "Hey!" My head was still swimming, but that wasn't going to stop me. "Apologize to her."

"No, Sydney, it's okay..." Ayana said.

"Sydney?" One of the guys smirked. "Isn't that a girly name?"

"So what if it is?" Lanei asked, getting to her feet. "You got a problem with girly names?"

"It ain't a girly name," I protested.

"We got no problem with girly names," the first man said. "But we do got a problem with things that aren't human trying to act like they're people."

Tenkou snorted. "Watch your tongue, little man. You do not want to make an enemy of me."

"Or me," Kaden said. He finished off his drink and stood up.

The man laughed. "Oh, right. Because if there was one person at this table I was worried about, it was the pretty boy." He turned back to Ayana. "Even the purple bitch might be able—"

I launched myself at him and smashed my fist into his jaw.

That was the last thing I remembered.

Chapter 17

SYDNEY

aden and I leaned on each other for support as we stumbled into the training room the next morning. It was the first time Kaden hadn't jumped out of bed wide awake and ready to attack the day. I would've enjoyed it more if I hadn't been throwing up at the time.

Lanei was sprawled on a stack of mats, her arm draped over her eyes to block out the light. Tenkou lay cross-legged on the ground, arms spread wide. It looked like he'd attempted to meditate and failed.

"Morning..." I mumbled.

Lanei groaned. "Shhhhh. Stop shouting."

The nearest chair was halfway across the room. Too far. I slumped against the wall instead. Kaden walked the eighteen miles to the chair and sat down. Show off.

"Someone tell Kaden he ain't never talking me into anything ever again," I said.

Kaden tried to laugh, but it turned into a hacking sound. "Kaden isn't here right now. Try back later."

"Niadhogr is the devil's breast milk," Tenkou said, his voice a weak rasp. "I knew not what hell I called forth."

Lanei peered out from under her arm. "You'd never had it before?"

Tenkou grunted. "My older sister claimed it was a rite of passage for all throldkin. I believe she was... playing a joke on me."

Lanei scowled. "I hate your sister."

Ayana skipped into the room. "Good morning, everyone!"

We responded with miserable groans.

She stopped inside the doorway. "Am I late? Did you already beat each other up?"

"How the hell are you so chipper?" Lanei scowled at her. "You drank as much as... some of us."

Ayana shrugged. "I don't know. I've never had alcohol before. Hey, maybe I'm immune!" She giggled. "Now wouldn't that be something?"

"Kill her..." Lanei muttered.

"Aww, you're silly." Ayana wrapped her arms around me in a big hug. I tried my best not to vomit as she squeezed. "Thank you for punching that guy last night. It was very heroic of you."

"Don't mention it..." I thought back on last night. "What happened after that? It's all fuzzy."

"You knocked him out," Kaden said. "One punch."

"Yay..."

"But then his friend laid you out with a pool cue," Lanei added.

"Boo..."

"So if you were wondering where that black eye came from, there you go."

"I have a black eye?" I touched my face. It stung. "Cool..."

"Don't worry, I took care of him for you," Ayana said. "It was only fair."

"And the others?"

Lanei gave what might've been a pained smile. "Don't worry. We make a pretty good team."

The door flew open and Reno strode in. "Come on, get up. It ain't that early."

Ayana beamed and stood in the center of the room.

When the rest of us didn't move, he shouted, "On your feet! Now!"

With great effort, we got to our feet and joined Ayana. Reno stared at us, hands on his hips. "This is how you turn up for squad training? A buncha hungover idiots? Is this the level of dedication I should expect from you?"

"No, sir." Lanei stood as straight as she could manage to try to mask her current state. Some miracles can't be asked for.

"Then act like it!" He marched down the line to Ayana. "Thank you for being the only responsible person here. Since everyone else needs a minute to sober the fuck up, I'll start with you. Get your tank out."

Ayana rubbed her neck. "Um, this doesn't seem like a Malbohr kinda morning. How about Mr. Drooly instead?"

I turned to Kaden and mouthed "Mr. Drooly?" He shrugged.

Reno shook his head. "No, we need to start with Malbohr. If you're going to work as a unit, he needs to learn teamwork more than your other demons. Bring him out."

"But—"

"Summon him. Now."

Ayana bit her lip and waved her makeshift staff. A portal opened. She hesitated a moment before whispering Malbohr's name. She waited a few seconds then turned to Reno. "Nope, guess he's not home. Should I try someone else?"

Reno gave her a stern look. "Call him."

Ayana sighed and repeated Malbohr's name, louder this time. After a few seconds, Malbohr slowly oozed out of the portal. He looked like jelly being poured over a windowsill. The goop piled up on the ground, and Reno took a step back so it wouldn't get on his boots. As the last of his slime dripped out of the portal, Malbohr took form. His features were twisted and out of place. The pile of ooze swayed back and forth.

"Um..." Ayana drummed her fingers on her staff. "Good morning, Malbohr. How are you today?"

Malbohr hiccuped. "Malbohr no feel so good. Think Malbohr drink too much magic bottle juice."

Reno glared at Ayana. "You didn't..."

"He was good!" Ayana insisted. "I promise!"

"Malbohr very good. Eat many magic juice bottle."

And then Malbohr spewed green slime all over Reno's shirt.

Reno looked from his shirt to Malbohr to Ayana.

"Ohhhh... Malbohr sorry." The demon tried to wipe the slime off Reno's shirt, but only managed to spread it further. "Malbohr try fix make better—"

"Ayana!" Reno shouted.

"Rightsorrytimetogo." Ayana waved her hand and the portal dropped down over Malbohr, scooping him up and ushering him away. "So, um... Want me to try Mr. Drooly?"

Reno touched his shirt. His hand came away slick with slime. He shook his head in disgust. "I was hired to teach students who are serious about doing good in this world. But I don't see anyone like that in this room. I didn't sign on for this shit."

With that, he turned and stormed out of the room. The door banged against the outer wall. It swung back and forth a few times before coming to a stop. We were either too smart or too ashamed to try to stop him.

Chapter 18

SYDNEY

None of us wanted to be the first to speak, so we left without saying a word. As we entered the corridor, Jeyla ran around the corner and slammed into Lanei. They went down in a heap.

Lanei shoved Jeyla off her. "Watch where the hell you're going."

Jeyla scrambled away. "Please, I'm sorry. I didn't mean... It was my fault, I'm..." The half-elf was on her knees, her eyes frantic. "Please don't... I..."

Lanei got to her feet. She sighed. "No, I'm sorry. I shouldn't have—"

As Lanei reached out a hand, Jeyla flinched back and scurried away.

I frowned. "What was that about?"

The concern vanished from Lanei's face, her expression neutral. "No idea. That girl's afraid of her own damn shadow."

"Sure about that? Cause it seems more like she's—"

"Drop it," Lanei said. "I'm not in the mood."

I held up my hands in surrender. I wasn't in the mood to press it, either.

Speaking of not in the mood...

Warren and his squad walked our way. They looked to be in good spirits. Yippee for them...

"Russo says we're in a league of our own here," Warren said, voice too loud to only be intended for his team. "The other squads aren't even close."

Milia grinned. "What do you expect? Look at the competition."

Milich laughed. "Sweet sister, you're too kind to call them that."

Warren's eyes gleamed as he looked us over. Couldn't blame him. We must've been quite a sight. He led his team into our path, blocking Lanei. "Now don't you wish you were with us Maldovans instead of the leftovers they stuck you with?"

Lanei narrowed her eyes. "Not a good time, Warren."

"No, I didn't think so. Why don't you talk to the headmaster? I'm sure we can find a way to make room for you. You know, one Maldovan to another."

"Oh, no, we can't do that to them." Milia laid a hand on Warren's shoulder. "You've seen their mentor. They're already at a handicap."

Before Milia could laugh at her own joke, Ayana let out a feral cry and leapt at her. She drove the taller girl to the ground, raining furious punches on her.

"Nobody talks about my brother like that! Do you hear—"

Warren yanked Ayana off Milia and hurled her through the air. She crashed into me and we hit the ground hard.

"Control your demon girl!" Milich shouted as he rushed to his sister's side. She slapped his hand away.

"How dare you!" Milia lunged at Ayana. Tenkou stepped between them and Milia bounced off like she'd hit a wall.

"Enough!" He held out his hands to separate the two girls. "There is no need for this. We are all here for the same thing."

The living mountain that was Katya pushed her way forward. "I am here to break the things that stand in my way."

I pushed myself back to my feet. This was getting to be a running theme. "C'mon, y'all actually talk like that up there? Smash, break, crush to tiny pieces?"

Katya smirked. "Hush, little farm boy. Put your raptor back in the stable where he belongs."

Tenkou growled, a low rumble that sounded like a passing train. "What did you call me?"

Katya stepped up to Tenkou. As large as she was, Tenkou still loomed over her. She had no problem getting up in his face, though.

"You are a large, overgrown raptor that needs to be broken in and shown—"

Tenkou shot his arm out and grabbed Katya by the throat. Selena and Warren were on him instantly. Warren drove an elbow into Tenkou's arm to separate him from Katya, and Selena jumped on his back, locking him in a chokehold. Kaden drove a knee into Warren's gut. I got shoved aside again as Ayana charged into Milia for the second time. I tried pulling them apart, but Milich shoved me against the wall.

"Oh, come on," I said. "Are we seriously doing—"

Milich threw a punch. I deflected with my forearm, leaving myself open for the shot at my stomach. I wheezed and doubled over in pain. Milich grabbed my collar and pulled me back up. At a loss for what to do, I put my hand in front of his face and summoned a ball of light. A bright flash made us both howl in pain, because I'm an idiot and it didn't occur to me to close my own dumb eyes before flashing a blinding light an inch from my face.

I stumbled away from Milich. The fight spilled out around me, grunts and curses from all sides. Through it all came a loud, piercing scream from Milich. For a second, I worried I'd done serious damage.

"Stop! Please, stop!" he pleaded.

"Call them off, Warren!" Lanei hollered. "Do it or I'll snap his arm in half!"

As my eyes adjusted, I saw Lanei and Milich on the floor. She had her legs wrapped around his arm and shoulder socket as she wrenched back. Milich screamed again. Across the hall, Milia let go of Ayana, eyes wide.

"Let him go!" she screeched. "Don't touch him!"

Warren dropped Kaden to the ground in a heap and intercepted Milia before she could do anything rash.

"Stop!" He said over Milia's head, holding her back. "We're done here."

Tenkou shoved Katya and Selena away. He snorted in disgust.

Lanei cast her gaze around the hall. Milich cried out in pain, still caught in her grasp. "Anyone tries anything and I'll finish this for good, understand?"

"Yes!" Milia's face twisted as Lanei wrenched her brother's arm. "Let him go, you bitch!"

Lanei locked eyes with Milia then released Milich. She rolled back and sprung to her feet. Milia rushed to her brother's side and cradled him in her arms.

"This is over!" Lanei commanded. "If any of you dare try something else—" She shot a look to Ayana. "And I mean *any* of you, I will end you. Do *not* try me on this. Am I clear?"

Grumblings.

"I said, *am I clear?*"

Murmurings of yes from both sides. Lanei nodded and turned to leave.

Milia caught her arm. Lanei looked ready to rip Milia's head off, but there was no fight left in Milia. It had been replaced with something else. Curiosity.

"Who are you?"

"I'm the baddest bitch here." Lanei moved to walk away, but Milia didn't let go.

"No..." The word came out slow and unsure. "I know you from somewhere. Where do I know you from?"

"Hell if I know." Lanei glanced at Milia's hand. "If you want to keep that—"

"Who are you?" Milia asked again. Lanei's eyes remained on Milia's hand. Milia reconsidered and pulled it back. "Where in Maldova are you from?"

Lanei hesitated. "Dresden."

Milia scoffed. "Please. Nobody from Dresden has a horse like yours."

"My mother left me an inheritance."

"Sure she did." Milia got to her feet and looked Lanei in the eye. "I don't care if you robbed some rich prick. Don't even care if you killed him. But you're lying. I will find out who you are."

They stared each other down. I was afraid they were going to come to blows again, but Lanei shook her head, stepped around Milia, and left.

Warren, Selena, and Katya left the opposite direction as Milia wrapped her arms around Milich and helped him up. I reached for Kaden but Milia put a hand on my shoulder.

"She's lying to you, you know." Despite everything, Milia's eyes looked sincere. "Are you sure you can trust her?" She left without waiting for an answer.

Kaden held his ribs and wheezed out a laugh. "Now that's the pot calling the kettle every shade of black in the book, isn't it?"

Trust... I'd gotten so wrapped up in classes and making friends I'd forgotten Lord Aguilar's warning: *Suspect everyone.*

Chapter 19

/LANEI

I was in the middle of my third set of sit-ups when Lucia opened the door to my room. The door I was absolutely certain was locked.

"It is time."

I shot her a look. "Why do you have a key to my room?"

The corner of her lip curled up slightly. "I don't."

Of course she didn't need a key. I'd have to take precautions against that. As much as I wanted to tear into her for entering my room uninvited, now wasn't the time to argue lock picking etiquette.

I followed Lucia outside. The courtyard was dimly lit by flickering lanterns. I hadn't expected anyone to be out at this hour, but Lucia evidently had other ideas. Chavo and Vanessa perched on different levels of the granite fountain, silently watching as Lucia led me past.

"You invited your squad?" I kept my voice low. "I thought this was between us."

Lucia tapped a finger to her temple. "Everything is a lesson."

Zeke and Jeyla stood under a lantern at the far edge of the courtyard. The big man's face was an unreadable mask, but Jeyla's eyes were wide as she cowered behind him. I bit back the urge to snap at her. She and I were going to have words one of these days if she didn't stop pulling this crap around me.

Lucia narrowed her eyes at Jeyla and gave a sharp shake of her head. Jeyla stepped out from behind Zeke and attempted to look brave. She failed. Hard to look brave when you're still clinging to the arm of someone twice your size.

We crossed the lawn toward Lucia's tower. It was situated near the forest, well-removed from the other buildings on campus. That was fitting. It sure didn't feel like it fit with the shiny, new exterior the rest of the school gave off. The stones weren't as smooth and uniform as the ones used everywhere else. They were larger and worn down with all the imperfections of age. Had it been built with the rest of the school? Or was it the remains of whatever had been here before Petrichor?

Nakato stood guard outside. She swung open the heavy oak door at the base of the tower as we approached. Her eyes remained locked on Lucia as we entered, not even glancing my way.

Mind games. Cool. Love that.

Lucia placed a hand on Nakato's shoulder. "Let nobody disturb us."

Nakato nodded and closed the door behind us. The room was sparse, just a few tapestries and a set of circular stairs leading up into the tower.

"I get it, you're very scary." I folded my arms and leaned back against the wall. "Is this the part where you make vague threats about all the ways you can hurt me?"

"Pain is fleeting." Lucia pulled aside one of the tapestries, revealing three dials embedded in the stone wall. She adjusted the dials, using the tapestry to block them from my sight. The dials clicked and the wall slid away, revealing a set of stairs leading down. "Shall we?"

I didn't feel great about it, but I followed Lucia down the stairs. We descended past two landings before she produced a set of keys on the third and opened an iron door. Metal ground on metal as the door gave way, hinges screeching in protest. The air beyond smelled stale and... wrong. I stepped into the corridor and peered into one of the empty holding cells. Lucia shut the door behind us.

"The dungeon," she said. "Well, one of them."

"Why does a school need a dungeon?" I grasped the steel bars on one of the cells and gave it a good shake.

"Why indeed. Surely Lord Aguilar wouldn't imprison his own students." She reached over my shoulder and grabbed the bar, her hand directly above mine. "Unless, of course, one of those students was from... a certain kingdom."

"Maldova."

Lucia nodded. "There is no love lost between the Lords Aguilar and Greyton. You and your compatriots must be aware of this."

Tensions between Maldova and Esperan had been high for years. Warren and the Levesque twins all came from notable families. They may be assholes, but they knew the lay of the land.

"These cells are old. He didn't build them for us."

"No. But he asked me to inspect them before you arrived." Lucia tightened her grip on the steel. "Coincidence, I'm sure."

"And I suppose he just forgot that you're Maldovan, too."

"Oh, no." Lucia let go of the bar. "He has never forgotten."

She inserted a key into the lock and swung the cell door open. It was small, containing only a bucket and a cot that was almost certainly full of spiders.

"So what's the lesson here? You're going to get me used to a cell before Aguilar locks us all up?"

Lucia smiled. "We Maldovans must look out for one another. But the cell is not for you." She stepped inside and shut the door behind her. "You have great potential, Miss Walker. I truly hope you live long enough to reach it."

Lucia pushed in one of the stones on the wall of her cell. A door opened at the far end of the room. Nothing but darkness beyond... and footsteps.

I shifted into a fighting stance. "What are you doing?"

"I am forced to pull my punches with most of your classmates. A soft, pampered bunch. But you..." She tapped her cheek. "You certainly didn't pull your punches with me. A true Maldovan." Lucia produced a dagger from her belt and tossed it to me. I snagged it out of the air. "Do not hold back."

I held her gaze a moment longer before facing the door. Whatever this was, I wasn't going to let her get to me. I was better than—

My breath caught in my throat as a figure shambled into the room. Its skin was gray and pallid, the eyes pitch black.

My blood turned to ice in my veins and my vision narrowed, blocking out everything except the zombie before me. I couldn't breathe or move. All of my training, everything I'd learned, everything I'd known in the last twelve years was gone.

I was no longer a warrior facing down a creature that had once been a man. Instead, my memories warped the image into a woman with dark brown, mottled skin.

I was once again a frightened six-year-old child staring into the dead, lifeless eyes of my mother.

Chapter 20

/LANEI

My brain screamed at me to move. My heart begged me to run. But every muscle in my body refused.

I couldn't tear my eyes away from the zombie.

Its pale skin was decayed and stretched thin over a jaw that hung limp on one side, exposing a mouth of rotten teeth. And those eyes... those empty eyes...

They were looking right at me.

Somewhere, a woman's voice shouted.

The zombie looked in the direction of the sound and shuffled toward it.

Another shout.

I tried to control my breathing. Anything to slow my heartbeat, to regain control of my body.

"Lanei!"

My entire body trembled as I slowly turned my head to Lucia. She stood in the comfort of her cell, not the least bit worried about the goddamn zombie coming her way.

"Are you with me?"

I swallowed hard, then nodded.

"Good. Then I suggest you get ready." Lucia took a step back as the zombie reached an arm through the bars toward her. Its fingertips clawed inches from her face. "You have perhaps ten seconds before it realizes it has a meal within reach."

"I... I can't..."

"You are a warrior of Maldova. I have faith in you."

Faith... This sadistic, twisted piece of shit had the nerve to—

The zombie stepped back from the cell and returned its attention to me.

I would deal with Lucia later.

I tightened my grip on the dagger, focusing on the leather handle. The familiar feeling of a blade in my hand helped bring me back to the present.

I wasn't a scared child anymore.

And this thing... this abomination... it wasn't my mother. It was just some other poor creature who'd been reanimated by a necromancer. Another victim of the unholy magic I'd sworn to eradicate.

I could start by putting it out of its misery.

I planted my feet as the zombie approached. It started at a slow shuffle, but with each step it got a little bit faster. When it was only a few feet away, it let out a vile, rasping sound and lunged at me. I ducked under its reach, dragging the dagger across its torso and darting past. It stumbled forward a few steps and then spun to face me.

"You cannot hurt it," Lucia said. "Strike to kill or disable. Anything else is wasted breath."

Right. Stupid. Can't whittle away at an opponent that doesn't feel pain.

I adjusted my stance so my free hand was in front. It lunged again. I smashed my right forearm against its arms to deflect it away from me. Pain lanced up my arm as I swiped the dagger across its neck. The blade cut a notch a few inches deep, but it wasn't the killing blow I'd been hoping for.

I shook out my right arm. "You know, this would be a lot easier if I had a sword."

"Oh, I know." Lucia rested her arms against the cell bars. "I didn't want it to be easy."

I snarled. Of course she didn't.

This time, I tried grabbing its arm so I could swing behind it for a direct shot at its spinal cord. I grasped its arm, but when I tried to twist it the creature didn't pivot with me. Instead, the arm I had in my grip snapped as the zombie shot its other arm forward and grabbed me by the throat.

I let go of its now broken arm and shoved my palm into its sternum, keeping distance from the zombie's snapping jaws as it tried to take a bite out of my face.

The creature's grip was stronger than it had any right to be. That strength didn't come from its decayed muscles, but from the unholy magic that empowered it. My throat ached from where its hand pressed my turquoise pendant against my trachea.

It inched its face closer to mine, the stench of its putrid breath so horrid I could taste the bile rising in the back of my throat. It opened its jaws again. I yanked back my hand that had been keeping it at bay. At the same time, I drove the dagger straight up through its chin and into its skull. The zombie's grip on my throat went slack as it collapsed to the floor.

"You were right." The cell door creaked as Lucia stepped back into the corridor. "Bad things do happen when someone touches your necklace."

I rubbed at my throat as I glared at her. "I should kill you."

"Many people should kill me. Many people will be disappointed."

"You're insane." I threw the dagger at her feet. "This is your idea of punishment?"

"No, Miss Walker. Everything is a lesson."

I had to bite back my response. If she didn't know about my mother, I didn't want her to know that she'd just made things personal. And if she did... "Explain."

"This school was designed to train the finest warriors in Nasan. And they do an excellent job. But you wish to be a knight of Maldova." Lucia looked down at the corpse. "And we Maldovans must be prepared for the worst."

"The undead?" I shook my head. "Ravenstone and Maldova are allies. Why would they attack us?"

Lucia gave me a pitying look. "The undead are older than Ravenstone. And King Draco is not the most powerful undead."

That took me a moment to process. I let out a long breath. "Shit..."

"You know how Lord Greyton feels about magic. The undead are a product of magic."

"He's going straight for the source..."

I had to give him credit, that was a ballsy move. Suicidal, maybe. But one I could get behind.

"That will not be the last undead creature you slay in service of Maldova." Lucia picked up her dagger and returned it to her belt. She smiled. "This concludes today's lesson."

Chapter 21

SYDNEY

I couldn't sleep. My body begged for it, but I couldn't shut my brain off. After lying awake for an hour, I gave up and rolled out of bed. I needed fresh air.

It hadn't even been a full week, but I already missed home. I had expected this place to be different from Laredo, but I wasn't prepared for how big a change I would face. It wasn't just life at Petrichor. Esperan moved at a whole different pace than I was used to. Nothing ever happened in Laredo. Which, you know, sucked. But here I struggled to keep up.

So little was expected of me back home because, well, little was expected of anyone there. You grow up, you follow in your parents' footsteps, and you die. That's the cycle. You don't break the mold. Trying to follow in my mother's footsteps instead of my dad's wasn't breaking the mold, but leaving home to do it sure was. Course, the way this week had gone, they might still ship me home and doom me to a life on the ranch. That wasn't a bad life, it just... wasn't mine.

Aw, hell. What was I getting myself into? I wasn't built to be a spy. Kaden. Kaden would make a good spy.

Or Lanei. She'd be good at skulking about and keeping secrets. She certainly had plenty of them.

I couldn't figure that girl out. One minute she was perfectly friendly, and the next she was moody or downright angry. For whatever reason, Jeyla was terrified of her. Maybe because of Lanei's outburst in class, but... I don't know. Hell, even Milia didn't seem too sure of her, and that was saying something.

Not that Milia's opinion was worth much. She and her brother acted like shits from the get go. Warren too. Maybe it was a Maldova thing. Maybe they were all wired to be miserable assholes half the time. If I was keeping an eye out for potential racists, it didn't take a spy to see that bunch kind of sucked as human beings. And with most of the issues starting in Maldova and spiraling out, they were the obvious ones to keep an eye on. Katya didn't seem much better. But she and Selena were from Ravenstone, which had close ties to Maldova ever since...

I shuddered. I didn't want to think about Ravenstone right now.

I still hadn't gotten used to walking around at night without a candle or magical firefly to guide me. Was it wrong for me to use The Light of Life as a candle? I'd have to ask Kasia.

The gas lights along the corridors were dim, but up ahead a bright light poured from one of the training rooms. The closer I got, the louder the grunting within.

Inside, Ayana wailed away on a punching bag. The bag swayed wildly on its chain as she threw punch after punch its way. Vadazach sat on a barrel next to her. The imp wore a handtowel draped over his shoulders and swung his legs back and forth as he watched her work.

Ayana let out a primal scream with her final flurry before wrapping her arms around the swinging bag and collapsing. Her thin white tank top was soaked through with sweat and stuck to the bag, exposing just enough purple skin to put a stop to whatever train of thought I'd been riding.

Vadazach leaned over the barrel to look at Ayana. "Feeling better?"

She glared at him, but didn't say anything.

"On the plus side, you sure showed the big bad bag o' sand who's boss."

Ayana kicked the barrel. Vadazach tumbled off and landed on his back. He rolled around and moaned dramatically like he fell off a cliff.

"Quiet, you," Ayana muttered.

Vadazach sat up. "I does what I can. Hows about you—" He spotted me in the doorway. "Hey! What's the big deal?"

Ayana jumped to her feet and spun around. Her high alert relaxed. "Oh. Hi, Sydney."

"Hey." I shifted from foot to foot. "I'm sorry, I didn't mean to—"

"No, it's fine. I was just... venting."

Vadazach strutted over to me. "Careful, buddy. One wrong move and *wap*! I'll fry ya faster than a fish on Friday, if ya get my meaning."

I held up my hands. "Yeah, I gotcha."

"Are ya sure? Because... *Fry*-day."

"Yeah, no, I get it. It's pretty literal."

"He's fine, Vaddie." Ayana stretched her arms behind her. "Why don't you get some sleep?"

The imp cast another look my way. He cracked his knuckles. "You sure?"

Ayana smiled. "Yes, I'm sure. Thank you for the company." She closed her eyes and a small portal appeared by him.

"Don't stress out too much, boss lady." Then, to me, he said, "Later bub." He tipped an imaginary hat and hopped into the portal.

"Don't mind him." Ayana waved her hand and the portal closed. "He's actually quite nice once you get to know him."

"Guessing that takes a while."

Ayana shrugged. "He moves at his own pace."

I rocked back and forth in the doorway. "Mind if I..."

"Oh! Yes. Yes, come in." Ayana righted the barrel and used the towel to wipe the sweat off her face. She took a long drink from her canteen and ahhhed. "Sorry. I just... I wasn't in the shiniest mood."

I laughed. "I get the feeling that's rare for you."

"Think positive, be positive. You know, except when I was positively trying to smash Milia's face open."

"Yeah, except for that."

Ayana plopped down on the mat. "I know I shouldn't let it bother me. Reno warned me people would treat me different because of what I am, but... I never imagined anyone would say bad things about him."

I sat across from her. "Some people got nothing better to do than tear others down. Milia and Milich and Warren... That's just what they do."

"But not to Reno!" Ayana clenched her fist and punched it into the mat. "They don't get to say that about him. They don't know him." She sighed and rubbed flat the little dent in the mat. "He's the only family I've got."

"You said you were adopted?"

She nodded. "Reno found me when I was three. My mother, she... She was hurt. Reno ran to get his parents, but... they couldn't do anything for her. So they took me in and raised me. Even despite all..." She waved her hand over her face. I didn't know if she was referring to her purple skin, blue hair, red eyes, pointy ears, or sharp fangs. It didn't matter. She traced a finger over the mat. "They died a few years later. It's just been me and Reno since then."

"I'm sorry."

Ayana shrugged. "It's okay." She tapped her head. "I've got all the memories here." She tapped her heart. "And here. There are plenty of people who have it worse than me. Who don't have *anyone* left. I'm lucky. I've got the best big brother who ever lived." She clenched her fist again. "And when I hear those stupid twins insult him, it makes me want to rip out their stupid blond hair and shove it down their stupid big mouths."

I smiled. "Sounds like a healthy reaction."

She raised an eyebrow. "Really? It didn't go so well earlier."

"I didn't say acting on it was a good idea."

Ayana smiled. "You punched a guy in a bar because he called me a mean name."

I shrugged. "Never said I was full of good ideas."

"At least I'm not the only one." Ayana sighed and leaned back on her elbows. Her shirt clung tightly to her chest, accenting every curve of—

I diverted my eyes to an interesting looking bit of paint on the ceiling.

"So... Why'd you seem so surprised about your magic yesterday?"

"Huh?" I craned my neck at an uncomfortable angle to keep my eyes from drifting south.

"When Miss Kasia said you were a healer. How come you didn't know?"

"Never had anyone to train me. Guess I saw the little glowing lights and figured I got the short straw of the magic game."

"No one ever trained me either. At first I was just making weird, swirly voids. But I kinda figured it out when demons showed up for tea."

"Yeah, about that... Your demons ain't like the ones I read about. Thought they were supposed to be all ferocious and bloodthirsty."

Ayana shrugged. "If you treat someone like a horrible monster, they're going to act like a horrible monster. Plus, I was six the first time I summoned Vadazach. All I saw was a weird little fella who talked funny. Nobody'd told me what to believe about demons yet."

"Lucky for you."

"Lucky for me." She shifted to lying on her side and propped herself up on one elbow. "Well, you know why I'm awake. What's got you up this late?"

Oh, you know, just terrified I was going to screw up and allow a mass genocide to happen. But Reno made it crystal clear what'd happen to me if I dragged her in, so... half-truths it was. "I'm just worried. About failing."

Ayana's eyes widened. "Oh my god, me too!" She sprung at me and hugged me. My mind blanked on what my hands were supposed to do. "I thought I was the only one!"

I tried to think of a witty reply, but the only thing going through my head was the smell of peppermint on her skin.

She sat back on her heels. "It's just that Lanei seems to do everything right, and Kaden's so sure of himself, and Tenkou's this awesome badass, and you're from *Laredo*, and—"

"Woah, woah, wait. How is me being from Laredo even close to any of those things?"

Ayana blushed. There was that color in her cheeks again. "Oh, um... I... like to read cowboy books." She held up her hands in apology. "I know, it's silly. But

I have lots of time to read and those stories always seem so exotic."

Now that made me laugh. "Ain't never heard anyone call Laredo exotic before."

She rolled her eyes. "Well, duh. You're *from* there! Places are only exotic if you've never been before." She puffed out her cheeks and let out a breath. "I guess the whole world's pretty exotic to me."

I gestured around the room. "You're here now. After this, you'll be ready for anything. The world's waiting."

"The world's waiting..." Ayana grinned. "I like the sound of that."

Her smile was infectious. I liked the sound of it, too.

Chapter 22

SYDNEY

Kaden woke me at the crack of dawn and dragged my groggy ass outside for a run. I know I'd told him not to let me make excuses, but dammit, that didn't include days when I just really didn't want to. And because torturing me wasn't enough, Tenkou was outside waiting for us.

"Kaden has expressed concern for my health," he said. "He believes my size hinders my stamina. I am here to prove him wrong."

An hour later, Tenkou and I were hunched over dry heaving while Kaden jogged in place beside us.

"Come on! Push through it! Feel the burn!"

I gasped for air, trying to contain last night's dinner. "If you... say that... one more time... I'm... going to have... Ayana's imp... set you... on fire..."

Tenkou nodded, an effort so great he almost collapsed. "What... sorcery... gives you... such energy... at daybreak?"

Kaden shrugged. "Years of hard work."

Bastard didn't even have the decency to breathe hard.

Tensions ran high in Reno's class. Warren's squad wasn't looking to show us up today. They were out for blood. I shouldn't have wasted all that energy running with Kaden.

Didn't help that Lanei was more on edge than usual. She went straight to the punching bag without saying a word to anyone.

Thankfully, Reno didn't have us sparring today. I think he was still pissed about yesterday, and most likely heard about our fight in the hall. Instead, he showed us moves and had us run down the line practicing on everyone.

We started with a simple hip toss into an armbar. Milia was quick to go first. Despite her smaller frame, she had no trouble getting Tenkou and Katya over. She gave Ayana a lion's smile before tossing her, letting their momentum carry them so Ayana landed on the hard floor instead of the mat. Milia wrenched her arm back hard, too, but released before Reno could bark at her.

When it was my turn, I didn't apply any pressure to the armbar on Ayana, but she still winced when she hit the mat. Warren wasn't going to make it easy, though. He planted his weight to keep me from lifting his huge frame.

I sighed. "Come on, man. You're seriously gonna do this?"

He grinned. "You want me to move? Move me."

I tried again. Nothing.

"Sydney!" Reno called. "Get to it."

"I'm trying, but he's got like a hundred pounds on me."

"Tenkou had more than that on Milia, and she got him over just fine."

"Tenkou wasn't acting like a little bitch..." I muttered. I attempted to lift Warren again. This time, he let me get him up off the ground, but once he was up he shifted his weight and crashed down on top of me.

"Who's the bitch now?"

"Enough!" Reno yelled. "Someone else."

Lanei stepped up. Warren was happy to be the first to go with her. Before he could try the same trick, she kicked her leg back and caught him in the crotch. He doubled over, and she tossed him over her shoulder and latched on the armbar.

"Don't try me, boy," Lanei growled. Warren squirmed, but she had it locked in. She released the armbar and kicked him in the ribs. He swiped a big hand at her, but she swatted it away and moved to strike back.

"Hey!" Reno stepped between them and caught Lanei's arm in his metal hand. "I don't care what issues you have outside this room. When you are in my class, you leave that shit at the door." He turned to the rest of us. "The next person I catch trying to injure a classmate answers to me." He shoved Lanei and Warren away with little effort. "You don't want to answer to me."

The rest of class was mercifully uneventful.

Chapter 23

SYDNEY

Fire was hot.

Major revelation, I know, but right now it was the only thing on my mind.

Fire was hot as hell.

Kasia was pushing Jeyla to see how much fire she could muster up and control at once. Turns out, that amount filled damn near every inch of the room not occupied by a body. At Kasia's command, Jeyla pulled the fire back in, channeled it, and released it in a directed burst that bored a hole straight through the concrete wall. When the smoke cleared, Jeyla walked up to the charred hole and peered through it.

"Woah," she murmured. "How did I..." She shook her head in disbelief.

Note to self: Stay on Jeyla's good side.

"Well done," Kasia said. "Let this be a lesson to everyone. What can be done on a large scale can also be condensed into a stronger, more powerful force." She tapped at the hole with her staff. "I suspect I should have someone repair this. Class dismissed."

In the hall, Lanei leaned back against the wall with one foot pressed into it. She nodded to us. "Sydney, can I—"

"Hi, Lanei!" Ayana wrapped her arms around Lanei. Lanei remained still and allowed it, her usual response to Ayana's hugs.

Lanei sighed. "Hello, Ayana."

"We are going to get food," Tenkou announced. "Would you care to join us?"

Lanei shook her head. "Not right now. I need to help Sydney suck less with a sword."

Ayana released the hug but not her smile. "Okay! Well if you want to come when you're done sucking, you know where to find us!"

I raised my hand to interject, but Lanei pushed it down and shook her head. I turned it to a wave as Ayana and Tenkou left.

"I need to suck less?"

"Yes." She crossed her arms. "You know this. I know this. Let's not make it a thing. If you're my second-in-command, I need to know you can—"

Jeyla stepped into the hall and let out a gasp when she saw Lanei. Her hands flew up defensively and she stumbled back into the door frame. "I'm sorry!" She looked down at her hands then quickly stuck them behind her back. "I didn't mean..."

Without another word, she took off down the hall.

I turned back to Lanei. "Okay, for real, what's going on with you two?"

"How should I know?"

"Because that ain't the first time she's turned into a big pile of scared-as-hell around you. Why?"

"I. Don't. Know." Lanei put her hands on her hips. "Believe it or not, I can't explain why everyone acts like freaks around here. Now, do you want my help or not?"

"But—"
"Yes or no?"

The sparring session turned out to be a whole lot of Lanei smacking me with the flat of her blade. By the time the hour was up, my wrists, forearms, elbows, and back of my head were all bruised. After a particularly rough blow sent me crashing to the floor, Lanei lowered her sword.

"The good news is, you're getting better," she said. "The bad news is, you're still the worst in our class."

I groaned, grabbing the side of my head where she'd rung my bell. "Thanks. You're so helpful."

"You're improving, though." She sat next to me. "But for the life of me I can't figure out what you're doing here."

"What's that supposed to mean?"

"No, I..." She shook her head. "It's nothing personal. It's just... How would you describe your fighting ability?"

I sighed. "The drizzling shits."

"There you go. You're a shit fighter, your magic's barely a concept right now, and you aren't exactly the faculty's favorite person. So, again, what are you doing here?"

Well, that was blunt. I took a sip from my canteen. "I want to help people."

"No, seriously."

"Yeah, seriously. Why is that so surprising?"

"Nobody just wants to help people. There's always more to it than that."

"My parents help people."

"And I suppose their reasons are purely altruistic?"

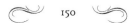

I opened my mouth to reply, but couldn't tell her she was wrong. My mom became a sheriff to atone for past mistakes. It was the same reason she and Dad became bounty hunters before settling in Chisholm.

Lanei nodded. "That's what I thought." She tossed her sword from hand to hand and held it out, peering down its length. "Everyone has their reasons. Doesn't mean they're bad ones, but I guaran-damn-tee you it's more than 'to help people.'" She gave me a crooked smile. "I didn't peg you as a 'just want to make my parents proud' kinda guy."

"I didn't say that."

"Please. You immediately jumped to 'oh, but my parents are good people.'" Her imitation of me was awfully high pitched. "Trust me, that's why you're here, whether you want to admit it or not."

"Yeah, well, there are worse reasons."

"Exactly. Just because it's not all pure and saintly doesn't make it a bad reason."

"What about you, then? Why are you here?"

Lanei was quiet for a moment as she lowered her sword. "Power." She let the tip drag across the floor. "Allowing... certain people to have near unlimited power is far too dangerous." She flicked the sword back up and held it in front of her face. Her smile vanished. "Someone has to keep them in check."

A barely contained malice simmered behind her voice.

I tried to keep mine as casual as I could muster. "Exactly what kinda power are you talking about?"

Lanei shook her head. "Forget it."

"What?"

"You're from Laredo." She stuck her nose in the air. "You couldn't possibly understand the kind of problems people deal with where I'm from."

"You mean Maldova."

"I mean places that aren't so far removed from the rest of the world that they have the benefit of ignoring what's really going on."

"Hey, what makes you think we're ignoring anything?"

"Give me a break. You come here with your 'I just want to help' attitude, but you don't know what that help entails, and you certainly aren't prepared to actually offer it. You can call me a bitch for saying it, but it's true." Lanei got to her feet and sheathed her sword. "Do yourself a favor, cowboy. Figure out who you're here to help. I don't know if you can see them from your little black-and-white world, but lines are being drawn in the sand as we speak. The people you think you're here to help may not be the ones who actually need it. Could just be they're the problem."

Chapter 24

SYDNEY

I woke up to a hand over my mouth and a knife to my throat. I did what any sensible person would do: I panicked. The knife pressed closer and pricked my skin. I ceased struggling.

"Shhh," a female voice whispered in my ear. "You're already dead. So is your roommate."

I tried to sit up, but she pressed me against the bed. I turned my eyes to Kaden's bed. He was sitting up without a hair out of place. He shrugged

"Sorry, mate. No free pass on my account."

What the hell? Why wasn't he freaking out or helping me or—

The knife pulled away from my throat. I tried hopping out of bed, but got tangled in my sheets and landed hard on the floor. Lucia Verdicci stood above me twirling her knife.

"Had I been an assassin, you would both be dead." Her voice was calm and steady, as if she'd just offered us tea instead of a slit throat.

"What. The. Fuck?" I panted. "What's going on? What time is it?"

"It is time for class. Today's lesson is to always be prepared, no matter the time or place. So far, you two are dead." She spun the knife one more time and sheathed it in her belt. "Get dressed and meet me in my tower. And do be quiet. I would hate for you to spoil the lesson for the others."

Instead of using the door, she slid out the window. The second floor window.

I stared after her. "She's insane. That woman is absolutely insane."

"Maybe so," Kaden said. "But she knows how to make an impression."

Chapter 25

SYDNEY

I decided to show up early for Russo's class. I'd made it through the week without any major ass-kickings, and I wanted it to stay that way. She may've hated my guts, but that didn't—

"...and you're sure nobody saw you?"

I stopped outside the door. I wasn't the first one there.

"I've been doing this a long time. I don't get caught."

I peeked through a crack in the doorway. Russo and Warren.

"Keep it that way. You came highly recommended, but that doesn't mean I want you attracting attention."

"The only people I'm talking to are you and my father. That's it."

"And Lord Greyton?"

"He knows my father's games."

"Try to avoid raising suspicion on yourself. Like, say, by brawling in the corridors."

Warren scoffed. "Oh come on. They're a bunch of freaks and nobodies. They're—"

"I don't care about the others. Just leave Lanei out of it."

Lanei? Why was Russo suddenly interested in her?

Warren shifted off the wall. "Why? She's—"

"Because I said so. Do you need more reason than that?"

"No. I just don't see what's so special about her."

"You don't need to. Just do as I say."

Warren sighed. "Yes, ma'am."

Footsteps behind me. I spun away from the door. It was Lanei.

"H—"

I did a cutting motion across my throat and she shut up. A faint thud came from the classroom. I grabbed Lanei by the arm and pulled her back around the corner.

"What was—"

"I'll tell you later." Great, now I needed to come up with a lie. Because I was so good at those. "Just act normal."

"You're telling me to act normal. Right."

I turned her back toward class and we walked around the corner together. "How about that chili in the mess hall today? Had a nice kick to it, huh?"

Lanei gave me a strange look that told me I definitely owed her an explanation for this, but she played along. "Eh, it was alright. A little runny. Could've used more meat."

Russo stepped through the doorway, arms folded. "Ms. Walker. Mr. Winter."

I cleared my throat. "Instructor Russo. Good to see you today."

"Is it, now?" She sniffed in disagreement. "The last time I saw you, you were certainly not happy to see me."

"Just trying to be polite."

"Don't. It doesn't become you."

Alrighty then. I nodded and walked past her. The classroom was empty. How did someone as large as

Into the Black

Warren manage to hightail it out of there so fast? And why he would bother? Russo was his squad's mentor. It would've been perfectly normal for him to show up early to chat. The fact that he'd try to hide that... It didn't add up.

I took a seat as far from the door as possible. Lanei slid into the chair beside me.

"Okay, talk. What the hell was that?"

"What was what?"

"Don't play dumb with me, Winter." She was breaking out the last name. Not a good sign. "You were spying on Russo."

"What? No. Why would I—"

"Maybe because she's had it out for you from day one. Maybe looking for a way to get in her good graces. Hell, maybe you've got a thing for old and wrinkly. Don't know, don't care. But you either need to learn to spy better or quit it, because I am not going to lose my place here because you suck at subtlety. Got it?"

"Got it," I said, relieved I hadn't needed to come up with a good excuse on my own. "It's the old and wrinkly. Really does it for me."

Lanei stifled a laugh. "Shut up."

"No, I'm serious. There's something about those varicose veins. I think it's the blue skin. So hot."

She punched me in the arm, but the anger had gone out of her. I relaxed back into my seat. Crisis averted for now.

Chapter 26

SYDNEY

The Arena looked like a stadium, only without all the seating. Several viewing booths were situated high above the arena floor, each large enough for a couple dozen spectators. Walls, obstacles, and other set pieces could be brought in to change the layout on the floor. Right now it resembled a ruined city that was all sorts of messed up. The detail was surprising, right down to barrels and crates filling the alleyways. No wonder Petrichor was the best place to train. They spared no expense.

Reno gathered us in one of the skyboxes overlooking the arena. "Sometimes you're gonna kick ass, sometimes you're gonna get your ass kicked. Today you'll have the opportunity to do both. The more you fail in here, the easier it'll be to find ways to come out on top when you're face-to-face with someone who's got the upper hand."

Failing was encouraged. Cool. Finally a lesson I could pass with flying colors.

"First up, Kaden versus Tenkou. Ranged weapons."

Kaden pumped his fist. Tenkou frowned.

"So you don't turn each other into pincushions, we're going to be using these." Reno pulled out a quiver of arrows, each tipped with a small black box with tiny metal prongs. "These are an invention of mine, so count yourselves lucky I'm letting you use them. They're a non-lethal deterrent, because not every asshole out there needs to die." He drew one out and flicked a small switch. A bright blue light jumped back and forth between the prongs. "That light is an electric charge. I've got it tuned down so it won't incap you or make you shit yourself, but it's still going to sting like hell. Just try not to shoot each other in the face." He handed one quiver to Kaden and another to Tenkou. "First to land seven arrows wins."

Kaden and Tenkou shook hands and took the lift to the arena floor. Once they'd positioned themselves on opposite ends of the field, Reno pushed a button on the control panel. A horn sounded.

Down below, Kaden and Tenkou took off. Kaden was a blur, running through the broken city, bounding over objects, and climbing walls like they were nothing. Meanwhile, Tenkou crept through the other side, an arrow already drawn and notched on his bow.

Kaden spotted Tenkou and darted out of his view, coming up on a ledge behind him. He notched and loosed an arrow faster than a raptor tearing into a squealing pig. Light flashed as the arrow caught Tenkou in the shoulder. Tenkou dropped his bow and yanked the arrow out. Tendrils of smoke wafted off his scales. By the time he picked up his bow, Kaden was behind him, firing off another shot that hit Tenkou in the back. Tenkou yelled and spun around, but Kaden had vanished.

This pattern continued until Kaden landed six shots on Tenkou. After the sixth, Tenkou roared and smashed his fist into a crate. He yanked out a large plank of wood and brandished it as a shield. He spotted Kaden as he fired off a seventh shot. Tenkou got the shield up in time to catch the arrow. It sputtered with blue light for a few moments before going out.

Kaden disappeared behind a wall. Tenkou spun and hurled the makeshift shield at Kaden when he reappeared on top. It caught Kaden in the chest and knocked him off the ledge. He landed with a thud. Ayana gasped at the impact, but Reno didn't look concerned.

Tenkou reached over his shoulder and drew out a fistful of arrows. He thundered across the arena, flipping the switches on the arrows as he went. My eyes flicked to his bow, abandoned in the dirt behind him.

Kaden hadn't moved as Tenkou rounded the corner, ready to drive all the arrows into Kaden in one fell swoop. But as Tenkou towered above him, Kaden rolled over to reveal he'd covertly nocked an arrow on his bow. Tenkou barely had time to register the "oh shit" moment before the arrow struck him in the chest. It jolted him back and onto his ass with such force that a cloud of dirt billowed around him.

The horn sounded. Just like that, the match was over. In the arena below, Kaden reached out a hand to Tenkou. The throldkin took his hand, but instead of allowing himself to be helped up, he yanked Kaden into the dirt beside him. Tenkou laughed, stood up, and reached his hand down to Kaden, who took it and got launched to his feet.

"Don't go anywhere," Reno said into the microphone. "Next up, hand-to-hand combat. It'll be Tenkou versus Kaden..." Kaden's eyes widened. Tenkou grinned. "... and Sydney."

My head snapped to Reno. "What? Why do I have to do it?"

"Because I said so. What, you don't like two-to-one odds?"

"I..." Okay, yeah, no good answer to that. I hung my head and took the lift down. Kaden and I faced off against Tenkou. "You have any—"

The horn blew. Tenkou charged. Kaden darted away. "Shit..."

Tenkou slammed his shoulder into me. The wall behind me crumbled as I flew through it. At least it broke my fall instead of my back. Tenkou stepped through the me-shaped hole, punching away the remaining plaster to make room for his larger frame.

Before Tenkou could reach me, Kaden dropkicked him from behind. It didn't even phase him. Kaden, being much smarter than me, ran off again. I took the opportunity to leap at Tenkou, but come on, the guy was built like an ox, so of course he didn't budge. I tried kicking him in the back of the knee, but I may as well have been a gnat. He grabbed me by the collar and lifted me off the ground.

"Would you like to concede now?"

"I'd love to, but I don't think Reno will let me."

Kaden ran at Tenkou from the side, but Tenkou swatted him away with a large backhand. Kaden flew into a stack of crates. Tenkou grunted. "No, that is unlikely."

I grabbed onto Tenkou's arm and swung forward to kick him in the chest. He caught my legs with his free hand and lifted my entire body over his head.

"Can you watch the face?" I asked. "I don't want another black eye."

"Of course."

Tenkou turned to Kaden as the Araspian deftly scaled the wall behind us. Tenkou waited until Kaden reached the top then hurled me through the air. I collided with

Kaden and we toppled over the back of the wall and landed in the dirt. Mercifully, Reno blew the horn.

"That'll be all," Reno announced. Ayana and Lanei's laughter drowned him out as it echoed through the speakers. "We'll work on fighting larger opponents."

Tenkou helped us up and we headed to the lift as Lanei and Ayana stepped off.

"What's he got you doing?" I asked.

"Melee," Lanei said, holding up a blunted sword.

Ayana grinned and held up one of her own. "Yep! This'll be fun."

Lanei frowned. "It's not supposed to be fun."

"That doesn't mean it can't be."

Lanei wrinkled her nose, but seeing as I'd gotten my ass kicked by a three hundred pound bruiser who wasn't even trying to hurt me, I had no sympathy for her not wanting to hear a few chipper comments.

Reno nodded to us when we returned to the observation booth. "Good work, Tenkou."

"Thank you."

"You too, you two."

Kaden rolled his eyes. "Yes, that went wonderfully."

"Did you learn anything?"

"Turns out the high ground isn't always safe."

"And you shouldn't just stand there when a huge person charges at you," I added.

Reno grunted. "Then you learned something. Good work." He turned back to the control panel.

Down below, Lanei and Ayana stood in a courtyard in the middle of the ruins. Lanei waited calmly, twirling the sword in her hand. Across from her, Ayana tried to mimic the action and dropped her sword. She looked up our way, gave an embarrassed wave, and picked up the sword. Reno sighed and pushed the button. The horn blew.

Ayana ran away.

Lanei dropped her stance and growled. "Oh, come on!" She glared up at the booth and gritted her teeth, but raised her sword and followed after Ayana.

"Notice Lanei's not running after her," Reno said. "She knows this isn't a chase."

Lanei made her way into the alley behind the courtyard. She certainly wasn't in any rush. I'd lost sight of Ayana when she ran off, but Kaden hadn't.

"There."

He pointed to the stack of barrels Lanei was approaching. A small patch of purple skin was barely visible from up here. As Lanei walked past the barrels, Ayana sneaked out behind her and took a swing. Still wasn't enough to catch Lanei off guard.

Lanei spun and caught the blade with her own. Ayana barely parried Lanei's return blow as she backpedaled away. Lanei swiped at Ayana's legs, but the smaller girl backflipped away with inhuman agility. Lanei took a swing at Ayana's midsection, but she pivoted aside. Ayana wasn't even trying to parry now. She merely danced away from Lanei's attacks.

"Stand and fight!" Lanei yelled, her voice taking on the same tone she'd taken with Warren's crew.

Instead of doing as she was asked, Ayana twirled away from Lanei, opened a portal, and jumped inside.

"Oh, bullshit!" Lanei kicked a barrel. It broke into splinters. She looked to us and threw up her hands.

Reno groaned. "Goddammit. What part of 'no magic' didn't that girl..." He shook his head and pushed the intercom button. "I'll talk to her when—"

Ayana's portal reopened in the air above Lanei and she dropped out. The sindari girl cried out and twisted her body as she fell. Lanei spun around and raised her sword.

Even a blunted tip can pierce flesh when someone falls directly on it.

Chapter 27

SYDNEY

Reno slammed his fist on the button for the horn, grabbed my arm, and hurled me onto the lift ahead of him. He pounded his fist on the wall as we waited second after agonizing second for the lift to reach the arena floor.

My mind hadn't registered what happened. Reno moved like a blur at the first sign of blood, before I could even tell if Ayana was okay or not. And why'd he grab me? If we had to get Ayana to a doctor, Tenkou was stronger and Kaden was faster.

Reno bolted out the doors as soon as they opened. "Move it!"

I took off after him. The lift whirred back to life behind us.

Lanei stood over Ayana, blurting out half-coherent apologies. Reno grabbed her by the arm and threw her back.

"Get away from her!"

Lanei caught her balance before she hit the wall. She took a step forward, cursed, and stayed back.

I got my first look at Ayana. The sword had gone through her right shoulder. It didn't look like it'd pierced anything important, but I wasn't an expert on internal organs.

Reno knelt beside Ayana and grabbed her hand. "Hey, talk to me. Are you okay?"

"I... I got stabbed." She sounded surprised. She turned her head to look at the sword sticking out of her shoulder. "Why did I get stabbed?"

"I'll take care of it. Sydney!"

I slid into the dirt beside them. Reno held Ayana down.

"This is going to hurt, but I need you to be still," Reno said. Ayana bit her lip and nodded. "Sydney, pull the sword out."

"Are you—"

"Do it!"

I took a deep breath, gripped the sword's handle, and pulled it out in as straight and clean a motion as I could. Ayana cried out in pain, tears welling up behind her eyes. I tossed the sword aside.

"Good," Reno said. "Now heal her."

"What? No, I... I don't know how it works yet. Kasia's still—"

"Heal. Her." It sure as hell wasn't a request.

The sword sliced through the strap on her tank top. I peeled away the remaining cloth and put my hand over the wound. "I've never done this before. I don't..." I swallowed hard. "I don't want to mess you up."

Ayana placed her hand on mine. Her lip quivered. "It's okay. I trust you." She gave me a strained smile. "It's not that bad, really. I can barely feel it."

"That's 'cause you're in shock."

She blinked. "Oh. That should make it easier then."

I closed my eyes, trying to focus on the Light. Kasia had shown me how, but never on an actual person. I was still trying to find my way to it when it found *me*. My hand jolted forward and fused with Ayana's shoulder. The warmth of her blood flowed over my hand and up my... no, wait... blood doesn't flow up.

I opened my eyes. A bright, golden light surrounded my hand over Ayana's wound.

Then the pain hit.

The sensation turned from warmth to burning heat as it shot up my arm and filled my body. A jolt as something moved from me to Ayana. My vision blurred and refocused. Another jolt. The light brightened and the heat turned to boiling water in my veins.

I screamed.

And then, just like that, it was over. The force holding me in place released and I collapsed. I looked at my hands, but didn't see any evidence of the fire I'd just felt burning through me. A dark purple scar covered Ayana's wound.

Reno patted my shoulder. "Good work." Then, to Ayana, "Kasia should be able to patch that up better. She can probably get rid of the scar."

Ayana sat up, holding the remainder of her tank top in place. She poked at the scar. "No, that's okay. I think I'll keep this one. It's a good reminder." She smiled at me. "Thank you."

"Welcome..." I gulped air into numb lungs. I could barely feel my fingers. I stared at them. Kasia never said anything about mind numbing pain. I'd have to ask her about that.

Reno turned on Lanei, punching his metal fist through the wall beside her head. "Just what the hell did you think you were doing?"

Lanei flinched but didn't back down. "It was an accident."

"An accident? You *accidentally* stabbed my sister?"

"Yes! I'm not the one who broke the rules of the fight. How was I supposed to know she'd fall on my sword?"

"I've seen how fast you move. You're saying you didn't have time to lower your weapon?"

"That's exactly what I'm saying." Lanei got right up in Reno's face. "What are you implying?"

Ayana cringed. "It's my fault. I shouldn't have—"

Reno ignored her. "Do you need me to spell it out for you?"

"Yeah," Lanei snarled. "I think you do."

"Sure you want me to do that in front of everyone?"

Lanei gave him a look that reeked of death. "How dare you. I am not..." She let out an exasperated grunt, pushed past Reno, and stormed away.

"It wasn't her fault..." Ayana said in a soft voice. "I shouldn't have used the portal."

Reno snorted. "Are you making excuses for the girl who just stabbed you?"

"No." Ayana frowned at him. "I'm making excuses for my friend."

As Kaden and Tenkou checked on Ayana, Reno grabbed my arm. My fingers may have been numb, but I sure as hell felt that. He looked at Lanei, then back to me. His mouth twisted as he shook his head.

Chapter 28

/LANEI

He knew.

The son of a bitch knew, and now he was threatening to expose me in front of everyone. No wonder he didn't believe it was an accident. And still he dared talk to me like that...

I shook my head. He had balls. If he kept pushing me, that's where I'd kick him.

I should've expected something would come to light and throw everything off. And just as I was making inroads... I took a risk coming here, but I wanted to believe I could do it without being scrutinized the whole damn time.

Showed what I knew.

I needed to get away from everyone. Maybe I'd take Ridley for a ride. Maybe I'd go wreck a punching bag or three. Maybe—

I ground to a halt as I turned the corner and came face-to-face with the last person I wanted to see right now.

Jeyla.

The stupid little half-elf raised her hands in surrender and cowered away. Again.

Not now. Not fucking now.

"Sorry, I... I didn't know you were here." Jeyla backed into a wall. She looked like a frightened animal. She looked like prey.

"What the hell is your problem?" I wasn't suspicious anymore. She knew, too. But I wanted her to say it. I had to hear it. "I've never done anything to you, so why do you freak the fuck out every time you see me?" She trembled as I advanced on her, but I didn't care. I wanted this to end. Magical energy sparked around her fingertips, but her nerves kept her from doing anything useful with it.

"Please, please, I..." She raised a hand, sparkling with red magic. I yanked her wrist away from my face.

"No! I'm sick of this. You've been running from me since day one. So how about you stop acting like a coward and we settle this now?" I let go of her hand. "Now tell me—"

She ran away. Again.

This had gone way past getting old.

And speaking of things that had gotten old...

A familiar laugh rang out behind me. I turned to see Milia and Milich, the perfect little twins with their perfect little faces in need of a perfect little beating.

Milich smiled. "You've done a marvelous job ingratiating yourself to the half-breeds."

"Mind your own business."

Milia draped her arm across her brother's shoulder. "Did you forget? This one thinks she's too good for the rest of us."

I scowled at them. "The girl with more power than either of you is terrified of me. Don't you think you should be, too?"

"Of course not," Milia said. "We're pure. You wouldn't hurt us."

"Don't be so sure of that."

Milich sauntered toward me like an old friend. "I don't see how you can stand to be grouped up with those... things. A tainted human, a reptile that should be caged, and... whatever that little purple demon is. You have more patience than I." He placed his hand on my shoulder conspiratorially. I looked at it then back at him.

"You want to find out how much patience I have? Leave your hand there. See what happens."

Milich smiled, but didn't remove his hand. Instead, he traced it down my arm. He must've severely misread the situation.

I grabbed his arm, twisted it behind his back, and wrapped my other arm around his throat, locking my fingers together. I swung him around to face his sister, but she leaned casually against the wall.

"You brought that on yourself, brother. Just relax and she'll let you go." Milia winked at me. "She doesn't really want to hurt you, after all. She's only showing you she can."

After a few more seconds of straining and groaning, Milich let his body go limp. I released the hold and shoved him, getting a foot under him to ensure he landed on his face.

I turned to leave. "Stop acting like you know me."

"We're more alike than you know," Milia called after me. "Or than you're willing to admit."

Chapter 29

SYDNEY

Flik planted his feet outside his pen and dug his claws into the ground, leaving deep grooves in the floor as I pushed. The brat didn't even strain to keep from budging. I finally gave up and dropped to the ground.

"I bet none of the other students have these problems with their horses..."

He responded with a clicking noise that meant he was mocking me. He bent his head down and nuzzled the side of my neck, although even a nuzzle from him knocked me clean over.

I'd taken him out for a ride around campus, which was a great way to collect strange looks. I caught Nakato and her squad returning from dinner. Nakato stared at him in awe, while the big man, Zeke, kept his distance. I expected Jeyla to pull her usual cowering act, but she seemed unfazed.

Our squad had a field exercise first thing in the morning, and I didn't want to be stumbling around like an idiot. I mean, I'd be doing that anyway, but I didn't want to add to it with sleep deprivation. Unfortunately,

I had a gigantic pet raptor who didn't much care about that and thought "mess with Sydney" was an appropriate game to play at all times, so...

I caved and gave him another hunk of meat from his icebox. He let out a low screech of thanks and entered his pen as if he hadn't just been acting like a huge pain in my ass. I scratched his head a few times and locked him in.

I was still feeling the effects from healing Ayana. My brain was running a couple seconds behind the rest of my body. I hoped a good night's sleep would fix it, but my body wanted to sleep for a solid week. I would have to adapt to using magic correctly, but if this was what I had to look forward to every time I used the Light, it needed a new name. The Light sounded way too pleasant for what I'd been through today.

As I left the stables, a scream pierced the night. Across the courtyard, the door to the main hall slammed shut. I sprinted toward it, stumbling over my numb legs as I took off. I cursed myself for being off my game, such as it was.

I threw open the door to the main hall and froze.

Jeyla lay in a pool of blood, a wide red mouth opened in her throat. I didn't need to get closer to know she was dead.

And there, kneeling over Jeyla's body with blood on her hands, was Lanei.

Chapter 30

SYDNEY

"What did you do?"

Lanei looked up, eyes glassy and distant. She looked at Jeyla then at her hands. "I... I didn't..."

I hauled Lanei to her feet. Jeyla's body hit the floor with a sick *thunk*. Her hair spread out around her, dyed red in the blood. "Lanei! What did you do!"

"I didn't do anything! I just... I heard a scream and ran this way but when I got here..."

I grabbed Jeyla's wrist. No pulse. I put a hand to the wound at her throat and tried to summon up the Light, but nothing came. I was either too tired or too late.

I punched the floor and stood up, face to face with Lanei. "Why?"

She shoved me away. "You think I did this?"

"Oh, come on. How many times did she run away from you?"

"I don't know why—"

"Stop lying to me!" My limbs trembled so bad I could barely stand. Only part of it was the dead body. I wasn't dumb. If Lanei decided I was next, I didn't stand much of a chance. "I don't know what was going on with y'all, but you sure as hell do. You're telling me she didn't have reason to be afraid?"

"What I'm *telling* you is I didn't do this."

"But not that she didn't have reason to be afraid."

Lanei clenched her fists. Her knuckles looked ready to break. "That. Is. Irrelevant." She spoke through gritted teeth, each word venom on her tongue. "I didn't do this."

I felt sick. Jeyla's blood surrounded us and we were standing here arguing. And yet... "If it wasn't you, then who was it?"

Lanei threw up her hands. "I don't know. If I knew, don't you think I would've said something by now?" Her shoulders dropped and the anger fell off her face. She tilted her head. "You really don't believe me."

"I..."

It looked bad, that was for damn sure. Jeyla'd been terrified of Lanei from the first time she saw her. Even if no one else saw this coming, Jeyla did.

The mugger from the train... Had I seen him attack Lanei? Or had the half-elf been defending himself? Lanei may've been rough around the edges, sure, but a murderer? It didn't feel right.

I'd been accused of being naive plenty of times before. Why ruin a perfectly good track record?

"I want to believe you," I said, "But you have to know how this looks."

"Of course I know how this looks!" Lanei thrust her hands at me. Droplets of blood spattered my shirt. "What was I supposed to do? Run away and wait for someone else to find the body?"

Heavy footfalls ushered Headmaster Kane and Caesar Hortez into the hall. Reno ran in behind them. They slowed to a halt when they saw Jeyla's body.

Headmaster Kane looked immediately to Lanei. Her eyes narrowed. "Lanei... Come with me."

"Headmaster, I didn't—"

Kane's hand locked around Lanei's wrist. "I said, come with me."

Lanei looked back at me as she was dragged away, a silent plea on her face to... what? Vouch for her? I didn't have much of a defense, except the fear on her face didn't look like a guilty person who'd been caught.

Once they were gone, Caesar walked over to Jeyla's body and checked her pulse. He shook his head.

"Goddammit." Reno couldn't tear his eyes away from Jeyla. "What happened?"

I told them about the scream, finding Lanei with Jeyla, and Lanei swearing innocence.

Caesar shook his head. "I can't imagine she'd confess to it if she had killed her." He ran his hand over Jeyla's face, closing her eyes. "Pity. She had such promise."

Reno tore a curtain down and draped it over Jeyla's body. "I knew this would happen if we let Maldovans in here. Greyton's got their minds so poisoned against non-humans this was bound to happen. We never should have let her in..."

"She's not the only Maldovan here, you know," I reminded him.

"Did you find anyone else next to a dead body?"

"That don't mean she did it."

Reno sighed. "Sydney, you're a good kid, but you may be dumber than shit."

I folded my arms over my chest. "You know, as much as you talk about Maldovan prejudice, you don't seem to have a problem lumping them all together."

"You're goddamn right I don't!" Reno shouted. "Count yourself lucky you lived your whole life in a desert and never had to deal with those Maldovan assholes."

"Maldovan assholes?" Even annoyed, Lucia Verdicci's voice purred.

I hadn't heard her approach. Reno opened his mouth to speak, but bit back his response.

"No, please, go on. You were saying something about..." Lucia's eyes landed on the blood pooling out from under the curtain. "What happened?"

"One of yours," Caesar said.

Lucia's cool demeanor vanished. She ran over and peeled back the curtain. "Jeyla..."

"Sydney found her. With Lanei."

Lucia looked up. "You were with Lanei when you found her, or..."

"He found Lanei with the body," Reno said.

I shook my head. "She didn't do it."

"You don't know that." Reno sat on a stone bench and flexed his metal fingers. "Just because you want it to be true doesn't mean it is."

Lucia pinched the bridge of her nose. "Caesar, will you please bring Nakato to me?"

He looked at me and frowned. "I should stay with Sydney."

"Caesar. Please."

Caesar rolled his eyes. "You're perfectly capable of—"

The door to Kane's office swung open and Lanei walked out, head hung low and without a trace of her usual swagger. But she wasn't in handcuffs. That had to be a good sign. We made eye contact for a brief moment before she looked away and kept walking.

Headmaster Kane followed her out. "Sydney, Reno. We need to talk." She looked at Caesar and Lucia. "Caesar, why are you just standing there? Do something about Miss Isthiru's body."

"Sadie, don't you think—"

"Yes, I do. And I *think* you should do something about the body before the students find out what happened and it draws a crowd. And tell Adelaide to see me at once. Lucia, gather your squad and inform them of what happened. Tell them we are still investigating."

Lucia looked back at Jeyla's body, but she nodded. "Understood."

Kane turned her attention back to me and Reno. "Inside. Now."

I didn't realize it was possible to ask so many questions about a two-minute interaction. No, I didn't see her do it. Yes, she already had blood on her when I got there. No, I didn't see a weapon. Yes, she and Jeyla had a history. No, I didn't know what that history was. Yes, Jeyla was afraid of her. No, I didn't know why...

After an eternity, Headmaster Kane stopped taking notes and set her pen aside. "Sydney, you were brought here for a reason. That reason was to prevent something like this from happening."

At least she wasn't making me feel like shit or anything.

"What did you expect me to do?" I tossed up my hands in frustration. "I have zero experience with this kinda thing. Zero. Did you really think you could just throw me into the deep end and expect results?"

"That's exactly what I expected," Kane said. "Darian Rankin assured me you could handle this."

"Yeah, well, you didn't give me the job because I could handle it. You've got nineteen other students who can handle it. You gave me the job because you can trust me."

"Then I need to trust that you can produce evidence that Lanei was behind this. Gain her trust, get a confession, whatever it takes."

I sighed. "I don't think she did it."

"You're trying to convince yourself she didn't do it," Reno said. "That's not the same thing."

"If y'all are so sure she did it, why didn't you arrest her? You've got enough to hold her."

Kane and Reno exchanged a look. They weren't telling me something. "It's more complicated than that."

"Then uncomplicate it for me."

"Sydney, we have entrusted you with an important task, but that does not mean you are privy to everything that goes on at this school." Kane placed her pen back in its inkwell. "I want to believe Lanei is innocent. I do. But—"

"Then act like it!" I snapped. "You're already assuming she's guilty!"

"*But*, as you said, you found her in a compromised position." She spread her hands out on her desk. "Either help find out who killed Jeyla or give me reason to believe Lanei is innocent. We will continue to investigate on our end, and we will not do so under the sole assumption that Lanei is guilty. But at present, we lack additional suspects."

"You've got three other Maldovans who've shown actual hostility toward non-humans. Why aren't you looking at them?"

"We will consider all possibilities, including them, but we have no proof any of them were involved." She heaved a sigh and folded her hands together. "Just as we will consider all possibilities, so should you. Do not be blinded by your familiarity with Lanei. It is not a coincidence that you two are on the same squad."

"What's that—"

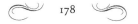

At a knock at the door, Kane's hand shot up to silence me. "Come in."

Russo opened the door and stepped inside. She snorted when she saw me. "Is this the killer?"

I scowled. "Bite m—"

"Sydney was just answering some questions about what he saw." Kane looked back to me. "Instructor Russo and I need to discuss how to proceed from here. You are dismissed."

"I—"

"You are dismissed."

I wasn't ready to be dismissed, but I also wasn't eager to talk with Russo around. So I nodded, pushed my chair back, and left. I felt Russo's eyes on me the whole time.

Chapter 31

SYDNEY

A sunrise never felt so wrong.

We decided to go through with today's training exercise, even though Reno gave us the option to cancel. Lanei didn't want to do it, but she got voted down. So far the only official word was that Jeyla had been murdered. Nothing about Lanei being the sole suspect. Yet.

The streets of San Domingo emptied before us as our squad rode through town. People saw Flik coming and pulled their horses off to the side to make way. A child reached out to touch him, but her mother yanked her away before she could get too close.

"He don't bite," I said.

The mother harumphed and dragged her daughter away. The little girl's eyes remained transfixed on Flik. For his part, Flik enjoyed the attention. He held his head higher than usual to soak it in. All the attention on Flik put Lanei at ease, though. Leave it to a raptor to take attention off a Clydesdale.

Tenkou still garnered his fair share of looks. People didn't shy away from him the way they did from Flik, but the sight of a throldkin riding an enormous boar had to be new to them all the same.

"You are stealing my thunder," he said. "This is not the reception I received when I arrived."

"Sorry about that. Flik's a sucker for attention."

The raptor chirped at the sound of his name.

Tenkou reached a large hand down and patted the side of his boar. "Abizboah does not seem to mind."

"So..." I bit my lower lip, trying to figure out how to phrase this in a non-offensive way. "Is there a reason you don't ride a raptor? I mean, they're native to Wismore, so I just assumed..."

He arched his brow. "Would you ride a gorilla?"

"Well, no."

"We share a common ancestor with the raptors. It would be disrespectful for us to ride them."

"I mean, I wouldn't ride a gorilla cause there's no good place for a saddle. And I never heard of anyone taming a gorilla. That sounds dangerous as hell."

Tenkou laughed. "Those are also valid reasons."

"You don't think I'm being disrespectful for riding a raptor, do you?"

"You treat the animal with respect. I am sure some throldkin would disapprove, but I am not among them."

"Oh. Uh, thanks."

He nodded and reined his boar in to slow down. Reno came to a stop in front of a large building with carved stone columns out front. A sign above the door read "Ascension." A familiar face stood in the doorway.

"Uncle Darian!"

I trotted Flik to him and hopped off. Darian greeted me with a firm handshake and a clap on the back.

"Sydney, good to see you." He waved everyone over. "Bring your horses or... whatever around back. Then we'll get started."

The others dismounted and we led our mounts to the stables. Ayana came up beside me. She raised an eyebrow and motioned between me and Darian. "Uncle?"

I shrugged. "It's like with you and Reno. Family's what you make it."

Ayana smiled, and I swear it made the red in her eyes light up like a fire. "You get it..."

I smiled back, and promptly walked into the edge of the door Kaden held open.

"Alright, listen up," Reno said. "This is Darian Rankin. Darian, as you may know, is the guild master of Ascension. He's also my former boss. So direct your attention to him."

Darian nodded his thanks. "You've got four suspects to track through the city. The first is carrying a briefcase. Stay with the case. Here are photographs of the first three suspects." Darian handed a folder to Lanei. She absently flipped through the photos with glassy eyes. "There is no photo of the fourth, because if you think you're always going to be that lucky, you're fooling yourself. To win, all you've gotta do is track the final suspect into their headquarters and block the exits. This next part is important: Do *not* attempt to confront, maim, or kill anyone. These 'suspects' are members of my team, and I promise you they will win. The first suspect was last seen in the marketplace. I suggest you start there. Any questions?"

Kaden raised his hand, but didn't wait to be acknowledged. "So we're just following people? That's it?"

Darian smiled. "You're following people who know they're being followed. If you're made, you're going to have a tough time maintaining a tail. Anything else?"

No response. Darian clapped his hands together. "Good. Then Lanei, share that folder with your team and come up with a decent strategy. You've got two team members who stick out like sore thumbs, so find a way to make sure that doesn't work against you. Head out!"

Reno pulled me aside after the others were out the door. "Do not let her out of your sight under any circumstances. Understood?"

His metal fingers dug into my bicep. It was equal parts command and threat. I nodded.

Darian placed his hand on Reno's shoulder. Reno released his grip.

"He's got this," Darian said. "Now go."

Chapter 32

SYDNEY

We spotted the first suspect sipping coffee on a cafe patio. The briefcase sat on the ground beside him. We formulated a plan while waiting for him to make a move. Lanei and I would follow as close as we could without being conspicuous. Kaden would go high. After seeing how well he moved through the ruins in the arena, this was as good a time as any to see how well he could scale and navigate the rooftops of a city.

Tenkou and Ayana were trickier. Some businesses employed throldkin as muscle or bodyguards, so Tenkou wasn't completely out of place. As long as he acted like he was out on business, and followed us instead of the mark, he shouldn't be too obvious. But in Ayana's case...

I hadn't seen a single other sindari in San Domingo. No way the suspect wouldn't put two and two together if he spotted her. It didn't help that Ayana was wearing a green tank top and shorts. Easy to move in, sure, but not so great for concealing purple skin. Lanei finally gave Ayana her coat. On Lanei, the hem of the leather duster fell just past her knees. On Ayana, it skimmed the ground. A pair of brown leather gloves later and the only skin showing was on her face and the front of her legs. If she stuck to the shade of vendor stalls, her race shouldn't be too apparent.

After what felt like forever, the suspect picked up the briefcase and left the cafe. He moved nonchalantly through the streets. The stupid part of my brain expected him to take off running, but criminals don't always act like criminals. If they did, there wouldn't be any need for this kind of training because they'd be super easy to spot.

We tracked him for half a mile through the city. He didn't seem to be in any hurry. He stopped to buy an apple from a fruit vendor and proceeded to talk with her for a couple minutes. Not even a sign he was looking for a tail. Maybe he was being nice and waiting for us to screw up before bothering to look for us. Or, alternatively, he knew exactly where we were and was just that damn good.

I was hoping for option number one.

He left the fruit vendor and zig-zagged through the street, moving from one large group to another. We followed him for a few hundred yards before Lanei came to a halt and raised a fist.

"What?" He hadn't done anything to—

"The briefcase."

I squinted. He carried... a bag from the fruit stand. Shit.

Tenkou pushed his way through the crowd. I couldn't see Ayana or Kaden anywhere.

"There was an exchange at the fruit stand." Tenkou ushered us into an alley. "Kaden saw the second suspect take it. He threw a rock at me and followed her."

"Ayana?"

He pointed to the far end of the alley. Ayana knelt to pick something up as we rushed to meet her.

Lanei looked around. "Where'd she go?"

"I don't know. I didn't see her face." Ayana held up a blonde wig. "She was wearing this. I lost sight of Kaden on the roof."

"How could you lose him?" Lanei snapped.

"It's a narrow alley, buildings are tall, and I'm short! What did you expect?"

Lanei cursed and kicked a trashcan. "We have to find them."

I scanned the rooftops, but couldn't spot Kaden anywhere. "He can't have gone far. If we split up—"

"If we split up, we'll never find each other again," Lanei said. "That won't do us any good when we have to block the exits to finish this."

Point. As I looked back down the side alley, light glinted off a metal object stuck in the dirt. I ran over to it and picked it up. It was a throwing knife with *K.A.* engraved into the blade. "Guys! This way!"

We exited into the street on the other side of the alley. People crowded around us, but still no sign of Kaden or the second suspect.

"There!" Lanei pointed to a wooden sign above a stall selling carpets.

"Tenkou," I said, "can you—"

"Got it." Tenkou plucked the knife from the sign. The vendor started to say something, but Tenkou silenced him with a look.

We made our way down the street. I caught sight of Kaden crouched behind a planter on a rooftop. He saw us and pointed to a fountain in the middle of the street. The second suspect sat on the edge, dipping a hand in the water. As we got closer, a man with a full beard approached her, knelt down to whisper in her ear, and stood back up. He now held the briefcase.

"That's number three," I said.

Lanei didn't respond. She remained focused on something behind us.

"Hey, Lanei—"

She raised a hand. "Shh!"

I followed her gaze. A pair of men stepped out of a fancy antiquities shop. One of them had a bulge in the front of his coat. He looked... familiar. I couldn't place his face, but something about it tugged at me. He stuffed whatever'd been in his coat into a satchel and nodded to the other man. They headed off.

Lanei moved to follow them.

I grabbed her arm. "What are you doing?"

She spun back to face me. "Let me go."

"What? No, we have a mission."

"I..." She looked again at the two men. "I think they just stole something."

"You don't know that."

"I intend to find out." She wrenched her arm away. The third suspect was on the move. From the rooftop, Kaden waved frantically at us to get our asses in gear.

Ayana stepped in Lanei's path. "You can't just leave! You're our leader. We need you for this."

"You'll be fine." Lanei's eyes tracked the two men up ahead. "A real crime is more important than a fake one."

"You don't know it was a crime," I insisted. "And if it was, fine, let's report it to someone."

Lanei shook her head. "There's no time." She gave us one last look. "I'm going." She pushed past Ayana and hurried into the crowd.

Crap. Double crap. I had to follow her.

Ayana's eyes welled up. "This is important to Reno. We can't let him down."

Kaden made his way further down the rooftops, still waving for us to follow. Lanei dashed down the street in the opposite direction.

I turned back to Ayana and Tenkou. "Then don't. Finish this."

I ran after Lanei.

Chapter 33

SYDNEY

Lanei glared at me when I caught up to her. "You should've gone with the others."

"I know," I said. "Trust me, I know."

"Just stay out of sight."

Right. Because I was planning to run up and say hello.

We followed in silence for several minutes. The men drifted away from the marketplace into a more industrialized part of the city. We had to hang further back to avoid drawing suspicion in the scarcer crowds. These two were acting more paranoid than the "suspects" we'd been following. I hated to admit it, but Lanei was right. They were up to something.

"We should get help."

Lanei shook her head. "No."

I sighed. "Okay, that's one argument. Care to say why not?"

"No."

"You know, after last night, I hoped you'd be more open with me about whatever the hell you're doing."

"Why, so you can throw accusations at me again?" Lanei scowled. "If you're so worried about me, leave. I'm fine on my own."

"I'm not..." God she was being difficult. "I'm not worried, I just... I found you with Jeyla's body last—"

Lanei grabbed me by the shirt and slammed me into the wall. "I didn't kill Jeyla! Get that through your damn head."

A sound came from up ahead. One of the men heard the racket. His head swiveled around.

Lanei cursed, pushed me against the wall, and kissed me. My mind went blank from shock. How'd she go from yelling at me to...

Oh, right. Blending in. That made much more sense.

Lanei broke the kiss and pulled away. "Sorry..." She looked back down the street. The men were gone. "Shit." She took off running.

It took me a second to regain my motor functions, but as soon as they came back I chased Lanei into an alley.

"No!" She punched a wall. Paint cracked over the plaster. "They were right there."

"Relax. If we don't find them—"

"If we don't find them, it's on you."

"Excuse me?" This shit was getting old. "How is it my fault?"

"If you would just believe me, really believe me, we wouldn't have wasted time arguing, and we wouldn't have drawn their attention."

"Then give me something to go off here! You keep telling me to believe you, so give me something to believe! Stop pushing me away and tell me what the hell is going on!"

"I can't!"

"Why not?"

"Because it won't help my case." Lanei sighed. "I'm tired of running. Tired of defending myself. But I need you—"

The distinct sound of steel drawn from scabbard rang behind us. I whirled to face the two men. Lanei didn't turn around. Her breathing accelerated as she flexed her hands open and closed.

"I knew we were being followed," the first man said. "You two've got about five seconds to explain yourselves before we come to our own conclusions."

My breath caught in my throat. Now that we were up close, I knew where I recognized him from. He was dressed in Esperanian garb, but even without the chain mail I recognized the thick handlebar mustache and scar on his cheek. One of the Maldovan knights from the train.

I glanced at Lanei. She still faced away from the men, her eyes closed.

"Five…"

I reached for my sword.

"Four…"

The second man pointed his sword at me and shook his head.

"Three…"

Lanei let out a slow breath.

"Two…"

She opened her eyes.

"One. Time's—"

Lanei turned around.

Both men's eyes widened. They lowered their weapons. The mustached knight swallowed hard.

"Your Highness…"

Chapter 34

LANEI

I could kill Sydney to keep him from talking, but I didn't want to. Yes, he'd been pissing me off since he found me with Jeyla, but despite that I liked him. He was a decent person, even if he currently looked like an idiot with his jaw hanging open like that. He was even a halfway decent kisser.

Goddammit. I never wanted it to come to this.

This was supposed to be my opportunity to make a name for myself away from my father, to stop being plagued by the Greyton name I never asked for and never lived up to, thank god. So what in the hell were two of his knights doing in Esperan?

Ian Pryce should have have returned to Maldova after escorting me here. His job was to make sure my father didn't suffer the embarrassment of a dead or kidnapped princess. So why was he back?

The second knight was younger. I didn't know him, but he sure as hell knew me.

"Your Highness," Sir Ian repeated, "what are you doing here?"

"You know damn well what I'm doing here." I stood at my full height, looking down my nose at them even though they were taller than me. It was funny how quickly I could shift back into princess mode. It made my stomach turn.

"You're supposed to be wasting your time at that bloody academy, not wandering around this slum hole of a city."

My lip twisted at the sound of my father's derision in his voice. "And you're not supposed to be here at all. Now hand over what you stole."

The younger knight nodded and reached for the satchel at Sir Ian's side. Ian yanked it away. "This is none of your business."

I gritted my teeth. I hated this next part. "In the name of your princess, Lana Greyton, I demand you hand over that satchel."

"No."

"But sir..." The younger knight cowered like a child. "She's the princess."

"We answer to Viktor Greyton," Ian said. "We obey his orders, not hers." He shot me a look that stank of disgust. "You've already shamed your family enough. Go back to Petrichor. Or, better yet, return home. Beg your father for forgiveness and forget all about this."

"That isn't going to happen."

We stared each other down. Neither of us was going to budge.

Sydney coughed. "Okay, uh... guys? *What the fuck is going on here?*"

"Sydney..."

"You're a *princess*? A fucking *princess*? How did this never come up in conversation?"

"I'll explain later."

"Oh, good, 'cause I was starting to worry you were hiding something from me!"

Ian laughed. "You didn't even tell them who you are?"

"My name isn't who I am. Not anymore." I held out my hand. "Now hand it over or we'll take it by force."

Sydney blinked. "We will?"

Ian rolled his eyes. "I don't know how Rilarde gave you the idea you were worth half a shit in a fight, but if you think—"

I charged him. Either he didn't expect it or he didn't want to kill me, because he didn't raise his sword. But he did bring his arm up to defend himself, which allowed me to slide under his reach and rip the satchel off his belt. Sydney drew his sword and advanced on Ian.

The younger knight dropped his sword and tried to grab me. I rolled to the side and got to my feet. Good. He didn't want to kill me either, and he was a shitty knight. I let him make another grab for me, caught his arm and yanked on it, driving my knee into his face. Blood erupted from his nose. I was pretty sure I'd just built some character for the poor guy.

The top of the satchel ripped open during the scuffle. I looked inside. I didn't know what it was, not entirely, but I had a good idea why my father wanted it.

"Lana!"

In the time I'd made short work of the young knight, Ian had done the same to Sydney. He crushed Sydney's head in the dirt with one boot, and pressed the tip of his sword into Sydney's neck. I stepped away from his partner.

"Your father *might* take issue if I hurt you, but he wouldn't give two shits if I cut this purple-eyed freak's head clean off." He pressed the point of his sword down. Sydney cried out as a trickle of blood ran down his neck.

"Leave him alone!" The royalty fled my voice, and all my authority along with it. "None of this is his fault."

"You're right. It's yours." Ian ground his boot into Sydney's skull. "So unless you want his blood on your hands, you'll hand over that bag. Now."

I looked at the satchel in my hands, and more importantly, what was inside it. If my father sent them all the way out here to steal... whatever it was... it must be powerful. No telling what his scientists could do if they were able to reverse-engineer it like the others. Best case scenario, it was a big battery. But if it was another weapon, I could be trading Sydney's life for the lives of thousands.

Okay, fine, so Sydney knew who I was and currently thought I was a murderer. Letting him get killed would solve that little problem. But he was also the first person to treat me like an actual human being, along with all the faults and suspicions that go with it.

What choice did I have?

I threw the artifact on the ground in front of Ian. I hoped to hear something break when it landed, but I wasn't that lucky. "Let him go."

Ian picked it up, never moving his sword from where it rested against Sydney's flesh. "Guess you're smarter than we all thought." He stepped back from Sydney, dragging the sword along his neck. "If you follow us, he dies. Your choice." Ian sheathed his sword, planted a boot into the back of Sydney's head for good measure, and took off. The younger knight ran after him, one hand clutching his broken nose.

I sighed and knelt beside Sydney. "You okay?"

He gave me a look of disbelief as he slowly sat up. "Well, let's see. I just had a sword jabbing my neck, got kicked in the back of the head, and oh, yeah, it turns out you're a freaking princess. So no, on a scale of one to what-the-fuck, I am most definitely not okay!"

"Hey, it's not my fault you got your ass handed to you." I stood up and backed away from him. "You didn't have to follow me. Hell, if you hadn't, those two wouldn't have gotten away."

"Seriously? You think you could've taken them both?"

"I could've at least gotten away with the bag if you hadn't been playing Mr. Hostage!"

"Wow, thanks. Yeah, you got me, that's exactly what I was doing. Definitely wasn't trying to help my friend out of a bind. And, you know, it ain't like the whole thing couldn't have been avoided if you'd just told me what was going on instead of keeping me in the dark."

"That's not import—"

"Yes it is!" Sydney shouted. "I mean... shit. You're Lana Greyton."

I shuddered at my name. *Lana*. "Please don't call me that."

He stared at me. "Why not?"

It was too late for me to deflect his curiosity. At this point, the best I could hope for was damage control. Of course, that meant coming clean. About everything. I didn't know if he'd accept it, but if half of what I'd heard about his parents was true, at least there was a chance.

As inept as Sydney could be in a fight, my initial impression hadn't changed. He wanted to do the right thing. I had to prove to him that I did, too.

"Because Lana is the name my father gave me. He and I aren't exactly on the best of terms, so if you still give even half a damn about me, call me Lanei."

Sydney pressed his tongue into his cheek. He nodded. "Alright. Why Lanei?"

"That's what my mother used to call me. It's what she wanted to name me, but Dad wanted the more formal *Lana*. Lana is who I'm supposed to be. Lanei is who I am..." I leaned against the alley wall and slid to the ground. "Or who I want to be, at least."

Sydney shifted to face me. "Why hide who you are in the first place?"

"I'm not hiding who I am. I only lied about my name. And... Well, you saw how Jeyla reacted to me. That's what the Greyton name means to anyone who isn't human these days."

"Did you—"

"No, I didn't know her. But there are a dozen ways she could've recognized me, and it's a little late now to ask her."

"I don't understand." Sydney frowned thoughtfully. "I keep hearing people badmouth Maldova and Lord Grey— your father. What's he doing that's got everyone so worked up?"

"Nothing. That's the problem. Are you familiar with the Children of Omek?"

Sydney nodded. "Yeah. That's the group that don't like anyone who ain't human."

I snorted. "Sure, if you want to sugarcoat the hell out of it. They're not a *group*, they're a racist cult spreading their filth all over Maldova. Instead of condemning them, my father encourages their rhetoric to push his own agenda. He wants the people to support technological expansion, so he implies that hey, maybe magic's holding humans back. Then he sits back and lets the Children fill in the details. When half-elves or sindari are run out of their homes or killed in the street, he does nothing to stop it because he needs the bigots on his side, so he brushes off each occurrence as an isolated incident or says they brought it on themselves.

"But you know what scares me the most? It's not my father spouting dangerous crap in his speeches. It's not the knights harassing the citizens they think are beneath them. It's the people. The way they buy into it or just... accept it. Let it happen. They stopped fighting back. Stopped standing up for what's right because it wasn't easy or convenient or... god, I don't know... socially acceptable. That's not a kingdom I'd want to inherit even if my father hadn't kicked me out of the line of succession."

Sydney studied me. Normally that'd make me uncomfortable, but right now I needed him to take an honest account of me. Because that would give me an honest account of him.

"And that's why you're here," he said. "At Petrichor."

I nodded. "I have to believe there's a better way. People who won't just accept things the way they are. Who believe that just because the world isn't perfect doesn't mean you shouldn't try." I grinned. "And enrolling here *really* pissed off my dad. He and Lord Aguilar despise each other, so if he was going to hate me no matter what I did, I was damn sure going to give him a reason."

"Why'd he let you come here? Kaden was shocked your father let *any* Maldovans join Petrichor, let alone his daughter."

"Honestly?" I shrugged. "I think he's hoping I get myself killed so I can't lay a claim to the throne."

Sydney's eyes widened. "That's horrible. Come on, you can't actually believe that."

"You haven't met my father. And you really haven't met my stepmother." I sighed. "It is what it is. I think he feels too much responsibility for me to have me killed, but I doubt he'd lose much sleep if something happened to me. He kinda lost all hope in me when

I refused to play the game and be a lady of the court eager to get married off to some noble as a political party favor. Even when he agreed to let his knights train me to fight, he was very clear that their real goal was to break my will. They started with this." I pointed to my nose, the bridge of which would never be straight again. "But then father told them to keep it off the face, in case I changed my mind and wanted to be a lady again."

"God help whatever poor bastard he set you up with," Sydney mumbled.

I shot him a look that sent him into panic mode.

"No, not like that! You're fine. You're great! I just mean, you know, you might try to, uh... maim him? Ain't that... Ain't that accurate?"

I rolled my eyes. I wasn't sure if Sydney was always this stupidly nervous or if they just didn't have girls in Laredo. But he wasn't wrong. "Yeah, that sounds about right. Anyway, I think he was glad to get rid of me. I didn't exactly turn out the way he wanted." I pulled one knee up to my chest and hugged it. "When I heard there were other Maldovans here, I thought he sent them to keep an eye on me. But now I don't think that's it."

"Why not?"

"They don't know who I am. Or if they do, they're doing a good job at playing like they don't. But it's only a matter of time." I hated the inevitable. "I don't think I've ever met Warren or Milich, but Milia and I took an etiquette class together when we were little."

"It didn't take."

I chuckled. "No, we both grew up to be obnoxious shits. But eventually she'll put two and two together and the whole school will know."

Sydney was quiet for a while. I let him think it over. Until I knew he was on my side, we weren't going back. One way or another.

He took a deep breath. "You were right, you know. About my parents."

I blinked. "What?"

"You said everybody's got an ulterior motive. And you're right. They do." Sydney stared at the wall above my head. "That's why Russo hates my guts. She knew them from... before. It was a long time ago, back before I was born. But they were bandits. Pretty famous ones, too, you might have..." He trailed off and shook his head. "No, probably not where you're from. Anyway, they robbed a bunch of banks, pulled off the first ever train heist... and they killed some people. Most were criminals... but not all of them." He pushed himself to his feet and brushed off his jeans. "They put that behind them a long time ago. Started a new life doing some good to shift the ledger in their favor. So I know what it's like to have people judge you because of what your parents did. A person's life ain't dictated by their past." He extended his hand to me. "I believe you. Your secret's safe with me."

I took his hand and got to my feet. "Thank you."

"Does anyone else know?"

"It was only supposed to be Lord Aguilar and Headmaster Kane, but I think Reno figured it out. Maybe Russo and Lucia, too. I arranged everything with Ricardo through private channels. Pretty sure he only agreed to piss off my father. Never really got the impression he trusts me. Kane... I've got no idea. Can't read her poker face."

"She's not sold on you," Sydney said. "When she talked to me last night, she was going on the assumption that you killed Jeyla. Guess I know why you got to walk free."

"Yep. She'd have put me in a cell until the investigation was over, but didn't want to start an international incident. She clearly overestimated my father's affection for me."

"So you don't have any idea who killed Jeyla?"

I shook my head. "None. Whoever did it got away fast."

Sydney frowned. "That'll make this difficult."

I raised an eyebrow. "Make what difficult?"

"Clearing your name," he said, as if it was the most obvious thing on earth. "Oh, I didn't make that clear. We're going to solve Jeyla's murder." He stuck out his hand. "Partners?"

No leads. No evidence. No faith from up above. Just me and a half-useless cowboy.

Yep, that sounded like my luck.

I clasped my hand around his forearm. "Partners."

Chapter 35

SYDNEY

I expected everyone to be furious with us when we met back up at Ascension headquarters, but Kaden hopped up and greeted us with a smile and a clap on the shoulder.

"You made it! Took you long enough."

Behind him, Darian and the rest of Ascension sat around talking with our squad.

"Uh, yeah." I shifted my collar to hide where the knight's sword had ticked my throat. "Sorry, it was..."

"A misunderstanding," Lanei finished. "I thought the one guy stole something, but he was just hiding it from his friend. Some sort of a gift. My bad."

Well, she was a better liar than me. That'd come in handy.

Kaden laughed. "That must've been embarrassing. Too bad you didn't get your first big bust."

"Sorry for abandoning you guys," I said. "But it looks like y'all made it through, so, you know, congrats!"

"What? Oh, no, we failed. Rather miserably, actually." He jerked a thumb toward Ascension. "The last part was impossible to finish with three of us. Ayana summoned

Malbohr to cover one of the doors, but even though Tenkou's big enough for two doorways, they weren't so generous as to put them right next to each other. So the last suspect got away."

"Oh. Sorry about that."

"Not to worry. Reno said, and I quote, 'I'm not gonna punish those of you who weren't selfish assholes and actually followed protocol.'" Kaden's Reno impression was horrible. "So he brought us here for a little Q and A. It's been quite eye-opening, actually. I'm sorry you missed it."

Reno slammed his fist onto a table with a loud thud. Everyone quieted. "I need the room."

Kaden may've been in a good mood, but Reno sure wasn't. Darian motioned for Ascension to follow him and they took their leave. Kaden let out a low whistle as he exited. Ayana gave me a reassuring smile as she and Tenkou followed Kaden out. Reno glared at us like a big, angry statue.

Lanei started in before Reno could say anything. "I'm sorry for abandoning the exercise. I saw someone suspicious and—"

"I don't give a hot steaming raptor shit what you thought you saw. Your job was to follow mission protocol. Want to take a stab at how you did?"

"Sir, I—"

"You failed. That's how you did."

"I thought there was an *actual* crime in process. I was under the mistaken impression that a real crime was more important than a fake one."

Lanei's temper wasn't an act. Noted.

"That's not your job," Reno snapped. "Leave that for the people who are licensed to deal with that shit. You are not one of those people, and if you keep this up, you never will be. Clear?"

Lanei narrowed her eyes. "Oh, I'm clear on a lot of things." She spun on her heel, threw the door open, and stormed out. She was good at that. Not one of the more useful skills to have in your wheelhouse, but it was something. And I could finally see where she was coming from.

Reno sighed. "Alright, tell me what really—"

"You knew!" I threw it right in his face. "You knew who she was and you didn't tell me!"

Reno stuck out his jaw. "Yeah, I knew. How'd you find out?"

"Oh, funny thing, it was on the cover of today's paper. How do you think I found out? She told me."

"Well, that was stupid of her. But now you see why she can't be trusted."

"Why she...?" I shook my head. "Are you serious? You think she can't be trusted because of who her father is?"

"Yes. And if you knew half of what her father had done, you'd—"

"Do you know half of what Darian's done?" I shot back. "I'll bet you do, because he don't hide it. People change."

"Not if you're a Greyton. Viktor's family tree is poisoned, and Lana is just the latest—"

"Don't call her that. Her name's Lanei."

Reno scoffed. "This is exactly what I was worried about when we brought you on board. You're too damn trusting for your own good."

"And you're not trusting enough."

"Maybe. But that's not going to get me or my sister killed." Reno shook his head. "She's got you wrapped around her finger. She's playing you."

"You're playing yourself. You made up your mind about her before you met her."

"She was found with a dead half-elf. You need more than that?"

"She didn't do it. I'm sure of it."

"What makes you so sure? You were still on the fence last night. What happened today?"

I ran him through today's events and our conversation about her father. To convince Reno the way she convinced me. He laughed.

"That's it? Goddamn, Sydney, you really are a fool. She. Played. You. Hell, she probably realized you were onto her and set that whole thing up to make you trust her."

I wanted to smack him, and I would have if it wasn't for the crippling certainty he'd kick my ass. "Look, maybe you don't like it, but Darian brought me onboard because he figured I was a good judge of character. Seeing as I'm the only one here who didn't have a preconceived idea about what type of person Lanei ought to be, I think my judgment beats yours." I took a breath. I'd laid a verbal smackdown on him and he hadn't kicked my ass, so that was something. "Lanei's innocent. I'd bet my life on it."

"I'd advise against that bet. If you're wrong, you might be next on her list." He stepped forward and got in my face. "And you'd better pray that you are, because if Ayana gets hurt after you trusted someone I *told* you not to trust, there isn't a god on this earth who can save you from what I'll do to you. Understand?"

I got right back in his face. "Understood. But that ain't gonna happen because you're wrong, I'm right, and if you don't want to believe me, that's your problem. But the smart move is bringing Lanei in. She wants to get to the bottom of this as much as anyone."

"No. Out of the question."

"Why? Why can't we question it?"

"There are too many unanswered questions about Jeyla's death, and Lanei is still suspect number one. Not just because she's a Greyton, but because she is literally the *only* suspect we have right now. You telling me you don't see that?"

"I see it. But I don't believe it."

Reno shook his head. "Then I question the faith Darian's placed in you."

"That sounds like your problem. Not mine."

I took a cue from Lanei and stormed out. I didn't do it as well as she did. There wasn't enough torque on the door for it to make a satisfying slam, but I mean, come on. It was my first try. Give me a break.

Chapter 36

LANEI

I spilled as much hay outside Ridley's stable as I threw in. I stomped at the loose piles, but they stubbornly refused to go inside.

Reno was such an asshole.

He knew about my father and didn't even have the balls to tell me to my face. He'd rather sit on his high horse and dig for reasons to hate me. I didn't need him on my side for what was coming, but it'd sure as shit make my life easier.

At least Sydney had my back. That was something. Not sure how much good he'd be, but it was better than nothing. It was a weird thought, knowing someone other than Cassius was looking out for me not because of some blind duty to my last name, but in spite of it. For years, I'd been cursed with lackwits who didn't give two shits about me hanging on because I was an "in" with the right people.

The right people... Well, that was a laugh, wasn't it?

I shut the door to Ridley's pen and leaned against the gate. The big horse nuzzled my cheek. I didn't even mind the slobber.

It was still light out. Plenty of time to get some training in. The day didn't have to be a bust.

At least, that's what I thought before Milia and Milich walked in, grinning like jackals. They sauntered my way like we were old friends. Just what I needed.

"Well, well, well." Milia clapped her hands slowly. "I wondered how long it would take before we saw the real you. Fine work last night, really top notch stuff."

I narrowed my eyes. "How'd you hear about that?"

"Word's all over school. Your good deed hasn't gone unnoticed."

"I didn't kill anyone."

Milia winked. "No, of course not. Innocent until proven guilty and all that. But just between us, you should have finished off your little purple-eyed subordinate. Or were you interrupted before you could finish your night's work?" Her eyes boiled somewhere between hunger and lust.

"Shove off." I walked between the twins, slamming my shoulders into them as I parted the sea of idiots.

"Hey!" Milich stumbled back. "Do you know who we are?"

"Why do you think I'm not remotely concerned with you?" I walked backward away from them while giving them the finger. I backed into something solid. It wasn't a wall.

"That's no way to treat your countrymen," Warren said. "Maldova first. You're smart enough to know that."

"What the hell is wrong with you people? I'm here to do some good."

Milia laughed. "So are we. One magic user at a time until the world is pure again."

"You're sick."

"Don't act like you're above us." Milich sneered. "You're the one running around slitting throats."

"It. Wasn't. Me. But if you want me to start, I know where to begin."

I reached for my sword, but Milia already had hers drawn. The point dug into my side.

"I think you've forgotten where you come from," she said. "Shall I remind you?"

I braced myself to act, but before Milia could do anything an arrow whistled through the air, tore through her cape, and pinned her to the post in the center of the room.

Yasir and Robia stood in the entryway. Yasir's sword was drawn and Robia already had another arrow notched on her bow.

"Before you do anything," Yasir said, "I should advise you that Instructor Hortez claims Robia can hit a fly off a wall at five hundred paces. As you three are significantly closer, I would suggest you not do anything she might dislike."

"How dare you!" Milich howled. "Do you know—"

Robia loosed the arrow. It tore through the epaulet that pinned Milich's cloak to his jacket. The cape fluttered impotently to one side. Before he could process what happened, she had another arrow ready to go.

Robia blew a loose strand of hair out of her face. "That's the kinda thing I might not like."

Yasir surveyed us. "So, now I ask you. Is there a problem here?"

Warren held up his hands. "No problem. Just confronting the murderer about her kill last night." He cocked his head to the side. "You've got a half-elf on your squad, don't you? Maybe you want a word or two with her?"

"If she was guilty, the headmaster would have taken her into custody," Yasir said. "Seeing as she did not, I am loathe to take your word over hers. What do you think, Robia?"

Robia grinned. Light glinted off the piercing in the center of her bottom lip. "I think I wanna see what happens if they make me waste another arrow."

"There you have it," Yasir said. "I suppose the choice is yours."

Warren looked at the other two and jerked his head to the entrance. Milich gathered up his cloak and followed, while Milia yanked out the arrow that pinned hers to the wall. She snapped the arrow in half and threw it at Robia's feet as she muttered something about the cost of designer capes.

After they were gone, Yasir sheathed his sword and bowed. "My apologies for the trouble. I assure you, not everyone is so quick to judge." He flashed me a smile that I'm sure dropped many skirts back in Araspia, but I'd long since gotten over noble charm.

"I didn't need your help."

He nodded. "Nonetheless, it was offered."

Robia slung her bow around her shoulder then tossed the arrow in the air and caught it in her quiver. Showoff. "Next time you decide to get caught with a dead half-elf, maybe get your alibi straight first."

I rolled my eyes. "Oh, hey, great advice. I'll be sure to use the buddy system next time I try to help someone."

Robia shrugged. I got the impression she didn't give much of a shit one way or the other.

A few seconds later, Kaden, Devi, Vigo, and Anji burst into the stable. Anji took one look at me and scowled.

Devi scanned the scene. "What's going on? The Maldovan brute squad just stormed through bitching about you two."

Kaden did a double take. "Lanei? What are you doing here?"

"What, you didn't hear? Everyone thinks I'm a murderer."

Kaden raised an eyebrow. "Why would they think that?"

I sighed. "It's a long story."

Yasir bowed again. He really liked doing that. "We shall leave you to tell it. If you ever have need of our help—"

"I won't, but thanks." I didn't know if he was waiting for me to bow or curtsy back, but he stood there dumbly for a few seconds awaiting a courtly mannerism that wasn't going to come. But instead of getting pissy about it, he nodded and exited with the rest of his squad behind him.

Kaden watched the others leave. "I wish I could've been here when all that went down."

I shrugged. "I was fine. They couldn't have hurt me if they tried."

"What? No, I just wish I could've seen Yasir in action. That must've been quite a sight."

I glared at him. "*That's* why you wish you'd been here? Not to keep me from getting my ass kicked?"

Kaden blinked. "No. Why would you need my help for that?"

I sighed. "You're an asshole, you know that?"

Chapter 37

SYDNEY

Jeyla's memorial was held at the end of the week. Her mother, a human from Kialen, attended. No sign of her father. I later learned from Nakato he'd left Jeyla's mother shortly after he learned she was pregnant. He likely had no idea she was dead. Or how she'd lived.

Headmaster Kane and Ricardo Aguilar both eulogized, but I wasn't listening. I spent the service scanning the crowd, trying to gauge the reactions of the people in attendance.

Jeyla's squad was a mess. She and Zeke had known each other since they were kids. The big man cried openly as Nakato attempted to console him. Nakato met the two of them the year before they joined Petrichor together. Her body shook as she held onto Zeke. The fire in her eyes burned with more than sorrow.

Lucia stood behind them with Chavo and Vanessa. She whispered to them throughout the service, directing their attention one way or another. At one point Lucia's words drew Vanessa's attention to me. We made eye contact. Vanessa narrowed her eyes but didn't turn away until Lucia whispered something else.

As they did with everything else, the Araspians remained formal and proper. Yasir, Devi, and Vigo kept their heads properly bowed throughout the service, as did Instructor Lightfellow. Anji, however, couldn't go long without casting a wary glance at Warren's squad or Lanei. He even seemed nervous about Lucia. He probably wasn't too keen on anyone from Maldova right now. His constant agitation appeared to annoy Robia. The more he fidgeted, the more she scowled. At one point she clapped a hand over his to stop him from drumming it against his thigh. When he resumed, she hissed something that finally made him stop.

Predictably, Warren and his squad acted put out by being there. Warren, Milia, and Milich traded jokes under their breaths. They didn't stop until Russo smacked Warren in the back of the head and murmured something to him. The words, more than the smack, silenced him. Katya and Selena observed the whole thing in silence. They weren't exactly mourning, but they had the good sense to not joke about the dead. They were from Ravenstone. Death had a whole different meaning there.

Kaden showed the same reverence as his fellow Araspians, but Ayana and Tenkou were on edge. Like Anji, they were potential targets. I supposed I was too, although at least Nakato and I could pass for full humans. There was no chance of that for Ayana or Tenkou. Not that appearance mattered much. Everyone here knew what we were. The idea that Jeyla'd been targeted because of her heritage hung over all of us.

I felt for Lanei. Since everyone knew she was the only suspect, Headmaster Kane needed to make a visible statement they were taking the investigation seriously.

Reno, Caesar, and Kasia surrounded Lanei. She may not have been in chains, but she sure looked like a prisoner. Didn't help that all three were armed. Reno had some contraption wired to his metal hand that sent a jolt of electricity through it when he flicked his wrist. Caesar had a bow strapped to his back and a pair of daggers on his belt. Kasia had her staff, but didn't need it to qualify as a weapon. The message was clear: Lanei wasn't off the hook. I would've appreciated a sign they were looking for other suspects, though.

Reno and Caesar ushered Lanei out after the service was over, and Kasia joined the other instructors in paying their respects to Jeyla's mother. I hung back and watched as Jeyla's friends said their last goodbyes. Zeke dwarfed Jeyla's mother in a hug. The darkness read plain on Ayana and Tenkou's faces. Neither of them wanted to be next.

As Nakato's squad hoisted Jeyla's casket onto their shoulders, it was clear something had changed in them. I didn't want that change spreading to anyone else.

Chapter 38

/LANEI

Instead of following in Jeyla's footsteps and cowering from me, Anji began treating me with outright disdain. I couldn't even blame him. So far Kane hadn't given any public sign they were looking at other suspects, which meant I was his only target. So I endured the snide comments and dirty looks. As long as he didn't try anything, I could deal with it.

Kaden's ranged skills were rapidly improving. He'd already been good with a bow, but he picked up the crossbow and throwing knives like a natural. He clearly enjoyed it, almost as much as he enjoyed outdoing his sister. Pride lit up Devi's eyes whenever he bested her, the sort of pride only an older sister can have for a younger brother. The kind when you want him to be so much more than he was raised to be...

I don't know. Maybe I was projecting.

Sydney and Ayana showed improvement. Not by leaps and bounds, but measurable. Bless that girl. Throughout all this, she never once voiced any doubt or treated me any different, which would've been understandable considering I'd stabbed her. Ayana couldn't hide an emotion to save her life. What happened to Jeyla scared her, but she never once directed that fear at me. I wasn't sure how much was her natural inclination to trust people or how much was Sydney assuring her I wasn't the enemy. Either way worked for me.

As I watched the two of them laugh together, Yasir walked up beside me.

"How are you?" he asked.

I sighed. "Fine." Since the stable incident, he'd taken it upon himself to ask me how I was every time he saw me. It likely had more to do with the accusations being flung my way than a misplaced desire to protect me, but at least for the latter I wouldn't be expected to *talk* about how I felt. "And how is your royal perfectness today?"

"I am not royalty. My father may be First Knight, but we are not royalty."

I noted he didn't discount the "perfect" part. But he was smiling that flawless smile and didn't have a hair out of place, so who was I to correct him?

"What does it make you?"

"But a humble servant of the realm."

Ugh. Even his answers were perfect. "Then shouldn't you be back in your own realm? Serving?"

Yasir laughed. "Well put. Sometimes the best way to protect your home is to go abroad and discover how you can improve the world around it."

Oh, puh-lease. Sure, that was more or less my reason for coming here, but did he have to make it sound so damned *nice*? No way was he for real.

Across the room, Caesar threw a knife at Robia. She caught it out of the air and hurled it into a target. She never missed. Not once. She even got into the habit of doing cool flippy shit while jumping. Kaden was right. Yasir's squad was the place to be.

"Teacher's pet seems to be doing alright." I tossed one of my throwing knives at a target. It stuck in the outer ring.

"Robia was born for this. I have never seen a truer shot in my life."

"Heh. I bet she'd be the first to tell you that, too."

Yasir nodded. "She would not disagree. But has she not earned that praise?"

I shrugged. "I suppose."

Caesar tossed a knife in the air. Robia leapt off a platform and caught it. As she spun in mid-air, our eyes met. Something flashed there and she was late on her release. The knife flew past the target, missing it entirely. Caesar yelled at her to do it again. As she reset, she threw another dirty look my way.

Why was Robia suddenly pissed at me? She had my back in the stable. I hadn't done anything to—

I glanced at Yasir beside me then back to Robia.

Oh. Oh, I see.

Tenkou stood in the hall waiting for us after class. "Reno would like to speak with everyone." He placed a hand on my shoulder and held me back. He waited until the others were gone then checked behind us to make sure we were alone.

I sighed. "I take it I'm not a part of 'everyone' now, huh?"

Tenkou shook his head. "I wish to speak to you about the rumors."

Fantastic. "I didn't kill Jeyla."

He studied me. "My family did not want me to come here. Did you know that?"

I shook my head. "We haven't really talked about our families."

"They believed that with the current situation in Maldova and Esperan, it would be best if I remained in Wismore."

"So why didn't you?"

"I wanted to see for myself. I did not want to believe such hatred as they described existed in this world. Not today. Not after what Omek did." The nostrils on his snout flared. "I was wrong. It exists. I see it in your countrymen."

"They aren't my—"

"They are," he said. "That may well be the only thing you have in common, but you do share that. I was led to believe all Maldovans hated non-humans. But they were wrong. You do not hate us. I see that." He snorted. "You may be arrogant, short tempered, and full of anger. But I trust you."

"Thanks... I think."

He nodded and continued down the hallway. At least he was honest.

"In addition to your classes and training sessions, you'll be participating in a series of exhibition matches called the Squad Games." Reno folded his arms over his chest. "For the record, I'm against it. The last thing you all need is another reason to stir up trouble with the other squads." He directed a glare at me. Or maybe Sydney. Either way, he wasn't wrong. "The first round is next week. You'll be going up against Nakato's squad."

Sydney and I exchanged a glance. I did *not* want to spar with Nakato's squad right now, not when they already thought I killed their friend. Win or lose, this couldn't end well.

Ayana's hand shot up and she started speaking before Reno acknowledged her. "Are we fighting them? Is it a marathon? Some kind of race? Do we—"

Reno held up a hand. "I don't know. The whole thing is designed by the headmaster, Caesar Hortez, and Kasia Windamier. You can ask them, but I doubt you'll get much of an answer. Each round will be different, and they'll test different aspects of your training. That's all I know."

Sydney raised a hand. Reno nodded to him. "How..." Sydney hesitated. "This ain't fair to Nakato's squad. They've only got four now."

Reno shook his head. "You'd have to take that up with the headmaster." He sighed. "Like I said, I'm against it."

"Well, I'm not," Kaden said. "Going head-to-head with the other squads is a great opportunity for growth." He grinned. "Plus we can show them we're the best, am I right?"

Reno shrugged. "Whatever makes you happy. Dismissed." He motioned for Ayana to follow him.

"I don't like it," I whispered to Sydney.

"Going against Nakato's squad?"

"Yeah. If I were them, I'd use the games to take me out."

Sydney nodded. "Better hope they don't think like you, then."

Chapter 39

SYDNEY

"Make no mistake. Your lives are all in potential danger." Kasia didn't waste any time getting to the point. "Now is a dangerous time to be a magic user, whether you are elven, sindari, or throldkin. Jeyla's death is a tragic reminder we must never become so complacent that we are blind to the prejudice and hatred in the world. There will always be those who do not understand us and have no desire to try." She shook her head and her voice softened. "Do not misunderstand me. Humans are not, and never have been, our enemy. The Children of Omek are our enemy. They will lie and say it is a war between humans and non-humans. Do not let yourself fall prey to the same lies that have poisoned minds against us."

"And when one of the Children is among us, what then?" Nakato asked. "Do we just wait for Lanei to kill again and hope she gets someone else first?"

"Lanei didn't kill anyone," I said for the hundredth time this week.

Anji snorted.

Nakato rolled her eyes. "Just because you want to bone her—"

"I don't want to..." My face flushed. Ayana raised an eyebrow. Nonono. "I don't—"

"Oh, please," Nakato said. "You were there. You found her. Why else could you possibly think she's innocent?"

"Nakato, this is not productive," Kasia scolded.

Ayana stood up. "Lanei didn't do it. She wouldn't kill anyone." She shook her head and blinked. "Okay, I mean, she *would*, but only for good reason! But she didn't kill Jeyla."

"Jeyla was terrified of her," Nakato said. "So scared she wouldn't even talk to her real friends about it. Smart money says she knew firsthand Lanei hates non-humans, just like all Maldovans."

"She doesn't hate non-humans! Tenkou and I aren't even a little human, and she doesn't treat us any different. She's my friend, and I won't let you talk about her like that."

"And Jeyla was my friend!" Nakato advanced on us. "But now she's dead and she's not coming back. So yeah, I'm going to talk about your racist murder buddy however I damn well please."

"That's enough!" Kasia slammed her staff onto the ground.

The shockwave sent me flying into a wall. Ayana landed on top of me. She tried to jump back to her feet, but I held onto her. Our eyes met and the anger drained from her. Heat flushed my cheeks as her body pressed into mine. We held each other's gaze a moment too long then scrambled to disentangle ourselves and stand back up.

"I will not have you all arguing like uncivilized beasts. This is what the Children want." Kasia turned on

Nakato. "We are investigating Jeyla's death. When we have something concrete, you will know. But we have no evidence Lanei is guilty, and until we do, you will refrain from casting judgment upon her or anyone else." Kasia knelt beside Nakato. "I know you are hurting. But if you strike blindly without regard for truth, you will only find vengeance, not justice." She placed a hand on Nakato's shoulder. A faint white light flowed from her into Nakato. "Do not become your anger."

Nakato closed her eyes and took a deep breath. She opened her mouth to speak. Instead, she started to cry. Kasia embraced her.

Ayana took a small, hesitant step toward Nakato. "I'm sorry. I didn't mean to upset you."

Nakato nodded, but didn't look up.

Kasia released her. "Rest. We'll work together later. Ayana, please summon your imp."

Ayana retrieved her staff. It was still crude, but it looked much better than when she first arrived. With Kasia's help, she'd stripped away the bark and sanded it down. The gaudy gemstone was gone. Turns out there wasn't any magic in costume jewelry.

She waved the staff around and muttered a few words. The familiar black and purple void opened up and she called into it. "Vadazach!" The imp didn't appear. "Vadazach!" Still nothing. She frowned. "That's weird. He always comes when I call him." She cleared her throat. "Vadazach!"

"Perhaps try a different demon," Kasia suggested.

"Um, okay." Ayana opened a new portal. "Malbohr!" No sign of the slime demon. Ayana furrowed her brow. "Malbohr! Where are you?"

"Is something wrong?" Kasia asked.

"Yeah, I just... This never happens." She opened a new portal. "Mr. Drooly?"

"You should consider binding your demons to ensure they come when summoned."

"I'm not going to enslave my friends. I don't know why they aren't coming..."

"We'll come back to you," Kasia said. "Sydney." She pulled out a knife and, without preamble, sliced it down her forearm. Blood spurted out like a stream. "Heal me."

"Shit! What?"

"Heal me," she repeated. "This is a deep cut. I need you to heal it before I pass out from blood loss."

"Yeah, but..." I looked at Ayana, the dark purple scar visible around the strap of her tank top. "I'm not good. It'll leave a scar."

"Practice is the only way you will improve." Her voice was too calm for someone leaking blood. "If there is a scar, I can re-heal it myself. I'm telling you to try your best."

My best or otherwise, I wasn't eager to try. Regardless, I placed a hand on the wound. Her blood was warm and seeped between my fingers. I closed my eyes and reached out for the magic. Once again, it found me first, like it sensed someone was hurt and needed me to tell it what to do. A jolt shot through me as my arm fused to Kasia's.

"Slow down," she said. "Take a breath."

But I couldn't. I couldn't breathe. The fire took hold and my whole body burned. I tried to pull away, but I was locked in.

"Sydney? What's wrong?"

I couldn't answer. Couldn't do anything. The Light made me its vessel. I didn't control it. It controlled me.

"Sydney."

The healing was working. I felt the veins closing up inside Kasia's arm. The severed muscle reached out to reattach itself. The blood...

"Sydney! Stop before you hurt yourself."

Someone grabbed my arm, cursed, and pulled away.

"He's burning up!" Tenkou. It was Tenkou.

I screamed as the fire consumed me. It was the only thing I could do. An eternity later, the Light finished. The connection closed and an unseen force shot me away from Kasia.

I hit the ground hard and stayed there. I didn't even have the strength to sit up. Ayana slid her knees under me and lifted my head into her lap.

Kasia's cut was healed, but as expected, my work left a nasty scar. She placed a hand on my heart and closed her eyes. Something tugged inside me. She shook her head. "That isn't how the Light is supposed to work..." She pulled the dagger out again, re-cut the wound, and healed it herself, leaving no trace of a scar. "Sydney, did you experience the same feeling when you healed Ayana?"

I coughed. "More or less..."

Kasia frowned. "I don't want you using your magic until we can understand why it's behaving like this."

"Don't have to tell me twice." I melted into a puddle on Ayana's lap. Doing anything else seemed like a real stupid idea right now.

Chapter 40

/LANEI

Lucia Verdicci was a sociopath. There was literally no other explanation for why she'd set off smoke bombs in our rooms at eleven at night to summon us to class. I don't even know how she got the bomb in there. If the lesson was catching her in the act, I needed to improve, especially if she was going to interrupt my relaxation time with this shit. She'd been on my bad side since day one when she put her hands on my mother's necklace, and she hadn't done a damn thing to work her way into my good graces since then.

Lucky thing I didn't have a roommate who had to deal with Lucia's insanity every time we had a class. One of my father's conditions for my enrollment was that I not have to share a room with someone he deemed beneath me. That was fine by me. I didn't like the idea of anyone else in my room, and that included Lucia. My father said I'd have at least one half-decent role model here, but I didn't know if that was because he knew her or just because she was Maldovan. Either way, I didn't trust her, and I did *not* want her poking around my room. If she was with the Children, I had too much research stashed away that could clue her into what I was doing. I barely hid my notes before Kane and Russo searched my room after everything with Jeyla. Maybe I should've let them see it. Maybe they wouldn't have been so quick to judge. Of course, if they were involved, they might have just slit my throat right there.

Fuck. Not knowing who to trust was exhausting.

Sydney and Kaden were waiting outside the forest when I arrived.

"Guessing she got you two first?"

Sydney shook his head. "Kaden's weird habits finally paid off."

"Oh, shut up. I saw it, didn't I?" Kaden rolled his eyes. "My weapons rack was closer to the wall than I like it—"

"Tell her why."

"I am not going to tell her why."

Sydney stifled a laugh. "The hilts must be exactly six inches from the wall. No more, no less."

I nodded. "That's a good distance. Less than that and you could drag against the wall if you have to draw in an emergency. More than that and you're just losing floor space. What's the problem?"

Sydney blinked. "Wait, you agree with him?"

"I mean, I don't take a ruler to mine every day, but it makes sense. How close do you keep your weapons rack?"

"Oh, uh..." Sydney's cheeks reddened. Maybe the boy didn't tan because he got enough color from embarrassing himself.

"Sydney didn't bring any weapons with him," Kaden said. "He just borrows from the armory when he needs them. I've been using his rack as overflow."

"And this has... *what* to do with the smoke bomb?"

"That's where she planted it. It was rigged to a pocket watch and set to go off at eleven." Kaden gave Sydney a cocky grin. "Powers of observation for the win."

Sydney shrugged. "I still think it's weird."

"You do realize I could've just left the room a few minutes early and let you deal with the bomb on your own, right?"

"Did I say weird?" Sydney backtracked. "I meant brilliant and astute."

"That's what I thought."

"Wait." I narrowed my eyes at them. "What did you do with the bomb?"

"I've still got it." Kaden held up the pocket watch. "I disabled the countdown. So, hey, free smoke bomb!"

"He's keeping it in his dresser." Sydney shuddered. "I don't want that thing going off anywhere near my stuff."

Kaden nudged Sydney and inclined his head toward the school. Lucia was headed our way with the other three in tow. But something about Nakato's squad seemed... off. Their silhouettes were wrong somehow. They stepped into the moonlight.

"What in the..."

They were dressed in identical black battle armor. I didn't recognize the material, but whatever it was looked lightweight and flexible. Then I saw the masks.

The effect was unnerving. Instead of their usual lovebird selves, Vanessa and Chavo looked like they'd stepped out of some animal nightmare. Vanessa wore a fox mask covering the top half of her face, with large eyeholes and an open mouth. Chavo's was a wolf with protruding fangs. Both masks were made of the same material as the armor plating, although Vanessa's fox was painted dark orange with intricate bronze designs, while Chavo's wolf was black with blue details.

My eyes locked on Nakato. Metal glinted beneath her hood. Her mask looked like someone melted the skin off her face and dipped her skull in dark metal. The sight of it jacked up my heartrate. The mask covered her entire face, and the hood was part of a cowl that blacked out her neck and slipped under her armor. There was no trace of skin anywhere. Anyone who saw her would only see death incarnate coming for them.

Death incarnate thought I killed her friend.

Fuck.

"I would like to congratulate Kaden and Nakato for finding the smoke bombs," Lucia said, unfazed by her squad's ghastly appearance. "The rest of you should take a lead from them and remember to always observe your surroundings. It is never safe to let your guard down."

Yeah, no shit. My eyes met Nakato's. They echoed Lucia's sentiment.

"For today's exercise, I have placed a series of traps in the forest. I have also hidden a fine bottle of Maldovan whiskey. You and a partner will navigate the forest. Whoever finds the bottle can either keep it or return it to me for face value." Lucia grinned. She was looking forward to this. There were a lot of things I was willing to do for good whiskey, but being murdered by a vengeful death squad wasn't one of them.

Kaden clapped me and Sydney on the back. "That bottle's as good as ours!"

"I never said you were working with your squad. I said you were working with a partner." Lucia tapped her fingers together. "So let's see... Vanessa and Chavo... Kaden and Sydney..."

Oh no... Oh shit no...

Lucia smiled. "Nakato and Lanei."

I looked at Nakato. Dead eyes stared back at me.

"May the best team win."

Chapter 41

/LANEI

akato didn't say a word as we entered the woods. Not that I was any better. How do you even start that conversation? *Hey, I know what you're thinking, but I didn't murder your friend.*

Yeah, that wasn't going to work with someone wearing a metal skull over her face.

Neither of us took point. I'd bet good money she didn't trust me behind her, and I damn sure didn't trust her behind me. So we walked side-by-side, like the worst best friends on the face of the earth.

The minutes crawled by. I kept my eyes forward, both to scan for traps and because Nakato was creeping me the fuck out. That lack of communication kept me from noticing she'd been inching away from me. My foot depressed something under a pile of leaves and twigs. Before I registered the sound of a cord being cut, a tree branch whipped forward and caught me in the stomach, knocking me on my ass.

I couldn't read any expression behind her mask as I groaned and picked myself up off the ground. She resumed walking.

I snarled. "You saw that!"

She turned back. Didn't respond. Just stared.

I was done with this shit. "You want to be that way? Fine." I advanced on her. "If you've got a problem—"

Nakato brought up her hands and a pair of blades shot out from her wrist guards.

I leapt back and drew the dagger from my belt, scanning my surroundings for Chavo and Vanessa. If this was a trap, I'd walked right into it.

Nakato must've read my mind. "This is between us." The skull's jaw moved when she spoke. Her voice was different, too. Unnatural. Inhuman.

"So this was your plan? Get Lucia to send us off together so you could stab me in the back?"

"You're alive, aren't you?"

"What do you want?"

"The truth."

She charged at me, blades dancing. I deflected one and ducked under the second. Instead of taking a second swing, she ran past me, halting at the tree line. She was testing me, feeling me out.

"I didn't kill Jeyla. That's the truth, and you're going to have to accept it."

"Make me a believer." Nakato raised her hands again and I readied myself for another attack. Instead, a sudden chill rose in the air as a ring of fog crept through the clearing. As it encroached, Nakato melted into it.

Aw, shit.

The fog filled the air until it was all I could see. I couldn't let her trap me like this. I didn't know if her magic let her see through the fog, but if not I wasn't going to give up my position by running. She'd expect me to back up, so instead I slinked right. I hadn't taken more than a few steps when she whistled past. One blade drew a shallow cut across my left arm. I bit back a curse, but didn't drop my dagger. A flash of metal skull and another slice, this time cutting my right arm. Then nothing.

"You want to talk? Let's talk." The cuts stung, but they weren't bad. She wasn't trying to kill me. Not yet, anyway. "Yeah, Jeyla was scared of me. So fucking what? That doesn't mean I killed her."

"Why was she afraid?" She was behind me now.

"That's none of your goddamn business."

I caught another flash of skull as she ran past. I raised my dagger to parry. She disappeared again.

"My friend is dead," she snapped. "So it is my business."

This was getting us nowhere. "She recognized me."

"And who are you?" Nakato was moving now, circling me.

"Someone I came here to forget."

Nakato darted out of the fog. I dropped to the ground as she swiped her blade toward me. I swept my leg. She jumped over it and kept moving.

"I'm here to help you remember," she said.

"You really don't want to do that."

"Because you're a killer?"

A branch cracked. I turned in time to see Nakato charge. I ducked under her swipe, stood up, and hooked an arm around her. I used her momentum to lift her in the air and slam her onto her back. I pinned one arm down, grabbed her other wrist and pressed the tip of the blade to her jugular.

"I don't know if I'm a killer." Whatever material that hood was made of, I bet if I pushed hard enough her blade would slide right up into her skull. I applied enough pressure to make sure she was aware of what I could do. She may have been wearing a mask, but I could see her eyes. She knew. "But I'm not a murderer."

I let go of Nakato and backed away. She sprang to her feet and brought her fists up. I readied myself for another round, but she didn't come at me. We stared at each other, barely visible in the fog. The tension left her body and the fog dissipated. Once it was clear, she flicked her wrists and the blades retracted into her armor. She reached up and both hands disappeared into the hood. With a *click* she removed the mask. Behind the skull hid the face of a girl my own age.

Nakato wasn't the enemy. She wasn't some highly trained assassin out to kill me. We probably had more in common than either of us cared to admit. Hell, for all I knew our mothers could have come from the same part of Kialen. All of that went right out of my mind when we fought.

Damn. That mask really worked.

Nakato looked me up and down. She nodded. "Now I know I can trust you."

"What?"

"You didn't kill me when I gave you the chance."

"When you..." I blinked. "What do you mean you *gave* me the chance?"

Nakato grinned. "Oh, come on. You think you could've caught me in the fog if I hadn't let you?"

"Damn right I could!" That wasn't the point, but I wasn't going to let her take that away from me. "If you thought I killed Jeyla, why would you let me catch you like that?"

"I had to know. I couldn't wait for them to finally accuse you and put you on trial. I had to know or it was going to drive me mad."

"That's insane." I shook my head. People don't do that kind of thing. "I could've killed you."

"If you were one of Omek's Children, you would have," she said. "But at least I would've died knowing.

And you'd have had a hell of a time explaining your way out of that one, so at least I would've gone out with a big 'fuck you.'"

I tried wrapping my head around her reasoning. "You know, there are other ways you could've cleared me without putting your own life at risk."

"I know. But my other option was to tie you up and torture you. I'm not ready to cross that line yet."

If those were her options, I was glad she went with the stupid one.

I pressed my fingertips to the cut on my arm, still wet with blood. "You could've done it without fileting me, you know."

"Oh, I barely nicked you. Stop bitching." She stuck out a hand. "So, can we put this behind us?"

"You done trying to kill me?"

Nakato nodded. We shook hands.

"So what's with the get up?" I asked, looking her over. "I mean, I like it, but it's a bit dramatic."

Nakato shrugged. "That's kinda the idea."

"Yeah, but why?"

She took a deep breath. "Jeyla was killed because of what she was. We don't want anyone to know who or what we are when we come for them." Nakato looked down at the skull in her hands. "Jeyla died for the face she showed the world. Our job isn't done until the day comes when people don't have to live in fear for existing. Until then, when we're on duty, our faces stay hidden."

"Where'd you get the gear from? That's top of the line shit you're wearing."

"Oh..." She blushed. "My mother's the lead engineer in Lord Kane's armory. The suits are prototypes. Something she's been working on." She flicked the blades out. "These too."

"Nice." I nodded my approval. "And the masks?"

"My father's an actor. They collaborated on those. Had them custom made and shipped over." She smiled and put the skull back on. It clicked into place. "Come on," she said, the unnatural voice returning. "I need a drink."

I smiled. "You read my mind."

As we left the clearing, leaves rustled above us. I couldn't see anything in the branches, but I was damn sure the noise wasn't my imagination.

Chapter 42

SYDNEY

was covered in dirt, sweat, cuts, bruises, and a blob of sticky sap that was going to take a patch of arm hair with it once I worked up the nerve to yank it off. To top it all off, we didn't even win. I was relieved when the flare went up and we could call it a night.

I think even Kaden was glad to be done. He'd done much better than me when it came to spotting traps, but he wasted too much energy freeing me from one or two or seven snares along the way. And one more on the way back.

"Who do you think won?" he asked once we had the edge of the tree line in sight.

"I couldn't care any less if I tried."

We were the last pair to make it back. Nakato's squad had removed their freaky masks and were having a laugh. With Lanei.

"Huh." I blinked. "They managed not to kill each other."

"Dude, they won." Kaden pointed at the bottle in Lanei's hand.

I opened my mouth to say something, but... Yeah. Still too tired to care.

Lanei smirked. "Took you guys long enough."

Kaden jabbed a finger at me. "Blame him. Even with his little night light powers, he still managed to step in every trap we came across."

"Hey, you're the one who had us walking in circles for hours."

Lanei stretched, exposing bandages on both her arms.

I pointed at them. "Woah, what happened to you?"

She glanced at the bandage. "Oh, Nakato tried to kill me."

My head snapped to Nakato. "What?"

Nakato rolled her eyes. "Relax. We worked it out like adults."

"With violence?"

Lanei laughed. "It's okay. We're good." She gave me a look that told me she'd explain later.

"Good work, everyone," Lucia said. "You've earned your night's rest." She motioned for us to follow her back to the main grounds, and I was all too happy to oblige.

At least, I was until I caught sight of a figure entering the forest down by the stables. Even in the darkness, I still recognized her.

"Is that Ayana?" Kaden asked.

"Yeah..." I looked back at him and Lanei. "You guys go ahead. I'm going to go warn her not to go too far." They stared at me. "Because of the traps."

Kaden grinned. "Suuuuuuure."

I fought back the urge to strangle him and hurried after Ayana.

What was she even doing out here? It had to be past two. With everything that'd happened lately, it wasn't a good idea for anyone to be wandering around late at night, especially non-humans. Which I guess included me.

Sydney Winter: king of great ideas.

I made my way through the trees. I lost her until a portal opened with a burst of purple light ahead of me.

"Vadazach?"

Ayana didn't sound angry with him for no-showing in class. She sounded worried. The little imp hopped out of the portal. His eyes darted around.

"Yo, this ain't home. Why ain't we home?"

Ayana raised an eyebrow. "What do you mean?"

Vadazach threw his hands up in the air. "We're still at that damned school, ain't we?"

"Of course we are. Why wouldn't we be?"

"Oh, uh, heh, no reason..." The imp put his hands behind his back and dug one cloven hoof into the ground.

"Why didn't you come when I called earlier?"

"I, uh... Well, we..." Vadazach sighed. "We figured if we stopped showing up, they'd make you go home."

"Why would they do that?"

"Well, ya know. You're here for the magic thing, and if ya can't do magic..." He shrugged. "Figured they'd kick you out."

Ayana placed her hands on her hips. "You were trying to get me kicked out?"

"After what happened to the half-elf, we was just..." Vadazach kicked the ground. "Shit, you know demons ain't good at this sentimental crap. We was worried about ya, okay? Not a lot o' people out there give a damn about guys like me." He plopped down on his butt.

"Vaddie..." Ayana knelt beside him. "Nothing's going to happen to me. It's very sweet of you to worry, but I'm fine."

"Yeah, ya say that, but you're an easy target! Ain't nobody gonna mistake you for anything but what you are. We ain't stupid, ya know. We knows what's goin' on out there. Can't ya just, ya know, stay home?"

Ayana smiled. "I could. But then I wouldn't be me, would I?"

"I guess not." Vadazach sighed. "Just, ya know, don't die. Not to be selfish, but that'd suck. We kinda like ya, kid."

"Aww, thank you." Ayana squeezed Vadazach in a hug.

The little demon's eyes bugged out. Hugs probably weren't a thing where he was from. He relaxed and put an arm around her, patting her on the back.

"Is that why the others didn't come either?"

"Yeah, I talked 'em into stayin' away, too."

"Even Mr. Drooly?" Ayana lowered her voice. "How'd you—"

"The son of a bitch bit me!" Vadazach spat on the ground. "Even for a demon, that guy's a real prick."

A mosquito landed on my arm and I smacked it. Vadazach shot to his feet and spun my way, eyes bright and a ball of fire in his hand.

"Who's there? Show yourself or I'ma burn this place to the ground!"

I held my hands in the air and stepped forward. "Woah, easy there, big guy!"

"Oh, big guy, huh? Tryin' to butter me up with flattery, huh? Think I'm gonna fall for that, *huh?*" He stamped his tiny feet. It wasn't intimidating.

"It's okay, Vaddie." Ayana placed a hand on the demon's arm. "Sydney's a friend. He wouldn't hurt me."

He looked at me through narrowed eyes. "A friend, eh? Well, you best watch yer step, cowboy." He looked me up and down. "Actually, looks like you shoulda watched your step already. For reals, the fuck happened to you?"

"Oh, uh... Stealth class."

"Wow..." Vadazach gave me a pitying look. "Yeah, you're okay. Pretty sure she could take ya if ya tried anything."

"Thank you, Vadazach." Ayana opened a portal. "Can you please tell the others I'll be fine?"

"I'll tell Malbohr, but you can tell the Droolbag yourself. I ain't goin' near that bitch." Before he hopped into the portal, Vadazach pointed at his eyes, then at mine, then back at his. "I'm watchin' you, punk." And then he was gone.

"He's really quite sweet when he wants to be." She glanced back at the fading portal. "Well, he never *wants* to be. But when he lets his guard down."

"Yeah, I get that impression." I took a seat on a tree stump before my legs gave out.

Ayana sat beside me.

"How do you do it?"

"Summoning? Oh, it's easy, I just—"

"No. How do you stay so upbeat about everything?" I shook my head. "I mean, I'm looking over my shoulder all day, and I barely register as part elf. Nakato and Anji are freaked. Tenkou's stoic as ever, but you don't even seem worried. How do you manage it?"

She tilted her head and gazed into the distance. "First time you saw me, what did you see?"

The most amazing girl I'd ever seen in my life... But I couldn't exactly say—

"You're trying not to say 'purple skin' or 'red eyes.'"

"No, that's not—" Not what I was trying not to say...

"It's okay." She looked into her lap and plucked at her clothes. "That's what everyone sees. I'm not exactly normal."

"I like not exactly normal," I blurted out. "Not exactly normal is good."

Ayana smiled. "Most people would disagree. Unusual is one thing. But most people today have never seen a sindari before. And when most people think sindari nowadays, they think..." She raised her eyebrows for emphasis.

I finished her thought for her. "Omek..."

She nodded. "Yeah. Mom and Dad—Reno's parents— explained it to me when I was old enough to understand. They told me there'd always be people who wouldn't like me because I was different, wouldn't see being sindari is what makes me special. You know, the parent thing. They told me I could either let the negativity get to me and turn into bitterness, or I could shake it off and think about all the good things in life." She sighed and looked up at the sky. "I choose to take tomorrow one day at a time."

"And you're not afraid?"

"Of course I am. But I'm here because I don't want to be afraid anymore. Just because I'm afraid doesn't mean I have to act like it." She placed a hand on my knee.

I dared to cover it with mine, and hoped she couldn't feel my hand tremble and sweat.

"Besides, I've got Reno and you and Lanei and Tenkou and Kaden and my own little army of demons. Who'd be dumb enough to mess with me?"

A gust of wind blew aside the branches overhead. Her eyes glowed bright red in the moonlight. I pitied anyone who could look into those eyes and not see how beautiful they were.

"Yeah." I swallowed. "They'd have to be pretty dumb..."

"They would..."

That's when I noticed I wasn't just looking into her eyes. She was looking into mine. The corners of her lips turned up and my pulse shot up about a thousand percent. She ran her hand up my arm.

This was it.

"Um, Sydney...?"

"Yeah?" I leaned in.

At a sharp tug on my arm, I looked down. Her hand was stuck in the patch of sap.

Ayana laughed. "I appear to be stuck."

I moved my arm. Her hand went with it. "Yeah, uh... Yeah. You are."

"Here." She grabbed my wrist with her other hand. "This might hurt a little."

"Wait—"

She yanked her hand free. I may or may not have screamed.

Chapter 43

LANEI

After I banged on Sydney's door for nearly a minute, Kaden finally cracked it open and peered out. His hair was uncharacteristically messy, and he was out of breath, shirtless, and, judging by the way he twisted his body behind the door, probably naked.

"Oh, Lanei. Hey."

"Hi." I folded my arms and raised an eyebrow.

"Do you... need something?"

"I'm going to go out on a limb and guess Sydney's not in right now."

Kaden shook his head. Beads of sweat dripped from his hair. "He, uh, had to meet with Reno about something."

I leaned against the doorframe. "So when I find him, how long do you want me to keep him away?"

Kaden glanced over his shoulder then back at me. "Can you handle him for another hour?"

I gave him a mischievous grin. "If you can handle another hour, so can I."

"Thanks. Oh, and can you not tell Sydney I had someone back here? I'm not certain his parents ever explained the birds and the bees to him, and I really don't want to have to do it."

I snorted. "My lips are sealed."

He nodded his thanks, closed the door, and got back to business.

I waited around the corner from Reno's office for a few minutes before Sydney finished up and walked out. He gave me a confused look.

"How'd you know where I was?"

"Kaden told me."

"Ah," Sydney said. "Was he still having sex with Vigo?"

I blinked. "Wait, that was Vigo in there with him?"

Sydney slapped his palm to his mouth. "Oh, shit, no, you didn't hear that." He cursed under his breath. "Kaden didn't want people to know about them 'cause he figured it'd be a conflict of interest. Different squads and all that."

I raised an eyebrow. "Who cares what squad they're on?"

Sydney shrugged. "I dunno. Maybe all Araspians are as competitive as him."

"Eh, more power to him," I said. "At least one of us is getting laid."

Sydney coughed. Birds and the bees...

"Nice of him to tell you, at least."

"Well, after the third time I walked in on them making out, he was fresh outta good excuses. To be fair, the first two excuses weren't any good either." He sighed. "Can you not tell him I know they're doing the ol' bedroom rodeo? I asked for a sign when I should stay out and he got all weird and bashful, acting like he didn't know what I was talking about. Don't want to embarrass him."

I pantomimed turning a key on my lips. "Come on. Got something to show you."

I led Sydney back to my room and locked the door, reasonably confident he wouldn't get any ideas. I took a deep breath. I wasn't used to honesty or openness in my life, but that's why I was here. I had to be better than I was raised.

"I told you I was here because I couldn't accept the path I was raised for. And that's true. But this is the real reason I'm here." I lifted a large pastoral painting off the wall and flipped it around, revealing a map of Esperan and Maldova covered in push pins with numbers painted on their handles.

Sydney stared at it. "You... want to be a cartographer?"

I rolled my eyes. "Yes, that's what this whole thing is about. I left home and joined a martial academy to fulfill my secret dream of making maps. Come on, get your head in the game."

"I'm just saying, some context would be great right about now. What is all this?"

"Violence and actions against non-humans. Anything that might be related to the Children of Omek." I pointed at the red pins. "Non-human murders." The green pins. "Elves or throldkin driven from their homes." The blue pins, far fewer, but numbered sequentially. "Theft of magical artifacts."

Sydney got close to the map to examine it. "Are these numbers..."

"How many have been killed or driven out. Yeah."

"Wow." He ran a hand over the pins for San Domingo. The number twelve was painted on the red pin, forty-six on the green. "I didn't realize it was this bad."

"Nobody does. Some of the cities in Maldova are triple digits, but the papers aren't reporting it. Just getting that information was nearly impossible for me, and my father runs the damn place." I pulled another painting off the wall and removed the back from the frame, producing a stack of papers. "I had to hide all this after Jeyla's death." I gestured to the paintings around the room. "They're all full. It's my research, everything I brought with me."

Sydney took the stack from my hand and flipped through it. "This is terrible."

I nodded. "It is. But I didn't come here because of the violence. Kane's not my favorite person, but she's doing good work here. Same with Darian and Lord Aguilar. Even that asshole Reno. But it's not the violence that worries me. It's this." I tapped one of the blue pins.

"The thefts?"

"These aren't normal thefts. They're stealing magical artifacts. Mostly sindari, but some elven and throldkin as well."

"Okay..." Sydney narrowed his eyes. "That don't sound worse than, you know, murder."

"Maybe not yet, but it's what drew me into this whole mess a year ago." I took a seat at the desk. "I overheard two of my father's advisors talking about reverse-engineering some sindari artifacts they'd acquired."

"Yeah, you're gonna need to back that up. Reverse-engineering?"

"The Children's whole deal is that the magical races have been using their magic in nefarious ways to prevent humans from reaching our full potential. It's bullshit, but it makes for a great scapegoat when the average citizen wonders why they can't get ahead, and it keeps them from thinking too hard about the real problem. Reverse-engineering means taking apart magical objects and figuring out how they work from a scientific perspective."

"Gotcha," Sydney said. "And that's worse than the actual artifact because...?"

"Because instead of having one object, they're looking for ways to duplicate them or make them bigger. And if it's not already a weapon, well, it will be."

"Oh." Sydney looked down at the sheet in front of him. "That could be bad."

"Yeah, no shit. I confronted my father, but he claimed he didn't know anything about it. Which is total bullshit. What I don't know is whether he gave the order or if he's turning a blind eye because he needs their support. What I do know is this." I pointed to the blue pin with a "1" on it. "The first artifact was stolen from right here at Petrichor. The next four were all taken from nearby. And the violence around here started at the same time." I turned a few pages on the stack of papers in Sydney's hands until he was looking at an old drawing of a staff. "That's a sindari staff that belonged to Kasia Windamier. She kept it here under lock and key until it was stolen. Want to guess who it used to belong to?"

Sydney's eyes widened. "You're shitting me."

I nodded. "Omek. You know Kasia fought in the war that dethroned him, right? Somehow it wound up in her possession. And I don't think someone broke in here to steal it. The next two artifacts were also stolen right out from Petrichor." I leaned in and lowered my voice. This was the part where he was going to tell me I was crazy. "I think one of the instructors is a member of the Children. And I intend to find out who."

Sydney opened his mouth then shut it. Opened it again, didn't say anything. He sighed. "Um... Yeah, about that..."

I raised an eyebrow. "What's that mean?"

He pulled up a chair to sit beside me at the desk. "Okay, so, I've got something to tell you, but... Can you promise not to be mad?"

"When you lead with that?" I didn't like where this was going. "No."

"Well, can you at least promise not to hit me?"

I frowned. He wasn't off to a good start. But, on the other hand, Sydney was supposed to be my ally, so the least I could do was not kick his ass. "Deal."

He looked relieved. "Alright. Uh... Where to start. I haven't been entirely, one hundred percent up front with you."

"Which part was a lie?" I asked. "The stuff about your parents?"

"No, that's all true. It's more... Well, you ain't the only one who's been keeping secrets." He bit his lip. "How surprised would you be if I said I didn't actually get into the school on my own merit?"

"Like, zero?" I laughed. "I mean, no offense, I like you, but you're not really the elite fighting force type this place seems to be looking for."

"Right. Yeah, I guess that's fair. I got in because my parents used to run with Darian Rankin back in the day. He's family. And Darian needed someone on the inside he could trust."

Someone he could... "Explain."

"Lord Aguilar and Headmaster Kane know there's someone dirty at the school. They tasked Darian with finding a trustworthy student to be their plant and find out who it is." He spread his arms. "Guess who lucked into that wonderful job?"

I stared at him. I know he expected me to be mad, but...

"That actually explains a lot." I rested my chin on my hand. "Why didn't you tell me sooner?"

"I wanted to! But I thought I should run it by Reno first."

I cocked an eyebrow. "And Reno was okay with that?"

"Oh, no, he shot it down right away. Still don't trust you. So I guess I'm, like, going rogue here."

"Thanks." That couldn't have been an easy choice. He could get in deep shit for bringing public enemy number one into the conversation. "So who all knows?"

"Why I'm here? Just Darian, Kane, and Reno. Darian was very clear not to trust anyone else." Sydney chewed on his lip. "So I guess I already broke that rule, because, well, you."

"What about Ayana?" I asked. "If Reno's involved, why didn't they just recruit her?"

"Would've been a smarter choice, huh?" Sydney shrugged. "Reno didn't want her involved. He's already worried about her enough as it is. He agreed to work here so he could investigate from that end, but he wants her as far from all this as possible."

"Fat chance of that," I muttered. "She's in the thick of it whether he wants it or not." This was good. If Sydney was already investigating the same thing, we just doubled our resources. "Alright, so once Kaden and Vigo are done riding the bone train, how about you go back and get your research so we can start filling in the blanks."

Sydney gave me a blank look. "My what?"

"Your research," I repeated. "You do have research, right?"

"I mean, I didn't know about any of this until I got here. Didn't give me time to prep."

"But you've compiled files or notes since you've been here, right?"

Sydney rubbed the back of his neck. "I mean, I'm keeping my eyes open, but I haven't turned any paintings into file storage. Right now it's all just..." He tapped the side of his head. The look I gave him must've been awfully judgmental. "Hey, they just threw me in here and said 'go investigate.' They didn't exactly explain how that's done."

I shook my head. This boy was going to be the death of me. "Then we'll start now." I grabbed a pen and paper. "Who are your suspects?"

"Russo. I've caught her and Warren talking a few times and it's always very hush hush. She's up to something. We all know where Warren and his squad stand on non-humans, and she's their advisor. It wouldn't take much for her to convince them to join the Children."

"Alright. Who else've you got?"

He tilted his head. "Else?"

"Yeah. Who else is on your list?"

"I mean... I don't have a *list*, per se..."

I sighed. "So you have one suspect?"

"As of this moment in time... Yes."

"Great. Well, we're going to go off the assumption that it might possibly be someone else, so let's look at the others, too." I continued making notes. "I already cleared Reno. I may want to punch him in the dick, but his sister's half sindari and half elf, and he obviously loves her. Plus you can vouch for him, so he's in the clear. I think we can both agree Kasia isn't a suspect."

"Agreed."

"That leaves Lucia, Caesar, and Miklotov," I said. "Lucia's at the top of my list. She's Maldovan and my father seemed okay with her as a role model for me. That's an automatic mark against her. And I'm almost positive she knows who I am."

"But she was Jeyla's mentor. She seemed pretty upset when she saw her."

That was true. "She's also a master of deception. Putting on a false face is second nature to her. For all we know, she killed Jeyla because she couldn't stand being that close to a half-elf all the time. Which means Nakato could be in serious danger."

Sydney considered that. "If anyone could've killed Jeyla and disappeared before you got there, it'd be her."

"Right." Now he was thinking. "Thoughts on Caesar?"

"He and Lucia don't get along. I dunno; I can't get a read on him. He's latched onto Robia, though."

I nodded. "Nakato says he's done the same with Vanessa and Milich in the other class. Very focused on creating the perfect archer. But I can't rule him out."

"And Instructor Lightfellow?" Sydney asked. "Kaden adores him. Apparently his family's a big deal in Araspia."

"I've got individual lessons with him. He's squeaky clean." And he was. He was the definition of courtliness, courtesy, and nobility. Everything a guy like Yasir strove to be. But... "I don't like it. Nobody's that inherently *good*."

"That's an awfully cynical view."

"It's a realistic view. If we want to get to the bottom of this, we've got to accept that the world's full of too much shit to not get yourself dirty."

I looked down at the list in my hand. Four suspects. Now we just had to narrow it down to one.

Chapter 44

SYDNEY

The arena'd been reconfigured since the last time we were here. It still resembled a ruined city, but the center had been cleared to make way for a metal ring twenty feet across. We stood in the ring face-to-face with Nakato's squad. Well, face-to-mask. Their squad showed up in full battle armor, and it was just as freaky as the first time I'd seen it. It was also the first time I'd seen Zeke's mask. The big guy was almost as tall as Tenkou and just as wide, so when someone that size wears a mask that looks like an angry demon, you question why you bothered getting out of bed.

"What kinda demon is that?" I whispered to Ayana.

"Not the friendly kind. If you ever see one, um... run."

Good. That was my default plan.

Headmaster Kane stood between our groups with Instructors Hortez and Windamier beside her. "To win today's match, you must control this ring for a total of five minutes. When members of only one team are on the point, it is considered to be under that team's control. Instructor Hortez will be the official timekeeper for this event." Caesar displayed a pair of stopwatches. Kane pointed to a glass disk suspended above the ring. "When Lanei's squad controls the point, Instructor Windamier will turn the disk blue. When Nakato's squad is in control, it will be red." Kasia waved a hand to change the color of the glass. "Now, I must repeat, this is an exercise. The goal is not to physically incapacitate your opponents. Sparring weapons only. If you receive a blow that would otherwise maim or kill you, or if you yield to an opponent, a whistle will blow. You will return to your base where you must remain for thirty seconds, at which point you will be released back into play. If you willfully cause anyone harm, you will answer to me." She turned her attention to Ayana. "Instructor Windamier says you have explained the concept of an exercise to your demons?"

Ayana nodded. "Vadazach and Malbohr understand. Well, they don't *understand*. They think the whole thing's silly. But they've agreed to behave." She rocked on her feet. "I, um, tried explaining it to Mr. Drooly, but I'm not sure he got it."

I wasn't eager to meet that demon.

"Then do not summon him," Kane said. "Return to your bases. You have two minutes to confer."

"This doesn't seem fair," Lanei muttered as we made our way to our base. "Without Jeyla, we're already a person up on them. Two if you count Ayana's demon."

Kaden's jaw dropped. "Are you suggesting we let them win?"

"I'm not suggesting anything. It just doesn't seem right."

"They agreed to go through with it," Reno said. "You better believe they won't just roll over. Lucia's gonna make sure they use that to their advantage."

"Let's just go straight down the middle to the point," Kaden suggested. "We've got the numbers. Just take it by force."

Lanei shook her head. "They'll expect that. It's the obvious play with the numbers advantage."

"Even if they expect it, what are they going to do about it?"

"I don't know, but I'll bet you they do. Sydney, what do you think?"

I pictured the layout in my head. "Three groups of two. One straight on and one circling in from each side. Even if they split into two groups, we'll be evenly matched if we run into them, and the third group will be able to nab the point."

Lanei nodded once. "I like it. Reno?"

Reno grunted. "It's sound. Ayana, bring out Malbohr. You'll need him if you run into Zeke. He's a beast in close-quarters. Unless your name's Tenkou, don't let him get his hands on you."

Ayana opened a portal and Malbohr schlooped out. Ayana smiled at him. "Now, Malbohr, remember what we talked about."

"Malbohr know." The poor demon looked dejected. "Malbohr no eat people. Malbohr no crush people. Malbohr no tear off tiny limbs." He sighed. "Malbohr no get do things Malbohr good at."

Ayana patted him on his slimy head. "And if someone blows a whistle at you, you have to return here."

"Magic whistle?"

"No, just a regular whistle."

"Why it make Malbohr return?"

"It doesn't *make* you return, but the rules say you need to."

Malbohr stared at her. He shook his head. "Demon world much simpler place..."

"Alright," Lanei said. "Ayana and Malbohr, go left. Sydney and Tenkou, go right. Kaden, you and I are going down the middle."

"Don't go rushing in there," Reno advised. "They're going to expect you to underestimate them. Don't."

A horn blew and the gates opened.

"You heard the man," Lanei said. "Don't do anything stupid."

Tenkou and I took off. We ran until we were about a third of the way down the field then stopped behind a wall. From there we crept from one cover to the next, peering out for any sign of opponents. A flash of blue light caught my eye. Lanei and Kaden must've gotten to the center already. No surprise. They both treated obstacles as optional.

"Come on."

Tenkou's head snapped up in the air and he raised a hand. "Wait." He set his polearm down, got on his knees, and laid the side of his head on the ground.

"What?"

Tenkou's eyes widened. He grabbed the polearm and jumped to his feet. "They're coming."

I drew my sword and waited as Tenkou counted down from three, following his lead as he kicked down the door we hid behind. I caught a flash of Chavo's wolf mask as he spun out from behind the door before it could crash down on him. I took a swing, but he slid out of the way. I spotted Vanessa on a rooftop, notching an arrow.

"Roof!"

Tenkou saw her as she loosed the arrow. Fortunately, the padded practice arrows weren't as swift as the real ones. Tenkou snatched it out of the air and threw it to the ground. He moved behind another wall to block Vanessa. I prepared to face off with Chavo, but he

feinted to one side and darted past me back toward Tenkou.

I dashed after in time to see Zeke step out from the wall Tenkou used as cover. Tenkou swung the polearm, but Zeke caught it in one hand and brought his fist down hard, snapping the head right off. Tenkou tossed the shaft aside.

"Behind you!" I shouted as Chavo closed in on him. Tenkou spun in time to catch Chavo in the gut with a backhand. The blow sent Chavo staggering back. I charged, but as soon as I emerged from behind the wall an arrow flew past my head. I ducked back behind. They were cutting me off from Tenkou. "Get to the circle!"

Tenkou jammed his shoulder into Zeke, driving him back a few steps. He must have sensed Chavo moving in on him again, because he swung his tail in an arc that took Chavo off his feet. Tenkou and Zeke exchanged blows. It was like watching two giants demolishing mountains. They were both going to feel it later.

I stuck my head out from cover to check the rooftops. Vanessa still had me pinned down. In the second I'd taken my eyes off the fight, a whistle blew. I looked back to Tenkou. Nakato stood behind him, both daggers drawn. Tenkou growled and shook his head, but he trudged off back to the base.

Well, shit. My turn now...

I raised my sword and prepared for them to come at me.

"Chavo, finish him!" Nakato called over her shoulder as she and Zeke vanished around a corner. I checked the roof. Vanessa was gone, too. Just me and the wolf.

And yeah, I was insulted they committed their entire team to taking out Tenkou then treated me like an afterthought. So either they greatly underestimated me or they made the smart call to not waste time. Time to find out which.

I wish I could say an evenly fought battle went back and forth as the judges wrung their hands in nervous anticipation, but Chavo was a much better swordsman than me. Granted, not a high bar to clear. Within fifteen seconds he'd disarmed me and sent my sword flying far out of reach.

Chavo pointed his sword at me and grinned, the fangs on his wolf mask turning it into mockery. "You can yield, you know."

The blue light up above went out. Somewhere in the distance a whistle blew. Chavo turned his head long enough for me to grab the shaft of the broken polearm.

Chavo laughed. "Or you could—"

I swung the staff. Chavo brought up his sword to block. He looked taken aback that I'd dare not let him finish mocking me.

I was done being mocked.

I took another swing, and another. Chavo backed up and I advanced again. Two more whistles blew back-to-back and the light turned red.

Something about the staff in my hand brought back memories of growing up on the ranch, seeing how fast I could spin a pitchfork instead of pitching hay like I was supposed to. Beating up scarecrows whose only trespass was being an inanimate object I could hit without getting in trouble. Now Chavo was my scarecrow.

I feinted like I was going to strike him in the head with one end of the staff. As he raised his sword to block, I swung the other direction, sweeping him off his feet. I slammed the butt of the staff into the protective plate on his chest.

A whistle blew.

Holy shit. I got one!

I reached a hand down to Chavo and helped him up. "Nice shot," he said. "Did not expect that from you."

Before my brain registered the backhandedness of the compliment, he was already jogging back to his base. I twirled the staff for effect, which is to say because it was fun, and made my way to the ring.

I tallied the whistles in my head. Tenkou was first. Three more before the light changed. That meant Kaden and Lanei, plus one more. Hopefully one of theirs. And then Chavo. Because I took out Chavo.

Hell yeah, I did.

Given how quickly they'd all abandoned me, their team probably figured the whistle was Chavo taking me down. So that gave me an advantage for about... a minute and a half, assuming he booked it both to and from the base. I could use that.

They'd be expecting Chavo to come from this side. That meant waltzing on in probably wouldn't be the best idea. But if they had two or three in the center, trickling in by myself would only get me eliminated. I needed to group up. That meant finding Ayana and Malbohr.

I turned down an alley and ran right into a wall of fog. It wasn't as thick as I'd seen Nakato pull off in class, but it did the trick. I was still a little ways from the center, so she was probably covering a much wider area than she was used to. The fog was thicker along the ground, so I crouched down as I moved to stay concealed.

I turned a corner and spotted Malbohr poking up out of the fog. The fog clung to him somehow, which shouldn't have been possible by any laws of science, but hey, demons. I flashed a ball of light and his head spun my way. Ayana peeked out from behind him and waved me over.

"It's just Nakato and Zeke in there," she whispered. "But I don't know where. Because fog."

"Yeah. Fog."

"Yeah." She bit her bottom lip and smiled. I smiled back. Time ticked past. "So... Plan?"

I blinked. "Right, plan. Maybe send Malbohr in to lure them out, and then—"

A battle cry rose from the mist behind us as Kaden charged past us into the center of the arena.

Ayana stared after him. "I thought his thing was stealth?"

I sighed. "In theory."

We ran after Kaden, losing him in the fog. Just before he reached the edge of the circle, he stopped yelling, launched himself off a platform, and climbed up the side of a building. Up ahead, Zeke stood tall above the fog, ready to grab Kaden when he ran into the circle. He was about to be in for a surprise.

I pointed to Zeke. "Malbohr, get him."

"Malbohr no take order from—"

"Malbohr, get him," Ayana echoed.

The slime demon hunkered low, condensed his mass into a disgusting blob, and slunk out of sight. He appeared moments later, leaping out of the fog onto Zeke.

"What the fuck? Get it off me! Get it off me!" The two rolled out of sight, lost in the fog. "It's sticky! Why the fuck is it sticky!"

A few wet thuds. Some more screams. Then a whistle.

"Oh, fuck this. *Fuck* this!" Zeke let out an impressive string of curses as he vacated the field.

Malbohr stood up to his full height. "That Malbohr whistle?"

Before he could get an answer, a dagger exploded from his chest, followed by Nakato's fist. A whistle blew. Malbohr looked down at the dagger protruding from where a heart should be.

"That Malbohr whistle?"

Nakato tugged at her arm, but it was stuck in the demon.

"Malbohr go now."

Malbohr headed back to the base, dragging Nakato with him. As she struggled to free her arm, the fog dissipated. With a gross *schluck*, her arm popped out of Malbohr's chest. Her dagger didn't pop out with it. She switched her remaining dagger to her right hand as she faced off with me and Ayana. Even behind the mask, she didn't seem the least bit worried. Maybe she didn't have to be. In a fair fight, she probably could've taken both of us without breaking much of a sweat. But she'd forgotten about the distraction that was Kaden. Before she had a chance to strike, he leapt out of the sky and landed behind her, swiping his blade across her back. The whistle blew and the light above turned blue.

Three things happened at the same time. An arrow flew through the air and struck Ayana in the chest. An arrow flew through the air and struck Kaden in the chest. And an arrow flew through the air and struck me in the chest. Okay, so it was the same thing happening three times at the same time. I don't know how Vanessa managed to fire that many padded arrows at once. Either she was an exceptional marksman or she had magic in her after all.

The light didn't change, though, as Lanei ran past us, dodging the fourth arrow. Kaden dragged me out at a run, but whatever Lanei did resulted in a loud crash and a fourth whistle.

"Hurry up," Kaden said, doing his usual thing of not even breathing hard at a full run. "If she and Tenkou can't hold it, we'll have to get back fast."

"Where's Tenkou?"

"Scouting."

Why was the biggest member of our team acting as the scouting party?

I got my answer when we reached the base. Tenkou sat outside the gate, symbols painted on the ground around him. Reno waved us inside and clicked a stopwatch as soon as we crossed the threshold.

"Pretty sweet, huh?" Kaden asked.

Ayana jumped on my back and leaned over to get a better look. She kicked her legs up in the air as her body pressed against me. Very tightly against me. I tried not to think about the fact that her extremely scary brother was five feet away.

"That's so cool," she squealed. "Look how much cleaner his runes are. Oooh, he's getting better at this." Ayana hopped off my back and threw punches at the air. "Is Malbohr already back out there?"

Reno sighed and pointed a finger ahead to where Malbohr slowly oozed his way to the base.

Ayana groaned. "I knew I should've brought Vadazach instead. He's much better with directions. Malbohr's usually more of a—"

"Go!" Reno flung the gate open and Kaden sprinted out. We ran after him. As we passed Malbohr, Ayana shouted for him to hurry up, and the big slime demon begrudgingly obeyed. As the center ring came into sight, a horn blew and the blue light flashed.

We had won.

Chapter 45

/LANEI

"Naw, man, scouting ain't fair when you can walk through walls!" Zeke laughed. "Lanei hit us before we knew she was there!"

Tenkou shrugged. "You eliminated me first because you believed I was only muscle. I was showing my... versatility."

"Yeah, well, you proved your point." Nakato finished filling glasses with the whiskey we won in our late night hunt. "But you gotta admit, we almost had you."

"We don't *have* to admit it." I winked at her. "But you definitely gave us a run for our money."

It was nice to push the petty bullshit aside and go out and celebrate, not as competing squads, but as fellow students. We all had reason to be proud. No reason to treat either team as the loser tonight.

Kaden had the idea to hit up Dragonfly. No surprise. Acting as a social butterfly may have been the only thing he took more seriously than competition. Knowing he was seeing someone from another team, he probably wanted to normalize the idea of socializing with the other squads. I doubted anyone else thought the idea needed normalizing, but hey. Araspians.

Nakato raised her glass high. "To a well fought match!" We echoed her and tossed one back, and holy shit that was good. Sharing this bottle may have made me and Nakato the most generous people in Nasan. Lucia had exquisite taste.

"You've got a good group," I told Nakato as we took a seat.

"I know. Got lucky with that." She nodded at Zeke, chatting with Tenkou and Kaden at the next table. "Known Zeke a while. Hell of a fighter, hell of a heart." She elbowed Vanessa next to her, almost knocking her off Chavo's lap. "Although the lovers can be trying sometimes."

Vanessa grinned. "Jealous?"

"Not even a little."

Chavo held a hand to his chest. "You wound me. I thought you wanted me to leave Vanessa and run away with you?"

"You wouldn't dare." Vanessa wrapped her arms around him.

"I wouldn't?" Chavo teased. "And why not?"

"Because if you did, I'd cut your balls off." To emphasize the point, she showed him the dagger she'd pulled off his belt. She traced it along his leg. "Wouldn't you rather I find another use for them?"

Chavo sighed. "Sorry, Nakato. She makes an excellent argument."

"I always do." Vanessa kissed his cheek and dragged him off to the dance floor.

"They're disgusting," I said.

"They are," Nakato agreed. "But they're here for the right reasons. And they grew up in San Domingo, so they come in handy."

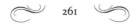

A flash of red fabric outside caught my eye as two people passed by the window over Nakato's shoulder. I glanced at Sydney, but he was too wrapped up in conversation with Ayana to notice.

"Excuse me a minute."

I hurried to Sydney's table. "Hey, come with me."

He looked from me to Ayana. "Um, can it wait?"

"No. Now."

I grabbed his arm and dragged him away before he could protest. I wanted to know what the twins were doing out in the city by themselves in the middle of the night.

Outside the club, Sydney jerked his arm away. "What's the big deal?"

I pointed to our targets up ahead. "Look."

Sydney raised his eyebrows as Milia and Milich turned the corner. "Little late for them to be out here."

"My thoughts exactly."

We hurried after them. The streets weren't as crowded at night, so we'd have to use the darkness for cover. I followed slowly, Sydney at my back. Milich carried a small package wrapped in brown paper under one arm. The twins turned down a few more streets but never once looked behind them. Either they weren't expecting to be followed or they were too arrogant to believe anyone would dare try.

They stopped in front of a nondescript storefront. Milia checked a piece of paper and nodded to her brother. They knocked four times, paused, then knocked twice more. The door opened.

Lucia Verdicci ushered them inside.

"Holy shit..." I muttered.

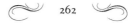

"What's she doing with them?" Sydney whispered. "She ain't their advisor."

"No, but they do have one thing in common."

Took a second for Sydney to get it. "Maldova."

We crept up to the building. Two windows faced front, both with curtains drawn. Fortunately, a sliver of a part allowed a small glimpse inside.

It was some sort of shop with dusty white sheets covering the counters. No sign the place had been open for years. But Lucia was using it for something.

Candlelight filtered in from a back room, illuminating their shadows on the walls. Their muffled voices were barely discernible. Not sure what they were saying, but it sounded like Lucia was chewing into them.

"Go around back," I said. "See if there's a window into the back room."

Sydney nodded and made his way behind the building.

If the mole at Petrichor was trying to recruit students into the Children, Milia and Milich were the perfect candidates. They didn't bother hiding their racism. And, loathe as I was to admit it, they were good. They had to be; they'd been raised for this. Their father, Aldric Levesque, was one of my father's best knights. I'd seen him often enough around the castle to know he was a world class asshole who'd be proud of the way his children turned out. The fact that the twins were secretly meeting with Lucia didn't bode well for any of them.

Sydney came back around front. "Nothing."

"Damn. Alright, stay close. We'll—"

Footsteps.

I spun back to the window. No more shadows in the candlelight. A figure passed the window.

"Hide!" I ordered.

We ducked around the side of the building and crouched behind a trash bin. It was barely big enough to hide one person, let alone two. We'd be counting on the cover of darkness here.

The door opened.

"Think about what I said," Lucia said.

"We will," Milia answered.

The door closed and the twins walked past the alley. Milich no longer carried the package.

I counted to ten then peered around the corner. "Come on."

Sydney followed me out of the alley. The twins leaned close to one another, talking quietly. I didn't want to risk getting close enough to listen in. We followed them in silence for a few blocks until it was clear they were returning to Petrichor.

"Let's go back to the club," Sydney suggested. "We're not gonna learn anything else here. Unless you want to beat it out of them." He rubbed at his neck. "To be clear, I don't wanna resort to that."

I did, but he was right. That wasn't the smart play right now. "Yeah. Let's go."

We turned to head back to Dragonfly. I cast one more look over my shoulder. At the same time Milia looked over hers.

Anger crawled over her face. She snapped something to Milich. He turned to look.

"Shit..."

Sydney stopped and looked back. Milich said something to his sister. She stared venom into my eyes before they took off.

Chapter 46

LANEI

Sydney was a puddle of exhausted Laredan on the floor of the training room. After Chavo told me how Sydney kicked his ass with the polearm shaft, I had to see it for myself. Turns out, he wasn't half bad. Still unrefined as shit, but his instincts were good and he handled it decently well. Might be able to make a fighter out of him yet.

The bo staff was the first weapon I trained with when Cassius Rilarde agreed to teach me to fight, instead of just blindly following my father's orders to break me and send me back to court as his other knights had done. God forbid a member of the royal family sully their hands with a sword. No, no. "*We kill with words, not weapons.*"

I never could get on board with that.

I was fortunate Sir Cassius always liked my mother more than my father or stepmother. He'd been assigned to Mom's retinue when I was young, so he saw a lot more of me than of my father. It probably helped that I took after Mom. Even if Cassius only helped me out of guilt, I was okay with it. He was a great teacher.

Even those early stave lessons were coming back as I worked with Sydney. I wasn't a proper trainer, but I could at least get him in a good place to start with Miklotov.

After three hours of beating the crap out of him, I peeled Sydney off the ground. We'd earned an unhealthy dinner.

But when we turned to the door, I knew dinner wasn't in the cards. Milia, Milich, and Warren stood inside the room. Warren's face was ugly as ever, but the twins' usual sour expressions had taken a turn for the worse. Katya and Selena stood guard in the doorway.

Milia wore a chain gauntlet on her right hand. She flexed her fingers and closed them into a fist. "I'm only going to ask once. Why were you following us last night?" Her voice was steady but lacked any sense of calm. Her restraint hung by a thread.

"Sydney, were we following them last night?"

"I don't think so," he said, still catching his breath. "We followed a dog for a while. Was that her?"

"No, different bitch." I snapped my fingers. "Oh, you know what, she's right, we did see her. Remember that girl in the skanky outfit we thought was a prostitute?"

"Thought that cleavage looked familiar."

"I'm sorry, Milia. I hope you weren't thinking we were interested. Unless..." I turned to Sydney. "You weren't interested, were you?"

"God no."

"You sure? If you're short, I could front you some—"

Milia's fist rudely interrupted me. I ducked under it, spun to grab her... and realized they'd prepared for this. Warren rushed in and grabbed my arms, twisting them behind my back. Milich intercepted Sydney with an arm drag and took him to the ground, hard. After three hours of intense training, Sydney wasn't in a place to put up much of a fight. They must've been waiting for us to tire ourselves out.

"Who's the bitch now?" Milia punched me in the gut. "Down, girl."

I had tightened my abs, seeing her telegraph the punch, but then Warren lifted me in the air and planted me face-first into the mat. It beat concrete, but you can't fight gravity. I didn't even get a chance to catch my breath before Warren rolled me over and Milia was on top of me. She yanked me up by my hair and punched me in the face with her gauntleted hand. The back of my head slammed into the ground.

"Why were you following us?"

I smirked through the stars swirling in my vision. "I thought you were only going to ask once?"

She punched me again. I tasted blood as my lip split open.

"I can do this all day. Why were you following us?"

"Just had to know where you bought those boots."

"You couldn't afford them."

"You'd be surprised."

I struggled to get free, but she punched me again. Maybe Sydney wasn't the only one tired from that workout.

"Warren, if you will."

Milich hauled Sydney to his feet. Sydney tried to break away, but Warren wrapped a meaty palm around his throat. Milich peeled the mat back. Warren lifted Sydney into the air like he was a child and slammed him on the exposed concrete. Sydney coughed and wheezed.

"Leave him a—"

Milia punched me again.

"Why were you following us?"

I spat blood in her face. "Fuck you."

If she wasn't pissed before, that did it. A sadistic smile crept over her face as she grabbed my eyebrow piercing and twisted.

A roar erupted from the doorway. Milia stopped her assault long enough for me to process Tenkou charging through Selena. Warren released Sydney and ran at him. The two collided like a pair of bulls locking horns. They struggled to overpower each other until Katya clubbed her fists into Tenkou's back. The big throldkin let out a pained cry and Warren drove him back, slamming him into the wall. Katya charged, crushing her bulk into my friend. Tenkou snapped his massive jaws, and Katya wrapped her thick arms around his maw to keep it shut.

Once they had Tenkou under control, Milia turned back to me. "Where were we?"

She raised her fist to strike me again.

"Stop right there!"

Yeah, sure. I wasn't going anywhere.

Yasir and Robia rushed into the room. Yasir pointed his sword at Warren and Katya while Robia trained an arrow on Milich. As soon as they backed off, I took advantage of the confusion, wrapped my fingers in Milia's hair, and yanked sideways. I rolled with it so I straddled her, grabbed her by the straps of that thing she called a shirt, and lifted her face directly to mine.

"If you dare accost me like that again, I will make sure you, your brother, and anyone else you drag in with you dies on the point of my sword. Tell me you understand."

Milia's eyes widened. She understood. But it had nothing to do with my threat.

"I do know you..."

"Shut up."

Milia laughed. "Oh, this is *priceless*. I knew you looked familiar, but I never expected—"

"Shut up!"

I punched Milia in the face. Robia dragged me off before I could strike again, but I had to. I had to shut her up. I couldn't let her—

"No! No more hiding!" Milia shouted, crawling to her feet. She didn't attack me again. She didn't need to. "I'd forgotten our beloved Lady Greyton wasn't Lord Viktor's first wife. The brown skin, the prissy attitude... I should have figured it out sooner."

"Shut up!" I strained to get at her, but Robia didn't let go. Sydney pawed at the ground by Milia's feet, still too dazed to do any good.

"You don't order me around. Not here." Milia spat the words like venom. She kicked Sydney's hand away and stared daggers at me. "Oh, I remember you. The little brat princess who thought she was too good for the other kids."

"Princess?" Yasir's sword hand wavered. He looked to me. "What is she saying?"

Milia smiled. "I'm saying there is no Lanei Walker. You're in the presence of Her Royal Highness Princess Lana Greyton of Maldova."

"Do *not* call me that." I yanked my arms away, and this time Robia let go. She stared at me like I was some kind of freak show.

"Why not?" Milia asked. "It's your name."

Robia shook her head in disbelief. "You're the goddamn princess..."

"That's not who I am."

"Yes it is!" Milia shouted back. "You may have turned your back on Maldova, but you will always be one of us. You know who you are. You just haven't accepted it yet."

I clenched my fists and bit back tears. It couldn't come out. Not like this. "I'm not—"

"You're a Greyton..." Tenkou's body had gone frigid. He knew the implications of that name.

I could continue lying to the others, but not to my friends.

I nodded.

Yasir pushed past Robia and dropped to one knee before me. He placed his sword on the ground at my feet. "Princess Lana, I beg your forgiveness for—"

I shoved him aside and ran out of the room.

I was getting good at running.

Chapter 47

*LANEI

I didn't want to move. I didn't want to get out of bed. I didn't want to fucking *breathe*.

My chance to have a normal life was gone. My chance to be treated like a human being instead of a title. Just like that, it had been ripped away from me. All because of that wretched blonde bitch.

If I were still in my father's good graces, I could finally make him proud by ordering her execution. Watch her led up the gallows and hanged by her pretty little neck until the last breath drained out of her. All because she pissed me off.

But I wasn't my father's daughter. I wasn't going to have someone killed just because it suited my mood.

I wanted to kill her my damn self.

Okay, so my humanity was a work in progress. At least I was aware of it.

I desperately wanted to ignore the knock on my door, but I couldn't hide in here forever. So I weakly told them to come in.

The doorknob turned, but the door caught on the bolt.

"Um, it's locked," Sydney said.

Ugh. Fine, I'll get up.

I unlocked the door and returned to my bed. I was back to burying my head in my pillow when he entered.

"Hey... You okay?"

I only bothered looking up because the pillow made it hard to glare.

"Yeah, I didn't think so."

"Does everyone know?"

He nodded. "Word got around fast. Milia made sure of that."

"That's that, then."

"All you can do now is face it head on," Sydney said. "Hold your head up and—"

"No, I mean that's it." I rubbed my hand over my face. "I can't stay here. Not now."

"What are you talking about?" Sydney sat down on the edge of my bed. "Of course you can stay."

"No, I can't. Nobody's going to want me around now. Why would they?" I sat up. "Come with me."

"What?"

"Come with me! We'll catch the next train out of San Domingo, take it wherever it goes. I'll finish out your training, get you up to speed. We can wander the kingdom helping people, righting wrongs, all that altruistic bullshit you love. Just... not here."

"We can't just leave the school."

"Yes, we can. I've got money, enough to cover our expenses until we figure something out. There's nothing keeping us here."

"And what do we tell the others?"

"Nothing! We just leave. Now, before anyone can stop us."

"Um..." He rubbed the side of his face. "That might not work."

"Why not?"

"I, uh, told them to wait in the hall."

I narrowed my eyes. "I hate you so much sometimes."

"So... does that mean I should bring them in?"

"Are you going to let me sneak out the window?"

"No."

I sighed. "Fine. Let's get this over with. Let the hate fest begin."

Sydney squeezed my shoulder and went to the door. I considered trying my luck with the window anyway, but didn't think I could pry it open and jump out before he got to me. So I propped myself up in bed and rubbed at my eyes, hoping they weren't noticeably red.

Not sure what I expected them to do when they stepped in. Angry accusations or yelling or good old physical violence. I did not expect Ayana to rush in, leap onto my bed, wrap her arms around me, and squeeze. I froze.

"I'm not gonna stop until you hug me back," she said, her face buried in my shoulder.

I smiled in spite of myself and returned the hug. "Better?"

"Better," she agreed.

Kaden and Tenkou entered behind her. The big man shut the door and leaned against it.

"Please tell me you're not actually leaving." Kaden sat on my desk and rested his feet on the chair. "I mean, sure, I'd welcome the promotion, but if Sydney goes up to squad leader, we're royally screwed." He winked at me. "*Royally* screwed. Because you're a princess, apparently."

I let out a small laugh. "Yes, I got it."

"Good, 'cause I had like six more lined up if you didn't." He dropped his hands to the desk and leaned back. "I know I talk a lot about family and lineage and all that. It's just something we do. But it's not only about who your parents are. It's about your whole line. Just because your father's a piece of shit doesn't negate everyone who came before him." He smiled. "Names have power. The Greyton name used to mean something different. Take it back. Make it mean what you believe it should mean, not what the world says it means."

"Thanks." It was about all I could manage to say.

I looked to Tenkou, his arms crossed, studying me. His nostrils flared as he let out a long breath.

"I told you once that I do not judge you for your countrymen. But that is not the same as your family."

I nodded. I couldn't expect him to brush aside the vitriol my father had spouted about the throldkin. That would be asking too much.

"To stand in opposition of your own people takes courage," he said. "To stand in opposition of your family takes a strength of character most do not possess. When that family is royalty..." Tenkou shook his head. "I cannot begin to understand how difficult that must be. I think no less of you for being a Greyton. I admire you even more."

"Why?" My voice was strained. "What's admirable about that?"

He cocked his head to one side. "You left a life of privilege and luxury because you knew in your heart it was not worth the cost. You could have followed your father's lead and ruled a kingdom. Instead you did what was right."

"Sounds kinda stupid when you put it like that."

Tenkou smiled. "Most wise decisions look stupid to those who lack wisdom."

"You're our friend," Ayana said. "It doesn't matter what name you go by. We'll call you Miss Petunia Cheeverfish if you want."

"Don't. Ever."

Ayana smiled. "The point is we love you for who *you* are. That's all that matters."

I hated this mushy shit, but I must have needed it. My body sagged as the tension drained out of me. This must be what it was like to have friends. Real friends. "Thanks, guys. That means more than you know."

"It's what we do." Kaden wagged his eyebrows at me. "Look good and brighten people's days."

Sydney sat next to me on the bed. "Think we can convince you to stay?"

"Yeah, I guess I can stay." I lifted my chin. "I've got a thing or two I need to prove."

To myself and everyone else.

Chapter 48

SYDNEY

Kaden and I found Lanei and Tenkou in the main hall. It looked like we were among the last to arrive. "Any clue why we're here?" I asked.

Lanei rolled her eyes. "Probably a public service announcement that I either am or am not a threat to everyone's safety."

Tenkou nodded. "Yes, that seems like an important enough matter to summon the entire school."

"Wait, was that sarcasm?" Kaden clapped Tenkou on the back. "It was! I guess you can teach an old lizard new tricks."

"We are the same age."

"Okay, he's got sarcasm, still working on humor. But it's a start!"

Ayana walked in with Reno. He joined the other instructors on the dais as she bubbled her way through the crowd to us, waving and giggling hellos to people as she passed. She wore a long, flowy, pale green dress that had all the hallmarks of something she'd made herself. The seams were frayed, the stitching was uneven... and she looked absolutely beautiful in it.

I caught myself staring. I had to stop doing that.

We never talked about that night in the woods, so I still didn't know if I'd completely misread the situation when I tried to kiss her. I had tried to kiss her, hadn't I? So much of that night was a blur, and only partially due to lack of sleep and possible concussions. Had she wanted me to kiss her? Had she desperately not wanted me to kiss her and purposefully stuck her hand in that sap to find an excuse to get away from me?

These were important questions to ask myself and *never* discuss with anyone else.

"Hiya!" Ayana practically hopped into place beside us. She smiled at me. "Hi, Sydney."

I gulped and may have said "Hi, Ayana" or maybe my lips just moved and no sound came out. Not sure, but it was definitely one of those things.

"Did Reno give you the inside scoop?" Kaden asked.

Ayana rocked on her heels. "What? Noooooo, of course he didn't. I'm just another student here. He'd never tell his adorably persistent little sister privileged information." She twirled, her dress flaring out around her. She was unfairly cute. "On a completely and totally unrelated note, my dressmaking is getting better, don't you think?"

"Very pretty." Yep, my eloquence was on full display.

Lanei rolled her eyes. "God, don't tell me it's more formal shit."

"Aw, okay, I won't," Ayana said. "But it looks like they're about to start, so I'll let them do it."

Headmaster Kane stepped onto the dais. She didn't even need to call for attention. Everyone in attendance quieted by the time she took center stage.

"This weekend, we celebrate the new year. And this year, more than ever, is a reminder of why we do what we do. It has been one hundred years since the calendar was reset. One hundred years since the kingdom lines were redrawn. One hundred years since Omek was overthrown." She looked us over. In those few seconds, I felt sure she'd made eye contact with every single student. "Make no mistake. If Omek were still alive, this school would not exist. Many of you would not exist. Omek's actions are a testament to why we must continue to fight against such oppression. You are all fortunate we have an instructor who was not only alive at the time of the revolution, but also played a key role in Omek's downfall."

Kasia nodded her thanks. "The headmaster overstates my involvement. I was merely a soldier. Most elves fled across the sea to Ilyn Themar before the war began in earnest." She scowled, a dangerous look on her. "They were cowards. They abandoned the Creed, running to preserve their lives instead of seeking immortality through their deeds. Thankfully, some of us still follow the old way."

I elbowed Kaden. "The Creed?"

"The Creed of Honor," he whispered back. "Old elven religion. If they achieved greatness, they could be canonized as gods." He raised an eyebrow. "You're part elf. How do you not know this?"

"My dad was an orphan. Guess nobody ever explained it to him."

"It's okay," Ayana said, voice quiet. "I never knew that part of my family either."

Kasia cleared her throat. "Omek was not always the monster we know him as today. He was arguably the most powerful sindari to ever live, and for hundreds of years he used that power for unquestionable good. People worshiped him as a god, and it was hard to say they were wrong.

"He was never the same after his twin brother, Kol, rebelled against him and challenged his claim to the throne of Rainess. After defeating his army, Omek pursued Kol north to the island of Salah, where he put an end to his brother.

"Upon returning home, Omek abdicated the throne and moved to a small estate in the mountains of Rainess. He remained there until well into the War of Unification, when his followers pleaded with him to put an end to the fighting. He obliged, and with minimal bloodshed, united all of Nasan under his rule. For the next three hundred years, Omek's rule was peaceful.

"Then reports came in of undead along Nasan's northern shore. Communication ceased with settlements on Salah as rumors spread of a necromancer building an island fortress and chasing out the living. After forces sent to the island vanished, Omek went himself to investigate. There he learned his brother had returned to life and turned Salah into his own desolate wasteland for the undead. He left his brother alive and forbade anyone else from venturing to the island.

"Instead, Omek assembled a task force to seize magical artifacts from throughout Nasan, believing such an object had allowed Kol to cheat death. His methods were harsh. Objectors were killed, with their bodies displayed as a warning to others. He sent forces into old sindari and throldkin ruins that had been abandoned since before the humans and elves made their way to Nasan, tearing them apart to find any traces of magical objects still buried within.

"Omek began viewing himself as a god. He bleached his skin until he looked more human than sindari. He removed all elves and sindari from his counsel, as well as the throldkin warriors who had been his royal guard for years.

"In five BCE, everything changed. Omek struck fast. He claimed the world would never be safe so long as magic was in the hands of those who could not wield it responsibly. His army, now made up entirely of humans, was sent out across Nasan to hunt down non-humans. Any soldiers who objected were summarily executed.

"The hunt lasted two years. Most of the elves fled rather than stand and fight. Some humans believed in Omek and followed him without question. Others disagreed, but were too cowardly to stand and make the hard choice because it did not affect them, and so turned a blind eye to Omek's campaign. But still others fought back.

"A coalition formed to overthrow Omek, led by his sister, Valeria. She gathered members of many prominent families who would go on to rule the kingdoms following Omek's downfall. Their names are legendary now for their bravery in the face of insurmountable odds, and thus we honor them. Cristobal and Herminia Aguilar, Lord Ricardo's great-grandparents. Manyara Kane, the headmaster's great-grandfather. The renowned throldkin shaman, Syren Stormtongue. Leonid Adwer, grandfather of the former king of Ravenstone. Cheyenne Brooks, first president of Laredo. Astrida Lebrante, the warrior queen of Araspia. And the last two members... We are fortunate to have their descendants with us today. Yasir's great-great-grandfather, Sir Orlandu Levenheit, sworn sword to Lady Astrida and one of the most fearless men I have ever seen on the battlefield. And finally, someone without whom the rebellion surely would have failed: Tommaso Greyton. Lanei's great-great-grandfather."

Every student's gaze pivoted to stare at Lanei.

Lanei looked up. "Uh... What?"

Kasia raised an eyebrow and addressed Lanei directly. "You are aware of your ancestor's role in the rebellion, are you not?"

"I... I knew he fought. My father, he... well, he never mentioned Tommaso except to talk shit about him for not carving out a larger kingdom."

"That is a shame," Kasia said. "Tommaso was a man of noble character and a tremendous strategic mind. Without him, the coalition would have suffered losses too numerous for us to succeed."

"Oh. Wow. I... didn't know that."

Kasia smiled. "Come see me later. I have something you might like to see." She returned to her story, addressing the whole student body. "The coalition did a wonderful job secreting non-humans to safety and fighting small battles where they could, but gaining the support of the populace was difficult. Omek's reputation had evolved from mere ruler to god. For many, fighting Omek was akin to fighting their deity.

"The final straw that turned the public against him and forced people to pay attention was when Omek unleashed the withering blight, the plague that killed every male sindari on Nasan, save for himself. At that point, it was no longer possible for people to stand by and pretend Omek wasn't committing these horrible atrocities. However, even with the support of the general populace, Omek's true believers outnumbered our forces.

"The turning point came when Kol joined the war. It was an uneasy alliance at best. Valeria was hesitant to enter into it, as Kol was the brother she never knew. But ultimately, the addition of Kol's undead forces turned the tide. A great battle took place when the coalition forces stormed Omek's palace. Valeria and Kol confronted their brother in the throne room, and with the assistance of Syren Stormtongue, Astrida Lebrante, and Orlandu Levenheit, Omek was finally killed. Kol took Omek's body to Salah, where he swore to guard it for eternity."

"Should've burned the bastard's body," Nakato said.

"We tried. Omek placed wards upon his body that made him immune to fire."

"How could you align with Kol?" Lanei spat his name. "The undead are a scourge that needs to be wiped off the face of the land."

Selena got to her feet. "Hold your tongue."

Katya stood up beside her. "You know nothing of the undead."

"I know plenty, you vamp-loving pricks," Lanei snarled.

"Enough!" The headmaster shouted. "Now is not the time or place for this."

"Fucking Ravenstone..." Lanei muttered.

In Laredo, the undead were one of those things we just didn't talk about. Other than the occasional zombie wandering in from the north, it didn't affect us. Maldova was the only kingdom to openly support Ravenstone's new regime when Draco Rhaetanis overthrew the last Adwer king. I guess I just assumed the whole of Maldova was on board with that. Lanei wasn't your typical Maldovan, though.

Kasia continued. "The war nearly wiped out Nasan's non-human population. Most of the elves escaped, but their half-blood offspring weren't so lucky. The throldkin population was decimated. And the sindari... will never recover.

"The people did not want another sindari ruler presiding over them, and Valeria did not want that burden. The decision was made to split Nasan into eight kingdoms, with the members of the coalition installed as their new rulers. Some of those, the Lebrantes and Adwers, were continuations of older ruling bloodlines. The Aguilars, Kanes, and Greytons became new dynasties. Cheyenne Brooks created a democratic government in Laredo, while Syren Stormtongue restored oligarchic rule to Wismore. Valeria resumed her role as queen of Rainess, ceding much of their land to Maldova and Araspia for their help in defeating Omek.

"That was a hundred years ago. A hundred years since the coalition gave Nasan a fresh start and reset the calendar to the Current Era in which we now live. Next Saturday marks the anniversary of Omek's defeat. To celebrate the occasion, and to show you there has been a point to this long tale, we will be holding a Centennial Ball. This will be a formal affair, and a time to not only honor the heroes from our past, but also to honor you, who I hope will become the heroes of our future."

Ayana squealed with delight. "Isn't it exciting?"

Kaden grinned. "Heroes of the future! I like the sound of that."

Lanei rolled her eyes. Tenkou remained stoic. They were each good at those things.

Chapter 49

SYDNEY

Kasia stopped me as we filed out of the main hall.

"Sydney, may I speak with you a moment?"

I froze in my tracks. What'd I do now? "Sure."

"The elven blood in your family comes from your father's side, is that correct?"

"That's the running theory, yeah." I shrugged. "His parents died when he was little, so we don't know for sure. But my mom can trace her lineage way back, so... yeah, probably my dad's side."

"I see. So you have no idea how much elven blood is in you?"

"Nope. Best guess is not a lot. Dad never showed any hint of magic. He didn't get the ears or eyes, either. Probably just a single elf a few hundred years back."

"You've never looked into it?"

I shrugged. "Never seemed important. I've got magic, so it's gotta be there somewhere." I frowned. "Except you're asking me about it, so maybe it is important?"

"It could be. I am not certain. I have never heard of anyone who wasn't a sindari or pureblood elf who could use healing magic. What I can tell you from our work together is that your connection to the Light is somehow fractured."

"I'm broken?" I turned my hands over, examining them. "Well, that figures."

"Not broken. Fractured. Fractured I can fix." Kasia produced a necklace from her robes and handed it to me.

"What's this?" I turned it over in my hand. It looked like a pair of faerie wings that had been woven together at the base. The metal was a bluish silver unlike anything I'd ever seen.

"This necklace came into my possession after the war. It was one of the magical artifacts Omek confiscated. Put it on."

I clasped the chain and let the pendant fall around my neck. I gasped as a surge went through me. Not like a shock from one of Reno's arrows, but like settling into a hot bath.

I blinked. "The hell was that?"

"It is a magical focus attuned to the Light, a way to channel and amplify your magic. Because your connection to the Light is fractured, this pendant should serve to bridge that gap and allow you to use your power safely." She gave me a warm smile. "You are the first student I have had with any connection to the Light. As my connection is already strong, and I have my own magical foci, I would like you to have it."

"Wow... Thank you."

"Now, there remains the matter of making sure it works." Kasia pulled out a knife and, before I could stop her, sliced her hand open. "Heal me."

Dammit, why didn't she ever ask if I wanted a test subject *before* doing something dumb like that?

I took a breath. "Here goes nothing."

Chapter 50

SYDNEY

The raging fire in my chest had been extinguished. I could use my magic without a side of crippling pain! Instead of making little more than glowy light balls, I might actually be useful now.

I couldn't wait to brag to Kaden when I got back to the dorms, but when I walked in he was pacing the room like a madman.

"Sydney! Perfect. Good. As much as I hate to admit it, I need your advice."

"Okay. Coulda phrased that better, but okay."

"Right. Yes, tact. That. Got it." He heaved a sigh that threatened to collapse his lungs. "Okay. So there's going to be a ball."

I waited for more, but apparently that was it. "Yeah...?"

He rolled his eyes. "That means we need dates to the ball!"

"What? No, we don't need..." I thought about Ayana's excitement before the assembly, the giddy squeal when the ball was announced... "Wait, do we?"

"Haven't you ever been to a ball?"

"We don't really have those where I'm from."

"Well, we do where I'm from. I've been to plenty of balls. I am an expert on balls."

I snickered.

Kaden held up a finger to shush me. "And let me tell you, you don't want to be the guy without a date. Do you know why they call it going stag?"

"No, but I'm sure you're going to—"

"Because if you're alone it means you've been castrated. Well, I am not going to be castrated. I like my balls. I would like to have my balls at the ball, thank you very much."

"Wow, okay. Just bring Vigo. You're, like, one of two actual couples at the school. What's the problem?"

"What's the problem? Dude." Kaden shook his head. "We're on opposing squads."

"And you are literally the only person in the school who cares about that." I couldn't help but laugh at him. "Seriously. It's fine. Nobody thinks you're undermining the team by dating him. I don't think it. Lanei don't think it."

"Lanei doesn't know about Vigo. How does Lanei know about Vigo?"

Oh, right. Shit.

"I mean, *hypothetically* Lanei don't think it. She's got more important things to worry about." Great recovery, Sydney. "I assume Devi knows?"

"She's my sister," Kaden said. "She knew something was going on before I did."

"And does she have a problem with it?"

"Well, no, but that's because Vigo and I were together before we got here."

"Who's the most competitive person at this school?"

"I am." No hesitation.

"And who's the second most competitive?"

"Devi." Again, no hesitation. I stared at him and waited. His eyes lit up. "Ooooooh."

"Yeah."

"So I should probably ask Vigo to be my date, huh?"

"If you still want to have a boyfriend this time next week, then yeah, you probably should."

"Yeah, I think you're right. Thanks." Kaden grinned. "You know, for a guy who's probably never been on a date, you're surprisingly insightful."

"For a guy who's all about etiquette, you suck at compliments."

Kaden shrugged. "I've always been better at receiving them. So, have you asked Lanei to the ball yet?"

I choked on the drink I wasn't drinking. "What? No. Lanei? No, why would you think that?"

"Well, the way you two disappeared the other night at the bar and came back looking all disheveled, I figured you ran off to get busy in an alley somewhere."

"No, there was no... getting busy involved."

"That makes more sense. I figured you had a thing for Ayana."

I rubbed my neck. "What makes you say that?"

"Well, your face just turned as red as her eyes, so that's a pretty good confirmation." Kaden slapped me on the back. "Dude, go for it. She's probably the only person as naive as you, which means it'll be a great fit for you and hilarious for me to watch."

I narrowed my eyes. "Man, you are really bad at this."

"I'm good at enough things as it is. I have to find a balance somewhere." Kaden flopped back on his bed. "But seriously, ask her."

"I don't know... I mean, have you seen us? I'm your standard issue Laredan, and she's... Well, there's nobody else like her anywhere."

"What, the half-sindari, half-elf thing? I mean, yeah, it's different, but she's still attractive if you're into that sort of exotic—"

"No, not that. Well, yeah, that too, but like... her." I sighed. "I mean, have you ever met anyone so hopelessly optimistic? So eager to see the good in people?"

"Oh god..." Kaden made a disgusted face. "I thought you just wanted to sleep with her. This is one of those mushy puppy dog things, isn't it?"

"I mean, yeah, she's gorgeous, I just—"

"Gorgeous?" Kaden shook his head. "Damn. Yeah, you're lost."

"What?"

"I was hoping for hot. Hot I can work with. Now you're just making me want to gag."

"Oh, come on. What's wrong with that?"

"There's nothing wrong with it, but I've gotta work with you guys! You've seen Vanessa and Chavo. That lovey dovey shit is just gross."

"Then ain't it convenient you and Vigo are on different squads?"

"Huh." Kaden turned that over. "Yeah, I guess you're right. Alright, you have my permission to ask Ayana out as long as you keep the mushy crap to a minimum. And so long as you don't get too weepy in the extremely likely scenario that she turns you down."

I really needed to find someone new to confide in.

I ran into Ayana on the way to Miklotov's class. She was sprawled across a bench in the courtyard reading one of those trashy Western novels I always rolled my eyes at and now thought I should probably read to figure out what

she saw in them. This was the perfect time to ask her. If she said no, I'd have a full three hours of getting my ass handed to me to be embarrassed about something else.

"Uh, hey, Ayana."

She looked up. "Sydney! Hi." She smiled, looked back down, tucked the book under her leg, and smiled wider, her pointy canines showing. "Um, how are you?"

"Good. I'm good." This was a mistake. Gotta get out. "Sorry, you were reading. I should—"

"What? No! No, I wasn't reading. I mean, I was reading, but I wasn't, like, *reading* reading." Ayana winced. "Is that a thing? Reading reading?"

"Sure. Yeah, I'm sure it is." No clue what she was talking about. "Is it good?"

"I like it. I don't know if it's good, but I like it. I like them all, though."

"Oh, good. That's good."

Yep, this was going real well.

"Is that new?" Ayana asked, pointing to my pendant.

"Oh, yeah. Kasia gave it to me to help focus my magic. Supposed to help bridge my, uh, broken connection to the Light."

"Really? That's so cool!" Ayana reached out and touched it. A pulse of white light flashed over the pendant, starting at the edges and flowing to her fingertips. She pulled her hand back. "Woah. What was that?"

"I... have no idea. It's old and elven and... well, that's about all I know." I'd felt something when I put it on, but it hadn't flashed like that. Ayana was half elf. Maybe it had something to do with that? Or maybe it was her sindari half. Or the demon thing. Or how cute she looked in that—

"Neat!" Ayana stopped my train of thought from careening off the tracks. "I haven't seen many elven artifacts."

"Me neither," I said. "We didn't see much magic back in Chisholm."

"Yeah?"

"Yeah."

"So..."

"So..."

Ayana rocked back and forth on the bench. "Is there... something you wanted to ask me?"

Something I wanted to... oh god, did she actually want...

I took a breath. Here goes.

"Ayana, would you—"

"Sydney! Ayana!" Tenkou thundered over to us. "I have been looking for you."

I gritted my teeth. "Well, you found us."

"Um, Tenkou..." Ayana made a dismissive hand gesture. "Could you maybe—"

"This is important," he said. "And you are the only ones who may understand." Before we could protest further, he said, "I need your support to convince the school to cancel the ball."

"What?" Ayana jumped off the bench. Her book fell to the ground, and she scooped it up. "Why on earth would you want to cancel the ball? It's a *ball*! I've never been to a ball before and it sounds so glamorous and fun!"

"It celebrates the near extinction of our races."

"What? No." I shook my head. "No, it celebrates our survival. Triumphing over evil. All that good stuff."

Tenkou snorted. "Which would not have been necessary if an evil dictator had not tried to exterminate us. You cannot celebrate one without the other."

"Yeah, I'm pretty sure you can."

"Where's this coming from?" Ayana asked.

"Omek slaughtered hundreds of thousands of throldkin. Our once proud race was reduced to its

knees." Tenkou frowned. "You should understand that more than anyone. The sindari are bordering on extinction. For as long as we live, there will never be another pure born sindari."

"Maybe not, but look at me." She held out her arms. "I'm proof the sindari don't have to die out. We can still survive."

"You are an anomaly," Tenkou said. "No one like you has been born in the last one hundred years. You are something new."

"But that's good!" I interjected. "It's change. It's healing. Without that, we'd all just kinda, you know, be."

"Just because it came from something sad doesn't mean you have to be glum about it," Ayana said. "The good has to come from somewhere, right?"

"In Wismore, the new year is a time for mourning, not celebration. Throldkin are not beholden to such things." Tenkou sighed. "I will not be attending. I would urge you both to reconsider." He turned and walked into the school.

I glanced back at Ayana. "Do you... are you still planning to go?"

"I would... I mean, I am. Still planning. To go. Are... you?"

"Yeah. I mean, I get what he's saying, but... Yes, I still think I'll go."

"Good."

"Good."

Ayana took a step toward me. "So..."

"Princess Lana!"

I couldn't win...

Lanei tried to duck inside before Yasir could reach her, but she was unsuccessful. Robia followed behind him, looking none too happy.

"What do you want?" Lanei snapped. "I need to warm up."

Yasir bowed. "I will only take a moment of your time, Your Highness."

Lanei cringed. "Don't call me that. And if you bow to me again, I'm going to kick you in the face."

Yasir smiled. "I believe you would. That is what makes you so peculiar, Princess Lana."

"My name is Lanei. I don't care how high and mighty your family is in Araspia. If I have to tell you that one more time, you're going home without all your teeth."

"My apologies. To the point. As you are a member of royalty, and my family has traditionally been linked to royalty, I would like to formally ask you, Princess Lanei, to be my date for the ball." Yasir's smile never wavered. Neither did Robia's scowl.

But the look of horror on Lanei's face sure did. "You what? No. No no no."

"No?" Yasir seemed genuinely confused, like he was asking for the definition of the word.

"No, I... I already have a date. Sorry, but he asked first."

"Oh? And which nobleman has the honor of escorting you?"

Lanei looked at me.

Oh no.

"Sydney. Sydney asked me, so I'm going with him. With Sydney."

"Wait wait wait—" I felt the weight of all eyes on me. A pleading look from Lanei. Shock from Yasir. Relief from Robia. And—oh hell—was that disappointment from Ayana? Oh shit, oh no...

"Yes, Sydney asked me practically right after the announcement. Couldn't wait, right Syd?"

"What? No. Yes. No, I... What?"

"You... already have a date?" Ayana bit her bottom lip, but she turned it into a smile. "You two will look very cute together."

"No, we won't, I—"

"Oh, don't be so modest, we'll look great. Just great." Lanei's eyes bugged out as she jerked her head toward Yasir. "Right?"

The last thing Lanei wanted was attention drawn to her, and the most surefire way to draw that attention would be an escort to the ball by Araspia's golden child. On the other hand, I was now almost entirely certain Ayana had wanted me to take her. I couldn't just *not* take her after working myself up to it and getting what almost counted as confirmation, could I?

Lanei's eyes were wide as she mouthed the word "please." This was important to her...

Dammit. I hoped Ayana would understand.

I sighed. "Yeah. Yeah, I'm taking Lanei."

Chapter 51

/LANEI

I couldn't tell if Yasir was more perturbed because Sydney was taking me to the ball or because Sydney was winning the match. The only thing saving Sydney's ass was that we were working with staves today. His extra training sessions with Miklotov had paid off. I was proud. It was good to see him on the giving end of a beatdown for once, especially against the prodigal son. Yasir kept charging in with more aggression than normal, and Sydney turned Yasir's mistakes against him.

Yasir wasn't used to losing, especially not against the universally acknowledged bottom rung of the class. But he was flustered and his judgment was off, plus he was distracted. He kept gazing over at me then he'd either make some comment to Sydney, get hit, or both. Sydney cast a glance my way from time to time, too, but his were less friendly.

I think I might be a terrible friend. I'm new at this. That's sort of an excuse, right?

I hated putting Sydney in this situation to begin with. I don't make the best decisions when I panic, but this had to be better than going with Yasir. Didn't matter how pretty he was, someone that skilled at trailing women along on his finger was trouble. The whole noble paragon thing didn't help his case any. I almost felt bad for Robia. Almost.

"You think just because you're a princess you deserve him?"

I hadn't even heard her approach. Kind of wished I wasn't hearing her now.

"What makes you think I even want him?"

Robia let out a dry laugh. "Of course you want him. He's as close to Araspian royalty as you can get without being a Lebrante. He's exactly the kind of match your father would want for you."

Now it was my turn to laugh. "Clearly you don't know the first thing about my father."

"I know enough."

I turned to face her. "And what the hell does that mean?"

"It means you don't deserve half of what's been handed to you. Pretty little thing, spitting image of the mother daddy loved. Bet he gave you everything you ever asked for, didn't he?"

"You don't know shit about me," I spat at her. "And if you mention my mother again, I'm going to rip that stupid piercing right outta your lip."

Robia grinned. "I grew up on the streets of San Domingo. Everything I have, I've earned. And everything I've wanted, I've found a way to get. Stay away from him."

"I don't want him. He's all yours." I stood, but turned back before I could think better of it. "You know, until I change my mind."

Robia was practically spitting blood when I left her to join Kaden and Vigo on the other side of the room. Continuing my pattern of being an ace friend, I eavesdropped on their conversation while adjusting my armor. Lucia would be proud.

"Are you sure you want to do this?" Vigo asked. "You don't have to prove yourself to me. Or anyone."

"If we don't go all out now, everyone's going to think I'm soft when they see us at the ball," Kaden said. "What'll they think when we face off in the Squad Games?"

"They won't think anything. They'll know you're too stubborn to pull punches when stakes are involved."

"And what about you?" Kaden asked. "Aren't you worried what they'll think of you?"

"For the millionth time, *no*. I've done nothing to sully my honor. Neither have you. We don't have to go above and beyond to prove that to anyone."

"Come on, please?" Kaden pleaded. "I know Devi says she's fine with it—"

"Because she is."

"But I don't want to take any chances! Not where our honor is concerned."

Vigo sighed. "Will it really make you happy if we knock each other senseless?"

"Yes!"

"Then I'll do it. For you. But don't say I didn't warn you."

"Thank you."

"Now..." Vigo took Kaden's hand. Kaden immediately looked around to see who was watching. As Kaden's eyes met mine, Vigo tugged his hand to bring his focus back to him. "Will you please stop worrying about what anyone else thinks and kiss me?"

"I..." Kaden only hesitated for a moment. As he looked in Vigo's eyes, I could see the weight fall from his shoulders. Kaden leaned in and kissed him.

I smiled. Across the room, Devi beamed.

Miklotov called them up next. True to their word, they went all out. Nobody in that room would've ever questioned that either held anything back.

I'd never seen Kaden so happy to lose.

Kasia's study felt completely out of place at Petrichor. It wasn't because the school was inelegant. The place rang of money and prestige. But stepping into Kasia's office was like walking into another world.

Calling it an office did it a disservice. It was more of a parlor. I gathered it was the entryway to her living quarters. If so, this was part office, part living room, part garden. A freaking tree was growing right in the middle of the room, and the dirt around it transitioned so seamlessly into a hardwood floor I couldn't tell where one ended and the other began. The ceiling was a curved glass dome, and I got the feeling I wasn't looking at the sky of San Domingo.

Shelves of old books lined the walls, along with glass display cases full of old weapons, artifacts, baubles... just about anything you could imagine. I stood in a museum the public was never supposed to see.

"Thank you for coming to see me." Kasia led me to a chair across from her desk. "I am sorry we have not been able to speak before now."

"Yeah, well, no magic." I took a seat and sank into a world of comfort I'd never known, even in my father's castle. Where had this chair been all my life? "Also, busy being accused of murder, so..."

Kasia glided around her desk, but did not sit. "I understand it has been a trying time for you. For what it is worth, the evidence I have seen leads me to believe you are innocent."

"Thanks..." Out of all the teachers, I'd have expected the elf to be the most wary of me.

Kasia smiled. "Sydney speaks highly of you. From what he has told me, there is more of your great-great-grandfather in you than you know."

"Yeah, you mentioned him. I don't know much about him..." I hesitated to say more, but something about Kasia made it feel safe to continue. "My father and I have never been close. That's the putting it mildly version. I was never interested in learning more about his side of the family." My hand gravitated to the turquoise pendant resting against my throat.

"And your mother's family?"

I rubbed my thumb against the smooth stone. "She was from Kialen. I remember my grandfather from when I was little. And an aunt. But I haven't seen either of them since..." I dropped my hand. "Maybe my father didn't want me to see anyone from the Walker side after... well. Maybe they were glad to stay away from Maldova. I don't know."

"I have never met your father, but I know his reputation," Kasia said. "Viktor Greyton is not well liked among my people."

I laughed. "He wants your people thrown out of his kingdom. I don't blame them."

"Your family has not always thought so poorly of the magical races. Tommaso Greyton was a good man and a friend to the elves and sindari. He was instrumental in convincing many of the elves to fight rather than flee."

"How'd he do that?"

"Because he was willing to die for one. He was ready to throw his life away for a woman he loved who would outlive him by many hundreds of years."

"An elf?" That was news to me. It also might explain why my father never spoke of Tommaso.

Kasia smiled, and her eyes glazed over. She was somewhere far away. "He really was a wonderful man."

My eyes widened. "You? You and my..." Holy shit. "Does that mean you're my..."

Kasia shook her head. "No, child. You are descended from his first wife. She had already passed away by the time we met. Tommaso and I never wed, never had children."

"But you... and he..." My head swam. I'd just assumed my family had always been like my father. When had that changed?

"We were together until the day he died. Which came far too soon." Kasia walked over to one of the glass cases and placed a hand on it. A glow of blue light and the case opened. "The world may never know another man as extraordinary as Tommaso Greyton. But if my instincts about you are correct, it may yet know a woman of such character."

Kasia removed a beautiful rapier from the case. The basket hilt was carved into a wonderfully ornate eagle. But what astonished me the most was the bluish silver metal. I knew that metal...

"That's elven steel," I whispered. "You hardly see those anymore..."

Kasia nodded. "Most of the art has died off, and the few smiths who still practice it left Nasan long ago. Brightclaw has been in my family for over a millennium. My mother gave it to Tommaso at the start of the war. When he died, it returned to me." She extended the hilt to me. "But I believe he would have wanted you to have it."

I let out a low breath. I wanted to reach for it, but my hand froze by my side. "I don't think I can accept this."

"You came to this school as Lanei Walker because you were ashamed of your given name. Because you wanted to hide who you were." She took my hand and placed the sword in it. "I am asking you to take this sword and leave this room not as Lanei Walker, but as Lanei Greyton. Show the world that love and bravery are more powerful than hatred and fear. Do not let the name of the man I loved fall into dishonor. You alone can restore the Greyton name to its former glory."

"I alone..." I muttered. "No pressure."

Kasia smiled. "With, perhaps, a little help from your friends."

Restoring honor to my family... It seemed an impossible task. Something I certainly wasn't up for on my own. But with my friends... with Sydney and Ayana... with Kaden and Tenkou and Nakato...

I wrapped my fingers around the hilt of the sword.

Maybe I could do this...

Maybe I could be Lanei Greyton.

Chapter 52

ALANEI

Just because the ball was tonight didn't mean Reno was going to give us the day off. We had the next round of Squad Games tomorrow, and we were going up against Warren's team. The last thing any of us wanted was to lose to those assholes.

As much as Reno tried to be neutral in class, it was obvious he wasn't fond of them. They hadn't exactly done a great job hiding their disdain for Ayana, and that was the fastest way to land on Reno's shit list. Fortunately, when we were in squad sessions, he didn't have to pretend to give a damn about them.

"Tenkou, again!" Reno yelled. "You may be stronger, but Warren's faster than you. You have to overpower him as soon as he gets in range! Do not give him any second chances."

Tenkou nodded, and Ayana had Malbohr reset. One of the nice things about his being a slime demon, and possibly the only nice thing about being a slime demon, was that Malbohr could alter his form and density. At present, he looked like a decent approximation of Warren. Malbohr had never actually seen Warren, so he was just going off Ayana's description. The size and shape were dead on, but his features were more bovine than human. The slime demon wasn't as technically proficient as Warren, but he could match him for speed and strength, and that was good enough.

Meanwhile, Kaden, Sydney, and I took turns double teaming each other in preparation for the twins. Our teamwork was good, but we were nowhere near their level of coordination. Even Selena and Katya had better synergy than we did. What they'd had years to hone, we'd been forced to cram into a couple of months. We'd come a long way, but it was hard to beat raw experience. Pretty soon Tenkou and Ayana joined in on the rotation.

Reno surmised their strategy would involve picking us off one-by-one, using double- or triple-team tactics to whittle us down. Much of our focus involved turning their momentum against them in a two-on-one situation, or slipping away and running for help if the odds were worse. As much as I hated the idea of running from a fight, it was the smart move.

Sometimes the smart move isn't the one that makes you feel good inside.

After six hours of rough and tumble, Reno decided we were in a good enough place to call it a day. That left five hours before the ball, just enough time to run into the city and pick up what I needed.

I returned to Petrichor with an hour to spare, plenty of time to bathe off the smells of sweat and horse. But before I went back to my room to clean up, I had one stop to make. I held the bag over my shoulder and knocked on the door.

Tenkou answered.

"Lanei. Hello."

"Hi. Can I come in?"

He arched a brow, but stepped aside. "Can I... help you with something?"

I stepped in and laid the bag across his bed. "Okay, so... I don't know if this is going to make sense, but I want to say it anyway. I think you should come to the ball." He opened his mouth to protest, but I held up a hand. "Hear me out. I know you have this moral objection to it, and I get that. I do. But for different reasons." I sat down at his desk and waited until he sat down on the bed. He glanced suspiciously at the bag. "We weren't big on new year's celebrations in my house. I mean, my mother would celebrate in her own way and my father would put up with it, but after Mom... after she was gone, my father wouldn't have anything to do with it. It wasn't a day of mourning. It was just like any other day. I hadn't thought of the new year as something worth celebrating until Kasia's speech. I was like you. I didn't understand why we were celebrating something that resulted in the loss of hundreds of thousands of innocent lives."

"And yet you are here." He folded his arms across his chest. "And you are going."

"I am. Because—and I don't say this often—I was wrong. All those lives that were cut short—throldkin and sindari and elven and human—they're worth celebrating. They're worth celebrating because every single one of them was worth dying for. The heroes who fought against Omek are worth honoring. And when I say heroes, I don't just mean the leaders of the coalition. I'm not just talking about Syren Stormtongue and Tommaso Greyton. I'm talking about everyone who fought so we could live in a world that isn't ruled by tyranny. I'm talking from every lieutenant like Kasia Windamier to every foot soldier on the front lines."

"I agree," Tenkou said, dropping his arms to his sides. "We honor all who fought and died, not only the legends."

"I guess what I'm saying is..." I let out a breath. "Until this week, I never knew I had someone in my family tree worth honoring, let alone celebrating. Now that I do... I think about the kind of world he would have wanted to see follow him. I don't think he would have wanted his legacy to be a day of sadness. What they achieved was amazing. They took down a man many believed was a *god*. We aren't celebrating the deaths of brave women and men. We honor their deaths by celebrating what they worked so hard to achieve."

Tenkou studied me. "Throldkin... do not have many celebrations."

"No?"

He shook his head. "We have many ceremonies. Many rituals. Few celebrations." He thought about it. "One celebration. A harvest festival in the autumn."

"What's that like?"

Tenkou smiled. "All the food you could ever wish to eat. The finest alcohol you could ever wish to drink." He must have seen my face, because he laughed. "Not Niadhogr. One of the northern tribes has a pumpkin cider that would make you question your religion. We eat, we drink, we tell stories... We do not dance, but we tell stories."

It was my turn to smile. "Think you'll have a story to tell when you go back next year?"

He laughed. "Yes, but who would believe it? A princess in disguise, a young sindari with demon friends, a human cowboy who rides a raptor, a man with a metal arm, an arrogant Araspian... I suppose that last one is not so far-fetched."

"Just think. You could add 'attended a ball' to that list."

"Throldkin do not dance."

"I'm pretty sure Laredans don't either, but Sydney's still going." I smiled and pushed myself to my feet. "Nobody will hold it against you if you don't attend. We understand it isn't a part of your culture, but... you're our friend. It won't be the same if you aren't there." I patted the bag on my way out. "Just think about it, okay?"

"I will," Tenkou said. "And Lanei?"

"Yeah?"

"I once told you that you were arrogant, short-tempered, and full of anger."

"Yes, I remember."

"You are still arrogant and short-tempered, and there is anger in you." He smiled. "But I believe you are no longer *full* of anger."

"No?"

"No," he said. "I believe you have just the right amount of anger in you to do some good."

I smiled. "I like the sound of that."

"As do I."

I closed the door behind me. Less than an hour. Time to work a miracle.

Sydney arrived at my door as I finished lacing up my boots. Perfect timing.

"Come in!"

I picked up my mother's turquoise choker from the dresser as the door opened behind me.

"Hey, you ready to— Wow."

I turned around in time to see Sydney's jaw hit the floor. I rolled my eyes. Tonight I'd decided to go with the Maldovan fashion for once. A red corset with a black brocade pattern, brass buckles down the front, and strings of brass chains along the side. A red high-low skirt with black trim that was exactly as high as I was comfortable with in the front and plenty long in the back. Black lace bracers with chains that connected to rings on my middle fingers, just in case I needed a little extra oomph flicking someone off.

"If this is worth a 'wow,' you're probably going to need to save a few 'holy fucks' for whatever piece of tape Milia decides to wear."

"No, it's just..." Sydney blushed. I had too much fun making him uncomfortable. "You don't usually wear dresses."

"Because we're training to fight. This isn't exactly fighting gear." I still had a dagger on me, but that was beside the point.

"Yes, right, no, but like... a Maldovan dress."

"Yes, I am sort of their princess. And the rest of my clothes are Maldovan, too. We don't all go as crazy as the twins. Just don't expect me to start wearing goggles any time soon." I took a second to look Sydney over and let out a whistle. "Sydney Winter, did someone finally learn how to dress for a formal event?"

He blushed deeper. "Yeah, I figured that'd be a good idea this time around. I mean, most of it was Kaden. All of it was Kaden. But, you know, I helped."

Kaden did well. I wasn't sure if they had formal wear in Laredo, but this was exactly what it should be. Although he still wore cowboy boots and a flashy steel belt buckle in true Sydney fashion, these were shinier and newer than his typical fare. He wore a charcoal suit with an embroidered trail of silver leaves starting at the shoulder and following down the lapels. Under that he wore a white shirt and a...

I took in a breath and reached out to examine the slide on Sydney's bolo tie. It was a silver circle inlaid with waves, and right in the center was a smooth piece of turquoise.

"It's beautiful." I rubbed my thumb over the stone. "Where did you get it?"

"Nakato," he said. "I asked Kaden if he had something that'd go with your necklace. Turns out he owns every type of jewelry except turquoise, but he remembered Nakato's pin from orientation. A little modification and..." He shrugged. "Voila. Fancy Sydney."

I smiled in spite of myself. "That was very sweet."

"Yeah, well. Apparently I asked you to the ball, so I thought I should make a little effort." He screwed up his face. "I mean, I don't *remember* asking you, but *someone* was very insistent that I did, so maybe I just forgot."

"Probably. It was very unmemorable."

"That would explain it, because I have literally no memory of it at all." Sydney pouted for a moment then rolled his eyes.

I was glad he wasn't sore about it. And he *had* made an effort, even though he really didn't have to. Trying to match my necklace was much more thoughtful than he needed to...

Oh shit. Oh hell. Oh shit shit shit.

I took a step back and held up a hand. "Um, look, before we go I just want to make sure I didn't, uh... give you the wrong impression."

"Okay..."

God I really didn't want to break his poor naive heart, but... I sighed. "The reason I said we were already going together was because I really didn't want to go with Yasir."

"Yeah, no, I got that," Sydney said. "It wasn't subtle."

"Alright, but..." Oh god, how to put this nicely. "I like you but I don't... like you like that."

"You don't?"

I shook my head. "No."

He let out a breath so massive it was as if he hadn't exhaled since setting foot in my room. "Oh, thank god. I don't like you like that either."

I gave him a pitying half smile. "That's sweet of you to say, cowboy, but I'll understand if you're devastated."

"No, I'm serious."

"Me too."

"Good."

"Good."

I watched him, looking for any sign of heartbreak. I didn't see any, but... "So, just to be clear, you're not—"

"No!" His exclamation turned into a burst of laughter. "You thought I...?"

"No!" I held up my hands. "I just wanted to make sure we're on the same page, that's all."

"Same page, same line, same word." He wiped a tear of laughter from his eye, and I was sure that was all it was. I heaved a sigh of relief. Sydney extended his arm to me. "Shall we?"

I smiled and hooked my arm through his. "We shall."

Chapter 53

SYDNEY

The ball was already in full swing when we arrived. Loud music and laughter greeted us as the doors swung open and we stepped into the great hall. I didn't know what was more impressive: the extravagant attire or the full banquet laid out at the far end of the room. There were dozens of faces I didn't recognize. Probably donors or state officials or local guilds who supported Petrichor. It felt strange being surrounded by so many people. We'd been isolated at the school for so long it was easy to forget we were only the starting point for the whole system.

The first familiar faces we ran into were Nakato and her squad. Well, the faces weren't familiar, but it was easy to identify the only people treating the whole affair as a masquerade ball. Rather than their usual creeptastic masks, they instead wore colorful, decorated masks that looked appropriately formal for a ball. A small painting of the wearer's second face was displayed beneath the right eye of each mask: Nakato's skull, Zeke's demon, Vanessa's fox, and Chavo's wolf.

"Hot damn, Lanei." Nakato whistled. "You should show those legs more often."

Lanei winked. "You can see them any time I kick you in the face."

"And Sydney! You should show, like, all that more often. Turn around for me."

I modeled my suit for her, finishing my turn with a little tip of the hat. I don't know where Kaden found a black suede cowboy hat in the middle of Esperan, but somehow he succeeded.

"I love the masks!" Lanei touched the gemstones along the side of Nakato's mask. "You don't look like a freaky death machine, but I still love them."

Nakato gave a mock curtsy. "Why, thank you kindly. Instead of being a death machine tonight, I thought I'd settle for being a knockout."

"Mission accomplished." Lanei draped an arm over my shoulder, somehow managing to stay in her corset in the process. "And thank you for loaning Sydney the pin. It was a sweet gesture."

Nakato winked. "Don't mention it."

We chatted with them until we spotted Kaden and Vigo step off the dance floor. They sat on a bench, and Kaden draped his legs over Vigo's lap. Lanei grabbed my arm and pulled me over to them.

"Kaden, you are a miracle worker," she said.

"I know, I know. Just one of my many talents."

I sighed. "Literally standing right here."

"Well, I for one am not surprised you clean up well," Vigo said.

"Thank you!" I gave him a head bow. "At least one person has faith in me."

Lanei gestured at the two of them on the bench. "So you're no longer worried what people will think about intersquad dating?"

Kaden nodded. "It has been brought to my attention by, well, a number of individuals that certain matters I believed were important are actually, uh..."

"A complete load of horse shit," Vigo finished.

"Yes. That." Kaden wrapped an arm around Vigo and kissed him. Then he crooked a finger at me. I leaned in. "Put a sock on the door if you and Lanei need some private time later."

I shoved him. Vigo caught him and they both burst into laughter.

Lanei leaned in to me. "Do I want to—"

"No."

Vigo's laughing ceased as he stared at the doorway. "Now there's something you don't see every day. Or ever."

I followed his eyes and forgot how to breathe.

Ayana.

The dress she'd been wearing when the ball was announced was now finished. The strapless gown fit her body perfectly. The pale green was the perfect contrast to her purple skin. Leaves of silver thread adorned the trim of the bust, and it occurred to me that maybe there was a reason Kaden sewed the silver leaves into my jacket. A sheer cape flowed behind her, attached to a high collar adorned with leaves.

"Yeah... she's... wow."

"No, not her," Vigo said. "We literally do see her every day. I meant the imp."

I blinked. Vadazach stood beside her in a tiny black tuxedo.

Ayana spotted us, waved frantically, and skipped over. Vadazach followed beside her, adjusting his cufflinks as if he wore a tux every day. As they walked our way, everyone stopped to stare. And even though most of the outsiders had never seen a sindari who looked like Ayana, most of the eyes were on Vadazach.

Those people were idiots.

Ayana wrapped Lanei in a huge hug, and Lanei didn't even try to pull away. "Oh my god, you look so pretty! The red and the floofy skirt! I love it!"

Lanei smiled. "Thank you. You did a wonderful job on your dress."

"Eeeeee, thank you!" Ayana spun around in a little dance. "I've been working on it all week. I was really happy with it. Kaden helped me with the leaves. I think it's a nice touch, don't you?"

I glanced at Kaden. He winked.

Ayana smiled at me. "Sydney, you're... you look very handsome."

"Thanks... You look—"

"Oh!" Ayana's eyes flashed. "You have silver leaves too! That's so cool!" She spun me around and posed with me. "Kaden, look! It's like we match!"

"Huh, it's like you do." He grinned. "Fancy that."

Ayana noticed the turquoise slide on my tie and looked over at Lanei's choker. "Oh, you two match, too. That's— Vadazach! Manners!"

Vadazach froze in place, his cheeks stuffed with crab puffs. Behind him, an unsuspecting party guest held an empty plate. Vadazach swallowed. He slowly reached for the man's wine glass.

"Vadazach..."

A man in a bowler hat walked past carrying a serving tray. Ayana pulled off a wine glass and handed it to the imp.

Vadazach cocked his head to the side. "Oh, I get it. It's okay for you to steal, but not me. Yeah, that makes sense."

"The people wearing the funny hats work here," she explained. "The food they're carrying is for the guests to take."

The imp jerked a thumb at me. "What about this guy? He's got a funny hat."

"My hat isn't funny."

"It's a little funny."

"No, it isn't."

"Come on, admit it. Kinda funny."

"His hat is perfectly fine, Vaddie." Ayana looked at me. "It really is. I like your hat."

"Thanks. I like your—"

"Will you look at what the cat dragged in," Kaden said.

Tenkou walked our way. I almost didn't recognize him. Instead of his usual rawhide look, he wore a finely tailored black suit with a green vest and black cravat. I didn't even know they made suits for throldkin, but apparently someone did.

"You came!" Ayana squealed, leaping up and wrapping her arms around his massive neck. "You look very dapper. Is that an appropriate word? Dapper? Because I would say you look dapper."

The big man smiled. "Thank you. I will accept dapper."

"Damn, Tenkou." Kaden circled him, taking in the suit. "You're making me look bad here. I mean, I knew I looked better than Sydney, but now you're making me think I'm not the best looking dude on this team."

"Still right here," I said.

"For real, where did you get that suit?"

Tenkou smiled and looked at Lanei. "A friend."

Lanei placed a hand on his shoulder. "I'm glad you decided to come."

"As am I," he agreed. "I believe it could make a good story one day."

Lanei laughed. "As good a reason to do anything as I've ever heard."

The music stopped and a murmur spread through the crowd. The sea of people parted as Yasir and Robia stepped into the ballroom.

Lanei rolled her eyes. "And that right there is why I did *not* want to be on his arm. Let pretty boy have the attention."

Although the rest of the school knew Lanei was the Maldovan princess, word didn't seem to have spread to the other guests. But everyone knew Yasir Levenheit. And boy were they getting a look.

Yasir wore a green and black velvet doublet with gold trim that may have been made from actual gold. His cloak was black velvet with, again, gold lining and trim. He acknowledged the crowd in a way that came off more noble than arrogant, which was no easy task. For a guy who wasn't technically royalty, he sure fit the part.

Robia looked right at home on his arm. She wore a sleek black dress with a plunging neckline. And a plunging back. Really, the whole thing was plunging. Supposedly she was human, but there had to be some magic at work there. Either way, she looked radiant, and happier than I'd ever seen her without a bow in her hand.

The band picked back up with a waltz, and Yasir led Robia to the dance floor. Others followed suit, Kaden and Vigo among them.

Lanei took my arm. "Come on."

"Oh, uh, sure. Dancing. Right."

She smiled. "Follow my lead. You'll be fine."

Ayana rocked on her heels. "Tenkou?"

Tenkou shook his head. "I am not quite ready for that." He eyed the buffet "I will try the food. That is a custom I am... accustomed to."

"Okey doke." Ayana stretched her hand down to Vadazach. "Want to show 'em how it's done?"

"Thought you'd never ask, toots."

We somehow managed two hours without having to deal with Warren and his squad. Those were a glorious two hours, but we knew it couldn't last.

The girls finally dragged Tenkou onto the dance floor. His moves were more lumbering than graceful, but every one of us gave him all the credit in the world for trying.

As the four of us left the floor, Warren slammed his shoulder into me. I spun around and almost collided with the twins. Milich wore traditional Maldovan formal wear, but Lanei hadn't been far off when she suggested Milia would just wear a piece of tape. It actually took me a second to realize she *was* wearing a dress. The top was completely sheer with strategically placed bead work. Below was... completely sheer with a similar amount of strategically placed bead work.

Holy fuck.

Lanei really could call it.

Milia looked Ayana up and down. "How cute. The little demon's trying to be a human."

Milich nodded. "Yes, I've never seen an imp in a suit before."

Milia tried looking innocent. It didn't work. "Oh, is there an imp, too? I hadn't noticed."

Vadazach pushed up his sleeves. "Alright, bitch, you and me are gonna—"

Ayana held him back. "It's alright, Vaddie. She's just upset because she lost her dress." Then, to her, "you should be more careful, Milia. Your Levesque is showing."

Milia scoffed. "This dress is worth more than your life. But I suppose most things are. Bad example."

"Come," Tenkou said. "Do not let them provoke you."

Milich rolled his eyes. "You put a raptor in a suit and suddenly he thinks he's civilized."

Tenkou stepped up to Milich, towering over the smaller man. "I am going to be civilized and walk away. If you want to die today, find me and call me a raptor one more time." Tenkou stared Milich down for several seconds until the Maldovan gulped uncomfortably. Tenkou snorted and walked away.

Lanei stepped in front of me and Ayana, shielding us from Warren's squad.

"Back off," Lanei said. "You do not want to go down this road with me. Not tonight."

Warren shook his head. "Your father must be so disappointed in you."

Lanei smiled. "That may be the nicest thing you've ever said to me."

"Well, we can't have that." Warren took a glass of deep purple wine off a passing server's tray and splashed it on Lanei's dress. It ran off her corset, but trailed long, dark streaks through her skirt.

Lanei looked down at her dress. For the first time in memory, she didn't get mad at being provoked. She looked amused.

"I am a fucking princess, Warren. I can buy a new dress anytime I want." Lanei picked up another glass of wine off the same tray and splashed it across the front of Warren's light gray suit, completely ruining it. "Can you say the same?"

He spluttered with rage. "You... bitch!"

Lanei laughed. "Besides..." She reached down and, with a few quick, practiced movements, removed the long portion of her skirt, turning the high low skirt into a very low skirt. She twirled it in the air and threw it in Warren's face. She held her hands out to the sides. "I make this look good."

Before any of the trio could respond, she turned on her heel and walked away. I could confirm that, yes, she did in fact make that look very good.

So good, in fact, that it wasn't long after we'd met back up with the others that Yasir approached Lanei.

Yasir started to bow but caught himself, gracefully turning it into a grand gesture of extending his hand. "Princess Lanei, may I have this dance?"

Lanei quickly latched onto my arm. "Oh, I would, but Sydney just asked me to dance with him."

He turned to me. "Surely you can spare her for one dance."

Looking more at Lanei, I said, "I mean, it's just one—"

"No, you were very insistent that you absolutely love this song and that you must dance to it."

"Perhaps you would like to dance with Robia?" Yasir offered. "She is a most nimble dancer."

I looked over at Robia, standing with her back to Devi and Anji, arms crossed, teeth bared, and casting the worst death glare at Lanei I'd ever seen in my life. I wanted no part of that.

"Yeah, no, I'm good," I said, allowing Lanei to pull me back to the dance floor.

The rest of the night was mostly a blur. Lanei must've had one eye on Yasir the whole time, because whenever he moved even remotely in her direction she dragged me out to the dance floor. To counter that, Robia had an eye on Lanei all night, and that eye was just shooting daggers the whole time. I didn't think one dance was the end of the world, but apparently three people disagreed with me, so hey, what did I know?

People trickled out as it passed midnight. The only instructors left in the hall were Reno and Kasia, laughing over wine on the dais. Warren and the twins had left shortly after our little run-in. I never even saw the two Ravenstone girls.

Lanei and Nakato returned from the dance floor. Nakato had given me a brief respite, insisting that Lanei dance with her before she called it a night.

"Good luck in the Games tomorrow," Nakato said. "Take it to those assholes."

"Oh, we plan to," Lanei said. "Good luck against the lovelorn pretty boy."

Nakato grinned. "No contest." She hugged Lanei and gave her a kiss on the cheek before heading out.

Tenkou rose on unsteady feet. "Ah yes, the Games... I believe that means I need to rest." He turned to me and Lanei. "Thank you. Both of you. This has been... an evening worthy of a story. And you have been friends worthy of legend." He placed a hand on each of our shoulders. "I love you both."

"You're drunk," I pointed out.

"Yes," Tenkou confirmed. "I am. But it is no less true."

Lanei laughed. "Love you too, big guy."

He smiled and stumbled his way to the door.

Lanei pushed me down onto a bench and took a seat beside me. "Successful night?"

"Successful night," I agreed, even though I only half meant it. I hadn't managed to get a moment alone with Ayana, let alone dance with her. Every time I tried, I got stuck running interference for Lanei. Ayana had spent the night dancing her heart out, twirling around the floor with Vadazach and Kaden and Devi and Anji and... not me.

I sighed.

Lanei nudged me with her elbow. "Thanks."

"For what?"

"For taking me," she said. "I know you really wanted to ask Ayana."

I had a moment of panic. "You knew about that?"

"Well, I have eyes and ears and a brain, so yeah, I noticed." She gave me a half-smile. "I'm sorry I sabotaged your plans. I just really hope I didn't mess it up for you."

"Trust me, if I'm gonna mess that up, I won't need any help."

Lanei leaned her head on my shoulder. "Eh, you ain't half bad. But... thanks. For helping me out."

I put my arm around her. "That's what friends are for."

"I'm still figuring that whole thing out."

"I'd say you're doing well so far."

"Aw, you're gonna make me blush."

We sat in silence watching the few pairs still out dancing. Yasir and Robia. Kaden and Vigo. Vanessa and Chavo. Devi and Anji. A band member announced that the next song would be the last.

Yasir said something to Robia. She grabbed his arm and tried to hold him there, but he gently disentangled himself and walked our way. She stamped her foot and stormed out.

I held out a hand to Lanei. "Looks like we've got one more dance?"

She shook her head. "No, we don't. You go find Ayana. I'll handle this."

Yasir reached us. He bowed graciously to me and then extended a hand to Lanei. "Your Highness?"

Lanei took his hand without argument and they made their way to the dance floor. I didn't see Ayana anywhere, but I spotted Vadazach at the buffet table, stuffing his tiny pockets with food.

"Hey, Vadazach."

He looked up at me, and quickly shoved his hands behind his back to hide the whole pie he was trying to pilfer. "This... this ain't what it looks like."

"It looks like you're stealing a bunch of food for later."

"Oh..." He shrugged. "Then yeah, it's exactly what it looks like. You gonna rat me out?"

I shook my head. "Nah, your secret's safe with me."

"Cool. Cool." He nodded approvingly. "You're alright, cowboy."

Approval from a demon. Not a bad thing to have. "Thanks." Awkward silence. "Hey, um... Do you know where Ayana is?"

The imp narrowed his eyes. "That depends... What are your intentions?"

"My... Intentions?"

"Yeah. Why you lookin' for her?"

"I, uh..." My father's stories of meeting my mother's parents flashed in my mind. Except last I checked, grandma and grandpa weren't demons. "I was hoping to ask her to dance."

Vadazach heaved a sigh of relief. "Oh, thank god. She hasn't shut up about you all night. Yeah, she just stepped out for a moment. Should be back any—"

A loud, piercing scream echoed from outside. Before the band even stopped playing, Reno leapt off the dais and ran full speed to the door. I sprinted out ahead of him, Vadazach at my side. My body reacted to her scream before my mind had time to process the voice. But now my mind had caught up and my throat constricted.

Ayana...

We found Ayana lying on the ground in the entrance hall, her pale green dress stained red. On the wall above her head was a message in blood: *OMEK'S WILL SURVIVES*

She was crying hysterically. Ayana raised her head slightly when she heard us, but kept her arms wrapped tight around Tenkou's lifeless body.

Chapter 54

/LANEI

No...

"I can't feel him!"

No, no, no.

"He's not... He's not there."

This isn't happening.

"Kasia!"

This can't be real...

"Kasia! Help me!"

Yasir placed a hand on my shoulder as I stood in the doorway. It shocked me back to reality. I ran toward Sydney and slipped on all the blood. I caught myself before I went down and knelt beside him. Sydney was blurry. Everything was blurry. Why couldn't I see?

Ayana's cries drowned out my thoughts. Reno had scooped her up in his arms and held her close, burying her face in his shoulder, muffling her sobs.

Those were my own cries I was hearing.

I became aware of hands on my shoulders pulling me back. Someone. Two someones. Kaden and Vigo. They held me as I screamed incoherently.

Kasia flew past us. Actually flew past us. Landed beside Sydney. Placed her hands on Tenkou's chest. And then nothing. Nothing. She shook her head.

"He's gone, Sydney. There's nothing we can do."

Sydney got to his feet, took a step back, and collapsed. He broke down. I wrenched free from Kaden and Vigo and ran to him.

"Lanei..." Kasia's voice.

I couldn't breathe. Couldn't speak. Couldn't respond.

Kasia laid a hand on my shoulder. "Lanei."

She pointed to Tenkou. I blinked back the tears. No...

Tenkou's jacket had been torn open. His white shirt was solid red. And protruding from his chest was my great-great-grandfather's sword. The sword Kasia gave me last week.

"No!" I gasped for air. "No! Kasia, I didn't do this! You know I didn't do this."

"Shhh," she whispered. "I know."

"Like hell you didn't!" Anji stormed toward me. "You're a Greyton. You—"

"Shut it, Anji." Vigo yanked Anji back so hard I thought Anji's arm would break. "She's been at the ball the whole time."

"How can you—"

"Because she is innocent!" Yasir shouted, getting in Anji's face. "And unless you have something of substance to add, you will remain quiet."

"How did..." I stammered. "How did they... My sword... Brightclaw... That's my..."

"Her sword." Anji spat on the ground. "Happy?"

"Quiet!" This time it was Reno coming to my defense. Reno. "Yasir, get him outta here. Now."

I don't know where they came from or when they arrived, but I was suddenly aware of the other instructors surrounding us. Headmaster Kane started barking orders.

"Adelaide, lock it down. Caesar, account for the students. Miklotov, same for the guests. Lucia, start interviewing. Kasia, see what you can find. Reno... take care of Ayana."

I watched as the instructors set about following orders. Every one of them. Including whoever among them was a fucking traitor.

One of them was responsible for Tenkou's death. It took everything in me to keep from flying into a rage. But I didn't. I held it in.

Someone used my ancestral sword to murder my friend. My *friend*.

Despite what some people thought, I was not, and never had been, a murderer. But when I found out who was responsible for this, I would be.

Chapter 55

⁄LANEI

There was no hesitation the next day when Reno asked if we wanted to postpone the Squad Games.

"We're doing this," I said. My throat was raw from crying and a lack of sleep. I was going to quench it with their blood. "Any other squad, we'd postpone. But it's Warren's crew. I'll be damned if they weren't involved."

"We don't have any proof of that," Reno said, but it sounded more like frustration than a condemnation of my comment.

"Why can't you lock them up?" Sydney asked. "You know how they feel about non-humans. They shouldn't be running free."

"Same reason Lanei wasn't locked up when everyone thought she killed Jeyla. No proof." Reno sighed. "And because they have powerful parents."

Reno hadn't said "when *we* thought she killed Jeyla." Between that and coming to my defense last night, maybe he was no longer sold on the idea of me as a killer.

"I don't even care about winning," Kaden said. "I just want to hurt someone."

Reno nodded. "I'm going to pretend I didn't hear that, and you pretend I didn't give you permission." He placed a hand on his sister's shoulder. "Ayana?"

She nodded. The poor girl hadn't said a word since last night. I knew how horrifying it was to find a dead body. But for it to be a friend... God, there was no comparison.

Voices came from behind us. I didn't bother turning. I didn't want to look at them. Not yet. But I didn't have much of a choice as Russo led Warren and company past us.

Milich and Milia slowed to a stop while the others kept going. Milich turned, a sly grin on his face. "I know this must be a tough time for you, but I have to ask. I'm looking for a nice pair of green raptor boots. Your friend's still around somewhere, isn't he?"

Milia stifled a laugh. I clenched my fists to keep from killing him, but Ayana wasn't having it. She screamed in fury and launched herself at Milich. Kaden and Sydney caught her before she could get her hands on him. Russo and the others turned at the sound. Milich laughed, but Reno backhanded him across the face with his metal hand.

"Reno!" Russo stormed over. "How dare you—"

"Shut it, Russo." Reno jabbed a finger at Milich, who clutched his face in disbelief. "I am two seconds away from ripping your boy's tongue out if you don't get him in check."

Russo glowered at him. She snorted. "The headmaster will hear of this."

"Damn right she will. As soon as this is over, I'm talking to her myself."

Russo fumed, but grabbed Milich and yanked him away to their side of the field.

Reno turned to us. "Fuck strategy. I want you to wreck 'em."

Capture the flag with a five minute time-out. The idea was to encourage more strategy and less rushing in blindly. Too bad we didn't give a hot shit about strategy.

There was no cityscape in the arena today. Only hills, cliffs, rocks, and a few broken down ruins. That meant we had a clear view of their whole team on the other side of the field. My eyes found Milich's. He grinned and tapped his boots.

Dead man walking.

The siren hit and I tore down the field. I didn't know where anyone else was. I didn't care. Only two people existed in my world. Everything else was a blur.

I ran right past someone big. Katya, I think. As I did, I felt a stinging blow of something on my chest, followed by a horn. Guess I'd been eliminated.

My eyes remained on Milich. He fired a practice arrow. Caught me in the gut. Another horn.

I kept running. Another arrow. Stop blowing that fucking horn.

Milich's expression changed. I saw the exact moment he realized I was playing for keeps. He dropped his bow and reached for the sword at his belt.

It was too late for him. I was already in the air, my arm drawn back. With all the force from my sprint behind me, my fist shot forward into Milich's face. He went down and I was on him.

I hit him again. And again. And again.

My world turned red.

Chapter 56

SYDNEY

Everything happened so fast. One moment Lanei was racing down the field, the next Milia and Selena were trying in vain to pull her off Milich. Headmaster Kane, Kasia, and Caesar burst out of the control room. Russo ran their way. Reno was on the field, cutting us off.

"Stay here!" he shouted. Ayana, Kaden, and I followed his orders and watched helplessly as Reno ran to join the other instructors.

Caesar had surprising strength for a man his size. He got his arms around Lanei's waist and hauled her off Milich, hurling her to the ground behind them. She tried to scramble back to her feet. Before she could get her bearings, Russo ran up behind her and put her in a choke hold.

Kaden yanked me back before I made two running steps.

"No," he said. "Reno's right. We'll just make it worse."

Reno ran in, pressed something on his metal arm, and grabbed Russo's shoulder. Blue light flashed. Russo cried out and dropped Lanei. She and Reno started screaming at each other to the point that the headmaster had to pull them apart. Meanwhile Caesar restrained Lanei and Kasia knelt over Milich, attempting to heal whatever damage Lanei had done to his face.

It took several minutes to restore order. Milich finally regained consciousness, and although his face was a bloody mess, Kasia helped him to his feet and led him off the field. Caesar and Kane escorted Lanei away. Reno returned to us, concealing a smile, while Russo stormed back to her squad.

"You saw what Lanei just did?" Reno asked. We nodded. "Well, don't do that."

"What's going to happen to her?" I asked.

"She'll be fine. They're making her sit out the rest of the match. Same with Milich. After I explained Milich's little comment, the headmaster decided Lanei's response was 'more reasonable than the situation warranted.' Russo wasn't happy about that, but hey, fuck her." He shrugged. "One rule change. Kane doesn't want this dragging out any longer than it has to, so when you're out, you're out. Go straight up to our holding room. And I do mean go *straight* there. The headmaster told Kasia to put an end to any further disputes, and you do not want to be on the receiving end of that. Wait for the horn and kick their asses." Reno gave us a nod and took the lift to join Lanei.

"Well, with Lanei out, you're the ranking officer," Kaden said.

I nodded. Kaden stared at me. I blinked. "Oh. Me. Right."

Kaden waited. "So... plan?"

I looked down the field at Warren and company. "We need someone on defense. Ayana, you're our heavy hitter. Have Malbohr guard the flag, and stay out of sight in the rear to sneak up on them when they go for it. Kaden, we can't afford to split up. Gotta go in together and try to get one—" The horn blew. "Damn. Let's go!"

Ayana muttered the spell to summon Malbohr as she ran back to the flag. Kaden and I ducked behind a rock. I peered out to see Warren retreating to their flag. Milia vanished over the ridge on the far side. Selena approached along our side. No sign of Katya. That worried me. It should've been more difficult to lose six and a half feet of solid muscle.

"Selena?" Kaden asked.

"Selena," I confirmed.

As we moved to her location, we lost sight of all the landmarks we'd been able to see only moments before. The layout had an optical illusion to it that screwed with visibility.

Selena found us before we found her. She didn't holler any battle cry as she attacked from the shadows, sword swinging. Kaden brought his sword up in time to catch hers. She parried my staff and danced out of the way. We advanced on her, and she did a commendable job fighting us both off. But she smiled the whole time. I wish I'd understood her smile before my foot depressed the ground.

I cried out as two pieces of steel snapped shut on my leg like a bear trap, thankfully without the teeth. I took a couple deep breaths and tried to feel it out. Hurt like hell, but my leg wasn't broken. The springs had enough pressure to keep me from yanking it out, though.

Selena tried to slip past Kaden and take me out while I was immobile, but he vaulted off a boulder and placed himself between us before she could reach me.

As they fought, I worked my staff into the trap and tried to pry it open. Couldn't get good leverage from this angle...

The horn blew. I snapped my head up. Selena cursed and stamped off to their team's lift. Kaden turned back to me, and as he did something moved around the corner behind him.

"Kad—"

Too late. A club swung out from the shadow and slammed into his back. He dropped to the ground hard.

Katya didn't waste any time. She bent over him, grabbed one of his legs, and wrapped it behind her massive neck. She hooked her arms over his leg, one pressing down on his ankle, the other on his thigh. Then she stood, hauling him in the air. He hung suspended, unable to do anything but cry out as she locked the fingers of her hands together, swung his body under her, and sat down on his back. Kaden screamed as she twisted his body in ways humans were never meant to bend.

I struggled with the trap, working at it with my staff. Kaden yelled out once more and frantically tapped his hand on the ground. The horn blew. Katya stood, lifting Kaden with her as she did, and dropped him in a heap on the ground. The giant woman set her eyes on me.

With one last desperate pull, I pried the trap open enough to remove my leg. It snapped shut on the staff, locking it in place.

I left the staff and hobbled back toward our base. I had to regroup with Ayana. I quickened into as much of a run as my leg would allow. Katya wasn't fast, but at her size even a jog was damned quick. I scrambled up a hill...

And ran right into Warren and Milia.

Milia's smile was feral. "Hello, stableboy."

I tried to dodge them, but Warren got his hands on me and yanked me off my feet, slamming me into one of the rock walls. I prayed the loud *crack* was the wall giving way and not my back.

I struggled to pry his hands loose, but Warren was a hell of a lot stronger than me. No way was I going to outpower him in a fair fight, so I stopped fighting fair. I drove my boot into his balls.

Warren crumpled to the ground. I landed on my feet, but Milia was right on me. She swung her sparring sword at my head and I blocked with the only thing I had available: my forearm. My entire arm went numb as the shock of the blow tore through me. She drove a straight kick into my chest, driving me back into the wall. The back of my head smashed into the rocks. My vision blurred. Milia dropped her sword and advanced on me with a dagger. I threw a punch, but I was too disoriented to get in a good shot. She sidestepped it, grabbed my hair, and yanked my head back. She held the dagger to my throat. The horn blew.

"Next time it'll be the real thing." She let the dagger fall to the ground. I'd only managed one step back to the holding area when Milia grabbed me by the throat and, without warning, licked the side of my face. I was too shocked to react, which kept me from doing anything when she dragged me to the ground, slamming the small of my back into the point of her knee. The horn sounded again and she stepped away from me, both hands raised in the air. I groaned and looked up at Warren, Milia, and Katya standing over me.

Three on one...

Kaden and I hobbled into the holding room as fast as we could. Lanei and Reno stood at the window looking down over the field.

"You two alright?" Reno asked.

"Sore, but fine."

"Same," Kaden agreed.

"Good effort." Reno never pried his eyes from the window.

Lanei patted Kaden on the shoulder. "I'm amazed you can move. That was a hell of a hold she had you in."

Kaden waved it off. "You win move of the day for that flying punch into Milich's face."

"He deserved it."

"Damn right he did."

"How's Ayana?" I asked.

Reno pointed to the end of the field with our flag. From up here we could see the entire arena. Ayana whispered something to Malbohr, too soft for the microphones to pick up, and headed midfield to Warren and Milia.

"What's she doing?" Kaden asked. "Why isn't she sticking with Malbohr?"

"I don't know..." Reno tapped his fingers on the wooden rail.

Ayana didn't try to hide her movements. Warren and Milia saw her coming and met her head on. Katya hugged the lower wall, moving around Ayana to our team's flag.

Ayana came to a halt ten feet from Warren and Milia. She didn't look the least bit concerned, but she muttered quietly to herself. They smirked at her.

"And then there was only the gnat." Warren's voice rang tinny through the speakers, but the words were clear enough.

"You're outnumbered, little girl," Milia said. "Should've brought your demon with you."

Ayana smiled. "That's okay. I have others."

She slammed the butt of her staff into the ground, sparking a flash of... not light. Darkness. Two portals opened up beside her. Vadazach hopped out of one and landed in a fighter's stance. He twisted his hands, and a ball of flame appeared between them.

"You've met Vadazach already," Ayana said. "But I don't think I've introduced my other friend."

A creature leapt out of the second portal. It landed on all fours, sank low to the ground, and growled. Warren and Milia took a step back.

Ayana reached down and petted the creature on its skeletal head. "I'd like you to meet Mr. Drooly."

A hellhound...

I'd read about hellhounds, but seeing one in person was... unreal. It was the size of a wolf, but instead of fur it had leathery, batlike skin with bony spikes protruding from its spine. But the head... the head was nothing more than a canine skull with fiery red eyes.

And Mr. Drooly definitely drooled.

The lack of skin covering his muzzle had a lot to do with that. Saliva dripped from his open mouth to the ground below, where it sizzled into a steaming puddle in the dirt.

"What are you doing..." Reno murmured. His fingers tapped faster.

Lanei pumped her fist. "That. Is. Badass!"

I frowned. "I didn't know she could summon multiple demons at once. Kasia said—"

"She can't." Reno punched the button for the loudspeaker. "Ayana! Stand down! Pull them back immed—" Reno stopped. His voice wasn't carrying out over the arena speakers. "Dammit." He banged on the window. "Ayana! Stop!"

If Ayana heard, she gave no indication. She left her staff planted in the ground and charged. Vadazach unleashed the fireball at Milia, who swung her cape around. It caught fire. In the time it took her to toss it aside, Ayana tackled her to the ground.

Warren had Mr. Drooly to deal with.

The hellhound circled him the way a wolf stalks a small rabbit. Warren thrust his sword out. Mr. Drooly snapped his jaws and hopped aside. Warren tried another swing. The hellhound pounced at him over the blade. The big man turned his body enough that he didn't take the demon's full weight, but Mr. Drooly's claws tore through his shirt.

Katya's battle cry signaled she'd engaged Malbohr at the flag. She threw heavy punches with much greater effect than anything I'd seen hit the slime demon so far.

The whole upper section had erupted. Reno banged on the window. In the control room, Kasia shouted into the microphone to no effect as Caesar furiously flipped switches on the board. In the next holding room, Russo shouted at Headmaster Kane through the window dividing them.

On the field below, Ayana got in a few good shots before Milia threw her off. Ayana rolled with it and landed in a crouch, breathing hard. Blood dripped from her nose. Milia hadn't even hit her. Why was she...

The demons. She couldn't handle summoning three at once.

Reno ran for the door and yanked on it. It didn't budge. He pulled it again, but it wouldn't move.

Ayana's eyes flashed red. Bright red. This time, it wasn't from the moon hitting them in the right way. The light shone from within. Her chest heaved with every breath. Ayana rose to her feet.

And continued to rise.

Milia's jaw dropped as Ayana levitated. Even Vadazach looked surprised. The fireball in his hand vanished.

"Hey, boss? Boss?"

The open portals wavered. Ayana raised her hands and the black, purple, and red energy from the portals flowed back to her and swirled in the air around her.

Reno banged on the control room window. "Open the fucking doors!"

"I'm trying!" Caesar shouted back. "The controls aren't working!"

Katya slammed her shoulder into Malbohr, driving him through a stone pillar.

Warren thrashed beneath Mr. Drooly, the flat of his sword the only thing between himself and the hellhound's snapping jaws. Saliva dripped onto Warren's chest. He howled in pain as his flesh sizzled and burned.

Vadazach yelled Ayana's name, jumping repeatedly to try to grab her feet.

Milia picked up her sword. "I knew you were just another demon, you—"

Ayana thrust her hands forward. All of the energy from the portals burst forth in a beam. The shadowbolt caught Milia in the chest and sent her flying through the air. She landed in a heap twenty feet away. Even from two rooms down, Milich's scream was piercing.

Ayana's body went limp and crashed to the ground.

"Stand back!" Reno placed his metal hand on the glass, pressed a button on the side, and turned his head away. A pulse of blue energy emitted from his hand, shattering the window. He jumped onto the ledge, grabbed a banner, and slid down it to the arena floor. The window of the control room shattered and Kasia flew out to the arena. I followed Reno out the window and slid down the banner. Despite the throbbing pain in my leg, I ran to Ayana faster than I ever had in my life.

Ayana going down must've acted like a beacon for her demons. Malbohr abandoned the flag and rushed to her. Vadazach knelt by her side shaking her, pleading with her to wake up. Mr. Drooly nudged her leg. She didn't move.

As one, the three demons turned on Warren.

Malbohr and Drooly charged him as Vadazach hurled a massive wave of fire his way. Warren held up his hands in a futile attempt at defense. He didn't stand a chance.

The flames dissipated against an invisible barrier mere inches from Warren's cowering form. Kasia held the barrier as Malbohr and Drooly beat and clawed against it.

Vadazach returned to shaking Ayana. "She's not... why ain't she moving?" Confusion and worry filled the imp's voice. "Why ain't she..."

"Sydney!" Reno yelled.

I was right behind him. I slid across the ground to Ayana and placed two fingers on the side of her neck. She had a pulse, but it was weak. No obvious physical damage to heal. I'd have to figure it out as I went.

I placed my hands on her and closed my eyes.

My pendant burned hot against my chest, channeling the Light through me. But I couldn't get it into her. The magic kept hitting a wall. I focused harder, pouring more energy into her, but it just washed away.

I opened my eyes. "I can't get through." I turned to Kasia, still keeping the demons at bay. "Something's blocking me!"

"It's the demons!" Kasia yelled back. "They're draining her! She can't sustain this many at once!"

I turned to Vadazach. "Vad—"

"On it." The imp ran to Malbohr and Mr. Drooly, both still tearing at the barrier. Balls of green light formed in Vadazach's hands as he ran, and he thrust them out at the other demons. Whatever it was, it shocked the hell out of them enough to refocus their attention on him.

Vadazach shouted something in another language. It was strange hearing a plea of compassion in a demonic language. The language wasn't made for that kind of message, not even a little bit. But it worked. They understood.

Vadazach led the other two back to us. "You a summoner, kid?"

I shook my head. "No. I can't open a portal."

He sighed. "That's what I was afraid of. Gotta do this the hard way." He barked an order. Malbohr nodded and knelt. Drooly growled, but complied. "Alright. You gotta kill us."

"What? I can't! You're her friends, she'd—"

"Relax. It just sends us back to our dimension. Won't be back for a while, but we'll live." The imp shrugged. "Manner of speaking."

"I'll do it." Reno drew his sword.

Vadazach nodded. "Tell her she can come visit until we're strong enough to return."

"I'll tell her. Don't worry."

"Thanks, bro." The imp cringed. "Can you, uh, do them first? It hurts like a bitch and I gotta build up a little courage."

Reno knelt beside Mr. Drooly and whispered something in his ear. He plunged the sword into the side of the hellhound's neck. The demon collapsed onto the ground and melted into a pile of goo.

Reno shouted an order to Kasia. She nodded. The air grew cold around us as the gem on her staff glowed light blue. All over the arena, the air shimmered. Then, in one loud burst, the energy shot into Malbohr in one concentrated burst, freezing the slime demon. Reno clicked the button on the side of his metal hand, placed it on the back of Malbohr's head, and shattered him into a thousand pieces.

Vadazach tugged on my sleeve. "Take care of her for me 'til I'm back, will ya?"

I nodded. "I will."

He heaved a sigh and dropped to his knees in front of Reno, sticking out his neck. "Make it quick, will—"

Reno brought the sword down fast, slicing off the imp's head. "Sydney, hurry."

I placed my hands on Ayana again and closed my eyes. The wall was gone. As the Light surged into her, it told me what was wrong. Trying to maintain more than one demon in our realm pulled directly from her life force. Summoning three demons at once was killing her.

The Light returned that life to her, and I was its conduit. I felt it enter me, and I felt it leave me. Somewhere in the back of my head, a voice told me to open my eyes. I did.

Everyone was staring at me. Lanei and Kaden stood with Reno and Kasia. Why were they were all looking at me like that? And why was it so bright?

I looked up. A beam of light shone straight down onto me. That was strange. The Arena had a roof. Why was sunlight pouring through like that?

The light vanished. I was done.

Ayana groaned. I put a hand under her back and lifted her into a sitting position. Her eyes fluttered open. She smiled.

"My hero..."

She curled up into a ball and fell asleep.

I smiled and held her closer. If I could be a hero in the eyes of someone as amazing and powerful as her, maybe there was hope for me yet.

Chapter 57

SYDNEY

I visited Ayana in the infirmary the next day. I meant to visit sooner, but after the Games I collapsed onto my bed and slept for a solid twenty-four hours. I only woke up when I did because Kaden wanted to make sure I was alive.

I poked my head into her room. She was sitting up in bed reading another western novel with a shirtless guy on the cover. I sneaked a peak at the title: *The Rose of the Loneliest River*. She looked paler than normal, but her eyes weren't doing the big red light show thing, so I took that as a good sign.

"Hey." My voice was hoarse. It didn't crack. It was hoarse.

She looked up from her book and brightened. "Hi!"

I sat in the chair by her bed. It was still warm. "How're you feeling?"

"Better. Good. Much gooder." She frowned. "I swear I was speaking fine a minute ago."

I laughed. "Then you're one up on me. I've been out cold since yesterday."

"Yeah, Kaden said. I told him to make sure you weren't dead."

Guess that explained it.

"That was really impressive what you pulled off yesterday."

"More like really stupid." Ayana set her book aside. "I knew better. I really did. But after Tenkou..."

I nodded. "Pretty sure Lanei was thinking the same thing."

"No..." Ayana shook her head. "I lost control. I never should have summoned that many at once. Now, it'll be weeks before they can visit again. Well, less for Malbohr. Slime demons reform quick, but..." She sighed. "I feel bad. I don't like when they get hurt."

"They don't like it when you get hurt either," I said. "Vadazach was really worried."

That made her smile. "See? He tries to act like such a tough guy, but he's really a big softy inside. Just don't tell him I said that."

"I won't." I chewed on the inside of my lip. "I didn't know you could... you know... that other stuff."

"That makes two of us."

"Seriously?"

"The last thing I remember was punching Milia. I think I blacked out for everything else." Ayana giggled. "Doesn't that just figure? Turns out I can levitate and shoot big balls of shadow void, and I don't even know how to do it!" She shrugged. "Kasia's going to work with me, see if I can control it. I won't have my demons for a while, so that'll give me something to focus on until then."

"Milia... is she...?"

Ayana rolled her eyes. "She's okay. I mean, she's not, she's a horrible meanie of a person, but she didn't break anything. I just knocked her out cold and gave her one more reason to hate me." A mischievous look crossed her face. "You should see Milich. He has to wear this protective mask from where Lanei shattered his nose. It's so awesome! I mean, not for him, but it is. Like, really awesome."

I took her hand. "I'm glad you're okay."

She squeezed mine back. "Me too. That you are, I mean." She blushed. "Thank you. For healing me. That was nice of you."

"I mean, I wasn't *not* going to."

"I know, I just... can I tell you a secret?"

"Of course."

She leaned in closer. "I'm glad it was you."

I smiled. "Me too."

I lifted my hand to her cheek and brushed my thumb across it. Ayana closed her eyes and nuzzled into my hand.

I leaned in and kissed her.

Sparks flew.

Not in a metaphorical way like in one of Ayana's books. But, like, actual sparks tingled our lips. Maybe it was leftover magic from healing her. Maybe something else. We probably should've been alarmed, but that'd mean stopping. Besides... it felt kinda nice.

A tendril of the magic clung between our lips for a second after the kiss ended. I opened my eyes.

Ayana's cheeks flushed, bringing color back to her skin. She bit her lower lip, one sharp canine pressing in. It made her look cuter.

"Hi..."

"Hi..."

She smiled. "Did you feel..."

"Yeah..."

"Do you know..."

"Not a clue..."

"Do you, um... do you want to see if it happens again?"

"God yes."

Ayana grabbed my shirt and pulled me in for another kiss.

There was definitely magic between our lips.

Chapter 58

/LANEI

I had no idea what to expect when Reno summoned me to Headmaster Kane's office. Even though he'd been cool to me the last few days, part of me still worried they were going to lock me up anyway. Despite the dozens of witnesses who could attest I never left the ballroom after Tenkou, the fact that he was killed by my sword still left a big question mark hanging over my head.

Reno opened the door to the headmaster's office and my heart sank. Darian Rankin was there. This was it. He was going to take me in. I considered bolting, making a run for it while I had a chance. A head poked around one of the chairs.

Sydney.

I breathed a sigh of relief.

"Lanei." Headmaster Kane motioned for me to take the seat beside Sydney. "Thank you for joining us."

"Wouldn't miss it," I muttered.

"Sydney tells us he has gone against his orders and informed you of his mission here at Petrichor."

I looked at Sydney. He nodded. "Yes. Yes, that's correct."

"He also tells us you were all too eager to assist him in his investigation."

"That is... also correct."

Kane steepled her fingers and leaned over her desk. "Tell me why."

"Oh, so he didn't tell you that, too?"

Kane gave me a hard look. Right. Not the time for sarcasm.

So I gave her the whole story. Everything I'd seen back home. My father's reactions. How I couldn't stand by and do nothing.

"So you left," she said.

I sighed. "Couldn't make a hell of a lot of difference there as the reject princess. I'd heard what Ricardo created here and... it seemed like a good place to start."

Kane stared me down with those unflinching eyes. "What are your opinions of Warren, Milia, and Milich?"

"They're a bunch of racist shits."

"I am inclined to agree," Kane said. "However, they were part of your father's price to allow you to come here."

That knocked the wind out of me. If they were responsible for what happened to Tenkou and Jeyla... then I was, too. I shrunk back in my seat. "That... really sucks."

"Yes. It does." Kane narrowed her eyes. "Is it possible for you to hide your disdain for them?"

I raised an eyebrow. "Why would I want to do that?"

"I'm fairly certain you wouldn't. But can you do it regardless?"

"Sure, I guess. But... remember how I just tried to break Milich's face? Because I'm pretty sure he does."

"It won't be easy. I have no illusions of that. However, despite your previous altercations, I believe you may be our best bet to get in with them and find out for certain if they are involved."

My eyes widened. "Wait. You actually want my help?"

"Yes."

"You... trust me enough for that?"

Kane turned her eyes to Darian.

"I've known Sydney since the day he was born," he said. "I've known his parents much longer. I trust him. If he says you're cool, then I'll put my reservations aside and trust his judgment."

Headmaster Kane spread her hands on her desk. "Instructor Windamier has also vouched for your character. I found that odd, as you are not in her class. But you have apparently made an impression. Fortunately for you, I hold her opinion in high esteem."

"Alright, so I'm in," I said. "What do you need me to do?"

"You are going to have to play a part. You will need to convince Warren and the Levesque twins you have had a change of heart regarding non-humans. It will have to be public. You're not convincing just them. You have to convince everyone, students and instructors alike. Everyone who may be involved needs to believe you are one of them."

I swallowed hard. "When you say convince them..."

"I mean that in the eyes of everyone at this school, you are going to have to become what you hate."

Fuck.

"Ayana and Nakato... They're my friends. You mean I'll have to..." I didn't even want to finish that thought. It'd taken me so long to allow people inside my life, people I could call friends. Now Kane was telling me I'd have to treat them with the same malice as the other Maldovans?

Kane nodded. "You will have to convince them as well."

"Can't I just tell them what's going on?" I asked. "You know for a fact Ayana's not involved in this shit, and there's like a zero percent chance Nakato's part of it."

Reno shook his head. "No. I don't want Ayana involved. Period."

"Agreed," Kane said. "And you will not tell Nakato. Ayana is the only student outside this room who we know we can trust, but she will have no part in this."

"But Nakato's part elf!" I blurted. "How can you possibly think she'd get involved with the Children of goddamn Omek?"

"It is unlikely; however, we cannot risk that she would say the wrong thing to someone and let on that she knows what you and Sydney are doing. The fewer people who know, the better."

I rubbed my eyes. She was asking me to give up the first friends I'd had since... ever. Everyone except Sydney was going to think I was a horrible human being. And there was no guarantee they'd forgive me once this was all over.

I wanted to say no. I wanted to refuse. I wanted no part of this.

But more than all that, I wanted to kill the son of a bitch who'd murdered Tenkou.

"Can you at least tell Kasia?" I asked. "I don't... I don't want her to think her faith in me was misplaced."

The headmaster nodded. "I will tell her."

"Thanks." I took a breath. "So what's the first step?"

"In light of the recent murders, we have sent out letters to all students' parents inviting them to visit the school. We want them to feel that their children are safe." Kane braced her elbows on her desk and steepled her fingers again. "Before you can convince the students and faculty that you hate non-humans, you must first convince your father."

Chapter 59

/LANEI

Making it through Tenkou's memorial service had been easy compared to this.

There'd been distance there. I had Sydney to lean on. Now I only had Reno with me, and he wasn't exactly my ideal support system. For him to be the only person by my side to meet Tenkou's family... I felt about two feet tall.

"Absolutely not," Tenkou's father said. "I will not allow you to defile my son's memory in such a way."

"I understand this is asking a lot," Reno said. "But we might not get another opportunity like this."

Tenkou's mother sneered. "My son is dead and you speak of opportunity."

"An opportunity to catch your son's killer," Reno clarified. "I understand that—"

Tenkou's father slammed his fist into Reno's desk. The wood cracked. "You understand nothing. If it were your sister, would you permit such blatant disrespect?"

Reno didn't answer immediately. Finally, he shook his head. "No. I wouldn't. I'm asking you to be better people than me."

"Tenkou was supposed to be safe here." His mother glowered. "Your headmaster assured us he would be in no immediate danger. Was that a lie?"

"It was no lie. We were wrong. I can apologize a thousand times for being wrong, but apologies won't bring him back. We will bring his murderer to justice. I am asking for your help."

"You ask for more than help. You ask for dishonor."

Reno's job was to do the talking. Mine was just to be here so they could see me. But I'd spent my whole life being seen and not heard. I was done with that life.

I cleared my throat. "I don't like this any more than you. Tenkou was my friend. What they're asking me to do is wrong. But I want to catch the son of a bitch who did this. I promise, no one will think less of your son. The only person I will dishonor is myself."

The weight of the fifth pair of eyes bore down on me. Tenkou's older sister, Saraya, had not spoken. She'd stared a hole through me the entire time. Saraya was nearly as large as her brother. While her parents dressed plainly in simple rawhide, Saraya wore a suit of leather armor adorned with crude medals that looked like they'd been hammered out of bronze chunks.

"Tenkou wrote of you." Her voice was even, measured. "He said you were a fountain bubbling with rage. Then he learned who you were. The princess." She leaned forward. "The *Greyton*."

Wonderful. My dead friend's sister was trying to intimidate me. I wasn't going to play along, not even for her sake. "I'm more than that. I am more than my father."

"Tenkou agreed. He trusted you. He believed you were meant to do great things. Now he is dead." Saraya pushed herself out of her seat. She towered over me. "Tell me why I should place that same trust in you."

I rose from my chair. Reno placed a hand on my arm, but I ignored it. I brought my face as close to hers as I could. "I came to this school because I believed it was the right thing to do. I wanted to change the world for the better. All that went out the window the minute they killed your brother. They made this personal by killing him with *my* sword. So right now, I don't give a damn about doing what's right. I don't care if I have to drag my own name through the mud to get to Tenkou's killer. Unlike Reno and Kane, I'm not looking for justice. I want vengeance."

Saraya stared down at me. She smiled. "Perhaps he was right. Perhaps you and I do have much in common." She pulled back and looked to her parents. "Let her do it."

Her father's eyes widened. "Saraya!"

"Tenkou desired to prove throldkin could thrive outside Wismore. He believed other cultures would accept us as equals and not just hired thugs. Perhaps he was wrong. But if he was right, I would see it with my own eyes."

"No!" Her mother shoved her chair back and got to her feet. "I will not stand by and watch my son's memory spat upon in this way."

"Then go home," Saraya said. "Take Tenkou with you. Return him to the earth. I will stay and do what needs to be done." She looked at me. "And for my brother's sake, so will you."

Chapter 60

SYDNEY

Meeting Kaden's family was all sorts of eye opening.

They arrived an hour before the festivities began. Punctual and early to rise, check.

His parents walked in the door wearing full suits of armor, covered with what looked like every medal or commendation they'd ever earned. His younger sister, Sari, was at a gawky early teen stage but looked like she was in princess training school. Has to make a grand first impression, check.

When they spotted Kaden and Devi, they sauntered straight to Devi and gushed over her accomplishments. Middle child syndrome, check.

Kaden's jaw quivered for a moment, until Sari leapt into his arms and fired off a series of questions. Kaden laughed, forgetting all about being ignored by his parents, and handed her a small box. She pulled out a small unicorn figurine and squealed with glee. Big heart, check.

Kaden's parents finally acknowledged him once Vigo and his mother came over to greet them. In fact, Vigo got a warmer welcome than Kaden had. Kaden's mother embraced Vigo like a second son. Sari raised her arms over her head and Vigo hoisted her in the air, sitting her on his shoulder.

After they'd chatted for a few minutes, Kaden waved me over.

"Sydney, these are my parents, Nerissa and Prabhat Ashworth, and my little sister, Sari Ashworth."

"Pleased to meet you." I tipped my hat to them.

"Ah, Sydney!" Nerissa bowed. "We have heard so much about you. Kaden says you ride a raptor! We really must see this."

"Oh, sure. My father trains them. I can introduce you—"

"How grand!" Prabhat said. "Humans with raptors. There really are no limits anymore, are there?"

"I like your eyes," Sari said, blushing. "The purple means you do magic, right?"

I smiled. "Sort of. It means I'm part elf. But yeah, I can do some magic."

The girl's eyes lit up. She was probably thirteen, old enough to have seen some magic, especially in Araspia. "Can I see it?"

"Sari!" Her mother shook her head. "You can't go around asking people to show you their magic. It isn't proper." She turned to me. "My apologies. She has the wildest fascination with magic."

"No, it's alright." I conjured a ball of light and flew it around her head a few times. She clapped her hands with glee. The little trick wasn't much, but it was nice to feel appreciated.

As more families trickled in, I excused myself and took a seat on a bench where I had a good view of the room. Until my parents arrived, this was a prime opportunity to see if I could glean something useful from the other students' interactions with their families.

Headmaster Kane greeted Nakato's mother like an old friend. That didn't come as a surprise. As Kialen nobility, she would've known anyone who was anyone over there. According to Lanei, Nakato's father was a famous actor, which explained all the heads he was turning. Apparently he was good, but as I'd never seen a play in my life, I'd have to take her word for it.

For all her glowering, moodiness, and piercings, I was surprised to see Robia's father arrive wearing the vestments of an Orynistic priest. He greeted her with a large smile and an even larger hug, which she was quick to break. Guess it didn't fit the tough girl persona. She dragged her father over to meet Caesar, who lavished her with seemingly endless praise.

There was no mistaking Warren's parents when they walked in. His father wore the armor of a Maldovan knight, although I'd never seen a knight his size. He had to be near seven feet tall, and, like Warren, more closely resembled a brick wall than a human being. His mother looked to be the source of her son's nasty disposition. She had the face of someone who'd scowled too much as a child and her face figured it'd be easier to freeze that way.

Warren's father raised a hand and a servant stepped forward with a large package. Warren leaned in, gave him orders, and passed him a key. The servant nodded and left. Interesting...

I did a double take when Anji's parents arrived. Both wore colorful robes in the traditional style of Rainess, but... they were human. Both of them. I squinted to get a better look, but there was no mistaking it. That didn't make sense, though. Anji was a full on half-elf. Er, half-on elf. Half an elf? I shook my head. Lineage was weird.

"His mother left when he was little."

I jumped at Ayana's voice.

"Hi. Hey. What?"

She sat beside me, bumping her hip against mine. "That's his stepmom. His biological mom was an elf. She left for Ilyn Themar when he was a baby."

"Oh. I didn't know that."

Ayana nodded. "We've got that in common. I think. I mean, I don't remember my dad. He probably ran away, too." She shrugged. "A lot of elves seem to do that."

I took her hand. "What about people who are only a little bit elvish? Do they run away?"

"Everybody runs from something." Ayana smiled and squeezed my hand. "I don't think you'll run very far, though."

"Oh? Why's that?"

"Because Mr. Drooly's faster than you."

I was about eighty percent sure she was joking. She giggled and kissed my cheek. Okay, eighty-five percent.

"Sydney!"

My parents waved at me from across the room. Just as Warren's parents were easy to spot, so were mine. After all, who else but the kid from Laredo would have parents walk into a ballroom wearing leather dusters and cowboy hats? My dad wore a vest, though, so points for effort.

I grabbed Ayana's hand. "Come on."

She held back. "Are you sure? You haven't seen them in months. Don't you want to catch up?"

"Well, sure. But I also want you to meet them because, um..." Words, Sydney. Use your words. "BecauseIkindalikeyouthat'sall."

Ayana's cheeks flushed. "I kinda like you, too."

I led Ayana over to my parents, and my dad wrapped me in a bear hug, giving my back a good crack in the process. Mom followed up with a regular hug like a normal person who didn't want to cripple her son.

Mom held me out at arm's length and smiled. The beginnings of tears shimmered in her eyes. "We've missed you."

"I've missed you, too. There's so much I need to tell you that I couldn't put in my letters, but, uh, first..." I took Ayana's hand and she stepped forward. "This is Ayana. She's... uh..." I froze. I didn't know what we were. I thought *maybe* we were a something. We'd certainly been *acting* like a thing since the Games. But I was now keenly aware we'd never used the B word or the G word or the R word. I looked to Ayana for silent clarification.

She must've read my mind. "I'm Sydney's—" She halted as Reno approached us. "*Teammate!*" she said, too emphatically. "I'm his teammate. We're teammates. On the same team. And mates." Her eyes widened. "Not that kind of mates! Friends. We're friends. Friendmates." She bit her lower lip and raised her eyebrows as if to ask how convincing that'd been. So she hadn't told Reno yet. That explained why I was still breathing.

My father raised an eyebrow and mouthed, "friendmates?"

I shook my head.

Reno gave us a strange look as he extended a hand to my parents. "Reno Isale. Pleasure to meet you."

"Brother!" Ayana blurted. "Reno is my brother." She looked at me and forced a smile, showing off her teeth. Between the two of us, we could almost form a complete sentence.

"Yes..." Reno narrowed his eyes at Ayana before returning his gaze to my parents. "Sydney's been an invaluable addition to the work we're doing here. Thank you for sending him to us."

"We're glad he's able to help," Mom replied. "Darian's kept us posted on his progress. He speaks highly of you, too."

Reno snorted. "Hell, he'd better after all I've done for him."

That made Dad laugh. He might've kept laughing if Russo hadn't picked that moment to walk past.

"Don't give them your good hand," she said. "You might not get it back."

Reno scowled. "Bite me, Adelaide."

Unfortunately, that made Russo stop, which opened up a conversation I sure didn't want.

"Far be it from me to warn you before you make a decision you'll regret." She sniffed in derision. "I merely wasn't certain if you'd read the boy's file. You can read, can't you?"

"I know sign language, too. Want to see?" He raised his metal hand and extended the middle finger.

Ayana stifled a laugh. My father didn't bother stifling his.

Russo's cheeks burned red. She brushed the side of her nose with her thumb and raised a shaky index finger at Reno. "Don't test me, Isale." She spun on my parents. "Celeste and Mathiu Winter, at long last. I don't suppose you recognize me?"

Mom didn't flinch from Russo's steely glare. "I've seen a lot of faces in my time. Ain't nothin' remarkable about yours."

"The Celestial Riders, indeed." Russo snorted. "This may be a foreign concept to you, but some of us were always on the right side of the law. Whatever you may claim to be now, I know who you truly are. And I know what your son is made of."

"I know who I am. I know what I've done." Mom stepped up to Russo, forcing her back a step. "I also know you struck my son."

"Your son—"

Mom put her finger to Russo's lips. "This ain't a conversation we're having here. This is me talking and you listening."

Shit. I knew that tone. "Mom—"

She ignored me. "My sins are my own. You got a problem, you come see me. But if you touch my son again, you can be damn sure I'll come see you."

"Are you threatening to put a knife in my back?"

"Nah," Mom said. "I want you to know it's me before I break your neck."

"Once a thug, always a thug." Russo shook her head and left the room, shouldering Reno on her way out.

After several moments of awkward silence, Ayana leaned into me. "I like your mom."

My dad laughed. "You and me both."

A commotion bubbled through the crowd as Sayid Levenheit entered with his son. The man cut a striking figure, that was for sure. He wore a suit of golden plate armor with a flowing green silk cape slung over his back. The golden sword that hung on his side was inlaid with rubies and emeralds. Like Yasir, Sayid was supernaturally good-looking. They had the same long black hair and chiseled features. It was pretty clear Yasir was going to age well.

Sayid smiled and nodded to all the gawkers as he walked through the crowd. He did a double take when he got to us. His smile faltered then turned into an amused grin.

"If I didn't know any better, I would swear I was looking at Celeste and Mathiu Winter." Sayid tapped a finger to his lips. "But surely I must be mistaken. I am mistaken, am I not?"

My mom grinned, already moving past her altercation with Russo. "Oh, absolutely mistaken, Sayid. He is mistaken, ain't he hon?"

"Oh yeah, definitely mistaken," Dad agreed. "Can't think of a single reason they'd ever come to a place like this."

Sayid laughed. "Well, that is a relief. But if you do see them, can you please remind them we have unfinished business we really must attend to?"

"Happy to pass the word along," Mom said. "On the off chance we see them, of course."

"Of course." Sayid bowed to my parents and headed off toward Instructor Lightfellow. Yasir and I exchanged one hell of a confused look. I guess there were still a few things from my parents' past I didn't know.

My father deftly changed the subject before I had a chance to ask. "So, Ayana, Sydney says you summon demons. What are they like?"

That got Ayana excited and she went into a lengthy and animated explanation about each of her demons, their personalities, favorite foods, you name it. I would've listened to her talk for hours, but we were interrupted by the sound of... something. It sounded like a tornado, and it was getting louder. People crowded near the window and stared up in awe. I moved closer to get a better look.

Awe didn't begin to describe it.

An enormous airship approached the school. I'd read about them, but words couldn't do them justice. Something so massive defying all laws of nature felt unreal. But there it was... And against the black hull of the ship was a large silver dragon. The sigil of Maldova.

Lord Viktor Greyton had arrived.

ʎLANEI

My father sure knew how to make an entrance. He could've just as easily taken the train here. Hell, he had his own private train specifically so he wouldn't have to associate with commoners. But he wanted to make an impression, and few people outside Maldova had ever seen an airship in person. He'd christened his first less than five years ago, but he'd been working toward them my whole life. What better way to show humanity's progress than by conquering the skies? Whatever else may be said of him, there was no denying my father was a scientific genius.

I shifted uncomfortably in a stranger's skin. Today I'd found myself in the unusual position of fretting over what to wear. Clothing made a statement in Maldova, and nobody knew that better than the princess who'd spent her life refusing to wear dresses. So today I wore one. But there was a balance to attain. If I went full on pretty princess, my father would know something was up. Even if I'd had a change of heart, that would've been too far out of character for me. I had no desire to show off Milia levels of skin, so I went with a brown high-low skirt over black leggings with a brown corset and white blouse. I'd worn a dress to the ball, but that was for me. This... was not me. But I guess that was the point. I was going to have to be a whole lot of "not me" for the foreseeable future.

The ship's motors died down and a ramp lowered from the deck. And there he was. My father. Lord Viktor Greyton.

Age hadn't affected him as much as he deserved. He was in good shape, but it was all for vanity's sake. He'd never trained as a knight. He believed fighting should be left to those less than royalty. As far as I knew, the only fighting he'd ever done had been with his older brothers when he was a teenager. They'd been trained knights and felt it was their duty to make a knight out of him as well, for how could one be a prince without first being a knight? My father disagreed.

I had no uncles.

The saving grace of my relationship with my father was that I looked nothing like him. I'd gotten my mother's brown skin, only slightly lightened by his pale complexion. I had brown eyes to his blue. My face had none of his hard angles. The only thing we had in common was our black hair, although his was cut short and flecked with gray, while mine was long and wavy. I dyed the blue streak in mine for a reason. I needed the separation.

My father made his way down the ramp flanked by knights. Ian Pryce stood on his left, unpleasant as ever. And to my father's right, Aldric Levesque... Milia and Milich's father. It was impossible to look at that man and not see a cruel piece of shit. Some people had a face you just wanted to punch. With the Levesques, it was hereditary.

I met my father at the base of the ramp and greeted him with my best curtsy. "Father." A hug would have been too much. My father wasn't the hugging type.

He gave me an appraising look. No doubt Sir Ian had told him about our encounter. I'd prepared an explanation for when that inevitably came up. I'd prepared explanations for every possible conversation I could anticipate. It was going to come down to how well I acted the part.

"Lana," he said. "You almost look your role."

"It's a recent change." I blinked slowly. "I've learned a few things in my time here."

"I find that surprising, what with Aguilar's involvement."

I smiled. "On the contrary. It's been an eye opening experience."

"In what way?"

"I now see what this place is. How they view me. How they view us."

"Us?"

"Greytons. Maldovans." I crossed my arms. "I was surprised to hear you were coming. I didn't think you wanted anything to do with this place."

"For once you're correct. However, I have been hearing disturbing reports and thought it best to come in person and make sure you didn't embarrass me further."

Breathe... breathe...

I bit back my retort. "You are referring to Sir Ian."

"Among other things, but yes, why don't we start there?"

This turned into an interrogation awfully fast. "If you had told me you were sending knights to the city, I wouldn't have gotten curious and followed them."

"Did you attack them out of curiosity as well?"

"I attacked them for their insolence." That part was true enough. I glared at Sir Ian. "Or did you not tell my father you dared to defy my orders?"

Ian glowered. "I had my own orders."

"Did those orders involve blowing my cover?" I asked. "My identity was supposed to remain a secret while I was here. So you either defied that order or you were never privy to it in the first place. If the latter, perhaps you should reconsider how highly you consider yourself to be in my father's trust."

"I—"

"Will apologize at once," I demanded. "Or perhaps you'd like to find a new line of work? I'm sure we can find a job for you in the sewers."

I raised my eyebrows and waited. I knew my father. He got off on demeaning and humiliating those beneath him. He rarely did so with a high ranking knight like Sir Ian, but showing I had the balls to do so had to work in my favor. I could feel the smile crawl up my father's face as the anger rose in Ian's.

"She does have a point, Ian. One way or another, you disobeyed an order."

Ian gritted his teeth, but his lord had spoken. "I apologize, Princess."

"For?" I had no problem milking this.

He narrowed his eyes. "For my insolence."

"Good. Now thank me."

"Why in god's name would I thank you?"

"For not taking your head off your shoulders." I stepped up to Ian and looked him over. "Because let's face it. We both know I could."

"Thank you, Princess," he deadpanned. "Your mercy is beyond measure."

"Oh, it's not mercy. I merely have no use for your head." I smiled at him. "At this time." I turned back to my father. "Shall I show you the grounds, father?"

"I have no interest in seeing the whole of this dump. Let's go in and get this over with. I have business to attend to."

I nodded and led the way. Aldric stepped in pace beside me.

"Perhaps you could clear something up for me, Princess." He spoke slowly, lengthening his words in unnatural places. "My children tell me you have been most inhospitable toward them. Do they exaggerate?"

"They do not. Perhaps you should have told them not to antagonize their fucking princess."

"They did not know who you were."

"And what was their excuse once they did? Why did they not beg my forgiveness?"

"Milia is quite headstrong."

"She's a stubborn bitch," I corrected. "She and I have that in common."

Aldric laughed. "Yes, I suppose that is true. But was it necessary to take your anger out on Milich's face? He doesn't have his sister's intellect. He needs his good looks intact." Aldric didn't seem angry or upset about my altercations with his children. Either he knew his place better than Sir Ian or he had remarkable objectivity.

"Milich brought it on himself." I shrugged. "Although his appearance may be slightly damaged at present, I too have appearances to maintain. In case you were not aware, there have been two murders here, and I am the prime suspect in both. If I had not responded as I did, people would have been suspicious. I cannot afford that."

Aldric smiled. "As I said, he is not as smart as his sister."

No shit. It's what made Milia so much more dangerous.

"Sir Aldric, I am afraid your children and I got off on the wrong foot. However, as you have seen, I am not one to merely brush insults aside. My father, your king, did not raise me to be so weak. That said, I have enough enemies outside of Maldova. I would prefer not to have them within the kingdom as well."

He nodded. "I understand, Princess."

We arrived at the doors to the ballroom. As I prepared to open them, my father placed a hand on my shoulder and pulled me back. Aldric and Ian stepped forward and threw the doors open. A pair of trumpeters in my father's retinue blared out an obnoxiously loud tune that brought everything inside to a halt. My father stepped past me and led me into the ballroom.

Once again, I found myself in the unenviable position of having all eyes on me. Warren and his parents pushed forward, eager for the chance to kneel before their lord. Milia and Milich sauntered into place beside them. The protective mask on Milich's face made him look significantly less pretty than usual. Katya and Selena stood with their families, one fist over their hearts in Ravenstone's salute.

A gorgeous middle aged knight who could only be Sayid Levenheit snapped his heels together and saluted; Yasir followed suit. I rolled my eyes and looked past them, but... they weren't saluting my father. Their eyes were fixed on me. I hid a smile. That's one way to show knightly respect while still working in a little defiance.

I looked for the rest of my team, finally spotting Kaden and his family. Kaden smiled, but looked uneasy. Araspian Knights or not, his family apparently wasn't bound to the same code of honor as Sayid. They folded their arms and stared daggers at me and my father.

But if looks could kill, Vigo and his mother would have been locked up on sight. Vigo's mother didn't look like a warrior, but I was sure that if Vigo hadn't been holding her wrist she would have attempted to exact revenge for her husband's death. Sir Ian must have seen it as well. He held his position between them and my father.

Sydney, Ayana, and Reno stood with the only two people in the world who could possibly have been Sydney's parents. They looked nice. From what Sydney had told me, we would've gotten along great. But here I was about to wreck my shot at a decent first impression.

Sydney gave me a reassuring smile and a nod, but we both knew it wasn't going to be okay. Ayana smiled and waved, eyes wide in awe of the spectacle my father presented. Even with all she'd heard about him, she reserved judgment. She still believed the best in people when she looked at them. I was going to miss that the most.

My father surveyed the room. He took his time. Even if this wasn't his kingdom, he held the authority here. Nobody would move or speak until he gave them leave to do so. It was a powerplay, one I'd seen him use countless times. He enjoyed it. He relished it.

And this was the first time I'd ever seen someone upstage him.

"Viktor!" Ricardo Aguilar stepped out from behind Nakato's family and strode forward to greet my father.

My father's lip curled. "That's Lord Greyton to you, Aguilar."

"But we go back so far, *Viktor*," Ricardo said. "We weren't always lords, the two of us."

"I was a lord long before my parents died. I still question whether you qualify."

"My people seem to think so. That must count for something."

"Less than you think." My father narrowed his eyes. To the rest of the room, he said, "You may continue." Conversations slowly picked back up, more to cover the awkward silence than any real desire to talk. My father only liked the spotlight when he was in control, and his control of this situation had been called into question. "Aldric, you may see to your children."

"My lord." Aldric bowed deeply and strode over to Milia and Milich.

"I trust you are aware of the situation your daughter is in," Ricardo said. "I say 'trust' because I've received no reply to my letters about our investigation."

"Your accusations warrant no reply."

"We have made no accusations. Merely investigations."

"Investigating the princess of a neighboring kingdom for murder is a fine way to wind up with an army on your doorstep."

"If she is innocent, there will be no need for that."

"My daughter is a princess. That places her above reproach of any foreign power."

"Your daughter is the prime suspect in one murder and a possible accomplice in a second. You should not be so dismissive of the situation."

"Nor should you so casually use words such as 'suspect' and 'accomplice' when describing a member of the royal family."

Ricardo smiled. "You haven't changed, Viktor. It's no wonder your daughter is so arrogant and entitled. Unlike you, however, she has actually proven herself to be a fine warrior. One of the best we have, in fact. She has certainly exceeded my expectations, given the stock she comes from."

"There is more to ruling than swinging a sword."

"Like a charming personality?" Ricardo asked. "Lanei takes after you there as well."

My father scowled. "Her name is Lana. There is no more need for false names."

"Only false faces."

"Careful, Aguilar. You would be a fool to believe you are safe just because we are inside your little school."

"You're right. That *would* make me a fool."

I'd been silent long enough. "I wonder what would be more foolish: Angering the ruler of a kingdom with a substantially larger army than yours, or angering a warrior who could kill you before your guards realized you were in danger."

Ricardo turned his gaze to me. "Is that a threat?"

"Oh, no, of course not. That would make *me* a fool. I'm far too smart for that. Just ask your instructors."

"I have. Their words were not encouraging when it came to how you use that intellect." He shook his head. "I'd hoped there would be more of your mother in you. It seems you only inherited her looks."

I fed him that line earlier. Even knowing it was coming, it hurt. But the smirk that played on my father's face told me I'd made the right call. If he still held any warmth in his heart for my mother, it was buried deep.

"Perfect," I said. "I'm told that was her best quality."

My father allowed himself a laugh. As much as it made me want to hit him, I'd brought it on myself. This was what I—

"Murderer!" Saraya's voice echoed through the ballroom. Time for the main event...

I turned to face the throldkin warrior as she pushed through the crowd. We were both unarmed. The drawing of blades would lead to others getting involved, and I didn't want my father's knights to jump in and stab her. Or me. No telling what orders he gave them before they arrived.

"I did not murder your brother, *raptor*," I called back. "Go spread your lies somewhere else."

"It was your sword that killed him. You are as much to blame as the one who stabbed him."

"If you believe that, throldkin really are as dumb as they say." I tried desperately not to notice Ayana in my periphery. "Go back to your jungle and leave me be."

Saraya turned her eyes to the knights who flanked my father. "Or what? You'll sic these cowards on me?"

I got in her face as best I could. "I won't need them. But you already knew that. I'm sure your brother told you I'm a much better fighter than he was."

She didn't miss a beat. She hauled me off the ground and threw me halfway across the room. Her throw was perfect. I rolled with it and slid into a crouch. The sound of steel cut through the room as my father's knights drew their blades, but Saraya stalked after me, staying out of their reach. The knights were there to protect my father, not me. As long as I never appeared to be in mortal danger, my father was unlikely to have them intervene. Even that was a big maybe.

I rolled out of Saraya's reach as she made another grab for me. I swung my leg around, catching her in the back of the knee. She staggered forward, but didn't go down. I jumped on her back, wrapped an arm around her throat, and dropped all my weight. I used her momentum to roll her onto her stomach. I wrenched back, my arm still locked around her neck. Any second now...

Right on cue, Sydney hauled me off Saraya and pulled me to my feet.

"The hell are you doing?" he yelled.

"Stay out of this!" I tried to push past him as Saraya got to her feet, but Sydney blocked my path. "You do *not* want to be in my way right now, purple eyes."

I made another move for Saraya. Sydney pressed his arm against my shoulder to stop me. I took a breath.

Kasia can fix it... Kasia can fix it...

I grabbed Sydney's arm, twisted it around so his elbow faced me, and thrust my palm straight into it.

Sydney screamed as his arm snapped.

It was his idea.

Kasia can fix it...

I didn't want to do it.

Kasia can fix it...

His scream was real and ripped at my guts.

How can I ever fix this mess?

I shoved Sydney away and faced Saraya. Reno struggled to hold her at bay as she snarled and thrashed. Miklotov rushed over to assist him as Caesar and Lucia stepped between us. I locked eyes with Saraya, gave her my best arrogant smile, and turned my back on her to make my dramatic exit.

Ayana stood in my path.

The sindari girl's eyes brimmed with tears. She wasn't readying for a fight. She stood there looking at me with the same look I'd grown accustomed to from Jeyla and Anji. But I never wanted to see it from her.

She was afraid.

She was afraid of me.

Ayana swallowed hard. "La... Lanei?"

The weight of a hundred eyes crushed me. I scanned the room.

Vigo gripped Kaden's wrist.

Yasir's mouth twisted with disgust.

The twins' eyes hungered for more.

Nakato, the friend whose trust I'd worked so hard to earn, seethed with rage.

I gave Ayana a hard look. "That's Princess Greyton, demon. Don't you ever forget who I am."

I slammed my shoulder into her as I passed. She stumbled. I didn't stop to see if she fell.

I wanted to vomit.

I wanted to scream.

I wanted to cry.

But I couldn't do any of those things.

I had a job to do.

Chapter 62

/LANEI

I expected my father to follow me back to my room, but it took half an hour before he showed up at my door. And he wasn't alone.

"Thank you, Adelaide."

Russo gave a small bow. "Lord Greyton." She turned her eyes on me. They were just as warm as ever. "Your father has pulled many strings for you to be here. Try not to let your temper cut them all." She bowed her head to my father and left, closing the door behind her.

"You always did have a temper." He scanned the room. Probably looking for something to disapprove of. He found it on my weapons rack.

Brightclaw.

My father picked it up in a tepid grip, as if he feared it would burn his hand. He examined the eagle on the hilt, pressing his thumb into the inlay.

"Where did you get this?"

"One of the instructors had it in her possession."

"The elf."

I nodded. "She decided to return it to its rightful owner."

He grunted. "But she gave it to you instead."

I stirred. "Sir?"

"Dominic is heir to Maldova. Not you."

Oh hell no. My father may have passed me over for the throne, but he was not going to take this from me, too. "I thought a true ruler had no need of a sword."

"Not for battle, no. But possessing a sword with a history makes a statement."

"Let me make the statement for him. A sword covered in blood is worth more than a sword covered by a sheath."

He considered it. After what felt like forever, he placed the sword back on the rack. "So you mean to continue this... madness?"

"It isn't madness, Father. This is the path you set me on."

He narrowed his eyes. "Explain."

"You robbed me of my inheritance," I said, stating it as fact rather than bitterness. "By laws of birthright, I should be the next ruler of Maldova. But when my brother—"

"Half-brother."

He never allowed that to slip by. "When Dominic was born, you named him heir instead. And did I complain?"

"You were seven. You couldn't have understood at the time."

"I was eight. Even a child knows what it means to be removed from the line of succession." I shook my head. "I understand why you did it. You wanted one of Catherine's children to succeed you. I'm not a fool. I know how you feel about my mother." Just the mention of my mother soured his face. "But I love my br... half-brothers. Dominic and Robert are welcome to the throne. I love and support them. But when you took away my birthright, you gave me something you never gave either of them."

"And what is that?"

"A need to prove myself worthy of something. Anything. Even with the Greyton name, nobles aren't looking to marry the child who's been disinherited."

My father scoffed. "Don't be so dramatic. Even without the throne, you're worth more than any lordling in the kingdom."

"I want to be worth more than gold. I have to prove my *own* worth, not just the worth I was born with. Here, in this world, merit is the only thing that matters. I'm proving that my merit is better than anyone's. I couldn't make you proud as a princess. Let me make you proud as a knight."

My father studied me. Everything I'd said was true. It wasn't the whole truth, but it was close enough that he wouldn't be able to read a lie into it. Having a shitty father-daughter relationship made that part easy.

Finally, he nodded. "Very well. Aguilar has agreed to let you stay, but do not draw any more suspicion on yourself. They're close enough to arresting you as it is. If I'm going to war, I'd prefer it not be to rescue you from a jail cell."

I smirked. "That might be the sweetest thing you've ever said to me."

He looked at me in a way that seemed... foreign. For just a moment, the disapproval I'd grown so accustomed to disappeared and I was looking at my father.

"Do you truly believe that?"

"I..."

He waved a hand, dismissing any response I had. Once again my father was gone and I stood before Lord Greyton. "No matter. I came here to see if you were embarrassing the family name with your latest rebellion."

"Your verdict?"

"I haven't decided. But I'm not wholly convinced this is folly."

"Thank you." I took a breath. "I had hoped you would bring Dominic and Robert with you."

My father shook his head. "Your half-brothers should not be exposed to this madness."

"All the same, I would have liked to have seen them."

"All the same."

There was a knock on the door and it swung open. Lucia Verdicci stood in the doorway.

"You wanted to see me, my lord?"

My father nodded. "Lucia. Yes. Wait for me outside."

Lucia bowed and shut the door. My father placed a hand on my shoulder.

"I do not pretend to understand why you are here or why you do half of what you do." He looked me in the eye. "But that does not mean I do not also waste far too many hours trying."

There were no big goodbyes, no hugs. But he gave my shoulder a squeeze. Even that small sign of approval was more than I could have hoped for.

Chapter 63

SYDNEY

I shouldn't be in charge of coming up with plans.

Kasia did a great job fixing my arm. It felt fine. You know, minus the throbbing pain. The arm knew it'd been broken and knew it shouldn't be fixed, so it was still sending out all the pain signals it knew should be there. The pain wasn't real, but my brain sure thought it was.

My brain sucked.

Fortunately, Kasia gave me some weird potion that made my head swim. Instead of feeling like any one part of my body was in pain, it felt like I was swimming through an ocean full of tiny pain fishes and the pain fishes were gently gnawing away as they whisked me into a nice little pain bed.

In other words, I was high as fuck.

"We never shoulda let Darian involve you in this." My mom's mouth was a tight line. "You shouldn't be here."

"He's fine," the blurry figure that was my father responded. "Darian's not gonna let anything happen to him."

"She broke his arm!"

"Only for an hour."

"That is not the point and you know it."

"He knows what he's doing."

"Does he? Look at him."

My parents stared at me. I smiled and gave them a thumbs up.

"That's just the drugs," Dad said.

"Oh, good. Just the drugs." Mom sighed. "We shoulda trained him sooner. He wasn't ready for this."

"Nothing we can do about that now. Just means we train the next one when it starts crawling."

"There's not going to be another one."

Dad put an arm around Mom's shoulders. "You sure about that?"

I tried swatting his arm down and somehow hit a table instead. "Just because I'm drugged don't mean you can flirt in front of me."

"You wouldn't even be here if it weren't for my flirting." Dad winked at Mom.

She rolled her eyes. "Ignore him. If your father actually believes his flirting is what got us here, he's the one on drugs."

"Speaking of flirting, why don't you tell us about your 'friendmate?'"

"Mathiu..."

"What? Can't a father inquire about his son's love life?"

"Not when your son is hopped up on—"

"She's pretty, isn't she?" I blurted out. "Her name is Ayana. Ayyyyyy ahhhhhn uhhhhh. Isn't that nice?"

"Yes, she seems very nice." Mom flicked another glance at Dad.

"She's soooooooo nice," I cooed. "Much nicer than her brother. Reno. Reno's her brother." I smacked my forehead. "He's not really her brother. Well, he is, but not, like, *brother* brother. She's a sindari. And an elf. An elfdari. A... sinelf." I rolled my head around. "She's pretty, isn't she?"

My mom nodded and patted my shoulder. "Yes, she's very pretty."

I rolled my eyes. "Mooooom. She's not just pretty. She's also sweet and nice and smart and funny and purple."

My dad barked out a laugh. "Yep, he's definitely my son."

"Was there ever any doubt?"

Dad put his arm back around Mom and kissed her.

"Sydney!" The door flew open and Ayana burst in. She leapt onto the bed, landing on her knees beside me. I bounced up and smacked my head against the headboard. She winced and wrapped her arms around me. "Sorrysorrysorry."

My mom smiled. "We're gonna go see Darian. We'll check back in on you before we go." She grabbed my father, who flashed me two thumbs up as Mom pulled him out of the room.

"Are you okay?" Ayana fussed to get the pillow back under my head. "Why would you let Lanei do that to you?"

"Why would I... what?" I tried to shake the confusion clouds from my head. "Whaddaya mean?"

"You just let Lanei hurt you. Why would you do that?"

"I didn't let... no, she's just better than me."

Ayana rolled her eyes. "No. Well, yes, but no. You two planned that." She sat up straight. "You did plan that, right? She didn't just go off script?"

"What? I... huh?"

Ayana sighed. "It's okay. I know. That wasn't Lanei. She'd never talk to Tenkou's sister like that. She wouldn't ever call me a you-know-what." She wrapped her arms around my neck. "And she wouldn't hurt you unless there was a reason for it. So you two planned it to trick her father."

I stared at her and then it hit me. "Ohhhhh. Reno told you!" I heaved a sigh of relief. "You have no idea how happy I am that he finally—"

Ayana leaned back. "What does Reno have to do with it? I just thought you and Lanei... What do you mean 'finally?'"

Oh shit.

"Um.... Reno? I didn't say Reno. I said... Gee, no, I don't know what you're talking about."

"Sydney?"

I swallowed. "Yeah?"

"You're high on magic painkillers. I won't have any problem making you talk." She didn't look angry, which was a relief. But she did have a mischievous look on her face.

"You're not going to torture me, are you?"

"Torture? Don't be silly." Ayana grinned and swung a leg over me, straddling me. She pushed me back on the bed and leaned over me until her lips were inches from mine. I could taste the peppermint on her breath. The fire in her eyes spread through my body as her lips drew closer. "I can think of a much better way to make you talk."

I was vaguely aware of the sound of a door opening.

"Sydney, I think we need—"

Reno's voice sobered me right up. Ayana tried to roll off to the right. I tried to roll her off to the left. In the end, she was still straddling me and we'd just made things look much, much worse. We froze.

Reno looked at me. He looked at Ayana. His eyes narrowed to slits.

"Oh, hellllllll no."

Chapter 64

SYDNEY

Reno dragged me out of the infirmary like a prisoner being led to execution. Ayana tried telling him to calm down, but seeing as telling someone to "calm down" has never once worked in the history of civilization, she didn't have much success. My head was still fuzzy, but my brain was working well enough to recognize one clear fact:

Reno was about to murder my ass.

He threw open the door to my room. The door hit the wall hard enough to knock a pair of swords off Kaden's weapons rack. He shoved me inside and slammed the door in Ayana's face. He turned the lock.

"Hey!" She shouted through the door. She rattled the knob and banged on the door several times. "You can't keep me out!"

"Quiet!" Reno shouted back. He turned to me. "Explain. Now."

"It's not what you think."

"Oh, really? Because it looked like you were making out with my sister."

"Oh, that's all it... Okay, yes. We, uh... were."

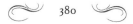

I tried my best apologetic smile. Reno's eyes hardened. If the sound of him cracking the knuckles of his left hand was bad, the grinding gears on his right was worse. I swallowed hard. This wasn't how I envisioned my death.

A swirling black portal opened beside us and Ayana tumbled out, crashing into me. I steadied her.

"Ayana!" Reno shouted.

"Don't you take this out on him," she shot back. "I was just as involved as Sydney. Probably more, considering the drugs."

"Medicine drugs!" I spat out. "They gave me drugs for my arm. I don't do drugs. Pain drugs."

"Shut it!" Reno turned on Ayana. "I have *told* you not to travel through the Void. It's too dangerous."

"Then you should've thought of that before you locked me out of my boyfriend's room."

Reno froze. He looked at me. "Boyfriend?"

I looked at Ayana. "Boyfriend?"

Ayana's mouth hung open. "I mean, I know we haven't really talked about it, but—"

"Maybe this isn't the best time." I didn't want Reno putting his fist through my skull.

"I told you to keep Ayana out of this." Reno's eyes tore a hole through me. "I was very clear."

"You were! And I did! I haven't said anything to her."

"Yeah, about that," Ayana said. "I'd kinda like to know what it is you two are hiding from me."

"It's nothing for you to worry about," Reno said.

"Oh, good. If you say I don't need to worry, then I guess everything's fine." She crossed her arms. "Tell me why Lanei's pretending to be all evil."

Reno glared at me. I held up my hands. "Hey, I didn't say anything."

Ayana raised a finger. "I mean, you kinda confirmed—"

"I was on drugs!"

"Both of you, shut up!" Reno pinched the bridge of his nose and took a deep breath. "Alright. Fine."

He explained everything. The Children of Omek. The mole. Why I was here. Lanei's role.

Ayana remained quiet and receptive throughout. When Reno was done, she smiled. "I knew Lanei was good."

"I'm glad you feel vindicated," Reno said. "Now say goodbye. You're going home."

"What?"

"You're leaving. It isn't safe here, especially now that you know what's going on."

"I'm not going anywhere." Ayana stuck out her chin. "You can't make me leave."

"I'm an instructor here. If I tell Kane you're done, you're done. Pack your things and say goodbye."

"No."

"That wasn't a request."

"I'm seventeen! You can't protect me forever!"

"I can damn sure try!" Reno yelled back. "There's a bunch of racist assholes out there hunting down non-humans, and you're the only sindari born in a hundred years. Believe me, I've looked. We've already had two deaths here. I will *not* allow you to be the third. I will keep you safe if I have to burn this whole kingdom to the ground to do it."

The anger melted off Ayana's face. She put a hand on Reno's arm. "I'm safe here. I have you and Sydney and Lanei and Kaden. Even with a killer on the loose, I'm safer here than at home by myself. And if I'm here, I can keep learning to defend myself better. This is the best place for me." She gave Reno a reassuring smile. "I'm not helpless. I'm half sindari, half elf, and one hundred percent Isale. Ask Sydney. I'm kind of a badass."

I opened my mouth to back her up, but Reno held up his hand.

"I ain't asking Sydney a goddamn thing right now." He sighed. "You can stay. But I don't want you involved in Sydney's mission."

Ayana shook her head. "You need me for this. I can help."

"Absolutely not."

"She's got a bigger target on her back than anyone," I said. "If we control the crosshairs, that might be the safest place for her."

"I know you did not just suggest—"

"Hear me out. If we make out like—"

"Do not use the phrase 'make out' in front of me ever again."

I swallowed. "All I'm saying is we should—"

A toilet flushed. The bathroom door swung open and Kaden sauntered in.

"So, we're spies now?" He walked past us and flopped down on his bed. He grinned. "Well, then you're in luck. You've got Kaden Ashworth on your side."

Chapter 65

/LANEI

I made a point of being the last person to walk into Reno's class. I hadn't seen Sydney since I broke his arm, and looking at him was a knife in my gut.

Kaden hovered over Sydney like the world's prettiest bodyguard. Sydney and Ayana sat together, holding hands. Guess that finally happened. I couldn't even give them shit about it. Or tell them I was happy for them.

Warren and his squad sat on the opposite side of the room. All eyes locked on me when I walked in. No sign of Reno. He'd be watching through the two-way mirror.

Sydney got to his feet and stalked toward me. Ayana tried to pull him back, but he shrugged her off. Although he favored his arm, it looked completely healed. Kasia did good work. I was going to have to buy her a drink after all this.

Sydney came to a stop in front of me. I wondered how much of the anger in his eyes was real.

This was it. Moment of truth.

I smiled. "How's the arm?"

He hit me with a right cross. "You tell me."

I touched my finger to my lip. It came back with a spot of blood.

Punch to the face. Our signal that the whole squad was in on the charade. It meant I didn't have to hold back.

"Who taught you to throw a punch, Winter? It sure as hell wasn't your mother." I feigned a right jab. He got his hands up to block it, and I decked him with a left hook. Ayana and Kaden rushed to Sydney's side before he hit the ground.

"What the hell is wrong with you?" Kaden snapped.

"Tell your boy not to start fights he can't finish." I looked at Ayana. "Unless you think you can finish them for him." I leaned over so my eyes were level with hers. I could taste the nerves in the air between us. "Want to see how much you're worth without your demons or big brother to fight your battles for you?"

"Shut up!" Ayana shouted.

"It's the fucking truth. Warren's squad didn't beat us because we were short an overgrown lizard. They beat us because you're nothing without those fucking demons. And you can't even keep them under control." I placed a finger on her forehead and pushed her back. "Maybe you're the one who should be on a leash, little sindari bitch."

Even if she was in on it, her expression showed the words hurt. Sydney sprung up and tackled me before I could reflect on what I'd said. The two of us hit the ground, Sydney on top. His fist shot back, but Kaden grabbed his arm and pulled him off. After pushing Sydney away, Kaden turned back to where I lay on the ground. And he spit on me.

I wiped the spit from my cheek and stared at my hand in disbelief. "How dare you! I am a goddamn princess!"

Kaden jabbed a finger at Warren and the twins. "You may be their princess, but you sure as hell aren't mine."

I rose to my feet and got in Kaden's face. "No, I am not. In Maldova, we have standards. I would never allow a common whelp like you to even entertain the idea of becoming a knight."

"Like those three are any better?"

"At least they have a pedigree. I know their families. Who the hell are you?"

"My family—"

"Is inconsequential. Nothing more." One by one, I looked down my nose at my three best friends. "Just like all of you."

I turned to leave as Reno entered the room.

"Where do you think you're going?"

"Back to my room," I said. "Tell the headmaster I want a new squad."

"That's not how this works."

"Then call me when they're in my league. Until then, stop wasting my time."

I pushed past him, and nobody made a move to stop me. I cast a glance at Warren's squad. Warren rested his chin on his large fists, but his eyes were alive as he watched. Beside him, Milia looked absolutely giddy. She whispered something to him and the big man nodded. She leaned over to her brother and ran a finger over the protective mask on his face before whispering something to him. He glowered but didn't say anything back.

Milia looked straight at me and smiled. I smiled back.

Bite that worm, you sick, racist bitch.

Three squads attended Caesar's class today. On the one side were Yasir, Robia, Anji, and Devi. On the other, Sydney, Ayana, and Kaden. I stood alone on the far wall, a squad unto myself. Nothing for me to do but what I do best.

Bullseye.

Bullseye.

Second ring.

Second ring.

Bullseye.

"You should be angry more often," Caesar said from behind me. "It improves your aim."

"I'll keep that in mind." My next arrow veered left into the third ring.

"Focus your emotions." He tapped my forehead. "If your mind is everywhere, your aim will be as well." He placed a hand between my shoulder blades. "Take a breath." I did. "Loose."

Bullseye.

"Good." Caesar placed a hand on my bow, pushing it down. "Regarding what happened with your—"

"I don't want to talk about it."

"No, I don't suppose you do. But you have friends outside your squad."

I gave a bitter laugh. "Oh yeah, I'm miss popular right now."

"You are a princess. Even if people only want to use you, you will never lack for options." Caesar produced a throwing knife and threw it blindly at the target. It hit dead center. "A word of advice: Be the one who does the using. Make the people you're using believe they are in control."

"Good advice."

Caesar took the bow from my hand and replaced it with a crossbow. "I may not have the flash of Instructor Verdicci or the pedigree of Instructor Lightfellow, but I have plenty to say worth listening to." He nodded to Robia, and the Esperan girl returned the gesture. "It has certainly helped Miss Castillo."

Caesar left my side to assist Sydney and the rest of my estranged squad. Robia watched him leave then said something to the rest of her crew. Anji snapped back a retort and Devi shook her head. But Yasir nodded, and the two of them came my way.

Yasir bowed, ever the gentleman even if his voice lacked its usual warmth. "Your Highness."

Despite my previous threats regarding the title, he'd decided it was now both accepted and expected. I went with it. "Yasir. Robia."

"Trouble in paradise?" Robia asked, just enough derision in her voice to show she was only talking to me because her mentor had shown the barest interest.

I snorted. "Nothing about that group was ever paradise."

"Yes, it did seem strange they'd pair you up with that lot. Kaden's the only one worth his salt, but even he pales next to his sister." Robia slid an arm around Yasir's waist. His discomfort was palpable, but he was of course too polite to say anything. She flicked her tongue against her lip piercing. "Or does this have something to do with Sydney and the sindari? A bit of jealousy perhaps?"

I couldn't help but laugh. Funny hearing Robia accuse someone else of jealousy. "God, no. I'd break that boy. She's welcome to him."

Yasir cleared his throat. "Princess, if I may ask, what happened between you and Tenkou's sister?"

"The throldkin have always been quick to anger." I shrugged one careless shoulder. "Listening to reason was never their strong suit."

"As you say. But, with respect, I did not witness an appeal to reason. I witnessed anger responding in kind."

"Am I not permitted to be angry when I've been accused of murder?"

"You are," Yasir conceded. "But perhaps there is a better way to resolve such disputes."

"The best route is the one that ends swiftly and with the desired outcome. Are you saying I failed in those goals?"

"No. I was merely unaware that what happened the other day was the outcome you sought." He bowed. "With your leave."

I nodded my permission and he returned to Anji and Devi.

Robia watched him go. "You really don't want him, do you?"

"Sydney?"

Robia shook her head. "Yasir."

"No. Frankly, I don't see the appeal."

"Hmm." Robia picked up a crossbow and pointed it at me while she twirled a bolt in her other hand. She slowly dragged the sight of the crossbow around the room, passing over the others until it pointed at Yasir's back. "Not interested in the knight, not interested in the cowboy." She flicked the crossbow back toward the target and loaded the bolt. "What does interest you, princess?"

"More important matters."

Robia handed me the crossbow. "Such as?"

I looked around the room. Caesar's back was to me as he worked with Kaden and Devi.

But Yasir and Anji were still watching. Factoring in Robia's big mouth, anything I did here would spread to the rest of the school.

I pointed the crossbow at Ayana and fired. The bolt shot inches past her face, close enough to make her hair billow. She gasped and spun to face me. Sydney jumped up and put himself between us.

I handed the crossbow back to Robia. "Things that matter to me."

Chapter 66

ALANEI

I woke to the scrape of a boot beside my bed moments before the knife pressed against my throat. Before I could think, I shoved the knife aside and sprang to my feet. Wetness covered my hand where it pushed into the dagger, but I couldn't see the blood. I couldn't see anything. I couldn't even see the fog filling my room. But I felt it. The chill hit me as soon as I was out of bed.

"You did it, didn't you?" Nakato asked.

I spun in the direction of her voice. "Don't do this."

Her knife slashed my arm with a flash of pain.

"Is that what Jeyla said before you killed her?"

I pivoted again, but her blade cut across my thigh. I grabbed for my bedpost to steady myself.

"Was I next?" she asked. "Is that why you pretended to be my friend?"

My blood leaked from three wounds, but none hurt as bad as those words. I wanted to tell her the truth. I didn't want her thinking I was a monster. "Please, Nakato, I didn't—"

"Don't lie to me!" Her gauntleted fist struck me in the face and sent me sprawling. "I trusted you! I believed you!"

"You don't understand! I'm not—"

"Liar!" Pain, not anger, filled her voice. "You killed Jeyla."

Glass shattered as she struck me in the side of the head with a picture frame. I didn't bother to check if my head was bleeding. I didn't care anymore.

"Believe whatever you want." I made no effort to get back up. "But if you're going to kill me, at least look me in the eye when you do it."

Silence.

The fog receded.

The spectre of death stared down at me. Her dagger dripped with my blood.

"Take off the mask."

"No." Her voice came out a low rasp.

I planted my good hand into the ground to sit up, but it slipped out from under me. I'd lost more blood than I thought.

"Take it off. Finish me."

"I'm not like you." Her mask may have hidden her features, but the moonlight reflected off her eyes. They were wet with tears. "I'm not a murderer."

There it was. I was a murderer. And I always would be in her eyes.

"What do you want?" The voice that came out was weak. It trembled. It wasn't mine.

"Confess."

I looked at my blood-soaked hand. I turned it palm up and watched as blood trickled out. More dripped from the wound on my forehead. "Will you kill me if I do?"

Nakato shook her head.

My cupped palm now held a lake of blood. "Will you kill me if I don't?"

She shook her head again. "You'll confess. I have all night."

"Yeah, well... I don't." I flung my hand up. The blood sprayed across her face and into her eyes.

Nakato staggered back and rubbed at her eyes. I grabbed my desk chair with my good hand and swung it. I had shit for leverage from this position, but the chair slammed into her shin. She went to one leg. I shoved the chair at her again, releasing it with as much force as I had in me.

It caught Nakato in her other leg. The world slowed as she toppled to the ground. Her natural instinct took over as she brought a hand down in front of her chest to break her fall.

Her instinct had forgotten she was still holding the dagger.

I had only a split second to react. I kicked at her, trying to do anything to stop the blade from sinking into her heart. I didn't know how good her armor was, but I'd felt that dagger enough times in the last minute to know how sharp it was. And gravity was unforgiving.

I wasn't fast enough to kick the blade out of her hand. Instead, my leg shot between her arm and torso. When she landed, it drove the blade straight into my calf. I screamed. She rolled aside, leaving her dagger stuck in my leg. She stared at it then looked at me.

The door flew open and light from the hall poured in. Lucia stood in the doorway, her own dagger drawn. She took in the sight for a fraction of a second before grabbing Nakato by the scruff and yanking her away from me with surprising strength.

"What the hell is wrong with you?"

"She... She killed..." Nakato shook her head as words failed her.

"Mask. Off!"

Nakato hung her head. She reached back and released her bloodied mask. It fell from her hands and clattered to the ground. "I... I just..."

"You just what?" Lucia spat. Nakato said nothing. "Answer me, goddammit!"

"I'm sorry..." She looked at me. "I'm..."

Lucia scooped the mask off the ground and shoved it into Nakato's hands. "Go to the headmaster's office immediately. If you aren't there when I arrive, I will see you expelled or worse."

Nakato nodded and hurried from the room, her resolve gone.

Lucia knelt beside me. Blood soaked into her pants. "Are you alright?"

I stared at her, looked at my leg, looked at the pool of blood, then back at her.

She shrugged. "Don't try to move. I will send for Kasia then we will sort all this out."

I nodded. "Thank you."

"There is no need for thanks." Lucia's lip curled up in a smile. "We Maldovans must watch out for each other in a place such as this, don't you think?"

Chapter 67

SYDNEY

I almost blew Lanei's cover when she walked in the door for Russo's class. Reno told me there'd been an altercation, but... damn.

On top of the stitches in her forehead and the bandage around her arm, she had one hell of a limp. She took her seat next to me and scooted her chair to the far end of our shared desk.

"Are you alright?"

"Go fuck yourself," she muttered, not even glancing in my direction.

"No, Lanei, what—"

"It's none of your goddamn business!" she snapped. "So mind your own."

I pulled back and stared at her. I couldn't tell how much of her irritation was real and how much was part of the act. But seeing what Nakato did to her... We had to put a stop to this, and soon.

The climate shift toward Lanei had been fast and definite. It wasn't all fear, either. Milia delighted in watching Lanei's interactions like some twisted voyeur, and while Warren didn't quite share her enthusiasm, he still enjoyed the chaos she caused.

I figured Yasir's infatuation with Lanei would vanish as soon as her attitude changed. It didn't. He stopped trying to court her, sure, but he still watched her every move. Robia's jealousy was gone, probably because Yasir had stopped fawning over Lanei, but she seemed to revel in the moments when Lanei set her fire loose on others. Guess she saw a kindred spirit in the short temper club.

Lanei tapped her fingers on the table several times then cast an angry glare my way. Our eyes met, she glanced at her hand, then back at me. I looked at her hand. She made a disgusted sound and turned away from me then ran a finger along the table. It traced an S. Then a T. Several seconds later, she stopped tracing letters.

Stop me.

She scowled at me. I nodded.

Lanei crossed her arms and commenced looking bored until Nakato and Chavo walked in.

Lanei didn't miss a beat. She leapt out of her chair the instant Nakato appeared. If her leg hadn't slowed her down, I never could've overtaken her.

I tried using my body as a shield between them. "Stop!"

"You don't tell me what to do. Bitch tried to kill me!"

Chavo collided with my back as he played peacekeeper on his side. "Now's not the time!"

"Like hell it isn't!" Lanei growled and reached for Nakato. I wrapped my arms around her and tried to force her back.

Warren and Milia sat back and watched, but Yasir and Robia leapt into action. Yasir vaulted a desk and spun behind me to put another body between Lanei and Nakato. Robia swung behind Lanei and helped me drag her away. Lanei cursed and clawed, but we were able to create distance between them. I glanced over my shoulder to see how much trouble Chavo and Yasir were having with Nakato.

They were having... none. They weren't holding her back. Nakato stood in the same place she'd been when Lanei first charged her. She hadn't moved, hadn't made any attempt to defend herself. She stood there stoic, no life in her eyes, no fight in them. Her skull mask had more life in it than she did.

I looked back at Lanei. She snarled and cursed, promising what she'd do if she ever got ahold of Nakato. One hand flailed wildly, but the other gripped my upper arm and squeezed. Her voice cracked.

I looked in Lanei's eyes, past the anger she forced to the surface. For the first time, I realized how much this was costing her.

Chapter 68

/LANEI

ven if Nakato hadn't succeeded, everything else had damn near killed me. The passive aggressive skepticism I'd experienced when people learned who I was didn't begin to compare to the full on hatred being thrown my way. The knowledge that Sydney, Ayana, and Kaden were playing along only did so much to lessen the hell of knowing everyone else wanted me dead.

So yeah. I needed a damn drink.

Dragonfly had become the regular place for most of the students to hit up after a long week, which meant if I were smart I'd have gone somewhere else. Unfortunately, I had a job to do, and that job included being public enemy number one. So Dragonfly it was.

An uncomfortable number of angry eyes looked me over as I walked inside. Milia and Milich sat at the bar, huddled close together and laughing. Sydney and Ayana sat with Kaden and Vigo near the front window. Devi sat behind her brother at a high top with Anji and Robia. Chavo and Vanessa turned their attention away from each other long enough to give me a death glare. No sign of Nakato, at least. Thank god for small favors.

I walked past Sydney's table, making a point of slamming a shoulder into him. He grabbed the table to keep from falling off his chair then jumped to his feet and squared off with me.

"Hey! Whatever your problem is, you need to get over it before the Squad Games tomorrow. I'm getting real tired of your attitude."

I held my hands to my face, feigning shock. "Oh no, am I angering the great and powerful Sydney Winter? What are you going to do? Heal me to death?" I rolled my eyes. "On your best day, you couldn't beat me on my worst. So sit your ass down." He didn't move. I turned to Ayana. "Demon, make your pet sit down before I put him down."

That brought Vigo to his feet. "Is that a threat?"

"I don't threaten. I promise."

Ayana tugged at Sydney's sleeve. She never looked at me. "Come on. Don't provoke her."

Sydney and I faced off a few moments longer before he let Ayana pull him into his seat. I turned my gaze to Vigo. At the next table, Devi, Anji, and Robia stopped talking. Their bodies tensed.

"Are you and I going to have a problem now?" I didn't want to push Vigo too hard. He wasn't in on the ruse, and I didn't want to have to hurt him. I doubted Kaden would forgive me if I did.

"That all depends on you," he said.

"Good. Because I don't have time for you."

I brushed past him and made my way to the bar. The bartender was a smart guy and placed a glass of whiskey in front of me in record time. I brought it to my lips and caught a movement across the bar. Milia and Milich raised their glasses. Milia tipped her glass my way. I mirrored the gesture. We all three took a drink. Milia waved me over.

Jackpot.

My whiskey and I joined them at their end of the bar. I didn't know what was in the glowing green cocktails they drank, but I was reasonably sure I wouldn't like it.

Milia ran a finger along the rim of her glass. "They turn so fast once they see the real you, don't they?"

"You noticed that too."

"It wasn't subtle." She took a sip and held the liquid in her mouth to savor it before swallowing. "You know, when we realized who you were, I told Milich I wished you could get a taste of what we've dealt with since day one. So I suppose I should thank you for granting me that."

I cocked an eyebrow. "From where I stood, it looked like you were the ones dishing it out."

Milich scoffed. "That's because you were standing on a pedestal."

"She's a princess," Milia said. "It's her job to look down on the rest of us."

I tried not to growl too loud. "If this is you being diplomatic, your diplomacy sucks."

Milia took a sip and let the martini glass rest in her hand. "I'm being honest. Sadly, honesty is the death of diplomacy."

"Then cut the vague shit and be honest with me."

"Very well. How many friends do you have outside of your squad?" She rolled her eyes and tapped her forehead, feigning forgetfulness. "Well, not now, obviously. But, say, two weeks ago. How many?"

"I'm not sure. A few."

"A few," Milia repeated. "The fact that you need to count only proves my point. My brother and I have been honest with you and everyone else here since day one.

We believe in the power of science, the end of magic, and the purity of the human race. We are proud of who we are, and not once have we tried to hide behind a false face for the sake of political correctness." She drained the last of her drink and set the glass on the counter. "Would you like to guess how many friends we've made outside of our squad?"

I said nothing, because that was the correct answer.

Milich nodded. "People may have thought you were a murderer, but at least they hated you for something you weren't instead of something you were." He smiled. "Although I suppose you know that feeling now, too."

"How do you know I'm not a murderer?" I asked.

"Because you're not that sloppy," Milia said. "If you'd killed the elf, your boy wouldn't have found you with the body. And if you'd killed the lizard, you wouldn't have been so dumb as to leave your sword behind."

Milich shrugged. "Don't be offended. We actually agree that you'd make a wonderful murderer. After all, who would dare arrest the princess of Maldova?"

I raised my glass and drank to that. "Aguilar fears my father. He knows Maldova's army could wipe Esperan off the map."

"He does," Milia agreed. "Just as we know you make a better ally than enemy."

"Most people would follow that with an apology."

"Most would," she said. "But, as I said, I've been nothing but honest with you. I have nothing to apologize for."

"I seem to recall you attacking me on multiple occasions."

"I seem to recall you breaking my brother's face."

I smiled. "Fair enough."

Milia nodded. "Fair enough."

Milich sighed. "Wonderful, I'm so glad we're all past that now."

Milia gave her brother a playful swat on the arm and leaned across the bar. "So tell me... how have you managed to put up with that band of misfits you were placed with? I could never feign civility near as long as you. Even with the lizard gone, you still have the demon and the purple-eyed freak to deal with. How did you do it?"

I shrugged. "Sydney barely qualifies as man or elf, so it's easy to pretend he doesn't exist. As for Ayana..." I gave the twins the best wicked grin I could manage. It was a decent imitation of Milia. "I don't think she's going to make it to graduation."

Milia took my hand. She rubbed her thumb across my fingers and smiled. My imitation of her grin paled in comparison to the real thing.

"What a coincidence. I don't think she will either."

Chapter 69

SYDNEY

"Come on, you're really telling me you two haven't..."

"No."

Kaden grinned. "No, you haven't, or no, that's not what you're telling me?"

"No, we're not having this conversation."

I'd spent the last twenty minutes staring out the window in the hopes that Kaden could take a hint. He couldn't.

"Hey, I'm just looking out for your best interests. Want to make sure you know what you're doing and all that."

I sat up straight. "Shut up."

"I'm serious! For all I know—"

"No, shut up!" I waved for him to look outside. "Kill the lights."

Kaden shot out of bed and turned off the gas lamp. A second later he was beside me at the window. "What is it?"

I pointed. In the courtyard below, Warren stepped into view. His head swiveled around on high alert.

"Little late to be out for a walk," Kaden mused.

"He's not the only one." I nodded to the other end of the courtyard where Russo walked his way. I cracked the window, but from this distance it was impossible to hear anything. I jumped up and hurried to the door. "Stay here."

"Where are you going?"

"Down there. It's time to find out what they're up to."

I reached the courtyard in record time but started kicking myself halfway there. I should've sent Kaden. He was better at the whole stealth thing. Too late to do anything about that now. Besides, this was supposed to be my investigation. I didn't want anyone else getting hurt on my account.

Warren and Russo had moved into an alcove. I slid around the side of the building and crouched low. I could make out their silhouettes through a gap in the hedges.

"...supposed to be keeping them in check," Russo said.

"I'm trying."

"Try harder. They're drawing too much attention."

"Milia's too headstrong to be controlled and Milich does whatever she says. How about you rein them in?"

"How about you remember who you're talking to?" Russo snapped. "Or have you forgotten the hell I could bring down on you?"

"I haven't forgotten anything. Maybe you've forgotten your hands aren't exactly clean either."

Silence. Despite being twice her size, Warren shrank away from Russo.

"Are you threatening me?"

"No, ma'am..."

"Then don't you ever speak to me like that again. My arrangement with your father is the only thing keeping my boot out of your ass right now, do you understand me?"

Warren nodded. "Yes, ma'am."

"Good. When I tell you to keep the twins in line, I don't want excuses. I want results. They're bringing attention on you, which brings attention on me." She took a step closer to him. He stepped back. "I will not lose my place here because of your incompetence."

"You won't. I'll tell them to be more careful."

"Yes, you will. Now, I believe you have something for me."

Warren reached into his jacket and pulled out a small box. He handed it to Russo. She lifted the lid and looked inside then reached into her pocket and passed something back to him.

"Get back to your room. We train at dawn."

Warren left without another word. Russo slid the case into the inner pocket of her coat and went off the other way.

I'd barely moved a muscle to follow her when a hand clamped around my mouth and something pointy pressed into my neck.

"Shhhh," a woman's voice whispered in my ear. "Go to sleep."

The needle jabbed into my neck with a sharp pain, followed by a burst of pressure. I tried to struggle, but my limbs wouldn't cooperate. My eyelids tripled in weight. I fought to stay awake, but it was no use. I collapsed to the ground as the strength left my body. Before I went under, Lucia Verdicci leaned over my body and lifted my head off the ground.

"Silly boy," she cooed. "Spying is my game."

Chapter 70

LANEI

My stomach roiled after palling up to Milia and Milich all night, and I wanted nothing more than to bathe off their filth and sleep until I could forget the whole thing.

So why the hell was someone knocking on my window in the middle of the night?

More to the point, why was someone knocking on my second story window at all?

I pulled back the curtains. Kaden clung to the sill outside my window. I opened it, careful not to smack him in the head and send him falling twenty feet to the ground.

"What are you—"

"Shh!" He pulled himself over the ledge and into my room with ease.

I looked out the window. No trees or anything within reach. "How did you—"

"Not important," he said. "Have you seen Sydney?"

"Not since he left the bar. Didn't he come back with you?"

"Yeah, but then he went to spy on Warren and Russo... He didn't come back here?"

I shook my head. "Should he have?"

"He should've done something, that's for sure. I couldn't see him from our room."

I frowned. "Are Warren and Russo still there?"

Kaden shook his head. "Long gone. I went to look for him, but nothing. I hoped he found something out and came to see you."

"No, he didn't... Shit." Now wasn't the time for Sydney to go off and get himself in trouble. But with everything that'd been going on lately and him being part elf... "We need to find him."

"Woah, no, we don't. You've gotta stay here."

"Sydney's my friend. I'm not just going to sit here while—"

"Sydney's not your friend. Not right now." Kaden placed a hand on my shoulder. "You've got a role to play, and that involves not giving a damn what happens to him."

"But..." Shit... he was right. If I went looking for him, it could blow everything we'd been working toward. But if anything happened to him... "Find him. Please."

"I'll wake up Reno and Vigo. We'll find him."

"And Ayana?"

"Nah, he wouldn't go see her this late. The game is weak with him."

"Not what I meant. Are you going to wake her, too?"

"Oh. Right. I'll... let Reno make that call. I won't be much use if he kills me."

"Smart." I sat on my bed. This fucking sucked. Sydney was the first person I'd opened up to in god knows how long. The first person to trust me, to accept me for me. He may have already been in the deep end with all this when he got here, but I was the one who tied an anchor to him.

"I'm sure he's fine. Probably off doing... I don't know, whatever he does when he doesn't know what he's doing." Kaden gave me a strained smile. "Are you okay?"

I laughed. "Not even a little. But I'll deal with it."

"Not alone, you won't. Now that I know I can climb that wall, just let me know if you need to chat by, I don't know, slapping me in the face or something." He shrugged. "Or slip me a note. That might be—"

I almost jumped out of my skin at the loud *bang* on my door. An envelope passed under it.

Kaden and I looked at each other. He mouthed *"Sydney?"* I had no answer, so I motioned for him to hide. He swung himself back out the window and dangled from the ledge.

I threw my door open. My heart dropped. Nobody there. I listened for footsteps, but... nothing.

I closed the door and picked up the envelope as Kaden pulled himself back inside. As far as envelopes went, it was fancy. My name emblazoned it in gold script. I tore it open and pulled out a plain white card with more gold writing.

Lana Greyton,

For your accomplishments at the Petrichor Martial Academy and your dedication to a better future for all of Nasan, you are invited to join an elite society reserved for the best Nasan has to offer. Meet us in one hour to learn how you can help create a better world for all. Speak of this to no one.

Kaden let out a breath. "You're in."

I nodded. There was an address at the bottom. A familiar address.

I crossed to my desk and pulled a stack of notes out of the picture frame sitting there. I flipped through them until I found what I was looking for.

"It's her..."

"Who?"

"That address. I've been there before, the night we followed the twins. That's where she met them." I handed Kaden my notes. "It's Lucia. She's the one behind this."

Chapter 71

/LANEI

The door to the abandoned storefront stood slightly ajar as I approached. Nothing good lay on the other side... So, naturally, I pushed it open and walked in.

The main storeroom looked as desolate as it had through the window weeks ago. And, like then, candlelight trickled in from the back room. Hushed voices stopped when I closed the door behind me. I walked into the back and was met with zero surprises.

The twins lounged on crates beside each other. Warren stood next to them, arms folded, looking more like a granite statue than a human being.

A grin spread across Milia's face. "Well, isn't this interesting? I knew there was more to you than you let on."

I raised an eyebrow. "Pardon?"

"Don't get me wrong, Princess. I'm flattered, truly. But why all the secrecy?"

I frowned and stepped into the room. "I didn't organize this. Are you saying you got a letter too?"

"Yes." Her voice wavered. "We all did."

"The best of the best," Milich said. "All from Maldova. I suppose that should come as no shock."

"No, I suppose not." It made sense Lucia would recruit from her own kingdom.

The door out front opened. We all shut up and waited to see who walked in next.

Yasir.

His hand flew to his sword. He didn't draw it, but I had no doubt he could be at the ready in plenty of time if it came to it.

"What is this?" His eyes scanned over the twins and Warren then fell on me. He gave a stiff nod. "Your Highness."

I nodded back. "Yasir."

"Would someone care to tell me precisely what is going on here?"

Milia laughed. "I would love to, dear knight. But you know what we know." She turned to Warren, lifting one leg onto the crate as she did. Her skirt parted, revealing her inner thigh in a way that was definitely not accidental. "We forgot the golden boy, Warren. How could we have forgotten the golden boy?"

Warren snorted, but didn't say anything.

"Are you planning to cut me down, sir knight?" I asked Yasir. "That wouldn't be particularly noble of you."

Our eyes met. Something hid there I couldn't quite place. It wasn't trust, per se... but he was looking to me for my lead. He was giving me the benefit of the doubt. He removed his hand from his sword.

"My apologies." He gave a short bow, his eyes never leaving mine. A question lurked there, but I didn't have the answer.

"Thank you."

"Not even your princess and you still bow and scrape at her feet." Milia traced a finger along her thigh as she eyed him. "I do love a man who knows his place."

Yasir cleared his throat. "My place is of no consequence to you, as you are of no consequence to me."

Milia's smile turned predatory. She leaned over, daring Yasir to break eye contact. "I can change that."

Milich sighed. "Can we not? I am sitting right here, in case you've forgotten."

"Of course, dear brother. How rude of me."

Yasir glared at them and walked over to me, deliberately placing himself between me and the others.

The front door opened and shut again. A chain rattled as it locked in place. Light footsteps approached. As everyone else leaned forward to see who had summoned us here, I waited for Lucia to walk through the door.

I was wrong. Yasir let out a sharp breath. Oh fuck...

"I'm glad you all could make it," Robia said. "We have much to talk about."

Chapter 72

SYDNEY

I woke up the same way I'd fallen asleep: Completely unable to move. At least I wasn't paralyzed this time. Just tied to a chair.

You know... At least.

Lucia Verdicci sat across from me. She didn't look at me, just continued picking her nails with a wicked looking dagger.

Nope. Not intimidating at all.

"Welcome back to the land of the living," she said. "Would you like to stay here?"

I looked around the room. "A little dark for my tastes. Bed looks nice. Those silk sheets?"

"Yes. Not what I meant."

"Yeah, I know. But it was worth a shot."

She smiled, but remained focused on the dagger. "I like you, Sydney. I do. So please know I am truly hoping you answer my questions in a way that makes me happy." The smile vanished and she finally locked eyes with me. "Keep me happy, Sydney. For both our sakes."

I swallowed. "Happy. Right. Gotcha."

She nodded. "Were you spying on Warren and Instructor Russo?"

"Yes." I know, you're supposed to lie under interrogation, but seeing as she caught me in the act, it'd be like trying to tell her my hair was green. Just wasn't going to hold up under scrutiny.

"Thank you for your honesty," she said. "Why were you spying on them?"

"Warren and I aren't exactly the best of friends."

"No, you are not." Lucia slashed the dagger down the back of my forearm. The cut was shallow and only opened a small slit, but it hurt like hell. "Why were you spying on them?"

I gritted my teeth. "Russo's a bitch."

"She is," Lucia agreed. She cut another slash in an X across the first. "Why were you spying on them?"

I winced at the pain. "I don't trust them."

"I believe you." She placed the point of the dagger in the intersection of the two slashes and pressed it into my flesh. "Why were you spying on them?"

"What does it matter? You caught me. If you're going to kill me, just get it over with. I've had a long day."

Something flickered in her eyes. The pressure on the dagger lessened. "Interesting. Thank you for that information."

I blinked. "What?"

"Who are you working for?"

"Who am I... I'm not working for anyone."

Lucia slashed the dagger down my other arm. It left a much longer trail than the last one. "Before you gave me half truths. Now you are outright lying to me."

I took a couple deep breaths to try to control the pain. "What makes you think I'm lying?"

"You do not belong at this school. You are not in the same league as the other students. Your parents are criminals."

"Reformed."

"Perhaps. But we both know you were not accepted to this school on your own merits." She placed the tip of the dagger against my chest. "Again, I like you. I hold none of that against you personally. But it does beg the question of how you got into this school, and, more importantly, who you are working for." She pushed on the dagger, and the tip pierced my chest. "I will have answers."

With a sound like thunder, the door exploded behind me, showering my back with splinters. Lucia spun my chair around and held the dagger to my throat.

"Drop it, Lucia." Reno stepped into the room. Blue sparks of light flashed down his metal hand. Kaden and Ayana stood behind him, weapons drawn.

"Reno?" Lucia hesitated. "He is with you?"

"Of course he's with me! What the hell do you think?"

There was a pause. "I think we need to have a chat, you and I."

"I think we can do that without a knife at Sydney's throat, don't you?"

"Oh, I do. But as there are three of you and one of me, it seems like an unfortunate necessity."

"Then you better talk fast."

"Was Sydney spying for you?"

"Damn right he was."

"Why?"

"Goddamn it, Lucia, we've got you. Put the knife down and—"

"I am curious. What do you think you've got?"

"I'm not playing games with you."

"Nor am I. But if Sydney is working for you, then I would very much like to change the tone of this conversation." The cold steel vanished from my throat. "Now, will you please turn your arm off?"

Reno eyed her then clenched his fist together and twisted his wrist. The electrical current shut off.

"Thank you. Normally I would ask you to step inside and close the door, but as I no longer have a door to close..." Lucia sighed and sliced the dagger through my ropes. "Let us take this conversation somewhere more private."

Ayana stepped forward, clutching her staff in both hands. "Why should we trust you?"

"Given recent events and who I am? You shouldn't." Lucia smiled. "But outside of Kasia Windamier, your brother is the only person at this school whose intentions I trust. And we have you to thank for that, little one."

Ayana narrowed her eyes. "What's that have to do with me?"

"Everything. After all, Reno would never allow the Children of Omek to get their hands on his little sister."

Kaden lowered his sword. "Wait... you're not with the Children?"

"Not all Maldovans seek to eradicate those who are not human. In fact, there are many of us who denounce the demagogue, Viktor Greyton." Lucia smiled. "And it's why I intend to place Lanei on the throne of Maldova."

Chapter 73

ALANEI

"Robia?" Yasir asked. "What's going on here?"

Robia beamed at him. "You have been chosen. You all have."

"Chosen by who? And for what?"

"By me and my master. To restore Nasan to its former glory. Not just Esperan or Maldova or Araspia, but all of it." She took Yasir's hands in hers. "We can do it together, Yasir. We can make all of Nasan great again."

"Araspia is already great. Everything I have seen of Esperan tells me the same." No mention of Maldova. No accident, I'm sure.

Robia shook her head. "They are trying to push us out, to make sure we never realize our true power. They fear us, what we are capable of. We must show them we will not rest until Nasan belongs to us again."

Yasir pulled his hands away. "What are you saying? Who are 'they'?"

"The sindari. The elves. The throldkin. The half-breeds." Robia spat on the floor. "All those races who have been hoarding their magic for centuries, keeping it out of the hands of the humans they hate. They see what we are building without their help and they are afraid. They know we can surpass them. They know we are better than them."

"Robia, this is not—"

"You're with the Children," I said. I needed to find out what was going on before Yasir put a premature end to this meeting.

Warren and the twins made sense. They'd made their feelings extremely evident. I made sense. As the daughter of Viktor Greyton, I'd be a natural ally for the Children. My recent actions should have alleviated any doubts they may have had about me early on. But Yasir... Robia was the only explanation. She wanted him on her side. She was infatuated with him, maybe even in love with him. She had to know he wouldn't share their views... but she probably believed he'd change for her. Stupid girl.

Robia turned her attention to me. "Yes. And soon, you will all have the opportunity to become Omek's children as well." She opened her arms in a welcoming gesture. "Milia, Milich, and Warren. You have already proven your dedication to a better, purer Nasan. Are you prepared to join the Children?"

Milia flashed her teeth, hunger in her eyes. "Oh yes."

"Of course," Milich said.

Warren cracked his knuckles and nodded.

"I expected no less." Robia looked to me and Yasir. "Lanei, you and I have had our differences. But my master believes you would be a powerful ally. And Yasir, my love..." Robia again took his hands. He'd never looked so uncomfortable as he did in that moment. "My master did not believe you would join our cause, but I promised you would. I know you will do it for me."

"Robia, this is wrong." Yasir tried pulling away, but she held tight. "I cannot—"

"You can!" She snapped at him. She placed one hand on his cheek. "And you will. I need you by my side. You need to be by my side." She glanced over her shoulder, looking into a mirror on the wall. "It's the only way to keep you safe."

"Safe from what?"

Robia leaned in and kissed Yasir. He did not return it. She took a step back. "This is not an offer you can walk away from, my love. You must accept. And you must prove yourself before you can meet my master and join our ranks." She looked back and forth between us. "Both of you must."

I looked at the mirror. The mole stood behind it, watching us. Robia was right. There was no turning this offer down, not if we wanted to walk out of here alive. Yasir, with his impossible sense of honor, wasn't likely to back down in the face of such an affront to everything he believed.

But that look he'd given me earlier... The way he'd been drawn to me after my identity was revealed. The way he acted disappointed instead of disgusted. Maybe I could save him from himself.

"We'll do it," I said. "Whatever you need, we're in." I gave Yasir a determined look and hoped he was better at reading expressions than I was. "Every princess needs a trusted knight by her side. Even if that knight comes from a different kingdom."

The protest in Yasir's eyes died, replaced with curiosity. He nodded and said, with only minor reluctance, "As she says."

Robia looked none too pleased that it took my interference for Yasir to agree, but she accepted it. "Good. Your task is simple. Tomorrow, our teams face off in the Squad Games. There will be an accident." Her eyes met mine, and they were full of sadistic glee. "Tomorrow, the demon bitch dies."

Chapter 74

SYDNEY

Reno glowered as he sat across from Lucia. "Why didn't Ricardo tell us you were working for him, too?"

Lucia smoothed out a wrinkle on Kaden's bed. "I suppose he did not want our separate investigations to taint each other."

"Maybe. Still, it's a dick move."

"It is also why we are stuck with Maldova's trash in our midst." Lucia sighed. "Ricardo believed the benefit of having Lanei close by outweighed the potential damage our countrymen could do here."

"He still think that?"

"Yes. He has not wavered, despite all that has transpired." She twirled her hand in the air. "He sees the big picture."

"And what about Tenkou?" I asked. "Wasn't he part of that big picture?"

"Tenkou's death was unfortunate. So was Jeyla's. But if we can put Lanei on Maldova's throne, there is no telling how many lives we can save."

"And where does Russo fit into all this?"

"I am not certain. However, her hands are not clean."
She reached into the pouch strapped to her thigh and
produced a small box identical to the one Warren had
given Russo earlier. She tossed it to me. My reflexes
were too dull to catch it at the moment, but Ayana's
were much sharper. She flipped open the lid.

"What's this?" Ayana pressed a finger into the box.
It came out covered in a white powder. She scrunched
up her face then held it to her nose to sniff it.

"Goddammit, keep that shit away from your nose!"
Reno snatched the box from Ayana's hands. "What the
hell is wrong with you? Giving drugs to my sister..."

Lucia shrugged. "I was giving it to Sydney. I did not
think their first instinct would be to try it."

"Drugs?" Ayana asked. "This is drugs?"

"Snowdust," I said. "I've seen my mom confiscate it."

Lucia nodded. "I pulled this off Adelaide last week.
Whether she is using or selling, I cannot say. But
clearly Warren is her supplier."

Ayana frowned at the powder on her finger and wiped
it off on my pillow. Admittedly, not the best place for
it. "So what does that mean? Is she—"

A knock on my window made Ayana jump into my
lap. Reno and Lucia snapped their heads to the window.
Kaden casually rolled off his bed.

"Don't get up, that's for me." He opened the window
and Lanei slid into the room as the rest of us gawked
at her.

"Thanks, I..." She froze when she saw Lucia.

"Nice way to get around, right?" Kaden chuckled. He
followed Lanei's eyes. "Oh, yeah, Lucia's cool. Sorry.
I know how much you wanted her to be evil."

Lucia looked amused. "How did your meeting go?"

"Well. And very not well." Lanei relayed what had
happened, ending with what they had planned for Ayana.

"No." Reno shook his head. "That's it. Ayana, you're done. I'm taking you out of here."

"I'm not going anywhere," Ayana said. "I'm not afraid."

"I don't care if you're afraid or not, you're done."

"Now wait," Lucia said. "Do not be hasty. If Ayana vanishes, they will know Lanei or Yasir informed you."

"Then we pull them too," Reno said. "The mission's over. I am not—"

"No!" Ayana leapt off the bed. "No! We are not pulling out. Not after what they did to Tenkou. If you send me home, I'm coming right back here to finish this. There's nothing you can do to stop me, so instead of trying, you should just accept that I'm a rebellious teenager with a mind of her own and access to a crazy amount of dark magic."

"He's got a point," I said.

Ayana turned to me, her jaw stuck out. As much as I didn't want to get on my girlfriend's bad side, I still wanted to have a girlfriend after tomorrow.

"They're planning to kill you. I ain't taking that risk."

"It's not yours to take." Ayana looked to Lanei. "How are they going to do it?"

Lanei shrugged. "No specifics. Just told me and Yasir to make an accident happen during the games."

"Okay... okay!" Ayana brightened up. "I got it. What if you guys kill me just a little bit and then Sydney brings me back, like, right away?"

"Woah, woah, no." I threw my hands up. "We are *not* resting this plan on my ability to bring someone back from the dead. I don't even know if that's possible. I sure as hell ain't going to test it out on you."

Ayana puffed out her lower lip and pouted. "Please?"

"No!"

"Killing you even a little is off the table," Reno said. "So unless someone has a better idea, we're going to can that one."

We were all silent for a long while. Then Ayana's head popped up.

"There might be another way." She looked at her staff, resting on my weapons rack. "Kaden, can you get a message to Yasir?"

Kaden nodded. "Nobody's going to bat an eye at me visiting Vigo in the middle of the night."

"Good." Ayana smiled, showing her fangs. "I think we can give them exactly what they want tomorrow."

Chapter 75

ALANEI

Ayana's plan was risky, to say the least. I still wasn't convinced it'd work, but it was the best we had. Ayana didn't look too confident either. She was sweating through her clothes, and perspiration dripped off her forehead. She hadn't said a word since we met in our holding area. That was to be expected. Hard to be talkative when you're building up the courage to die.

The format for today's games would play in our favor. Each team started with one member in play. Every two minutes, a horn would blow and another team member would be released into the field. Eliminations only occurred when a team member verbally gave up or was knocked unconscious.

We won the coin toss, so we'd get our second member first. Yasir and I would start things off, followed by Ayana, then Robia. That's when we'd ensure Ayana's accident. Which meant I had to buy about two minutes to get Sydney out there in time.

Piece of cake...

Reno walked into the holding cell. He passed Sydney and Kaden then stopped in front of Ayana. He looked her over, sighed, and shook his head. He turned to me.

"Are you ready for this?"

I shrugged. "Nope. But it's not like I have a choice."

"Just stick to the plan." He stuck out his hand. "Good luck."

I shook it. Luck was only the start of what I needed.

The horn blew, signaling Robia's entrance into the games.

"Come on." I motioned for Ayana to follow me to the southwest corner of the Arena. Robia assured us there was no visibility there from the rest of the stadium, so it was the perfect place for something to go wrong. Ayana took slow, languid steps. She was barely holding it together. Only a little longer...

Yasir was there waiting for us. He looked over his shoulder. No Robia yet, but I didn't want to risk him saying something that could tip her off if she suddenly appeared.

"Two on one, golden boy," I said. "Sure you don't want to wait for your girlfriend?"

"She is not..." He huffed out a breath and got with the program. "Do not test me, Princess."

"Don't 'princess' me. You want to prove you're the big dog here?" I drew my sword. "Bite."

Yasir's sword flashed out of its sheath. "You cannot bait me into foolishness."

"Maybe I can bait you into something else..." I winked at him. He raised an eyebrow. I'd lost track of who I was playing in this whole mess. I needed this to be over. This much deception was exhausting.

An arrow whistled past me. Ayana let out an unnatural gasp as it caught her in the calf. She dropped to one leg and pawed at it, panicking. It was an actual arrow, not a practice one. That wasn't supposed to happen. Robia was supposed to let us handle it. Ayana's mouth opened and closed, but no words came out. The blood seeping from the wound looked wrong, darker than it should've been.

Shit.

Robia stepped into the alcove with us, hidden from the sight of the rest of the arena.

"Poor little demon," she said. "You shouldn't exist. You're an abomination. The product of two inferior races. The first and last of your kind."

Ayana began hyperventilating. She lifted her staff, and I kicked it from her grasp. It skittered away. She looked up at me with wide eyes, mouth opening and closing dumbly.

"Speechless? Good. The world doesn't need your last words." Robia nodded to me. "Finish her."

In the distance, a horn blew. Sydney would be sprinting our way now. I prayed he would get here in time.

I jerked Ayana up by the ponytail. The smooth blue shank was slippery and wet, making it tough to get a solid grip. I looked in Ayana's eyes, and they were the eyes of a stranger. The optimistic and joyful girl I knew wasn't there. These were the eyes of someone who knew they'd agreed to a plan that wouldn't end well for them. Too late to turn back now.

I grabbed the arrow in Ayana's leg and gave it a sharp tug. It pulled out with much less resistance than it should have. Ayana whimpered but managed not to scream. I tossed the arrow back to Robia, hoping she had the good sense to return it to her quiver. The wound that remained could have easily been made by my rapier. Incriminating Robia wasn't part of the plan.

"This world belongs to the human race." The words tasted like ash in my mouth. "It's time for you to become extinct." I whispered, "I'm sorry" in her ear and drove the sword through her lower back. I left it there, sticking out through her gut as Yasir approached. Uncertainty filled his eyes, but I nodded for him to continue. He drove his sword into Ayana's chest, directly through her heart. She coughed and dark red blood erupted from her mouth. She exhaled her last breath and collapsed onto the ground. The light left her eyes.

Hurry, Sydney...

"Congratulations. You've just earned yourselves a meeting." Robia traced a finger along Yasir's jaw, turned his face to her, and kissed him. "And we take care of our own." She looked down at Ayana's body.

Hurry...

"As for this... thing..." She slung her bow over her shoulder and drew a dagger from her belt.

Hurry!

Sydney burst into the clearing. Robia deftly slid the dagger back into her belt and spun behind me. "Sydney!" she cried. "You have to help! Please!" The speed with which she cranked up the concern gave me whiplash.

Sydney ground to a halt in front of Ayana. He dropped to his knees and looked at me. "What did you do?"

"It was an accident," I said. "Can you..."

Sydney placed his hands on Ayana. They emanated a golden glow and fizzled out. "Come on..." He tried again. His hands lit up, but as he placed them on Ayana the light shot away from her as if repelled by an unseen force. "No... no no no..."

Robia ran out of the alcove, waving her arms frantically. "Help! We need help! It's Ayana! Help!"

Sydney placed his hands on Ayana one more time. I held my breath as he attempted to pour the Light into her. Her body rejected it with such force that it sent him flying. He hit the ground hard and rolled several feet.

"What did you do?" Sydney asked again.

"I'm sorry! It was..."

"An accident?" He spat the words. "You're going to tell me this was a fucking accident?"

"She wasn't supposed to— She should have..."

He charged at me. I braced myself for a fight, but Yasir stepped between us. He caught Sydney and used his momentum to slam him into the ground.

That was when Reno showed up.

Reno rushed straight to Ayana. He placed two fingers along her neck. When he looked at me, his eyes were fire.

"You..."

He didn't say anything else, just stormed my way. Yasir stood in his path, but Reno hurled him aside as if he was a child.

"Reno, I—"

Reno moved insanely fast for someone his size. He struck me with a flat palm to my chest. The force coupled with the electric shock launched me back faster than a crossbow bolt. I shattered the arena's retaining wall, flying through and showering the area with splinters. That hurt. That hurt like a bitch.

He stalked me, fist erupting in blue sparks. Reno backhanded the wall surrounding the hole I'd made and it flew apart. Debris rained down on me.

"I'll kill you!" Reno screamed. As he was about to leap through the hole in the wall, a translucent barrier sprung up between us. Reno hit it and stumbled away. His nostrils flared and he beat against it. "You're dead! You hear me! Dead!"

He continued pounding against the barrier as Kasia stepped in, followed by Headmaster Kane and the other instructors. Lucia and Miklotov tried to get a hold on him, but the big man was too strong. He tossed them aside and beat furiously at the barrier, his metal fist sparking with each hit.

"Kasia, restrain him!" Russo shouted.

Kasia waved her staff and the barrier folded over itself. It wrapped around Reno, binding him in place. The barrier warped the light around it, resulting in what looked like a thick band of glass strapping Reno's arms to his side. He snarled and cursed, but couldn't free himself. That allowed Lucia and Miklotov to take him down and pin him to the ground.

"What happened here?" Kane demanded.

Yasir stepped forward. "It was an accident... We didn't mean to..."

"I don't give a damn what you meant!" Kane snapped back. "You two have a lot to answer for."

Russo grabbed Yasir by the arm and hauled him to his feet. "Shall I take them into custody?"

"Do it," Kane said. "Caesar, take Lanei. I want them in the dungeon and out of my sight."

Caesar nodded and stepped through what was left of the retaining wall. He pulled me to my feet and dragged me back to Russo and Yasir.

"Come on," he said. "You two aren't getting out of this so easily."

As they led us away, I looked back to see Sydney and Kaden lift Ayana's body off the ground. I was glad Robia wasn't still there to see the puddle of slime on the ground where her body had been.

Chapter 76

SYDNEY

Kaden and I hurried into the holding area and dumped Ayana's body on the ground. The door slammed shut behind us.

"Clear!" Nakato called.

Not a moment too soon. Ayana's features collapsed into a writhing pool of thick slime. The slime twisted and reshaped itself into Malbohr. The demon flailed around on the ground, huffing and wheezing as he readjusted to his normal form.

The mists that had kept the room shrouded in darkness dissipated and shifted to cover the windows into the arena. Ayana rushed to Malbohr's side. She placed a hand on the side of the demon's face.

"Shhhh, it's okay. You're okay."

Malbohr gasped for air. He coughed up something that could've been a lung, but was more likely a chunk of solid slime. "Malbohr do good?"

"Malbohr do very good." Ayana smiled down at him. "That has to be a new record! I've never seen you hold a form that long."

"Human bodies strange," Malbohr said. "Hard be so fragile."

Ayana wrinkled her nose. "I'm not human."

Malbohr's shoulders lifted in something close to a shrug. "All mortals same to Malbohr."

The door flew open and Reno stormed in, followed by Lucia and Kasia. Kasia removed the magical restraints binding Reno. The big man didn't say anything, just immediately went to Ayana and wrapped her in a hug. She smiled and hugged him back.

"What do you think?" I asked. "Did it work?"

Lucia winked. "Like a charm. Lanei has the key to the holding cell in her boot. After they escape, you will use Kasia's tracking spell to locate them. I am going to stake out my safe house in case they decide to use it again. Good luck to you." She bowed and exited.

Kasia returned Ayana's staff to her. Over the last few months, it had been carved into a proper staff and adorned with runes and stones. Ayana looked like a full fledged sorcerer as she held it. It was kinda hot.

Kasia produced a small crystal ball from her robes. "Treat it as a compass. It will lead you to them. When it glows green, that is where you will create your doorway."

Ayana raised an eyebrow. "Aren't you coming with us?"

Kasia shook her head. "I am not welcome there. I would still caution against this plan. It is incredibly dangerous."

"I've done it before," Ayana said. "I'll be fine."

"And what of them?" Kasia gestured at the rest of us. "Have you ever taken someone with you before?"

"Well, no... But it'll be okay. I can—"

The crystal in Ayana's hand flashed red.

Kasia frowned. "They're off course."

"Off course?" I asked. "What's that supposed to mean?"

"It was supposed to flash blue when they reached the prison..." Kasia lifted the crystal ball into the air, turning around as she did. "They are going the wrong way. And fast."

"Russo?" Reno asked.

"Or Caesar." Kasia handed me the crystal ball. "You must go now. Be careful." She placed a hand on Ayana's shoulder. "If the situation looks bad, create a doorway and leave immediately. Do you understand?"

Ayana nodded. "I got this."

Kasia took a step back as Kaden and Nakato lined up behind me. Reno helped Malbohr to his feet.

Ayana took my hand. Then she raised her staff, whispered quiet words in a language I didn't understand, and opened a portal to the Void.

Chapter 77

/LANEI

Russo and Caesar hadn't cuffed me or Yasir, which was a small blessing. If they were on the up-and-up, they knew how delicate a situation this was. We were the two highest profile students at Petrichor. The princess of Maldova and the son of Araspia's first knight arrested for the murder of the only sindari to be born in a century... that'd make quite a story if it was true.

"You're making a mistake," I said. "It was an accident."

"Save it," Russo replied.

"Do not make this worse for yourselves," Caesar said. "The less you say now, the better."

"When my father hears about this..."

"He will surely congratulate you on a job well done," Russo said. "Now keep your mouth shut."

Yasir gave me a sideways glance begging me to comply. To his credit, he knew he sucked at deception. Silence was his best friend right now.

As we approached Lucia's tower, my instincts screamed at me to run. I hadn't returned to the holding cells since Lucia's sadistic punishment, and I wasn't eager to spend any more time there than was absolutely necessary.

Just don't put me back in that cell. Any cell but that one...

Caesar stepped forward with a ring of keys. He inserted one into the lock and turned it, but the door didn't open. He put his shoulder into it. Still nothing.

"What's wrong?" Russo asked.

"The door is stuck," Caesar said. "I can't get it open."

Yasir and I exchanged a look. Something was wrong.

"Do you have the right key?" Russo asked.

"Of course I have the right key," Caesar snapped. "The door is—"

"Instructor Hortez! Instructor Russo!" Robia sprinted our way, breathless.

"Robia?" Caesar said. "Now is not the—"

"You have to let Yasir go," she pleaded. "He didn't do anything wrong."

"Miss Castillo, please. You know he and Miss Greyton are responsible for—"

"It was an accident! Yasir's not a murderer."

"This is highly inappropriate," Russo said. "You can speak your case to the headmaster later. Right now, we must take him to—"

Thunk.

Russo's body slumped forward into Yasir's back. Yasir caught her and set her limp form on the ground. Blood pooled out from the wound on the back of her head. I turned to see Milia and Warren.

"You're late," Caesar said.

Oh. Oh shit.

I'd been so focused on Russo and Lucia with their brash personalities I hadn't given much thought to Caesar Hortez as a potential suspect. He was just so

unassuming, so quiet, so... precise. And whenever things went south, he was always just one step behind the more obvious suspects. The perfect spy.

I was an idiot. All the attention Caesar lavished on Robia... It wasn't just because she was the perfect archer. He saw her for what she really was: the perfect sociopath.

Milia shrugged, tossing aside the brick she'd used to bash in Russo's skull. "She wasn't supposed to be here."

"No. She wasn't."

Warren knelt beside Russo and felt for a pulse. "She's still alive."

"Then finish her off."

"She doesn't know you're behind anything," Warren said. "For all she knows, you were attacked too."

Caesar shook his head. "Russo's no idiot. She'll piece it together. My cover here is likely blown, but that doesn't mean I want to leave any loose ends." He pulled aside his coat to reveal a crossbow at his waist. "Don't make me waste a bolt when you're perfectly capable of finishing her yourself."

"Is that really necessary?" I didn't like Russo, but this was no way to go out. "She's probably going to bleed out as it is."

"'Probably' isn't good enough."

Yasir started to choke out a protest, but Robia wrapped her arms around him and put a finger to his lips. She shook her head.

Warren hadn't moved. He looked back and forth from Caesar to Russo's unconscious body.

Milia sighed. "God, don't tell me you grew attached to the old bitch." She drew her sword. "If you won't do it—"

"I'll do it," Warren said. "I owe her that much."

He turned away from us and lifted Russo's head off the ground. He wrapped both arms around her neck.

"Wait," I protested, desperately searching for something that might stop this. "She's human! I thought we were just taking out—"

Crack.

Warren dropped Russo's body into the dirt, letting out a nearly inaudible cry of anguish as he did. I stared at Russo's unmoving form. I may not have been the one to end her life, but I was directly responsible. I should have been able to stop this.

"If you're not with us, you're against us," Caesar said. "Now, Miss Greyton. Are you with us?"

I took in a breath and strengthened my resolve. I looked him in the eyes and nodded.

"Good," he said. "Milich is waiting with our carriage. Let's go."

As we ran from the tower, I looked at the company I was keeping. Caesar Hortez. Robia Castillo. Milia Levesque. Milich Levesque. Warren Malenko. All the people I would need to kill to wash Russo's blood from my hands.

Chapter 78

SYDNEY

The friendly faces of Vadazach and Mr. Drooly waited for us on the other side of the portal.

An imp and a hellhound. Those were the *friendly* faces waiting for us.

Think about that for a moment.

When you hear about a place called "the Void," you don't go in with high expectations. I'm not even sure what I expected. Maybe a big swirling darkness surrounded by nothing. Maybe a cave spiraling forever downward.

What I got was too surreal to wrap my brain around.

We were in what looked like a forest. I say "looked like" because even though the things around us looked like trees, they seemed to be made out of black glass. It was dark, which suggested nighttime, but the sun was high in the sky. It didn't seem to be giving off much light, which may have had something to do with it being a deep purple. If this was daytime, I didn't want to be here once night kicked in. Not just because it was bound to be darker. No... At night, I wouldn't be able to see all those pairs of eyes staring back at us through the obsidian trees.

Wait, scratch that...

Some of the eyes didn't come in pairs. Some were flying solo. Some were clustered together in large bunches.

Screw night. I didn't want to be here now.

"Nakato..." I whispered.

"On it."

Nakato raised her hands and a slow curtain of fog rose from the ground. She hissed in pain.

"What's wrong?"

"The fog... It's different here."

I felt it, too. As the fog surrounded us, the air didn't cool. It burned.

Nakato expanded the ring, pushing the fog further from us so we weren't boiling in the heat. It distorted everything outside the ring, but didn't fully conceal us from the demons outside.

"There's not enough to pull from," she said. "The atmosphere here is just... wrong. I don't like it."

"Then let's not waste time standing around," Reno said.

"And don't do anything dumb," Ayana said. "They're not all bad. Some of them are friends."

"Yeah, hey, right here." Vadazach sauntered over to Ayana and hugged her left knee. She smiled and gave him a hug back. Mr. Drooly bounded over after him, tongue lolling out, and she patted him on the head. Vadazach turned to the rest of us. "So, welcome to my home. Well, not my *home* home. I've got a nice little hovel staked out in the hellmarsh, but you get the idea." He gestured back behind where the portal had been. "If you head deeper in the woods to the north, you'll find the lair of the spiderlings. Nice guys, if your definition of nice involves eating anyone who offends you. And they're easily offended. To the east, you got the sludge caves. That's Malbohr's people over there." He slapped Malbohr on the back, and his hand stuck in the demon's mass. Vadazach tugged it out and wiped it off on my jeans. "Looks like you need to recharge, bud."

Malbohr nodded. "Malbohr feel not so good."

Ayana gave him a hug and managed to step away without any slime on her. "Go on home. You've earned a rest."

Malbohr waved a little goodbye and collapsed into a puddle. The slime puddle absorbed into the ground and vanished.

"Now that's how you travel in style," Vadazach said. "Anyway, back to the tour. To the south you've got—"

"Um, maybe let's not tell them what's to the south," Ayana said.

Vadazach looked at her. His eyes lit up. "Oh. Oh, right. Heh, yeah, yeah, there's nothing down that way. Just a bunch o' rocks and shit. Nothing to worry about."

Kaden and I exchanged a glance. He gulped and gave a dramatic tug at his collar.

I looked down at the crystal ball. "Looks like we're going west. What's that way?"

Vadazach looked from me to Ayana. "Uh... how far west?"

I shrugged. "I don't rightly know. It don't work that way."

Now he just looked at Ayana. "How far west?"

Ayana cocked her head to the side. "Vaddie, come on. We have to move."

The imp shuffled his feet. "Hey, cowboy, you didn't happen to bring that raptor o' yours, did ya?"

"No..."

"Well, that's a shame," he said. "I hear they run fast."

Nakato did a fine job keeping the heat off the rest of us, but she'd worked up a bad sweat as we picked our way through the obsidian forest. She had her mask flipped up, but she still wore her full battle armor, which had to make things even more uncomfortable. The mists did their job, though. The demons we passed either didn't see us or paid no attention to the vague shapes behind the fog.

Vadazach walked with me and Ayana at the front of the pack. The imp kept nervously glancing at the crystal ball, as if dreading where it was going to point us next. Knowing there were places in the Void even demons didn't want to go was a might worrisome.

I took Ayana's hand. "So, uh... you come here often?"

She smiled. "Not really. It isn't exactly the happiest place to visit."

"Coulda fooled me."

"The forest is pretty tame. There are much worse parts." She glanced back at Reno, who brought up the rear with Kaden. "I made the mistake of showing Reno when I was little. He forbade me to come here after that."

"How'd that work out?"

"I got better at keeping secrets," she said. "But I was also more careful. I mean, he wasn't wrong. I've got friends here, and I think there are more good demons than anyone realizes. But I'm not dumb. There's evil here, too. A lot of it."

Mr. Drooly padded up to her. She scratched the side of his exposed skull and he wagged his little flaming tail. Funny how a hellhound didn't fall into Ayana's classification of evil.

"How many types of demons are there?"

"Hundreds. Thousands." Ayana shrugged. "The Void's a big place. I've only seen a fraction of it. Who knows what all's out there."

Vadazach snorted. "Heh, yeah, that's a thread you wanna leave untugged. Trust me. Not all demons are as fun at a party as me, kinda like you mortals ain't all exactly balls o' sunshine." He looked again at the crystal ball. "We're, uh, gettin' near the edge of the forest. Any chance we're getting outta here before then?"

The crystal ball was slightly brighter than when we'd arrived, but I had no idea how that translated to actual distance. Magic wasn't an exact science. Or maybe it was, and I just didn't understand how that science worked. I told Vadazach as much and he scrunched up his face.

"Well, if you can figure out some way to make it do its thing before then, that'd be swell."

"Why? What's on the other side of the forest?"

Vadazach chewed on the inside of his cheek, but didn't respond. I looked to Ayana and raised an eyebrow.

"Buldarak Temple." She patted the imp's shoulder. "Vaddie used to be a slave there."

I frowned. "I didn't know demons enslaved each other."

"What, you thought elves had the market cornered on demon slaves?" Vadazach huffed. "Nah, we been doin' it to each other longer than anyone remembers."

Nakato cried out behind us. I spun in time to see Kaden catch her as she collapsed.

"What's wrong?"

Nakato took several deep breaths. "Can't... keep it up. Something in the air... it's fighting me."

Vadazach snarled. "We're too close to the temple. They got wards against elven magic, and your girl's swimmin' in it. Surprised she kept it goin' this long."

"Can you walk?" I asked.

Although the color had drained from her face, she nodded. "Yeah. I just don't know if..." She raised her hand to try to steady the mist before it settled around us. The air surrounding her hand sizzled and fought back against her. Reno placed a hand on her arm and lowered it.

"You've done enough," he said. "I don't know what those wards are capable of, and I ain't gonna risk you to find out."

Kaden put an arm under Nakato's shoulder, helping her to her feet. "You're lucky I'm here. I've got enough stamina for the both of us."

Nakato smiled. "I know. Vigo talks."

"Let's move," Reno said. "I don't want to stay here any longer than—"

Reno stopped short as Mr. Drooly snapped his head around, arched his back, and let out a menacing growl.

With the mists down, we could now see what they'd been concealing. It may have been hundreds of yards behind us, but even the combination of darkness and distance couldn't hide a demon the size of a small house. Humanoid. Bat-like wings. Limbs as large as trees. Bull-like head. A face that matched Zeke's mask.

It stared right back at us.

"What... is that?" Kaden asked in a hushed voice.

Ayana swallowed. "Behemoth... But I've never seen one so far from—"

Vadazach interrupted her. "Hey, you know how I said we shouldn't go anywhere near the temple?"

"Yeah?"

"Run to the temple!" The imp bolted headlong through the forest.

We didn't ask questions. We burst into a run after him.

I didn't need to look back. The sound of trees shattering behind us was all the motivation I needed.

Three things happened as we reached the edge of the forest:

A massive, hellish structure came into view in the distance, exponentially larger than any castle or palace I'd ever heard of.

The behemoth let out a primal roar, so close the heat of its breath scorched my back.

And the crystal ball glowed bright green in my hand.

Chapter 79

/LANEI

The carriage doors opened. We weren't in front of Lucia's safehouse. Shit. She wouldn't be here for backup. It was up to Sydney and Ayana.

Instead, we'd pulled up in front of a modest Orynistic church. Robia led us up the steps and unlocked the padlock on a set of thick chains barring the front door. She tossed them aside and swung the doors open. The doors themselves didn't have proper locks, so once we were inside Robia slid a tall candleholder between the door handles to keep out pesky intruders.

The church was in fine shape, unlike the old storeroom. As we walked down the aisle, I saw why there'd been chains on the doors. A lone chair sat in front of the church's altar. A priest sat strapped in the chair, his head hung low with a gag covering his mouth. His vestments were spattered with dried blood. I'd only seen him once before, but I recognized him.

Robia's father.

He lifted his head weakly, too exhausted to give much of a reaction. His eyes passed over the group of us and settled on Robia as she made her way through the pews.

"Have you had time to think over our discussion, Father?" Venom laced that last word. Robia knelt in front of him. "You should be grateful. I am giving you a chance to repent from your false god, to make up for all the years you placed him before me. Your god is made of lies." She gestured to Caesar. "Master Hortez has shown me the truth. Allow me to open your eyes as he has opened mine."

Robia pulled out a knife and slid it between her father's cheek and the gag. She twisted the knife, slicing off the gag and cutting a thin line down her father's face. He didn't even wince, just stared into his daughter's eyes, searching for someone who wasn't there.

"Renounce your false god," Robia said. "Pledge yourself to Omek and lead your congregation into his arms." She placed the tip of the dagger under his chin. "It is the only way for you."

Yasir shifted uncomfortably beside me. "We're not letting this happen," he whispered.

"I know. Let me think."

Caesar sat patiently in the first row of pews, allowing Robia this moment with her father. Milia and Milich stood in the aisle next to him. Warren, however, kept his distance. He'd sat up front during the carriage ride, so I hadn't seen him since we'd left Russo. Since he'd killed her. Warren's face was grim and colorless. He took deep, slow breaths as he clutched one arm to his chest.

"What happened to you?" The priest's voice was cracked and dry. "This is not you."

"This is the only me!" She sneered. "Not the shell you tried to fill with lies. I am done being a sheep in your mindless flock. You've poisoned their minds with the lie that all races are equal before god. Equal! As if we could ever be mere equals to overgrown lizards or demonspawn!" Robia spat on the ground. "We have achieved more than they could ever dream of, and we did it without magic. And you sit there and call us equal? That's what they want us to believe! They know we could destroy them if we only realized how much greater we are."

"Destroy them?" Her father shook his head. "Stop this madness. It's not too late. You can still turn back."

"I already have. I turned back from your false god to serve the only god that matters. Omek's will survives through me."

Omek's will survives...

"His will calls for the death of magic. The end of the elves and sindari. The end of the throldkin." Robia smiled and leaned in to her father. "Your god could never make me feel as alive as I did when I put a sword through that lizard's chest."

Tenkou.

My blood boiled. A hundred thoughts flashed through my mind. Things I wanted to do to Robia. Things I *would* do to her. I finally had a target to direct my rage.

The priest's face fell. "You didn't..."

"He will be the first of many," Robia said. "A new age has begun, Father. The Children of Omek will deliver this world to its rightful heirs. Master Hortez has shown me this is bigger than any of us. Bigger than me, bigger than him, certainly bigger than you." She pricked the knife into the skin under his jaw. "You are with us or you are against us. Decide."

Robia's father looked back at her. "If this is what you have turned to, then I am sorry. I have failed you. But I can no sooner deny my god than deny the air we breathe."

Robia sighed. "I thought you might say something stupid like that. Then I suppose this is goodbye." She turned the dagger over in her hand. Her arm tensed as she prepared to push it through her father's throat.

"Stop!" Yasir stormed down the aisle. I cursed and rushed after him. No more need for pretense. We had all the proof we needed. What we didn't have was weapons. Or a way out. Or numbers on our side.

Robia froze at Yasir's voice. Milia and Milich drew their swords.

Caesar glanced over his shoulder, appearing bored. "Control him, Robia."

"This is something I have to do, sweetheart," Robia said, honey in her voice. "Omek requires—"

"Damn Omek!" Yasir snapped. "Let him rot in hell and be forgotten. You can join him there for all I care."

Robia's eyes widened. "Darling, what are you—"

"Enough! I am not your darling. If you think I could ever love someone like you, you clearly have no idea who I am or what I stand for."

Robia clenched her jaw. "You don't mean that. You're just feeling conflicted about killing the demon bitch."

I heaved a loud sigh. "Damn, girl, you can't take a hint. He's not into you! He's never been into you! And all of this..." I waved my arms around. "I am going to put an end to all of it. Starting with you." I smiled. "I'm not with you guys either, in case you didn't get that."

Caesar frowned. "I am sorry to hear that, Princess." He looked past me and nodded. A sword pressed into my back.

"Don't move," Warren said. He sounded drained. "Is this what you've been after this whole time?"

I was confused for a moment, until I realized he was talking to Milia.

A grin spread over her face. "Yes. This is only the beginning. When the Children spread—"

Warren huffed. "Yeah, fine, whatever. Do your thing. I won't bother asking Milich. He's never been much for independent thought." The sword's pressure vanished from my back. "You're still my friends. But this isn't why I came here." Warren stepped beside me. Now that he was no longer clutching his left arm to his chest, I got a better look at it. His hand fell at an unnatural angle.

His wrist was broken.

The confrontation with Russo... The sound of bone snapping...

He couldn't go through with it.

Warren hurled the blade aside. It hit the wall and clattered to the ground.

Milia's face twisted. "What are you doing?"

"Kill them yourselves," Warren said. "Come find me again when you realize how stupid you sound right now."

I gritted my teeth. "You could have handed me the sword."

Warren scoffed. "Yeah, right. Like I give two shits about you or the golden boy." He turned and walked away.

Caesar sighed and pulled the crossbow off his belt. "If you want something done right..."

A crackle of magical energy shot through the air as a portal opened up between us. Kaden and Nakato leapt through, crashing into Milia and Milich. The four of them hit the ground hard. Yasir was on them right away, disarming the twins. Reno barreled through next, followed by Vadazach, Mr. Drooly, and Sydney. Ayana tumbled out last, landed in a roll, spun, and closed the portal as an eardrum-shattering roar emitted from it.

Reno took a second to assess the situation. The twins pinned down by Kaden, Nakato, and Yasir. Warren sitting in the back row of the church minding his own business. A bleeding priest hostage. And then Robia and Caesar. Reno's gaze settled on Caesar.

"You," Reno growled.

Caesar smiled. "Hello, Reno." He raised his eyebrows to Ayana. "Aren't you supposed to be dead?"

Ayana, still panting with exertion, shrugged. "It didn't seem like much fun."

"Pity you don't have a choice in the matter." Caesar looked back at Reno. "Thank you for bringing her to me."

He pointed the crossbow at Ayana and pulled the trigger.

Caesar's shot was perfect. The arrow went straight for her throat. Ayana's last breath would have been a painful one if Sydney hadn't jumped in front of her. The bolt took him high in the shoulder, the force of it spinning him into the first row of pews. Ayana rushed to his side as Reno and I charged Caesar.

The fight, if you want to call it that, lasted about three seconds. I kicked the crossbow out of Caesar's hands, Reno grabbed him by the throat, lifted him off the ground, and slammed him on the floor. Reno flicked the wrist on his metal arm and blue current sparked through it.

Caesar laughed. "Go ahead. Arrest me. The Children will have me free by this time tomorrow."

Reno held his sparking fist up to Caesar's face. "Then you'd better start talking or you're gonna have a real long day."

The sparks made Caesar flinch, but his demeanor remained unchanged. "There's nothing you can do to—"

"Vadazach, fetch!" Ayana opened a portal and the imp hopped in.

Caesar glared at her. "What are you doing?"

"You shot my boyfriend," Ayana said. "That was a mistake."

A moment later, Vadazach sprinted back through the portal, Flik hot on his heels. "Get me outta here! Get me outta here!"

Ayana opened a second portal and Vadazach dove into it. The raptor stopped and looked around, disoriented by his new surroundings. But then he saw Sydney on the ground with the crossbow bolt through his shoulder.

And holy shit, you do not want to be the guy to shoot a raptor's best friend.

Sydney pointed to Caesar. "Flik, hold."

Reno stepped back to allow Caesar a moment to scurry away. He didn't get far. Flik leapt over the twins and collided with Caesar, pinning him against the altar. The raptor bared his teeth and growled.

Sydney grunted as Ayana helped him to his feet and led him toward Caesar. "I don't normally let him eat people. It ain't a moral thing." He coughed and grabbed his shoulder. "Nah, I just don't let him do it 'cause it's real messy. Plus he's slow about it. Likes to keep his meals alive as long as possible so the meat stays warm."

Caesar's eyes widened. "You... you're bluffing. You wouldn't do that."

"Be a shame to lose whatever information you've got," Reno said. "But after everything you've done, I can live with that."

Caesar dared to look in Flik's eyes. The raptor screeched and flicked its tongue at him. Caesar snapped his head back to us.

"Alright! I'll talk! Just don't—"

Robia's dagger shot through the air and buried itself to the hilt in Caesar's throat. He gagged once then his head rolled back.

"I'm sorry, master. This is bigger than me or you." Robia turned on her heel, bolted toward one of the large stained glass windows, and dove through, shattering the glass and showering the ground with shards. Yasir burst past me and leapt out the window after her.

Before I could follow them, Milia grabbed my ankle and tripped me. I yanked my foot away and kicked her in the face. By the time I got to the window, Robia and Yasir were gone.

Chapter 80

SYDNEY

The last few weeks at Petrichor passed without incident, relatively speaking. Robia got away, but the twins were taken into custody. They fought and spat and cursed the whole time, but I hadn't seen them since, and that was good enough for me.

Given the circumstances, Lord Aguilar dropped the drug trafficking charges against Warren. He was, however, kicked out of the academy for "behavior unbecoming of one charged with upholding the law." He packed his bags and left without a word to anyone. Katya and Selena remained as the only members of his squad, although they were kept under heavy scrutiny and were respectively moved into Nakato and Yasir's squads for the remainder of the term. They still weren't particularly friendly or likable in any way, but they were less hateful, so I guess that was something.

Russo remained in a coma for two days following the attack. When she woke up, she was put on indefinite suspension and forced to undergo treatment for her drug addiction. It spoke to Headmaster Kane's faith in her that she wasn't outright fired for employing a student as her drug dealer. I wouldn't have been half as lenient, but hey, she was a bitch to my parents, so I'm biased.

For all my unrealistic dreams of grandeur, I hadn't planned ahead for what came after Petrichor. Fortunately, someone else had plans for me.

Reno asked the four of us to join him in the training room. I expected a celebratory toast, some shots to say, "hey, congrats on not dying." I was *not* expecting to find my parents and Uncle Darian waiting for us along with Lord Aguilar.

"What are you doing here?" I asked. "I didn't think I'd see you until I got home."

Mom smiled. "That's what we thought, too. But then we talked to Darian, and..."

"Well," Dad continued, "it seemed like a good idea to come up now."

I raised an eyebrow. "Why? What'd he say?"

Mom shrugged. "We'll let him tell you."

Lord Aguilar cleared his throat. "Thank you all for your assistance. Petrichor is in a better place now that Caesar Hortez can no longer use it as a breeding ground for his propaganda. It is unfortunate he died before we could get more information from him. Esperan and the rest of Nasan are not yet safe from the Children, but with Petrichor freed from their grasp we are in a better place to fight back."

"That's where you come in," Darian said. "You all did good work. And while you've still got a ways to go to reach your full potential, I'd like to offer you a job working with Ascension here in San Domingo. Reno will be rejoining us, and I'd like you all to work under him."

Reno nodded. "Ayana, Sydney, you two will be able to continue training with Kasia. You won't find a better magic teacher anywhere outside Rainess. Lanei, Kaden, I don't know if you planned to return home, but there's a place for you here if you—"

"I'll take it," Lanei said. "I'd rather be on the streets fighting the Children than stuck in some castle tower where I can't do a damn thing about it."

Ayana gave her brother a puzzled look. "You're going to let me fight?"

Reno snorted. "Like it'd do me a hell of a lot of good to tell you not to."

"It wouldn't," Ayana agreed. "I'm a rebellious teenager who can't be controlled. Next thing you know I'll be doing drugs and getting face tattoos." Her eyes widened in horror and she turned to my parents. "Only kidding! I wouldn't actually get a face tattoo. Or do drugs! That's much worse. I don't do drugs. Please don't think I do drugs."

My mom gave Ayana her best stern look then burst out laughing.

I didn't need to do a whole lot of thinking on the matter. This was a chance to make a difference. It didn't hurt that I could stay here with my girlfriend and best friends.

"I'm in," I said.

Reno looked from me to Ayana. He sighed. "Yeah, I thought you might be. Kaden?"

Kaden took a second to respond. "I appreciate the offer. I'm grateful for everything you all have done for me. I really am. But Araspia's my home. My family and friends are there, and I've still got a knighthood to earn. A world without a Sir Kaden Ashworth would be a terrible place to live."

"Think we could convince you to stay?" Lanei asked.

"And let my sister hog all the glory back home?" Kaden flashed a marvelous smile and winked. "I have to go pack before my train tonight. But I'll say goodbye before I leave." He bowed and left.

Ayana slumped her shoulders. "He's leaving? Just like that?"

"He's got his own destiny," I said. "I'm sure this ain't the last we'll see of him."

Ayana came to my room after Kaden moved his things out.

She gave me a small wave. "Hi."

I smiled back. "Hi."

Ayana stepped inside, twirling so her dress spun around her, and plopped down on the bed. "So..."

"So..." I sat next to her.

"You're staying?" The question was hesitant, like she expected me to pull the rug out from under her.

"Looks like it, yeah." I grinned. "Hope that ain't a problem."

"No! No, I just, um..." She blushed, purple rising in her cheeks. "Can I tell you a secret?"

"Sure."

"I don't actually know how this..." She motioned her hand back and forth between us. "...works. I mean, I know how *this* works. You and me. But not, like, *this*... dating thing."

"Well, to be fair, I don't think we've gone on an actual date yet."

She bit her lower lip. "I took you into the Void. Does that count?"

"A giant demon tried to kill us. Let's not set that as our standard."

"Oh, right..." She brushed a strand of hair from her face. "Sorry. You've probably gone on lots of dates before."

I snickered. Clearly she hadn't talked to Kaden. "Why do you think that?"

"I mean, the cowboys in all my books have a different lady in every town, and I just figured, well..."

"Oh, yeah, you know me. Got like six girls waiting for me back in Laredo."

"Oh..." Her face dropped. "Sorry, I guess I should've expected that."

"What? No!" I waved my hands frantically. "I was kidding. There's nobody waiting for me. Like, at all."

"Really?"

"Of course, really! You're giving me way more credit than I deserve."

She smiled, but it only lasted a moment. "It's just... Are you sure you wouldn't prefer a girl who's more..."

I knew what she was getting at. "Human?"

Ayana nodded. "Milia wasn't wrong. I'm a freak. I know that. Even if I was a full sindari, I've never heard of a human and sindari who could... you know..."

"So what? If you're a freak, then you're the most beautiful freak I've ever seen." Wait. No. Damage control. "Not that you're a freak! I mean, if you're a freak, then I'm a little freaky too, right? I may only have a sliver of elf in me, but that's at least something we have in common. Besides..." I pointed at my eyes. "I think purple and red go well together, don't you?"

Ayana grinned, threw her arms around me, and kissed me.

Phew. Saved it.

We fell onto the bed together, and at least for the moment, everything was right with the world.

Just as I rolled her onto her back, Ayana pulled away from me. "Did you feel that?"

"Oh, um, sorry, I—"

"No, not that!" Ayana's cheeks flushed. She took my hand and placed it on the headboard. It was vibrating.

I looked out the window. There in the distance, floating toward us like some monstrous beast, was Viktor Greyton's airship.

Chapter 81

/LANEI

I stepped outside as my father's airship touched down. I wasn't alone. It appeared everyone else had the same idea. Yasir, Kaden, Vigo, and Devi stopped loading their bags onto a carriage to watch the scene unfold. Yasir whispered something to the others, and one-by-one they reached into their belongings and re-equipped their swords. Nakato's squad appeared from the courtyard in full battle armor. Sydney and Ayana ran out from the school and, in the least subtle way possible, stood next to me like the world's least intimidating bodyguards.

So much for a private family talk.

Lord Aguilar walked out of the school flanked by Kasia, Miklotov, Kane, and Reno. His bodyguards were much scarier than mine. At least, until Ricardo sent his heavy hitter, Kasia Windamier, to back me up. I mean, it was my father, so I was hoping backup wouldn't be necessary. But, then again, it *was* my father.

The ship's deck was uncharacteristically empty as the ramp lowered, but now the doors to the interior opened and rows of soldiers piled out. They lined up all along the railing. They didn't draw their weapons, but each had crossbows in plain sight. My father was sending a clear message: Don't fuck with me.

Áldric Levesque and Ian Pryce stepped into view next, with my father following directly behind them. This time, he wasn't making a point of being the center of attention. They were his shield. A handful of knights followed behind them as they made their way down the ramp.

I took a step his way and Sydney grabbed my wrist. He shook his head.

"It's fine," I said. "Don't worry."

I gently pulled my arm away and approached my father.

He walked right past me. I turned to watch in stunned silence. I knew my father would be upset with me, but I was expecting a lecture. He never passed up an opportunity to tell me how much I'd disappointed him.

Lord Aguilar met my father in the middle of the field.

"Viktor."

"Ricardo."

The space between them was the iciest five feet on the planet.

"If you came for graduation, you're about two days late."

"You know why I'm here," my father said. "Sir Aldric's children have been unlawfully detained. I want them released immediately."

"They were a part of a conspiracy that resulted in two dead students."

"They were not responsible for either of those deaths and you damn well know it. The last time I checked, Robia Castillo and Caesar Hortez were from Esperan. That makes them your problem, not mine."

"They may be from Esperan, but their ideals came straight out of Maldova. It was you and yours that poisoned their minds."

My father sneered. "Like you poisoned my daughter's mind? Filled it with the ridiculous notion that humans should treat the lesser races as equals?"

I stepped forward and inserted myself in their conversation. "They didn't have to 'poison my mind.' In case you forgot, one of my parents actually had a heart."

My father finally acknowledged my existence. "The only good thing your mother ever did was die before she could fill my bloodline with more disappointments."

I slapped my father across the face.

"That is the last time you insult my mother in front of me." I kept my eyes on him, aware that a hundred crossbows had been raised in unison and pointed my way.

My father lifted his thumb to his lip. When he pulled it away, a spot of blood came with it. He looked at me through narrowed eyes. "They have turned you into an insolent brute."

"I was already insolent. It's why you couldn't break me."

His mouth twisted in disgust. He turned back to Lord Aguilar. "Bring Milia and Milich Levesque to me immediately or it will be considered an act of war. And make no mistake, it is a war you cannot win. If recent events have taught you anything, it's that more of your people follow me than you'd like to believe."

Lord Aguilar stared him down. "Follow *you*."

"Yes, me. The world is changing. It needs someone strong, someone with vision to return it to its former glory." He jerked his head toward Ayana and Kasia. "Someone who understands the threat their kind poses to the world."

"So it's true," I said, not wanting to believe it. "You're with the Children."

My father studied me. "For years, Omek's children have been pushed into the shadows. They've been told their beliefs are wrong. I'm here to give them a voice. You may not understand now, but one day you'll thank me for the world I have created."

Lord Aguilar spat on the ground at my father's feet. "That's what I think of you and your world."

My father kicked dirt over the spittle. "Leaders like you have been a disaster for our world. I'm just cleaning up the mess you've made. Now bring me the twins unless you want to start a war you can't finish."

Lord Aguilar stared him down, but finally cursed and waved a hand. The heavy sound of a door swinging open echoed across the field, and Lucia emerged from the tower with Milia and Milich in tow. They didn't look any the worse for wear. Milich scowled as they walked our way, but Milia bore a look of pure triumph. Sir Aldric embraced them each in turn and led them back to the airship. Milia winked at me and blew a kiss as she boarded. My father's eyes remained fixed on Lord Aguilar the whole time.

"The world is changing, Ricardo. I suggest you change with it."

"The world you want and the world I want cannot coexist."

"Well, then. I suppose that's a problem, isn't it?" My father turned to face me. He looked me over from head to toe and held out a hand.

I scoffed. "I'm not going with you. I don't belong in Maldova. Not anymore."

"I couldn't agree more," he said. "You've chosen the freaks and half breeds over your heritage. You are no daughter of mine. But you have something that belongs to me." He nodded to the sword at my hip.

I put my hand on Brightclaw's hilt. "Tommaso Greyton is more my ancestor than yours. Everything he died for is everything you loathe. So if you want *my* sword, you're going to have to kill me first." I took a step forward and got in my father's face. Sir Ian and the rest of my father's guards put their hands on their swords. "I don't like your odds."

My father held my gaze for several moments. "Elvish junk. I hope it's worth everything you've given up." He spun on his heel and marched back to his ship. His knights held their places until he was on board then followed him on.

I didn't realize my hands were balled into fists until Sydney and Ayana came up to me. Ayana took one of my fists in her hand, unclenching it for me.

"I'm sorry." The sindari girl clutched my arm, resting her cheek against it.

"I'm not," I said. "This is my home now. There's no place for me in Maldova."

As we walked back inside, Lucia caught my eye and nodded. I nodded back.

My father was right. Things were going to change.

Even though Yasir and company had been prepared to leave when my father's ship arrived, they stuck around for a few hours after he left. I guess they were waiting to see if he'd turn around and come back. Which I guess was a nice thought and all, but not remotely necessary. My father wasn't coming back. He'd said what he wanted to say, did what he wanted to do. There was no reason for him to come back.

Yasir made his exit in typical grandiose fashion. He didn't even have to try, it was just his default setting.

He made the rounds saying his goodbyes to everyone gathered outside. And I do mean everyone. Cooks, servants, you name it, he greeted each one by name, gave them genuine thanks, and a fond farewell. It would've been sickening if I didn't believe he actually meant it.

He finally stopped in front of me, drew his cape back as if he were going to bow, then stopped and smiled.

"Do I have your permission to bow, Your Highness?"

I grinned. "Hey, you do you. But I'm pretty sure my princess card has been revoked."

"On the contrary. I believe you have proven yourself more worthy of the title than ever."

"I never wanted the title."

"That makes you no less worthy." Yasir flashed his perfect smile again and bowed. "Princess or not, if you ever find yourself in need of a loyal knight, you have one at your service."

"Who, Kaden? Yeah, I know, he already told me."

Yasir looked flustered as he tried to determine the proper response. I might actually miss that about him.

"Thank you. I'll be sure to let you know."

He took my hand and kissed it. "Until we meet again, Princess."

"Until then, sir knight."

Yasir smiled and strode off to his waiting carriage. To my surprise, it left as soon as he was inside. I ran over to Sydney.

"Did Kaden seriously just leave without saying goodbye?"

Sydney looked at the carriage pulling away from the school. "Son of a..." He sighed and shook his head. "Yeah. Yeah, I think he did."

A pang of pain shot through me. "I can't believe he'd do that."

"Yeah, well..." His shoulders dropped. "...me neither."

We watched the carriage drive out of sight. After everything we'd been through, for Kaden to just up and leave like that...

Nakato tapped my shoulder and pulled me out of my head.

"Hey. Can we talk?" She took my hand and led me away from Sydney so we could have privacy. "I never actually apologized for trying to kill you that night."

"Well, don't. I deserved it."

"No, you didn't. I know I was supposed to think you did, but you didn't. I never should've reacted like that."

"You walked through a land of demons to bail me out. I think that makes us even."

"It's not about being even. It's about..." She let out a sharp breath and looked down at her feet. "I should've given you the benefit of the doubt. Then, and before, and... I lashed out at you when I should have listened. You deserve better than that, and I'm sorry."

I took Nakato's hand and she looked up at me. It was easy to forget that beneath the armor and the mask was a teenage girl with the same insecurities as me. "Thank you. Not for the apology, because fuck that, you still don't owe me one."

She laughed a little.

"Thank you for trusting me when you did and for being my friend when I needed one. It meant a lot."

I wrapped my arms around her and she hugged me back. Her breath was warm on my neck as she exhaled slowly, releasing the weight of guilt. After a few moments she sniffed and took a step back. She blinked away tears before they had a chance to form.

"So, what will you do next?" I asked.

"We're going to stay in San Domingo. There's a lot of work left to do, and I think I'm needed here more than in Kialen." She smiled. "I hear you're sticking around, too."

"Yeah. Going to work for Darian Rankin. That should be quite the adventure."

"Ascension's the best guild in the kingdom. You'll fit right in." She chewed on her lower lip. "I guess this means I'll be seeing you around."

"Yeah, I guess so."

"Good." Nakato smiled. "I'm really bad at goodbyes."

"Me too," I said. "Me too."

I found Sydney sitting on the roof of the Academy, looking out over San Domingo. I climbed out my window and scaled the stone wall up to where he sat. He blinked several times as I pulled myself over the ledge.

"Hey," I said.

"Hey..." He stared at me, jaw agape. "You know there's an access door back there, right?" He pointed over his shoulder to one of the turrets.

"Oh, yeah. Yeah, I just wanted to... climb... something."

"No clue, huh?"

"Not a one."

I sat beside him, our feet dangling over the edge. The sunset painted the whole city in gold and orange. It was a beautiful sight. We each took in a long breath and let them out simultaneously.

Over the last several months, I'd met elves and sindari and throldkin, murderers and drug dealers, knights and lords. And yet, despite all that, somehow this wannabe hero in a cowboy hat was the most peculiar. By all rights, he didn't belong here. No one could argue that he was suited for this life. Maybe that's why I was so fond of him. We had that in common.

And yet, here we were. Together, we exposed the traitor at the school and put a stop to the rash of murders. It wasn't all golden. Robia was still out there somewhere. My father was still planning... who knows what. There was a long road ahead of us.

"So. You ready for this, cowboy?" I asked.

Sydney took a moment to think it over. "Yeah. Yeah, I think I am. I mean, I'm not *ready* ready. But I'm up for the challenge."

"That's worked out pretty well so far."

He laughed. "Yeah, sure, minus all the injuries and near death experiences."

"Right, minus that."

Another voice chimed in behind us. "Did I hear near death experiences?" Ayana skipped across the roof in a manner that was far too carefree on a raked surface this high off the ground. She sat down next to Sydney. They shared a quick kiss and held hands, because they were disgustingly cute. "I've had a couple of those. Oooh, remember when you stabbed me with a sword?"

"Doesn't ring any bells," I said. "I remember you teleporting above me and *falling* on my sword."

"Are you sure?" She cocked her head to the side. "I distinctly remember you stabbing me."

"You're thinking of Malbohr. I stabbed Malbohr with my sword."

"Ohhhh, right." Ayana smacked her forehead. "Right, that's it. I get the two of us confused all the time." She giggled.

"How's Reno feel about us working for him?" Sydney asked.

"He's looking forward to it. I think he really wants to get back in the field." She cleared her throat and added, in a fast, quiet voice, "And I think he wants to make your life hell for dating me, so there's that."

Sydney blinked. "Wait, what?"

"He says it'll be good times!" Ayana smiled, trying to look reassuring while flashing her pointy teeth.

"I'm a dead man, aren't I?"

A hand clapped down onto Sydney's shoulder. "That's why you've got me here to look out for you."

I spun my head around as Kaden slid onto the roof next to me. I smiled at him. "I thought you left."

Kaden grinned. "What, and leave you all here to suffer without me? I couldn't do that with a clear conscience."

I punched Kaden in the arm then hugged him. "You're an asshole for making us think you left without saying goodbye."

"Yeah, I know."

"Major asshole," Sydney added.

"Yes, I got it."

"You... stupid idiot." Ayana stuck out her tongue. She couldn't even fake anger well.

"You know, there's still a train leaving for Araspia tonight, if you prefer I take it."

"Don't you dare," I said. "You're one of us now."

"One of you all, eh?" Kaden shrugged. "There are worse things to be."

"What about Vigo?" Sydney asked.

"He understands. He knows you'd all fall apart without me. Besides, Araspia's not far by train. We'll figure things out after he's knighted."

"What about you?" I asked. "I know how important a knighthood is to you."

"Are you kidding? With everything I'm going to accomplish here, they'll be throwing titles at me! They may even give you lot something just for being around me."

"Oooh, can I be Lady Ayana of the Shimmering Void?"

"That's not quite how titles—"

"Lord Sydney the Lightbreaker?"

"Guys, no, there's a system to this."

Ayana laughed. "Lies! Hey, Lanei, what do you want to be called?"

I looked at my friends and couldn't help but smile. "Lanei. Just being Lanei is fine by me."

And for the first time in my life, I actually believed it.

Acknowledgements

That's a wrap! It's hard to believe that this book is finally done. It's taken quite a journey to get here, starting with its life as a (very short-lived) web comic 18 years ago, all the way back in 2004. So first off, I would like to thank Marissa Trudel, who was the artist on that original project and has been this story's biggest fan for all these years. I have always appreciated your enthusiasm for Sydney and Lanei, and your artwork has helped me put into words the characters I see in my head. You can see some of Marissa's work in the pages of this book, with the sword and hat designs on the chapter titles.

Thank you to my editor, Kelly Schaub, whose guidance and feedback was invaluable in shaping this book. Thank you to my beta readers: Jessica Holloway, Misty Thompson, Michelle Luby, and Amberly Coker. I loved hearing your enthusiastic reactions throughout this entire process, from your excited calls and texts to the ones forever cursing my name. You kept me going to the finish line.

Thank you to all the Icy folks for giving me an awesome community to grow up and be weird in, back when the internet would let just anyone run a major website. It was fun growing up with y'all and sharing a love for JRPGs that influenced so much of *Into the Black*. Now please do me a favor and forget absolutely everything about teenage/early-twenties Brian. That dude was duuuuuuumb.

Thank you to Sean & Zeke for inspiring two of the characters in this book. I wish you could be here to read it, and I hope that some small part of you lives on in these pages.

And finally, thank you to my mom, Lynne Work. As an artsy kid with big dreams, I couldn't have asked for a more supportive role model.

Made in the USA
Middletown, DE
04 December 2022

16954421R00279